WITHDRAWN

THE ANNOTATED FRANKENSTEIN

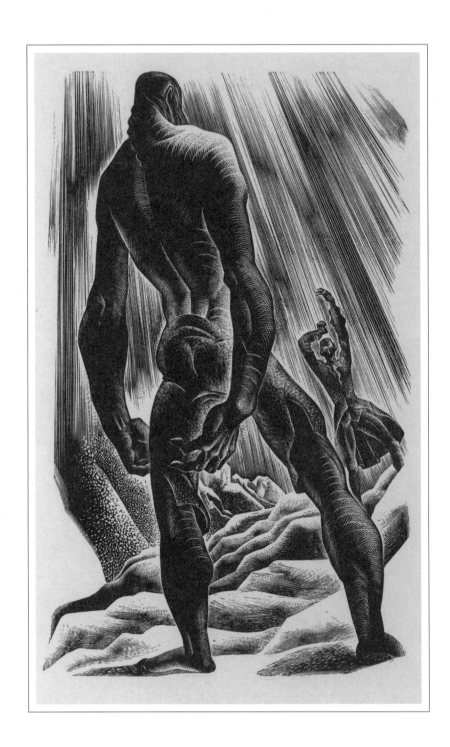

MARY WOLLSTONECRAFT SHELLEY

THE ANNOTATED

Frankenstein

EDITED BY *Susan J. Wolfson and Ronald L. Levao*

THE BELKNAP PRESS OF HARVARD UNIVERSITY PRESS

Cambridge, Massachusetts, and London, England   2012

DESIGN BY ANNAMARIE MCMAHON WHY

Frontispiece: The Creature confronts his maker, wood engraving by Lynd Ward.
Courtesy of Houghton Library, Harvard University

Library of Congress Cataloging-in-Publication Data

Shelley, Mary Wollstonecraft, 1797–1851

   [Frankenstein]

   The annotated Frankenstein / Mary Wollstonecraft Shelley ;
edited by Susan Wolfson and Ronald Levao.

     p.   cm.

   Includes bibliographical references.

   ISBN 978-0-674-05552-0 (alk. paper)

   1. Frankenstein, Victor (Fictitious character)—Fiction.   2. Frankenstein's monster
(Fictitious character)—Fiction.   3. Scientists—Fiction.   I. Wolfson, Susan J., 1948–
II. Levao, Ronald.   III. Title.

   PR5397.F7   2012c

   823′.7—dc23   2012024171

CONTENTS

ABBREVIATIONS

For full information on items indicated in brief, see Further Reading and Viewing.

1817/History/Tour	Percy Bysshe Shelley [and Mary Shelley], *History of a Six Weeks' Tour, Through a Part of France, Switzerland, Germany and Holland: With Letters Descriptive of a Sail Round the lake of Geneva, and the Glaciers of Chamouni* (London: T. Hookham / C. and J. Ollier, 1817). *Tour,* from July 28 to September 13, 1814, is by "M." (Mary). *Letters* (from the summer of 1816) are by both: Letters I (May 17) and II (June 1) by "M."; Letters III and IV (July) and the poem *Mont Blanc* ("June 23") by "S." (Percy Shelley).
1818	*Frankenstein; or, The Modern Prometheus,* 3 vols. (London: Lackington, Hughes, Harding, Mavor, & Jones, 1818) [anonymous].
1823	Mary Wollstonecraft Shelley, *Frankenstein: or, The Modern Prometheus,* "A New Edition," 2 vols. (London: G. and W. B. Whittaker). Available in photo facsimile reprint: Oxford: Woodstock Books, 1993; and on Google Books.
1831	Mary W. Shelley, *Frankenstein: or, The Modern Prometheus* (London: Henry Colburn and Richard Bentley; reprinted 1832 [our text]); available also on Google Books.
1931 *Frankenstein*	Directed by James Whale, with Boris Karloff (Creature) and Colin Clive (Frankenstein).
Bible	The Authorized King James Version: book, chapter, verse.
Crook	Nora Crook, ed., *Frankenstein; or The Modern Prometheus.*
Davy	Humphry Davy, *A discourse, introductory to a course of lectures on chemistry delivered in the theatre of the Royal Institution on the 21st of January, 1802;* reprinted in *Early Miscellaneous Papers* (London: Smith, Elder, 1839) 2: 311–326.
Journals	*The Journals of Mary Shelley, 1814–1844,* ed. Paula Feldman and Diana Scott-Kilvert. Percy Shelley wrote in these journals. Pages 84–103 give Mary and Percy's reading lists from 1814 to 1818.
Knoepflmacher	U. C. Knoepflmacher, "Thoughts on the Aggression of Daughters," in Levine and Knoepflmacher.
Letters MWS	*The Letters of Mary Wollstonecraft Shelley,* ed. Betty T. Bennett, 3 vols. (Baltimore: Johns Hopkins University Press, 1980–1988).
Letters PBS	*The Letters of Percy Bysshe Shelley, Containing material never before collected,* ed. Roger Ingpen, 2. vols. (London: Isaac Pitman & Sons, 1912).
Levine and Knoepflmacher	*The Endurance of Frankenstein,* ed. George Levine and U. C. Knoepflmacher.
Lyrical Ballads	[William Wordsworth and Samuel Taylor Coleridge; anonymous], *Lyrical Ballads, With a Few Other Poems* (London, 1798).
Mellor	Anne K. Mellor, *Mary Shelley: Her Life, Her Fiction, Her Monsters.*
ms /*Notebooks*	The 1816–1817 manuscript of *Frankenstein,* ed. Charles Robinson, *The Frankenstein Notebooks.*
OED	Oxford English Dictionary, online.
Paradise Lost	John Milton, *Paradise Lost* (1647), in the 1747 edition Mary Shelley used as she wrote *Frankenstein* (see Textual Note).
Wolf	Leonard Wolf, *The Annotated Frankenstein.*
Wollstonecraft, *Rights of Men*	Mary Wollstonecraft, *A Vindication of the Rights of Men, in a Letter to the Right Honourable Edmund Burke; Occasioned by His "Reflections on the Revolution in France,"* 2nd edition (London: Joseph Johnson, 1790).
Wollstonecraft, *Rights of Woman*	Mary Wollstonecraft, *A Vindication of the Rights of Woman: with Strictures on Moral and Political Subjects,* 2nd edition (London: J. Johnson, 1792).

THE ANNOTATED FRANKENSTEIN

INTRODUCTION

"But lo & behold! I found myself famous!—Frankenstein had prodigious success as a drama," exclaimed Mary Shelley to a friend, only a bit wryly, after seeing a musical melodrama of her novel in London on August 29, 1823, just before her twenty-sixth birthday. "I was much amused, & it appeared to excite a breathelss [*sic*] eagerness in the audience . . . & all stayed till it was over."[1] She was witnessing only the first moments of her novel's fame.

Frankenstein may be the most famous, most enduring imaginative work of the Romantic era, even of the last two hundred years. First published in 1818, it has inspired legions of writers, theatrical producers, and filmmakers, rewriting the fable of Prometheus as a modern myth, reflecting the excitements of scientific idealism, and exposing more broadly anxieties about ambitious schemes run disastrously out of control. From the novel's first decade of published life, "Frankenstein" offered a byword for the promises and premonitions of technology, new science, or any radical shift in the structure of consciousness, social framework, and social relations. "Frankenstein" language continues to form cautionary tales, to haunt allegories of aliens and alienation, and to name any half-acknowledged human "other."

This conflict of high ideals and tragic horrors is rooted in the novel's biographical genesis, the complex background of the young woman who would repeatedly sign herself in print as "The Author of *Frankenstein*."

Mary Wollstonecraft [Godwin] Shelley, 1797–1851

"It is not singular that, as the daughter of two persons of distinguished literary celebrity, I should very early in life have thought of writing," remarks Mary Wollstonecraft Shelley on the first page of a new Introduction she undertook for the 1831 revised *Frankenstein; or, The Modern Prometheus*.[2] Writer and "Author" amounted to different identifications, however. "Author" was more Percy Shelley's ambition for her than her own. "My husband," she wrote, "was, from the first, very anxious that I should prove myself worthy of my parentage, and enrol myself on the page of fame. He was for ever inciting me to obtain literary reputation." Yet with an active imagination, and inspired by the brilliant company that populated her life with Percy (especially their new friend of 1816, the celebrated poet Lord Byron), teenage Mary Godwin became interested in the prospect of being an author. As a girl she explored her father's considerable library, and listened in when his friends would visit for hours, conversing about literature, politics, philosophy, and science. Sneaking downstairs one evening, she hid behind the couch to hear Samuel Taylor Coleridge recite *The Rime of the Ancient Mariner*—a poem that would stay with her as she wrote *Frankenstein,* imprinting its narrative structure, key scenes, and nightmarish anxieties.

Mary's "worthy parentage" proved, however, as much a scandal in the public eye as a celebrity-credit in the circle of Percy Shelley's friends. William Godwin and Mary Wollstonecraft, two of the leading political writers of the 1790s, were distinguished by daring social criticism and calls for radical reform. Wollstonecraft first caught attention in 1790 with a caustic attack on Edmund Burke's *Reflections on the Recent Revolution in France* (1790), a passionate denunciation of a disastrous turn in European history, the Revolution of 1789. Wollstonecraft's rapid response, *A Vindication of the Rights of Men* (1790), preceded Tom Paine's famous *Rights of Man* by several months. It made her name. Her most important work by today's lights, however, is her second vindication: the first English manifesto of feminist philosophy (before the notion of "feminism" was formulated). Published in 1792, *A Vindication of the Rights of Woman* exposed the neglect of women's "rights" by many enthusiastic supporters of the French declaration of "The Rights of Man." Advocating a "revolution" in society's attitudes about women, Wollstonecraft developed a philosophical argument with the skill of a penetrating literary critic, exposing the contradictions in works both conservative and progressive, from standard conduct manuals, to Milton's *Paradise Lost,* to Rousseau's *Émile, ou*

Mary Wollstonecraft, 1790–1791, by John Opie. Mary Shelley's mother is portrayed as a serious, forceful woman of letters, at about the time William Godwin first met her, when she became famous as the author of her polemic on the principles of the French Revolution, *A Vindication of the Rights of Men* (1790).

l'Education. "Mary Wollstonecraft Godwin" was her daughter's homage and chosen signature before marriage.

William Godwin's fame from the 1790s was his blazing "anarchist" tract, *An Enquiry Concerning Political Justice.* Anarchy (no governing head) was his proposed alternative to the pervasive evils and corruptions in existing institutions. Godwin contended

E. Vere Nicoll
Shipton

A
VINDICATION
OF THE
RIGHTS OF WOMAN:
WITH
STRICTURES
ON
POLITICAL AND MORAL SUBJECTS.

BY MARY WOLLSTONECRAFT.

LONDON:
PRINTED FOR J. JOHNSON, N° 72, ST. PAUL'S CHURCH YARD.
1792.

Title page of Mary Wollstonecraft's *Vindication of the Rights of Woman* (1792), the first English manifesto for a rational treatment of women. Her daughter Mary Godwin read this as a teenager, and again with her lover Percy Shelley, who admired Wollstonecraft and this work.

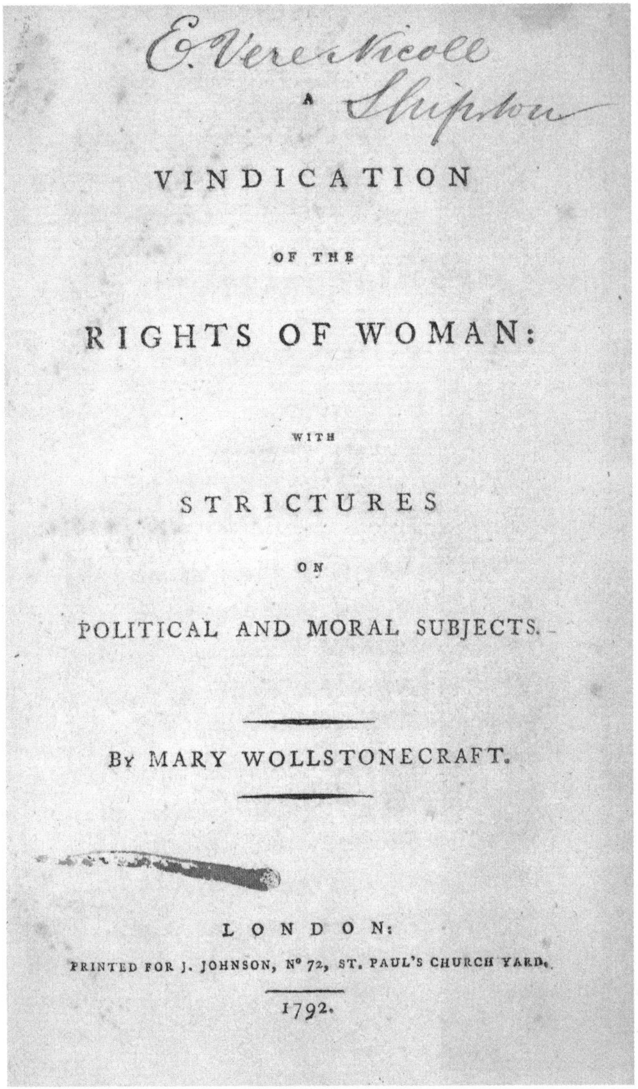

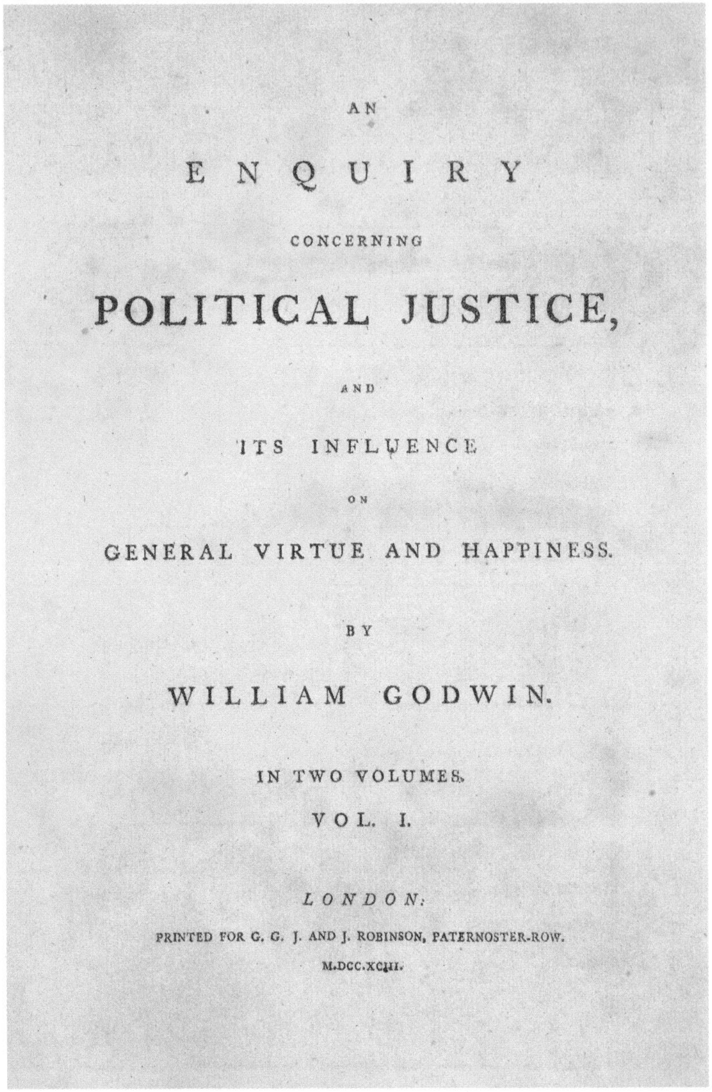

AN
ENQUIRY
CONCERNING
POLITICAL JUSTICE,
AND
ITS INFLUENCE
ON
GENERAL VIRTUE AND HAPPINESS.
BY
WILLIAM GODWIN.
IN TWO VOLUMES.
VOL. I.
LONDON:
PRINTED FOR G. G. J. AND J. ROBINSON, PATERNOSTER-ROW.
M.DCC.XCIII.

The title page of William Godwin's *Political Justice,* 1793. This "anarchist" treatise (a critique of government as a set of corrupt and tyrannous institutions) ignited a generation, including Percy Shelley, who decided he had to make Godwin's acquaintance.

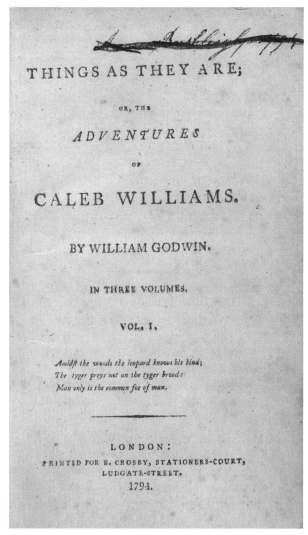

J. W. Chandler's portrait of William Godwin (1798), by this time a widower, father of infant Mary, and stepfather to Fanny.

Title page to William Godwin's gothic-political novel, *Things as They Are; or, The Adventures of Caleb Williams.* The verse, apparently by Godwin, is "Amidst the woods the leopard knows his kind; / The tyger preys not on the tyger brood: / Man only is the common foe of man."

that rational men, pursuing the common good, could deliberate without the interference of government, law, and religion; he would even abolish contracts of marriage and private property. *Political Justice* electrified progressives in the young generation, including Wordsworth, Coleridge, Byron, Percy Shelley, and the "Author of *Frankenstein*," who took a calculated risk by dedicating this novel to her father.

Godwin's most infamous publication was not *Political Justice,* however. It was *Memoirs of the Author of a Vindication of the Rights of Woman* (1798), which he began immediately after Wollstonecraft's horrific death in 1797 from septic poisoning ten days after Mary's birth. Working through his grief and naïvely devoted to a principle of honesty, Godwin recounted several biographical details that proved such a scandal that Wollstonecraft's reputation—and in the bargain, the cause of the Rights of Woman —was ruined for a century. The scandals went well beyond her "improper" independence (living on her own in London and Paris) and immodesty (publishing controversial work under her own name): readers were shocked to learn of her tormented obsession with artist Henri Fuseli; her passionate affair with American adventurer and gun-runner Gilbert Imlay, and their daughter born out of wedlock; two attempted suicides as this affair fell apart; a premarital affair, including pregnancy, with Godwin; and no statement of habitual church attendance. While she and Godwin did marry five months before Mary's birth to insure legitimacy to both Wollstonecraft's daughters, this made it clear that the eldest had been born out of wedlock. Some friends terminated their acquaintance, including the renowned actress Sarah Siddons. Those who had never liked Wollstonecraft's politics and philosophy in the first place rushed to declare her death from childbirth the work of divine correction of a rebellious woman. Godwin's *Memoir* had in effect produced a moral monster or, in the terminology of one reviewer, an "Unsex'd Female"—deviant avatar of Lady Macbeth.

In his grief, Godwin may well have viewed little Mary as a dreadful error, her birth into the world entailing the loss of his beloved wife. Even without this catastrophe, Mary's parents may have been a bit disappointed; they were so sure that their child would be a son that they had already determined to honor him with his father's name, William.[3] No wonder Mary Shelley would grow up to write a novel about a being rejected from its first breath, and pattern Frankenstein's Creature partly on Milton's Eve, the odd female in a male order of creation, ironic counterpart of the only other female, Satan's daughter, condemned to be the monster "Sin." Maybe no wonder, too, that the Creature's first victim, though with no malice aforethought, is an adored son named William.

Portrait of Percy Shelley, by Amelia Curran, 1819: "the Romantic Poet," with pen and dramatically flared collar.

For all his heartbreak, William Godwin did his best with the two girls now in his charge. He became a loving and involved father, and Mary adored him. But he soon wanted help with parenting and homemaking, and (after a few rejections) his choice of wife, with whom he was already involved, was the boisterous Mary Jane Clairmont, mother to a son and a daughter, their fathers unknown. The new Mrs. Godwin, preferring her own children, had no ready sympathy for stepdaughter Mary. For her part, Mary resented the more populated household and her father's divided attentions. Godwin took cover in the domain of his library. When Mary, more temperamental than her elder sister, Fanny, reached her teens, Godwin took steps to relieve the tensions by sending Mary to live with the family of one of his admirers in Scotland. Sentenced to exile on "the blank and dreary northern shores of the Tay, near Dundee," as she writes in that 1831 Introduction, Mary also found unexpected happiness amid a stable and affectionate family, even a "freedom" that issued "airy flights of . . . imagination" and her first pieces of imaginative writing. When she went back home for a visit in 1812 at age fifteen, she impressed her father as "singularly bold, somewhat imperious, and active of mind. Her desire of knowledge is great, and her perseverance in everything she undertakes almost invincible."[4] She was worthy of her parents after all—and it wasn't just Godwin who noticed.

On a later visit, in 1812–1813, Mary opened the door to meet an ardent Godwin-disciple: wealthy, brainy, idealistic nineteen-year-old Percy Bysshe Shelley. Expelled from Oxford in 1811 for publishing and distributing his pamphlet *On the Necessity of Atheism,* he appalled his father no less than he adored Mary's father. He wrote to Godwin in January 1812 to introduce himself to his hero. His heart beat to Godwin's "inestimable book on 'Political Justice'": "it opened to my mind fresh and more extensive views; it materially influenced my character, and I rose from its perusal a wiser and better man." For his part, Godwin took the full spiritual and economic measure of the young acolyte who presented himself as "the son of a man of fortune in Sussex" with whose "habits of thinking" he "never coincided" and who, convinced he had "duties to perform," also had the evident means: "I am heir by entail to an estate of £6,000 per annum . . . My father's notions of family honor are incoincident with my knowledge of public good."[5]

Godwin, always financially strapped, welcomed such an acquaintance and realized that his daughter was an asset. To Percy Shelley, the bright, lovely offspring of Godwin and Wollstonecraft was an unexpected delight. When Mary visited London again in spring 1814, they kept happy company. She was only sixteen; he was twenty-one and stuck with a wife he had married on principle, to liberate her from a father who refused to educate her. "The irresistible wildness and sublimity of her feelings shewed itself in her gestures and her looks," sighed Percy of Mary to the college friend who was his collaborator on that *Atheism* pamphlet; "I speedily conceived an ardent passion to possess this inestimable treasure."[6] The sweethearts met at Wollstonecraft's grave for reading,

conversation, and intimacy.[7] By the summer Mary was pregnant. At the end of July 1814 (fifteen years to the month after the French Revolution), they declared their erotic freedom and eloped (without marrying) to France for a six-week adventure, taking along Mary's restless stepsister, Claire Clairmont, for cover with the family, companionship, and the resources of her fluent French. It was an exciting adventure through towns, villages, and the natural landscapes of a Europe scarred by the Napoleonic wars. "[I]n the summer of 1814, every inconvenience was hailed as a new chapter in the romance of our travels," Mary recalled in 1826.[8] Back home, the Godwins fumed at the subterfuge and transgression, and refused to receive Mary and Percy when they returned. It was not until they married, at the end of 1816 (following the suicide of Percy's first wife), that Godwin would see his daughter again (though he did not stint, in the interval, to

An engraving of St. Pancras Churchyard in 1815–1816. Teenage Mary Godwin frequently visited her mother's grave in this churchyard and read her works there, as if to commune with her; in 1814 the gravesite would be the location of amorous meetings with Percy Shelley.

George Gordon, Lord Byron, by Richard Westall, 1813. Byron, theatrically alluring, in Hamlet-like meditation, painted in the first year of his international fame following the overnight sensation of *Childe Harold's Pilgrimage, A Romaunt* (1812). Engravings based on this portrait made this one of the most widely circulated images of the poet.

press Percy for funds, making Mary quite sensitive to the slander of his *"selling his daughter"* to Shelley).⁹ After the marriage, it was not "Wollstonecraft" that Mary dropped from her name but "Godwin." She now signed herself "Mary Wollstonecraft Shelley," sometimes in correspondence as "M.W.S."

From 1814, Mary's life with Percy was intimate, liberating, exciting, stressful, and often painful. That first pregnancy issued a premature birth; the infant died a few weeks later on the night of March 5, 1815, and was buried without being named. Mary's grief was acute and haunted. On March 19 she wrote in her journal, "Dream that my little baby came to life again—that it had only been cold & that we rubbed it by the fire & it lived—I awake & find no baby—I think about the little thing all day."¹⁰ The dream

Villa Diodati, tinted steel engraving, 1833, printed by Byron's publisher John Murray. In the "Frankenstein" summer of 1816, Lord Byron rented this lavish villa (where Milton was thought, incorrectly, to have resided), on the south shore of Lake Geneva, Switzerland, about four miles from Geneva. Percy Shelley, Mary Godwin, Clare Clairmont, and J. W. Polidori were daily companions. This image, rendered just two years after the publication of the revised *Frankenstein* (1831) with an Introduction recounting the generative events there in June 1816, envisions a romantic literary retreat, a poet and lute in the foreground. Although it was originally known as Villa Belle Rive ("Beautiful Shore"), Byron named it Villa Diodati, after the family that owned it, distantly related to Charles Diodati, close friend of Milton. "Belrive" is the name Mary Shelley gives the Frankenstein family home on Lake Geneva.

would return more than once in *Frankenstein,* as warmth or fire animates the dead, or near dead, into life. Mary soon became pregnant again, and named the baby born in January 1816 William, a gesture fraught with her complex relation to her father.

Strong-willed behavior continued to shape Mary's life, as did its sensational and sometimes cruel consequences. In spring 1816, Claire made a play for the celebrity Lord Byron, recently separated from his wife of scarcely more than a year. He was about to leave England (forever, it turned out), but first obliged Claire's sexual overture. Wanting to use her connection to Percy Shelley to hold Byron's attention, Claire maneuvered Mary (who was agreeably fascinated with this brilliantly talented bad boy), Percy, and little William to a summer residence at Lake Geneva near Byron's Villa Diodati. Percy Shelley became fascinated with Byron, too, and when the poets met, a close friendship blossomed; they spent long weeks touring and conversing about everything late into the night. Claire, pregnant by Byron, gave birth to their daughter back in England in January 1817, naming her Alba Allegra ("Alba" echoing "LB": Lord Byron). In summer 1818 she and Percy took Allegra to meet Byron in Venice. Byron found Claire too flighty, and exercising his legal right, claimed Allegra and sent her mother packing. He then decided that Allegra would be better off living and being educated in a convent, to which he sent her, barring her mother access. The Shelleys defended his decision but were appalled when Allegra died there at age five from typhoid.

Family catastrophes accumulated. In October 1816, Mary's half-sister Fanny (acutely aware that she was no blood relation to anyone in the Godwin household) committed suicide. In December, Shelley's first wife, Harriet, pregnant by someone other than the husband whose wedding ring she still wore, drowned herself. While this sad event did enable Mary and Percy to marry, and so be reconciled to their parents, Percy's behavior and controversial publications cost him the custody of his two children by Harriet—an extraordinary ruling in an era when fathers had presumptive claim to all children (including illegitimacies). Mary entered a life of serial pregnancies and in 1822 almost died from the miscarriage of her fifth. Little William, a toddler when she was writing *Frankenstein,* died from malaria in 1819; Clara, born in 1817, scarcely survived infancy, dying of heat exhaustion in 1818, at the end of a summer of traveling to keep up with Byron. By the time of Mary's miscarriage, moreover, Percy (though he saved her life by stemming the bleeding with ice) had been growing distant, caught up in ever new erotic fascinations. A few weeks after the miscarriage he drowned in a storm at sea, along with the common-law husband of the woman who was his latest infatuation.

Portrait of Mary Shelley, by Richard Rothwell, circa 1840. This image of the established woman of letters, in her early forties, was exhibited in London at the Royal Academy in 1840. It was captioned "child of love and light," a phrase from Percy Shelley's dedication "To Mary" in *The Revolt of Islam,* published in January 1818, the same month as *Frankenstein.*

Percy Shelley's death was quickly politicized, his champions casting him as a martyr to liberty and his detractors hooting that the atheist was off to be rebuked by his Maker. Mary was devastated. "I have now no friend . . . Oh, how alone! . . . no eye answers mine," she wrote in the first entry of a notebook that she titled

The Journal of Sorrow—
Begun 1822
But for my child it could not
End too soon.

The feeling would never leave her. As late as 1838 she could sigh, "Shelley died, & I was alone—my father, from age & domestic circumstances & other things could not *me faire valoir*" [be supportive of me]; she "sunk . . . in a state of loneliness no other human being ever before I beleive ~~ever~~ endured—Except Robinson Crusoe."[11] She had become the agonized reflection of the Creature of epic loneliness in *Frankenstein.* Her second-most-famous novel, *The Last Man,* begun in 1824, was published in early 1826, its protagonist the sole human survivor of a global plague.

Wracked by grief, impoverished, with one surviving child (Percy Florence) to support, Mary Shelley returned to London in 1823 at age twenty-five. She channeled her grief into a determination to redeem her husband's reputation by bringing his unpublished works into publication, and so managing a new, more sympathetic reception for this misunderstood idealist. This was tricky because Percy's father wanted to keep his scandalous son's name out of the public eye, and as a condition of the small annuity of £100 he supplied to Percy Florence, Mary was enjoined from publishing anything at all about her husband. Her own name, too, was tainted by the circle of scandal, which extended to Claire, Byron, and Polidori. Poet Laureate Robert Southey was rumored to have slandered the whole Geneva party of 1816 as a "League of Incest," and in 1821 he branded in print their "monstrous" "Satanic school" of poetry.[12] A quarter of a century after her death, Wollstonecraft's reputation was seemingly beyond repair, and Godwin, though his controversial 1790s fame had faded, was still regarded as an eccentric radical. It was no small challenge for Mary Shelley to fashion herself into the professional writer that her lost husband desired. Although she never matched the genius or fame of *Frankenstein,* she did develop a productive, steadily busy career across several genres: imaginative tales, essays, reviews, travel books, encyclopedia articles, more novels, poems, and a mythological drama. In the same year *The Last Man* was published, 1826, Percy's eldest son (by his first wife) died. With Percy Florence now the heir, Sir Timothy took stock and gradually enhanced his annuity.

Mary Shelley's most deeply devoted labors were her several editions of Percy Shelley's works, beginning in 1824 with *Posthumous Poems.* While this publication was scarcely out before it was quickly bought up and pulped by an angry Sir Timothy, his paternal ire abated with advancing age, and Mary Shelley was able to develop a multi-volume *Poetical Works of Percy Bysshe Shelley,* threaded through with prefaces offering biographical details, personal anecdotes, and thematic commentary. This full edition appeared in 1839, complemented in 1840 by an edition of Shelley's letters, essays (including the first publication of his influential *Defence of Poetry*), translations, and prose fragments. Mary's commitment to these editions helped her to sustain a sense of relationship with Percy and to prove herself worthy of him, as the vehicle of understanding and advocacy to new generations of readers. As she hoped, her editions helped recreate a political recreant into a poet of visionary idealism and exquisite verbal beauty. While there would be editions of a more scholarly cast later in the century, these would not have been possible without Mary Shelley's determined rehabilitation and foundational textual labor. Later editors often reprinted her narrative notes, the interest deriving not only from her intimate knowledge of the poet but also from the steadily expanding fame of *Frankenstein.*

Frankenstein; or, The Modern Prometheus

"The Author of *Frankenstein*" was Mary Shelley's claim to fame, her signature on the title page of all her subsequent novels and the byline to the stories and tales she published from 1829 to 1835, before she was confident enough, as an established woman of letters, to sign her work "Mrs. Shelley." Although she had collaborated with Percy Bysshe Shelley on a travelogue (1817) drawn from their adventures on the Continent in 1814 and 1816, only his name appeared on its title page. The first edition of *Frankenstein* (1818), in modest run of 500 copies, outsold and made more money than the sum of Percy Shelley's lifetime publications.[13] Even so, Mary Shelley would have been astonished at its subsequent fame.

Stage plays, beginning with the one she attended in 1823, took over the basic fable, sheared off the novel's literary complexities, and gave what a novel-text never could: a visibly realized Creature. Far more people knew "Frankenstein" from the stage than from the page. Even so, the London stage success prompted the ever alert Godwin to secure a new printing of the novel in 1823 (now with "Mary Wollstonecraft Shelley" on the title page). With its fame increasing across the 1820s, Shelley herself negotiated a revised, expanded version for Bentley's Standard Author series. To help promote this

1831 *Frankenstein,* she wrote an Introduction that reads like a supplementary short story, or stage script, about the gothic genesis of the tale back in 1816.

The Introduction drew to a close with an envoy of authorial pride that also sounds like a parental blessing: "And now, once again, I bid my hideous progeny go forth and prosper." Prosper it did. The 1831 version ran into the thousands, with many reprintings. Charles Dickens could invoke *Frankenstein,* without naming it per se, in his best-known novel, *Great Expectations* (1861), and exercise some wry turns on the tale. Pip finds that his new identity as a London "gentleman" is a manufacture by an unsuspected benefactor, the shabby transported convict Abel Magwitch. When Magwitch secretly returns to London to reveal himself to Pip, he beams in pride at his creature's accomplishments:

> he would ask me to read to him—"Foreign language, dear boy!" While I complied, he, not comprehending a single word, would stand before the fire surveying me with the air of an Exhibitor . . . appealing in dumb-show to the furniture to take notice of my proficiency. The imaginary student pursued by the misshapen creature he had impiously made, was not more wretched than I, pursued by the creature who had made me, and recoiling from him with a stronger repulsion, the more he admired me and the fonder he was of me. (chap. 40)

Part of the wit of Dickens's *Frankenstein* allusions lies in their repeated role reversals. Here, Pip the creature shrinks in horror at his creator. In an earlier episode Pip is the haunted creator of a misbegotten pastiche, a botched attempt to reflect his recent rise in status in his makeover of another poor boy:

> For, after I had made the monster (out of the refuse of my washerwoman's family) and had clothed him with a blue coat, canary waistcoat, white cravat, creamy breeches, and the boots already mentioned, I had to find him a little to do and a great deal to eat; and with both of those horrible requirements he haunted my existence. (chap. 27)[14]

These allusions assume a familiarity of reference and make it clear, too, that *Frankenstein* had come to public consciousness not just by force of its astonishing fantasy but also with its range of implication: the definition of "monster," judgments that derive virtue or villainy from class origins and accidents of physical appearance; the responsibility of creators to and for their creations; the responsibility of society for the anger of those to whom it refuses care, compassion, or just decent regard; the relationships of parents and children—and all this arrayed with an eerie, brilliant intuition, a century before Freud, about the psychological dynamics of repression, transference, condensation, dream-work, and alter egos.

In the animations of early cinema, a medium of dreamlike silence, *Frankenstein* inspired Thomas Edison, the genius of electricity, to make the first film adaptation, in 1910.[15] Many modern readers first encountered *Frankenstein* in childhood, in cinema or the afterlife of the creature-feature on TV. Still the most prominent movies are the 1931 *Frankenstein* (directed by James Whale, with Boris Karloff in the performance of a lifetime as the Creature) and the tender, campy 1935 sequel, *The Bride of Frankenstein*. These generated serial resurrections in the horror-filled pre- and postwar 1930s and 1940s (*Son of, Ghost of, House of,* and so on). Then, the notorious *Abbott and Costello Meet Frankenstein* (1948); the Gary Conway puberty trauma *I Was a Teenage Frankenstein* (1957); the full-color British Hammer revivals of the 1950s, 1960s, and 1970s; Paul Morrisey's ghoulish, sadistic film *Andy Warhol's Frankenstein* (1974); Mel Brooks's vaudevillian *Young Frankenstein* (1974); the transvestite Dr. Frank-N-Furter of *The Rocky Horror Picture Show* (1975); the 1980s-feminist *Making Mr. Right* (Dr. Frankie Stone trains android John Malkovich in being human); and Kenneth Branagh's 1994 extravaganza, with Robert De Niro as the Creature, *Mary Shelley's Frankenstein* (it wasn't). As recently as summer 2011 (and fated to be outdated), *Frankenstein*-referring characters and fables excited movie audiences with *X-Men* and *The Rise of the Planet of the Apes*. There are no signs of abatement. At the time of this writing, seven more *Frankenstein*-themed projects are in development.[16]

"Frankenstein" has multiplied in allusive force to label any disturbing development in science and technology, as well as in history and politics, sports and fashion, and just about everything else—with various and sometimes overlapping senses of amusement, alarm, awe, and admonition. Hardly a month passes without some new iteration. "For all we know, we have created a Frankenstein," murmured one reporter on the horror of Hiroshima, in August 1945. A half century on, this power of massive de-creation would be complemented by disturbing new creations. The child in William Blake's *Songs of Innocence* who asked back in 1789, "Little Lamb who made thee?" might be stunned by "the creation of Dolly, the lamb formed by cellular biologists in Scotland and fused into life by electric shock, as was the Monster in . . . *Frankenstein*," to quote William Safire,

The EDISON KINETOGRAM

VOL. 1   LONDON, APRIL 15, 1910   No. 1

SCENE FROM

FRANKENSTEIN

FILM No. 6604

EDISON FILMS TO BE RELEASED FROM MAY 11 TO 18 INCLUSIVE

The cover of the March 15, 1910, issue of *The Edison Kinetogram* (vol. 2, no. 4), a semi-monthly magazine-catalogue that the company published to promote its new films. This is the London edition, published a month later, after the American premier on March 18. The short, silent film starred Charles Stanton Ogle as the Creature, Augustus Phillips as the Creator, and Mary Fuller as the fiancée. Across the nineteenth century, the Creature was dehumanized into the kind of figure represented here. Though often regarded as the first horror film, Edison's *Frankenstein* was released with assurances that the "repulsive" horrors of Shelley's novel had been purged, sensitive to the concerns of a newly formed Board of Censors (a collaboration of film industry executives and religious leaders). To those who know the novel, "it will be evident that we have carefully omitted anything which might by any possibility shock any portion of the audience . . . the Edison Co. has carefully tried to eliminate all actual repulsive situations and to concentrate its endeavors upon the mystic and psychological problems that are to be found in this weird tale." Even so, striking special effects render the Creature's emergence from a smoking cauldron. Two well-conceived mirror scenes imply that the Creature and the fiancée are rival reflections of Frankenstein's psyche.

for whom this event provoked "head-breaking thoughts about good and evil, God and humanity."[17] If in retrospect this Lab-Lamb seems just one more step in the sophistication of genetic engineering, the initial template was *Frankenstein*. "The *Frankenstein* Myth Becomes a Reality: We have the Awful Knowledge to Make Exact Copies of Human Beings" was the tabloid title of an article in the *New York Times Magazine* in 1972.[18] Anxiety about genetics' replacing Genesis was hard to shake off. When President George W. Bush was about to veto federal funding for stem-cell research on the grounds of the blasphemy of playing God, Safire relented a bit but continued to warn "of the real dangers of the slippery slope to Frankenscience."[19] In 2005 Dr. Stephen

INTRODUCTION

19

Despite the lumbering gait, the poignancy of Karloff's acting emerged through his eloquent gestures and the facial expressions clearly visible through Jack Pierce's makeup. Later versions coarsened the emotion, and even Karloff's third and final performance, in *The Son of Frankenstein* (1939), reduced the hand gestures to a formula.

Levick turned the tables but kept the myth. In a letter to the *New York Times Magazine* he asked, "Which is the real monster? chimeric stem-cell science or the *political* [his italics] use made of it by opponents to all embryonic-stem-cell research? . . . to see the researchers as monster-creating Dr. Frankensteins" is to "risk inflaming the public to unthinkingly torch the whole hopeful enterprise."[20]

No less remarkable than the expansive vitality of the Frankenstein myth is its genesis in the imagination of the brilliant young woman who distilled into her novel her personal traumas, her reading, her attention to current European history (intellectual and political), and her excitement by the poets and the philosophical debates of her day. Her world included the writings of her parents; the death of her mother from complications in her birth; her father's alternating affection and distance; her infatuation with the passionate idealist Shelley; her pregnancies and the deaths of three of her children; her exhilaration and anxiety amid a company of somewhat older, brilliantly talented

Illustration for *Frankenstein* by Lynd Ward. American artist Lynd Ward (1905–1985) is noted for his expressionist woodcuts. His illustrated edition of *Frankenstein* appeared in 1934, in the same decade as James Whale's *Frankenstein* and *The Bride of Frankenstein.* With a strong design, Ward depicts a Creature of athletic power, superhuman massiveness and mobility. The Creature is at one with the rugged natural world in which he manages to survive.

men; their extreme commitments to their passions and ideals and their willingness to subordinate family and domesticity to these excitements; and, above all, their speculative conversations about the principle of life, the reanimation of corpses in myth and recent electrical experiment, and the manufacture of a living creature.[21] Mary's adventurous reading coursed through the Bible, classical authors, Dante, Shakespeare, Milton, novels, ghost stories, as well as political tracts, and accounts of modern science and polar exploration.

All this was in the heady air of an evening's entertainment during a spell of rainy weather in June 1816, at Byron's villa on the Alpine shores of Lake Geneva, Switzerland. As Mary Shelley tells the story in the 1831 Introduction, the party—herself, Percy Shelley, Lord Byron, Byron's personal physician, John William Polidori, and Claire Clairmont—had been reading volumes of ghost stories when Byron proposed that they try their own skill. Claire came up dry; Shelley soon gave up; Byron dashed off a fragment of a vampire tale; Polidori jettisoned a tale about an ill-fated peeping Tom, then, working on Byron's idea, eventually "vamped up" (said one of their friends) his own fuller vampire story.[22] Mary, eager to prove herself, embraced the challenge. "I busied myself *to think of a story*"; but she was soon tripped up by writer's block, a "mortifying

From Whale's *Frankenstein,* 1931. The relay shots of Creator and Creature viewed through the gears of the windmill at once evoke the doubling of these characters and effect a meta-cinematic spectacle of flickering, framed images. The publicity poster for *Frankenstein* at London's National Theatre, 2011 (reprised 2012), is a savvy sequel to Whale's relay shots. On the top half, eight head shots left to right morph from "Benedict Cumberbatch as The Creature" to "Jonny Lee Miller as Victor Frankenstein"; on the bottom half the same array morphs from "Benedict Cumberbatch as Victor Frankenstein" to "Jonny Lee Miller as The Creature." The actors alternated the roles every night, ingeniously staging the theme of Creator and Creature as alter egos.

negative" to the question asked of her each morning, *Have you thought of a story?* A way of saying "acutely embarrassed," *mortifying* is a loaded term, forecasting the struggle for animation at the heart of the story to come. A still uncreative Mary found herself unable to sleep, but her "imagination, unbidden" came to life, starting to work with a "vividness far beyond the usual bounds of reverie":

> I saw—with shut eyes, but acute mental vision,—I saw the pale student of unhallowed arts kneeling beside the thing he had put together. I saw the hideous phantasm of a man stretched out, and then, on the working of some powerful engine, show signs of life, and stir with an uneasy, half vital motion . . . I recurred to my ghost story,—my tiresome unlucky ghost story! O! if I could only contrive one which would frighten my reader as I myself had been frightened that night!
>
> Swift as light and as cheering was the idea that broke in upon me. "I have found it! What terrified me will terrify others" . . . On the morrow I announced that I had *thought of a story.* I began that day with the words, *It was on a dreary night of November.*"

The germ of the "story" produces Frankenstein's climax of daring creation (Vol. I, Ch. IV). Writing with retrospective knowledge of the novel that issued to fame, Mary Shelley tells a story of creating herself as an Author.

No small terror of that night vision was "the effect of any human endeavour to mock the stupendous mechanism of the Creator of the world." If the artist-creator as a second God is a traditional Neoplatonic conceit, Mary Shelley's Introduction refreshes this conceit not only with a literal enactment but also with one that draws an anxious parallel between a female author and the transgressive creator. She recognizes that "invention" draws on a "capacity for seizing on the capabilities of a subject" and "the power of moulding and fashioning ideas suggested to it" in order "to invent the machinery of a story." The language evokes Frankenstein's assembling his creation from parts of other creatures. Author Shelley and author Frankenstein (he calls himself thus in the novel) are both in the business of creating a "hideous phantasm"—Frankenstein his Creature, Mary Shelley the creation named *Frankenstein.*

In more ways than this, *Frankenstein* is a novel assembled from component parts, sutured with sequential narrations, beginning with the visionary polar explorer Robert Walton's letters to his sister Margaret Saville. Her initials, we realize, must be M. W. S.,

the very signature at the end of Mary Wollstonecraft Shelley's 1831 Introduction, and so a ghostly proxy for the Author.[23] Walton's letters enfold Victor Frankenstein's story of catastrophe, which recounts, verbatim, his Creature's autobiography. "Listen to my tale" is the repeated petition, internally to some auditor and rhetorically to the reader. Each narrator—Walton, Frankenstein, the Creature—tells a tale as an "Author" whose needs, grievances, and desire for understanding shape his story. As audience to them all, readers contend with sequentially new information, with corresponding effects of disjunctive sympathies and judgments both on the events narrated and, more crucially, on the protagonists, Frankenstein and his Creature.

Prometheus Creating Man (L'Homme formé par Prométhée et animé par Minerve, détail) was first painted in 1802 by Jean-Simon Berthélemy, and again by Jean-Baptiste Mauzaisse in 1826. Evoking Michelangelo's famous image on the ceiling of the Sistine Chapel of God infusing life into Adam, this is an idealized image of Promethean creation, the gift of fire illuminating human intelligence, an act witnessed by Minerva, goddess of wisdom.

What's in a Name? Identifying, Imaging, Picturing

The title page of the 1818 novel reads *Frankenstein; or, The Modern Prometheus,* and features three lines of verse from Book X of John Milton's great seventeenth-century epic *Paradise Lost,* excerpted from Adam's long complaint to his Creator about his punishment for disobedience. In the implied background of the two printed names, *Frankenstein* and *Prometheus,* then, are God and Adam, and shadowing them, Satan and Eve—all figuring in the narrations to come. On the obverse of the title page is a dedication by the novel's "Author" to the "Author" William Godwin. Each of these names is pregnant with significance or (more often) conflicting significances.

Yet for all this, the spectacular absence on these front pages is the novel's most famous figure, its unnamed Creature. Generations of readers have given him his creator's name. In November 1830, *Fraser's Magazine,* for example, referred to "an unnatural body of the species of the Frankenstein monster" (481). What makes such conflations so canny is Shelley's own insistent linking of Creator to the Creature, the science to its product. For those who know the novel, this link ironically gives the Creature the patronym that his horrified creator never would, never even naming him at all, except with a barrage of derogatory epithets. The habit of calling the Creature "Frankenstein" in effect performs the denied paternal acknowledgment. The "creator and creature are in some sense two sides of one personality," comments Martin Tropp, nicely advancing the common error of double-naming into a psychoanalytic intuition.[24]

Creature? Frankenstein Monster? just *Frankenstein?* Everyone who writes about, discusses, or teaches this novel or its avatars has to think about what to call the abject being. It is unique in having no given name, first or last—and by implication, no social identity by nation, clan, family, or legitimate species. In 1838 Prime Minister William Gladstone described hybrid mules as "Frankensteins of the animal creation" but with a poignant, critical qualification: "Sympathy, however, they have; and with a faint yet wild and unnatural neighing they will sometimes recognise relationship."[25] From first breath to last, the being in Shelley's novel rarely has this recognition, hailed instead with derogations that repel relationship: catastrophe, wretch, demon, daemon, Devil, hideous phantasm, fiend, vile insect, abomination, monster. All these namings react only, but irrevocably, to a visual impression shocking to human norms. The only person who responds to the Creature as "a human creature" is one who is "blind, and cannot judge of [his] countenance" (Vol. II, Ch. VII). We feel the importance of these negatives against what is always posited: "I beheld the wretch," moans Frankenstein as his science project stirs into life, "the miserable monster whom I had created" (Vol. I, Ch. IV).

This is the first, but hardly the last, event of the word *monster* in *Frankenstein.* Its etymology is potent, working back from the French *monstre* to the Latin root *monstrum* (a portent, prodigy, wicked creature, atrocity), down to the verb-base *monere:* to warn (of something ominous). This is the matrix of definition, post-*Frankenstein,* that appears in the OED: "Originally: a mythical creature which is part animal and part human, or combines elements of two or more animal forms, and is frequently of great size and ferocious appearance. Later, more generally: any imaginary creature that is large, ugly, and frightening." There is also an inaccurate but verbally appealing etymology from the closely lettered Latin verb, *monstrare,* "to show or point to" (as in a de*monstra*tion). Monsters are spectacles.[26]

Yet if *Monster* has become the most popular epithet, the novel constantly puts this naming forward as a problem. The term appears almost three dozen times therein, mostly for Frankenstein's Creature—but with two arresting exceptions. A young woman unjustly convicted of murder is harassed by her confessor "until I began to think I was the monster that he said I was" (Vol. I, Ch. VII), and a close, sisterly friend, dismayed by this miscarriage of justice, scans a courtroom of men "who seem monsters thirsting for each other's blood" (Vol. II, Ch. I). The force of these deviations is critical, exposing "monster" not as innate depravity but as a name for behavior perceived as depraved.

Being and *Creature* bid fair as neutral terms, foregrounding the fact that this being has been created but making no assumptions about its character. Even so, *Being* still implies a distinction from Human Being. *Creature* has ethical force in reminding us of a *Creator,* the bond of the two words failing to convince the creator Frankenstein of the bond of responsibility for his Creature. It is telling that *creature* appears nearly sixty times in *Frankenstein,* yet scarcely more than twenty referring to Frankenstein's Creature. The reference, with cruel exclusion, is instead to creatures and fellow-creatures in the community of human beings. Restoring a pathos to the character after a century of demonizing stage representations, Boris Karloff preferred *Creature* as the designation in the 1931 *Frankenstein,* and conveyed this especially with his plaintively gesturing hands. Yet only an innocent child reacts to him without alarm. The Creature was not listed in the film's opening credits, and in the closing cast list was designated by "?". He is forever indeterminate, exiled, nameless, unnamable.

Peter Paul Rubens, *Prometheus Bound* (1611–1612), depicts Prometheus not as heroic creator but as eternally tormented transgressor.

On the program of the play that Mary Shelley attended in 1823, R. B. Peake's *Presumption: or the Fate of Frankenstein*, the Creature had a similar sign, a blank dash. "The play bill amused me extremely," she noted, "for in the list of dramatis personæ came, ———— Mr T. Cooke: this nameless mode of naming the unameable is rather good."[27] What kind of embodiment bears this "unameable"? Performances from Cooke to Karloff, whatever the variables, have two notable characteristics: gone is the Creature's skilled literacy, while the extraordinary body is crudified into a giant or ugly phantasm, somatic sign of inherent menace. The first cinema Creature was the silent-film specter of Edison's *Frankenstein,* an exact inversion of Shelley's movingly speaking

M^r. T. P. COOKE.
Of the Theatre Royal Covent Garden.
In the Character of the Monster in the Dramatic Romance of Frankenstein.

A poster for *Presumption; or, The Fate of Frankenstein,* by Richard Brinsley Peake, staged at the Lyceum Theatre (English Opera House), summer 1823, starring Thomas Potter Cooke, a prominent actor noted for his athleticism and good looks, as the unnamed being. The costume directions indicate "Dark black flowing hair—*à la Octavian*—his face, hands, arms, and legs all are, being one colour, the same as his body, which is a light blue or French gray cotton dress, fitting quite close, as if it were his flesh, with satin colour scarf round his middle, passing over one shoulder." The poster exaggerates the Creature's size. Three years before, in 1820, Cooke was celebrated for his role as Ruthven, the hero of *The Vampire,* a play based on another tale from the Villa Diodati night, June 1816, by John William Polidori, Byron's personal physician and companion.

Cover illustration of Richard Brinsley Peake's *Frankenstein,* the performance text, when it was published in Dicks' Standard Plays, No. 431. The Creature is not particularly monstrous, but rather large, boyish, and strangely flirtatious.

Frontispiece to Henry M. Milner's *Frankenstein, or the Man and the Monster!* (1826). Milner's play, originally titled *Frankenstein; or, The Demon of Switzerland,* was also staged in the summer of 1823, at London's Royal Coburg Theatre, which had almost 4,000 seats. As the Creature, Richard John O. Smith wore a "close vest and leggings of pale yellowish brown heightened with blue, Greek shirt of dark brown, and broad black leather belt."

Mr. O. SMITH as the MONSTER.
in
FRANKENSTEIN.

Creature. Even Karloff's portrayal of pathetic confusion and inept delight was consumed in a final brutishness. His Creature is huge, lumbering, inarticulate, and while quite moving, a constant reminder of the potential for violence lodged in that powerful body. Shelley, by contrast, conceived a Creature of supernatural athleticism and agility, qualities that at times give him a hallucinatory grace and mobility as he crosses rough terrain. Aware of this superiority to human beings—bigger, more powerful, more supple, more resistant to the elements—the Creature has a pride of physical being that evokes Adam's account in *Paradise Lost* of awakening in Eden, delighted in his physical existence. Yet the differences matter mightily. The Creature's pride in his power and resilience alternates with his horror at his deformity and loneliness, while Adam is pleased to learn that he is graced with the image of a divine Creator-Father, a lodge in Eden, his momentary loneliness quickly healed with a spouse to love and angels to guide him.

Without a precise image of the Creature, Shelley's readers are closer to the old blind father M. De Lacey, the Creature's best hope, he realizes, for a sympathetic reception. On this depends his social life and death. While we inevitably sift some imagination of the Creature from the stark descriptions and expressions of horror, we never actually "see" him, and our reception of his words is spared this disturbing interference. The novel's verbal medium allows us to encounter him firsthand in the language of an articulate, poignant storyteller, a penetrating student of *Paradise Lost* with an eloquence that conveys an unanticipated humanlike, even fellow-human, sensibility. Not only has the Creature mastered the "god-like science" of language (as he calls it) but his humanity is the most surprising, most disturbing, and ultimately most moving aspect of his character. One of the elements lost to our history of the Creature is the humanity of the

ENDLESS ENTERTAINMENT.

A SERIES OF ORIGINAL
COMIC, TERRIFIC, AND LEGENDARY
TALES.

No. 7.   FRIDAY, JUNE 17, 1825.   Price 2d.

Contents.—THE MONSTER.

See page 101.

THE MONSTER MADE BY MAN;
OR, THE PUNISHMENT OF PRESUMPTION.

IN every age of the world woman's curiosity has been equalled by man's presumption, and one of the most astonishing events produce'' the latter quality is related in Germany, that native country every thing non-natural.

In one of the most romantic parts of it resided Wallberg, a

H 2

Endless Entertainment; A Series of Original Comic, Terrific, and Legendary Tales, a weekly magazine costing a mere twopence, was published by G. Herbert, 88 Cheapside, London. Each of the eighteen numbers presented a tale with a "Spirited" woodcut illustration by J. March. This is the cover for Number 7, Friday June 17, 1825 (97–119), featuring an anonymous tale: "The Monster Made by Man; or, The Punishment of Presumption." As the title may suggest, the picture is based on *Frankenstein* as filtered through Peake's *Presumption,* with "Ernest" as the too-inquisitive hero. The scientist is "Ernest Wallberg"; the kneeling figure at the left is the lab assistant, Frantz, invented by Peake as "Fritz" (memorably performed in the 1931 film by Dwight Frye). The woodcut here illustrates the Monster's awakening: "its perfect proportions were enlarged to an unnatural size, its regular features were distorted into hideousness, the eyelids opened, and displayed two green balls, bedded in a yellow fluid, and the alabaster whiteness of its exterior turned to a leaden blue colour" (101); "at length in a hollow voice, in which was discernible none of the usual tones of human nature, he uttered, 'I am the punishment of thy presumption'" (103).

George Cruikshank, *The Modern Prometheus, or Downfall of Tyranny* (print published in London, 1814). In 1814, the coalition against Napoleon invaded France, forcing this self-styled emperor to abdicate and exiling him to the island of Elba in the Mediterranean. In less than a year, Napoleon escaped and returned to power but would be vanquished at the Battle of Waterloo in 1815, and thereafter exiled to the island of St. Helena in the Atlantic Ocean, where he died in 1821. In this moralizing political cartoon Napoleon (lower right), the archetypal over-reacher, suffers the fate of transgressive Prometheus while Justice prevails.

THE MODERN PROMETHEUS, OR DOWNFALL OF TYRANNY.

This Print Presented gratis to every Purchaser of a Ticket or Share at Martins Lottery Office & Cornhill

first visual representations. These are not horrifically monstrous. In the frontispiece image for the 1831 novel, he is fairly human-looking, just dazed and disoriented. The plays of the 1820s had human-scale actors in human form, with the body difference managed by colored garments or greasepaint. This coloring could bring to mind racial otherness, but if so, the closest company to this "other" look are the marginal population of tinker-gypsies. In the 1823 play these characters were clad in goatskins and possibly body makeup (one is named "Tanskin"), and so akin in this animal way to the nonhuman creature. The kinship is doubly forceful, exposing the arbitrariness of naming any marginal creature a "monster."

What of the nameable? Frankenstein's first name turns out to be "Victor." Mary Shelley has clearly calculated an irony—not only the delusion of being a scientific *victor* but also the recoil of this delusion into a chiming opposite, *victim*. The name of fame is of course *Frankenstein*. Possibly inspired by a Castle Frankenstein (near Mayence on the Rhone River, down which Mary and Percy traveled), it means, literally, "stone (stronghold) of the Franks." In French, the Frankensteins' native language, *frank* means "free" —and in character, "honest, open, candid."[28] On this thread, Mary Shelley deftly weaves

FRANKENSTEIN.

"By the glimmer of the half-extinguished light, I saw the dull, yellow eye of the creature open; it breathed hard, and a convulsive motion agitated its limbs. *** I rushed out of the room."

Page 43.

London, Published by H. Colburn and R. Bentley, 1831.

T. Holst, del. / W. Chevalier, sculp.

The first image of the Creature to be published with the novel shows not so much a hideous "monster" as a dazed and disoriented human-like being, whose bulging eye is very much like the eyes of his horrified Creator.

frank-words into the Frankenstein family affections. The polar explorer Walton feels encouraged to speak "frankly" to his mysterious guest; Victor Frankenstein admires the "air of frankness" in his favorite teacher; Justine is welcomed into the family as "frank-hearted"; adopted cousin Elizabeth is admired for her "great frankness of disposition." In *History of a Six Weeks' Tour,* Mary records having met a young woman who seems her very model: "at one of the inns here we saw the only pretty woman we met with in the course of our travels. She is what I should conceive to be a truly German beauty; grey eyes, slightly tinged with brown, and expressive of uncommon sweetness and frankness" (70). The family name *Frankenstein* does not appear in the novel until Vol. I, Ch. IV, and here just five paragraphs after the science student names his creation "monster." The two names arrive in close company, the dream of openness and liberty in the wide family of man always coupled to its nightmare of abjection.

The other name on the title page, *Prometheus,* was, like "Frankenstein" today, fraught with a complicated legacy. In the old Greek myth, this Titan deity violated divine law by creating man from clay. In anger, the king of the gods, Zeus, visited various abuses on this new creature, and in pity the creator Prometheus stole fire from heaven and gave it to humankind. In the myth, fire is the actual spark that raised human beings above brute existence, and in its symbolic aura it signifies the light of human civilization: hearth and home, science, art, learning. Enraged even more by the theft of divine fire, Zeus condemned Prometheus to perpetual torment and sent humankind Pandora's box of evils, saved only by the last gift, hope. It is no wonder that writers and artists throughout the Middle Ages and the Renaissance drew from and projected onto Prometheus a spectrum of identities: God the Creator, Christ the Redeemer, Satan the tempter, man the restless inquisitor.

The Prometheus story bears some of the same mythic elements found in the Book of Genesis. God creates man from the earth ("Adam" means *clay* or *red earth*), and though God expels man from Eden and condemns him with mortality for heeding the serpent's invitation to forbidden knowledge, He also sends hope in the form of a divine son who undergoes torment for man's sake, even as Prometheus suffers a form of eternal crucifixion, chained to a mountaintop where a vulture feasts on his liver (or heart) every night. For some Renaissance philosophers, Prometheus's punishment signifies the "continuous gnawing of inquiry" that advances civilization at the cost of "torture and anxiety of mind"—an ambivalent legacy inviting both praise for benevolent enlightenment and condemnation for presumption.[29] Yet in its largest arc, the figure of Prometheus comes to embody human reason itself, his theft of fire representing the sudden awakening of intellect out of a brutish natural state, with all the promises and perils.

What is the template for Frankenstein? Is he a punished transgressor or a daring, tragically ennobled creator? All aspects are reflected in Shelley's narrative. The passion of Frankenstein's science is to "pour a torrent of light into our dark world. A new species would bless me as its creator and source" (Vol. I, Ch. III). This light-bearing is twinned in Walton's belief that his benefit to humanity will be finding that the ocean at the top of the globe is a region "of eternal light" (Letter I), and light-bearing even shapes Mary Shelley's story of inspiration, coming "swift as light" after a midnight's reverie. Light-bearing is vital excitement. And fire-bearing, literally or metaphorically, enacts comfort and care-giving. A campfire is one of the Creature's happiest discoveries in the winter woods, and his benevolent service to the winter-weary De Lacey family is supplying "firing" (firewood) to their home. With different balances of attributes, both Frankenstein and Creature have a claim to the epithet "Modern Prometheus."

But fire is also hell-torment, as *Paradise Lost* reminds us: once the brightest of angels, the light-bearing "Lucifer," Satan is condemned to the misery flashing in his eyes and burning in his heart, even in the Garden of Eden. It is the torment of Satanic suffering that forms the subtlest, and ultimately the strongest, bond between the Creature and his creator. Each reflects in his own way a momentously historical "Modern Prometheus," Napoleon Buonaparte, who was alternately the heroic liberator from monarchal tyranny and the type of Milton's Satan.[30] In a world-victor doomed to end his life imprisoned on an ocean island (where he was exiled in 1815), readers in 1818 could well see types of Victor and his Creature, remnants of a shattered Promethean idealism living out their final act as exiles on an ocean wilderness. Like Napoleon, the Creature wreaks devastation across half a continent; like Napoleon, Victor Frankenstein finds his last chapter of life on an island-like fragment of ice.

As Milton's Satan figures into the psychological torments of these characters, so too does the Romantic fascination with Satan's defiance. While Milton's epic narrator identifies Satan as Arch-Fiend, sworn enemy of God and mankind, Shelley's era often focused on how much Milton gave the devil his due, allowing God's Providence to be shaped into a subject of debate. Romantic readers found in Satan's speeches and soliloquies a resonant sarcasm about divine-right rulers, arbitrary tyranny. Blake's satire, *The Marriage of Heaven and Hell,* begun in 1790 just after the French Revolution and published in 1793, guessed that Milton was really writing for "the devil's party": in the mea-

Benjamin West, *Benjamin Franklin Drawing Electricity from the Sky,* circa 1816. This is the heroic "New Prometheus" (as Franklin was called by Kant and others) receiving a dangerous electrical charge as the risk for advancing scientific knowledge.

sure of poetry, imagination, and republican politics, Satan seemed to Blake to be the true hero of *Paradise Lost,* the magnificent antagonist of a vengeful oppressor who happens to have the name God. In the age of the American and French Revolutions, Blake was not alone in remembering that, notwithstanding the "high argument" of *Paradise Lost* about the sin of disobedience, Milton had also written in vigorous defense of

Cromwell's regicidal revolt of the 1640s. In *Rights of Woman,* Wollstonecraft echoed Satan's antimonarchial arguments, going further than her male contemporaries in questioning the ways of God to woman: she compared the life of a woman educated just enough not to bore her husband to Satan's exile in Hell, a place of "no light, but rather darkness visible": "would it not be a refinement on cruelty only to open her mind to make the darkness and misery of her fate *visible?*"[31] Godwin's *Political Justice* (1793) joined the party of Blake and Wollstonecraft in admiring Satan's political heroism and his fortitude in his torments. And then there was Milton's poetry itself, expressing the character of a great modern antihero: daring, transgressive, intellectually adroit, agonizingly alienated, eternally tormented, self-tortured—in sum, a sublime psychology rendered with unarguable dramatic power.

If this reception was selective and willful, having to ignore or to transvalue Satan's evil agenda and its informing sins, the fable of Prometheus seemed, despite its ambiguities, more available for sympathetic treatment. The tortured but adamantly resistant idealist was the hero of Byron's "Prometheus," a meditative lyric of sympathy for this "Byronic" hero, composed in July 1816, just weeks after the ghost-story contest. In 1818, the year *Frankenstein* was published, Percy Shelley began writing and devoted himself whole-heartedly to a visionary lyric drama, *Prometheus Unbound,* presenting an intensely idealized hero, of greater poetic appeal than Milton's Satan for being "impelled by the purest and the truest motives to the best and noblest ends."[32] A quite positive "Modern Prometheus" in the mortal world—one, moreover, with a surname-link to *Frank*enstein—is Ben *Frank*lin, famous for capturing lightning from heaven to pioneer the world-changing technology of electricity. The animation-scene in James Whale's 1931 film is a laboratory rife with electrical instruments shocked into activity by lightning, to which the 1935 *Bride* adds large kites. In 1755, Immanuel Kant dubbed Franklin "The Prometheus of modern times" and continued to admire this "second Prometheus," who "stole the spark immediately from heaven."[33] Other admirers of Franklin noted the continuity with his work for the American Revolution: *Eripuit coelo fulmen sceptrumque tyrannis* (He snatched the lightning from the sky and the scepter from tyrants), wrote the French statesman Anne-Robert-Jacques Turgot, in 1778, for an inscription on a bust of Franklin. And in 1791, scientist Erasmus Darwin (Charles's grandfather) hailed Franklin, the heroic scientist: the forces of heavenly lightning "wreath'd the crown electric round his head"—matching "Immortal FRANKLIN" the heroic revolutionary, whose "patriot-flame with quick contagion ran, / Hill lighted hill, and man electrised man."[34]

Victor Frankenstein's science, however, highlights the ambiguity of the myth. Although idealistically creating a being that would be immune to the diseases and ravages of ordinary human flesh (with his mother's death a recent memory), or even creating a new race with this immunity, his Promethean science becomes a project of monstrous egotism: "A new species would bless me as its creator and source; many happy and excellent natures would owe their being to me," he murmurs, even after he knows the outcome (Vol. I, Ch. III). This egotism is a presumption of divine prerogatives, a blasphemy that horrified the first reviewers, notwithstanding Mary Shelley's giving it a severely critical edge in the human creator's monstrous failure of ethical responsibility. In the months before Frankenstein animates and abandons his Creature, Shelley signifies trouble in the monstrosity of the research: grave-robbing, vivisection, and the devolution of the researcher into antisocial physical collapse. In his "workshop of filthy creation," Frankenstein does not see that his project is taking shape in horrifying form, nor does he see the full degree of his own self-transformation into a hideous thing: "my eyeballs were starting from their sockets in attending to the details of my employment. The dissecting room and the slaughter-house furnished many of my materials; and often did my human nature turn with loathing from my occupation" (Vol. I, Ch. III). In a surreal logic of modern genetics, the helpless Creature's monstrous aspect shimmers as a manifestation of his creator's moral monstrosity. It is a gothic mirror of Genesis: "And God said, Let us make man in our image, and after our likeness" (I: 26).

Social Mirrors

This is not the only mirroring in *Frankenstein*. Mary Shelley deftly composes the novel with an array of mirroring scenes that double one another in repetition and antithesis: scenes of animation, scenes of care-giving, scenes of rejection. These correspondences expand into a symbolic logic across the novel, and no one is a more alert reader of correspondence than the Creature, uncertain of his identity. As secret student in the De Lacey's home, he learns about "the strange system of human society . . . the division of property, of immense wealth and squalid poverty; of rank, descent, and noble blood":

> The words induced me to turn towards myself. I learned that the possessions most esteemed by your fellow-creatures were, high and unsullied descent united with riches. A man might be respected with only one of these acquisitions; but without either he was considered, except in very rare instances, as a vagabond

and a slave, doomed to waste his powers for the profit of the chosen few. And
what was I? . . . I knew that I possessed no money, no friends, no kind of property.
(Vol. II, Ch. V)

The Creature is nothing if not a social critic, the internal locus of the novel's historical
reflections.

Frankenstein mirrors two historical periods in particular: the fictive setting, in the
1790s, and its years of composition, 1816–1817 and 1823–1831. When Mary Godwin/
Shelley began the novel, in June 1816, Europe was still scarred by the long wars of aggression waged by Napoleon, who was finally defeated at Waterloo in May 1815. As
noted above, he was a hero to some, a monster to many, and one whose feats ended
with bitterly ironic results. The Treaty of Versailles restored all the old monarchies,
which applied fresh repressions to secure their power. The English monarchy, now triumphant as the premier world power, was intent on squelching civil unrest at home,
especially from its horribly poor famished classes, who were subject to brutal suppres-
sion rather than parliamentary representation—classes regarded by those in power as a
population of miserable wretches. When the novel's events conclude in the late 1790s,
these circumstances are just coming into being. In May 1797, Napoleon signaled his
imperial ambitions by invading Venice and extinguishing its long independence as a
Republic. Before the end of this summer Mary Godwin was born, and her mother died.

The world of *Frankenstein* is set to anticipate these events, and more generally the
turmoil in the first decade following the French Revolution. Events within the novel
counterpoint this history. Victor Frankenstein was born in the early 1770s in the Republic of Geneva, home of Jean-Jacques Rousseau, whose writings inspired the French
Revolution. His scientific studies begin in 1789, the year the Bastille was stormed and
the Revolution exploded. *Monster* was a political keyword in the Revolution. To its
champions, the *ancien régime* was a monster of tyranny, decadence, and corruption.
Godwin depicted its feudal system as a "ferocious monster, devouring . . . all that the
friend of humanity regards with attachment and love."[35] Tom Paine excoriated "the
monster Aristocracy."[36] Wollstonecraft described the despots of modern Europe as a
"race of monsters in human shape."[37] To conservatives, however, it was the Revolution
that was "monstrous." Burke, who supported *our* Revolution, recoiled at the revolu-
tionaries as "miscreant parricides," broadcast Revolutionary France as a "monster of a
state," with a "monster of a constitution," "monstrous democratic assemblies," and Regicide France as "the mother of monsters."[38] Abbé Barruel published a scathing critique

of the Revolutionary society called the Illuminati at the University of Ingolstadt, the university of Victor Frankenstein's monster-generating scientific studies. Barruel excoriated the Revolution as the monster of the age: "before Satan shall exultingly enjoy this triumphant spectacle, which the Illuminizing Code is preparing, let us examine . . . [w]hat share has it borne in that revolution which has already desolated so many countries, and menaces so many others. How it engendered that disastrous monster called *Jacobin,* raging uncontrouled, and almost unopposed, in these days of horror and devastation." When Percy Shelley read Barruel in 1814, his heart turned not against the Revolution but against Barruel's slanders.[39] While there is no reference to the French Revolution in *Frankenstein,* its first readers, less than twenty years on, would have felt the force of making the 1790s its setting, a decade for a sequence of catastrophes descending from idealism gone wrong.

No less pertinent to the daughter of Mary Wollstonecraft, the 1790s was the decade of the first political arguments for the rights of woman, and metaphors of deformation played a part in this polemic, too. In *A Vindication of the Rights of Men* (1790)—Wollstonecraft's brisk rebuttal to Burke's conservative alarm—she described the man privileged in the system of aristocracy as "an artificial monster."[40] Her sequel of 1792, *A Vindication of the Rights of Woman,* highlights monstrosity as a category for women in all social classes: in the deformations wrought by poverty and brutal labor, in the corruptions of upper-class luxury, and even in the middle classes, in the prevailing system of education which doomed young women to the weird brand of monstrosity that her disciple Mary Hays cartooned as "Perpetual Babyism": a girl's mind in a woman's body.[41]

Wollstonecraft's preferred term for the domestic and political subjection of women was *slave*—the social determinism of a body, whether by race or sex, in subjects with no civil rights, destined to lives of labor and tyranny. England abolished the slave trade in 1807, less than ten years before Shelley began her novel; but the issue was by no means settled: slavery was still legal in Britain's colonies until 1833. And in this debate, too, notions of monstrosity were integral to the high stakes, no less economic than moral. Defenders of slavery (including those who profited from slave labor or who enjoyed its products) liked to insist that the African captives were more animal than human, innate monsters who would be improved by conversion to Christianity and an ethic of labor. Abolitionists countered that it was the capitalists, investors, and masters who were the real brutes and savages, the moral monsters of the modern age.

This scene, of a torch-bearing village mob setting fire to the windmill in which the Creature is trapped, suggesting both a lynching and a crucifixion, is the one that director James Whale intended to be the closing frame of *Frankenstein* (1931). Instead of this disturbing image (in the 1930s vigilante justice was not uncommon in parts of the United States), the producers insisted on a vignette of happy domesticity: "Henry" Frankenstein (renamed from Shelley's "Victor") is recovering in his bedroom from his nearly fatal struggle with his Creature, while his father the Baron leads a toast in the hallway outside, to "the House of Frankenstein!"

The Creature captured by the villagers. In this early scene in *The Bride of Frankenstein* (1935), Whale returns to the Creature's implicit crucifixion.

Conceived, published, revised, and republished in the era of abolition debates, *Frankenstein* traces the terms of *master* and *slave* into the Creature's petition and his ultimate revenge. Shelley's Creature was summoned directly into the abolition debate. "In dealing with the negro," the ultra-conservative foreign secretary George Canning cautioned Parliament in 1824, "we must remember that we are dealing with a being possessing the form and strength of a man, but the intellect only of a child. To turn him loose in the manhood of his physical strength . . . would be to raise up a creature resembling the splendid fiction of a recent romance" (the term then for "fantasy" fiction).[42]

When the Creature gets called *Monster,* repeatedly and by all kinds of human beings, the term links the novel to a larger world in flux. This is not to say that the Creature is an allegory of the French Revolution, or the Rights of Woman, or of slavery. It is to say that the word "Monster" is intrinsic to the polemical language and imagery of the day. The connection endured. One hundred years after the publication of the revised novel, the Whale/Karloff *Frankenstein* entered movie-houses in an era when a black man could be lynched on suspicion of menace. Whale wanted the final scenes to evoke this atrocity: a drunken, torch-wielding village mob, with no evidence that the Creature has murdered a child (her death is actually an accident of his miscalculated playfulness), chases the frightened, tormented man-child into a windmill in a scene that evokes both a lynching and a crucifixion. This scenario is revived in *The Bride of Frankenstein,* where the Creature (not dead after all) is chased through a surreal forest of bare, limbless trees, caught, and strapped on to a log in a cruciform figure, jeered at and battered by a village mob that seems equally, or more truly, monstrous.

Allegories of Parenthood

The title-page epigraph for *Frankenstein,* from *Paradise Lost,* Book X, after the Fall, is a child-parent scenario. Adam addresses a now absent God,

> Did I request thee, Maker, from my clay
> To mould me man, did I solicit thee
> From darkness to promote me?

This complaint is one that contrary children think profoundly original and case-closing: "I didn't ask to be born!" (It's as old as Adam, destined himself to be a parent hearing this.) The verse appears on the title page of each volume of the 1818 *Franken-*

stein, with a progressive deepening of meaning. Not only does the question become recalibrated as the Creature's, but we also measure his claim to it when contrasting what God has provided for Adam to what Victor Frankenstein has not, for his Creature. The mortal creator is a poor double for the God of Genesis—all pride, with no providence for his creation. He is great in self-pity, and flagrant in his incapacity to imagine the world from any point of view other than his own shattered ideal.

Failing to create a being whom he could bear, Frankenstein recoils from him as a monster to be abhorred and aborted (the Creature will later call himself an "abortion"). Adam wakes in Eden; the Creature wakes into hell on earth: rejected by his creator, abandoned in the shambles of a workshop, thence to fend for himself in the stormy woods of a German November. This story, obscured in Frankenstein's narration, emerges later in the novel in the Creature's voice; but some of it is retrievable beneath the scrim of his creator's account. It is the novel's most famous, most iconic scene:

> It was on a dreary night of November, that I beheld the accomplishment of my toils. With an anxiety that almost amounted to agony, I collected the instruments of life around me, that I might infuse a spark of being into the lifeless thing that lay at my feet. It was already one in the morning; the rain pattered dismally against the panes, and my candle was nearly burnt out, when, by the glimmer of the half-extinguished light, I saw the dull yellow eye of the creature open; it breathed hard, and a convulsive motion agitated its limbs.

This is the scene the movies adore, with storms, electricity, mechanical contrivances, explosions, and light-shows, beginning with Kenneth Strickfaden's creations in the 1930s. In the novel, it is private, subdued, and psychologically chilling as the "thing" assumes life, like a dream taking form in the silent half-light of a candle. What Shelley highlights is the creator's monstrous egotism: "*I* beheld the accomplishment of *my* toils"; "*I* might infuse a spark of being into the lifeless *thing*"; "the creature . . . *it.*" *Creature* is as good as it gets. In revulsion at his highly invested failure, the naming quickly descends into the negative details of disgusted aversion—a grotesque of that Renaissance form called the *blason,* the poetry of a young man enumerating and doting on his beloved's beauties:

> How can I describe my emotions at this catastrophe, or how delineate the wretch whom with such infinite pains and care I had endeavoured to form? His limbs

were in proportion, and I had selected his features as beautiful. Beautiful!—Great God! His yellow skin scarcely covered the work of muscles and arteries beneath; his hair was of a lustrous black, and flowing; his teeth of a pearly whiteness; but these luxuriances only formed a more horrid contrast with his watery eyes, that seemed almost of the same colour as the dun white sockets in which they were set, his shrivelled complexion, and straight black lips.

Defending his aversion as a reflex of "human nature," Frankenstein's chief labor in this birth-narrative is to evoke sympathy for his horrified disappointment:

> I had worked hard for nearly two years, for the sole purpose of infusing life into an inanimate body. For this I had deprived myself of rest and health. . . . but now that I had finished, the beauty of the dream vanished, and breathless horror and disgust filled my heart. Unable to endure the aspect of the being I had created, I rushed out of the room.

Against the narrator's "breathless" self-pity of injured vanity, Shelley unfolds the bitter fate of his breathing creature, doomed solely by his unendurable physical aspect.

Here is another parent-tuned text, some of which Ellen Moers excerpts at the head of her influential essay "Female Gothic":

> A baby at birth is usually disappointing-looking to a parent who hasn't seen one before. His skin is coated with wax, which if left on, will be absorbed slowly and will lessen the chance of rashes. His skin underneath is apt to be very red. His face tends to be puffy and lumpy, and there may be black-and-blue marks. . . . The head is misshapen . . . low in the forehead, elongated at the back, and quite lopsided. Occasionally there may be . . . a hematoma, a localized hemorrhage under the scalp that sticks out as a distinct bump and takes weeks to go away. A couple of days after birth there may be a touch of jaundice, which is visible for about a week. . . . The baby's body is covered all over with fuzzy hair. . . . for a couple of weeks afterward there is apt to be a dry scaling of the skin which is also shed. Some babies have black hair on the scalp at first, which may come far down on the forehead.

This is no horror story. It is from the 1957 edition of Dr. Benjamin Spock's household familiar, the best-selling *Common Sense Book of Baby and Child Care,* preparing parents for the possible letdown, even recoil, from a normal newborn.[43] And what of a baby who is physically abnormal or deficient? Or just the wrong sex? Frankenstein's shocked recoil is the extravagant nightmare of this anxiety. Shelley's novel imprints the Creature with this nightmare and it spawns a history from which this Creature cannot awaken, nor can his creator, who bequeathed it to him as his only birthright.

The first monster in *Frankenstein* is not this Creature, however. Routinely elided in theater and cinema, it appears in the frame tale. The famous Creature is a peripheral ephemeron, glimpsed by the crew on Walton's polar adventure as a near mirage on a far-distant ice-plain: "the shape of a man, but apparently of gigantic stature," driving a dogsled (Letter IV). The immediate astonishment (reported three paragraphs on) is the appearance the next morning of a haggard being off the side of the ship on a fragment of ice, alone in a sled but for one dog, asking which direction the ship is headed. Learning that it is northward, he consents to come on board. "Good God! Margaret, if you had seen the man who thus capitulated for his safety, your surprise would have been boundless," writes Captain Walton to his sister; "His limbs were nearly frozen, and his body dreadfully emaciated by fatigue and suffering. I never saw a man in so wretched a condition." This is the first dreadful wretch in Mary Shelley's novel, and soon the star of its first "Frankenstein" moment. The wretched being faints dead away, then is revived, animated, by the crew:

> We restored him to animation by rubbing him with brandy, and forcing him to swallow a small quantity. As soon as he shewed signs of life, we wrapped him up in blankets, and placed him near the chimney of the kitchen-stove. By slow degrees he recovered, and ate a little soup, which restored him wonderfully.

This crew brings life out of death. In a body dreadful to behold, teeth-gnashing, mad, wild, Victor Frankenstein receives concerned parental care as a fellow human being. Everything he recounts hereafter bears this tremendous irony. Monsters are not born, the Author of *Frankenstein* proposes; they are made and unmade on the variable scales of human sympathy.

1. To Leigh Hunt, September 9–11, 1823 (*Letters* 1: 378).

2. For Shelley's 1831 Introduction see 331–340.

3. "William is all alive," Wollstonecraft assured Godwin on June 10, 1797; *The Collected Letters of Mary Wollstonecraft,* ed. Janet Todd (New York: Columbia University Press, 2003), 420.

4. C. Kegan Paul, *William Godwin: His Friends and Contemporaries* (London: Henry S. King, 1876) 2: 214.

5. January 10, 1812, *Letters* 1: 218–221.

6. To T. J. Hogg, October 3, 1814 (PBS *Letters* 1: 401–403).

7. Mary was already in the habit of reading her mother's works at her gravesite, a practice that, however morbid it might seem, reflects a desire for imaginative and intellectual connection. Before the development of public parks, churchyards often functioned as pastoral sites within the urban world.

8. Unsigned review of three books, *Westminster Review* 6 (October 1826), 326.

9. Letter to Percy Shelley, November 3, 1814 (*Letters MWS* 1: 4).

10. *Journals* 70–71.

11. *Journals* 428–429, 555; style elements *sic.*

12. For Byron's anger at Southey's slander, see his letter to his close friend J. C. Hobhouse, November 11, 1818, in *Byron's Letters and Journals,* ed. Leslie Marchand, vol. 6 (Cambridge: Harvard University Press, 1976), 76. For Southey's Satanizing of Byron's and Shelley's poetry, see his Preface to *A Vision of Judgement,* in *The Poetical Works of Robert Southey, Collected by Himself,* 10 vols. (London: Longman & c., 1838), 10: 203.

13. For these statistics, see William St. Clair, *The Godwins and the Shelleys: The Biography of a Family* (New York: Norton, 1989), 360.

14. We thank Garrett Stewart for this subtle insight. See also George Levine, "The Ambiguous Heritage of *Frankenstein,*" in Levine and Knoepflmacher, 22.

15. For this silent film, see www.archive.org/details/FrankensteinfullMovie.

16. See Harout Harman, movieweb.com/news/Frankenstein (accessed September 2, 2011).

17. *New York Times,* op ed, February 27, 1997.

18. Willard Gaylin, *New York Times Magazine,* March 5, 1972, 12.

19. *New York Times,* July 5, 2001.

20. The course of cultural mediation is apparent in Dr. Levick's upgrade of the undergraduate to a professional colleague, "Dr. Frankenstein." Torches still flicker on less momentous fronts. "Frankencat," the genetically engineered debutante of the 1995 New York Cat Show, had furry stubs in place of legs, a "cute" commodity created without concern for its capacity of self-preservation. In a food court of appeal reported by the *New York Times* in January 2003: "The judge ran down the ingredients of several McDonald's products, including Chicken McNuggets, which in addition to well-known additives common to processed foods, contain some less-

familiar substances like TBHQ and an 'anti-foaming agent'"; "McNuggets," he intoned, "are a McFrankenstein creation." See also Molly O'Neill, "Geneticists' Latest Discovery: Public Fear of 'Frankenfood,'" *New York Times,* June 28, 1992.

21. She recounts these conversations in her 1831 Introduction (336).

22. The punster of *vamped up* was Byron's friend, and later biographer, Thomas Moore. *The Vampyre, A Tale* was published in a *New Monthly Magazine* in 1819. When it was attributed to Byron, he objected and Polidori acknowledged the thing of darkness as his own. On the London stage an adaptation preceded (by three years) *Frankenstein.* Bram Stoker, the author of *Dracula* (1897), was inspired by Polidori's tale.

23. Mellor makes this sharp observation (54).

24. Martin Tropp, *Mary Shelley's Monster: The Story of Frankenstein* (Boston: Houghton Mifflin, 1976), 8.

25. Gladstone read *Frankenstein* in 1835; his tour of 1838 is cited in *A Handbook for Travellers in Sicily* (London: John Murray, 1864), xlvi.

26. Shakespeare's enraged Antony gloats over Cleopatra's fate to be displayed by Octavius Caesar as "the greatest spot / Of all thy sex. Most monster-like be shown" (*Antony and Cleopatra* 4.12.35–36). For a survey of Shakespeare's language of "monster," see Chris Baldick, *In Frankenstein's Shadow: Myth, Monstrosity, and Nineteenth-Century Writing* (Oxford: Clarendon Press, 1987), 10–15.

27. *Letters* 1: 278.

28. In classical-era Gallic France, *Frank* referred to the dominant group, the one "free" from subjection; the denotation of character (analogous to another term of esteem in this novel, "noble") is class-inflected. The Western European character is also the "meaning" of *Frank*-based names, such as *Frank, Franklin, Francis, Franco, Francisco.*

29. See Olga Raggio, "The Myth of Prometheus: Its survival and metamorphoses up to the eighteenth century," *Journal of the Warburg and Courtauld Institutes* 21.1/2 (1958): 44–62.

30. Byron's *Ode to Napoleon Buonaparte* (London: John Murray, 1814) compared him both to Prometheus, "the thief of fire from heaven," and to Satan's pre-Fall existence as Lucifer, the light-bearer of the arch-angels (stanza XVI).

31. *A Vindication of the Rights of Woman: with Strictures on Moral and Political Subjects,* 2nd edition (London: J. Johnson, 1792), 196; her italics, alluding to *Paradise Lost* I.63.

32. He is "a more poetical character than Satan, because, in addition to courage, and majesty, and firm and patient opposition to omnipotent force, he is susceptible of being described as exempt from the taints of ambition, envy, revenge, and a desire for personal aggrandisement, which, in the Hero of Paradise Lost, interfere with the interest. The character of Satan engenders in the mind a pernicious casuistry which leads us to weigh his faults with his wrongs, and to excuse the former because the latter exceed all measure. In the minds of those who consider that magnificent fiction with a religious feeling it engenders something worse. But Prometheus is, as it were, the type of the highest perfection of moral and intellectual nature, impelled by

the purest and the truest motives to the best and noblest ends" (London: C and J Ollier, 1820), viii–ix.

33. The first quotation is from Epes Sargent, *Selected Works of Benjamin Franklin* (London: Phillips, Sampson, 1853), 21; the second, from Kant's *Essays and treatises on moral, political, and various philosophical subjects;* English trans., 2 vols. (London: William Richardson, 1799) 2: 186n.

34. Erasmus Darwin, *The Botanic Garden,* 2nd edition (London: J. Johnson, 1791): *Part I: The Economy of Vegetation,* Canto I.388; Canto II.365–368 (pp. 37–38 and 91).

35. *Enquiry Concerning Political Justice,* 2nd edition, 2 vols. (London: G. G. and J. Robinson, 1796), 2: 96.

36. Paine, *The Rights of Man,* 8th edition (London: J. S. Jordan, 1790), 73–74. In *Common Sense* (Edinburgh and Philadelphia, 1776), Paine defended the American Revolution as an escape from "the cruelty of [a] monster" (34).

37. Wollstonecraft, *An Historical and Moral View of the . . . French Revolution* (London: J. Johnson, 1794), 516.

38. Burke, *Letter to a Noble Lord* (London: Owen/Rivington, 1796), 75; *Reflections on the Revolution in France,* 2nd edition (London: J. Dodsley, 1790), 283, 310; *Two Letters [on Peace with Regicide France]* 10th edition (London: Rivington, 1796), 66.

39. Abbé Augustin Barruel, *Mémoirs, pour sevir à L'Histoire du Jacobinisme* (1797), translated by R. Clifford as *Memoirs Illustrating the History of Jacobinism* (Hartford: Hudson & Goodwin, 1799), Part III, Volume III: *The Antisocial Conspiracy,* 251. For Percy and Mary's reading of Clifford's translation of Barruel on their European adventure of summer 1814, see Mary Shelley's *Journals* 18–19.

40. Wollstonecraft, *A Vindication of the Rights of Men* (2nd edition, 1790), 59, on the misery visited by political tyranny.

41. Hays, *Appeal to the Men of Great Britain* (London: J. Johnson, 1798), 97.

42. Canning, March 16, 1824; for Mary Shelley's awareness of his reference and for the citation in Hansard's *Parliamentary Records,* see *Letters MWS* 1: 417–418.

43. Benjamin Spock, M.D., *Common Sense Book of Baby and Child Care* (New York: Pocket Books, 1957).

TEXTS AND AUTHORSHIP

The present text is based on the first edition of *Frankenstein; or, The Modern Prometheus,* 3 vols. (London: Lackington, Hughes, Harding, Mavor, & Jones, 1818), in the collection of the Princeton University Library. We retain idiosyncratic spellings (for example, "avelanche"), but we correct, without comment, obvious printer's errors, checked against the manuscript, the fair copy, *1823,* and *1831.* Such errors typically involve dropped or mis-set letters (for example, "surrouuded"), dropped or mis-set punctuation marks, and, repeatedly, "De Lacy" for "De Lacey" and "Ingoldstadt" for "Ingolstadt" (the ms. has the second spellings). We retain all original punctuation, except that we follow the modern convention of giving both opening and closing quotation marks. From time to time, our annotations address interesting textual issues, corrections, and local variants and revisions in *1823* and *1831.* The Sample of Revised Passages provides some of Mary Shelley's most notable *1831* revisions.

The text for *Paradise Lost,* also in Princeton University Library, is Mary Shelley's own copy, inscribed "Mary W. G. from Percy B. Shelley, June 6, 1815."[1] This is the first of a two-volume collection, *Poems of John Milton* (Dublin: S. Powell, 1747). The first volume is titled *Paradise lost. A poem in twelve books.* Compared with the authentic editions, and revised by John Hawkey.[2]

Henri Fuseli, *Milton Dictating to His Daughter* (1793–1794). The blind poet dictated his epic *Paradise Lost* to his daughters. This magnificent poem figures throughout *Frankenstein,* from its title-page epigraph, through several direct echoes and allusions. Mary Wollstonecraft had a romantic infatuation with Fuseli at about the time of this painting.

Mary Shelley's copy of *Paradise Lost*, given to her by Percy Bysshe Shelley on June 6, 1815.

Frankenstein 1818

Encouraged by Lord Byron, Percy Shelley took *Frankenstein* to Byron's publisher, the establishment house of John Murray. After Murray declined the offering (a mistake rivaled by Thomas Cadell's rejection, unread, of Jane Austen's *Pride and Prejudice*), Shelley tested his own publisher, Charles Ollier, who also declined. His next approach was to Lackington & c, a firm with a huge inventory, and hospitable to works on occult and supernatural subjects. James Lackington proved receptive, thinking *Frankenstein* was a good addition to his catalog of popular genres: science fiction and ghost stories, with such titles as *The Magus; or Celestial Intelligences; a complete System of Occult Philosophy, being a Summary of all the best Writers on the subjects of Magic, Alchymy, Magnetism, the Cabala &c.; Lives of the Alchemystical Philosophers with a Critical Catalogue of Books on Occult Chemistry; The Life, Prophecies, and Predictions of Merlin Interpreted; Apparitions; or, the Mystery of Ghosts, Hobgoblins, and Haunted Houses Developed;* and *Tales of the Dead*—this last, an English translation of the volume of ghost stories that sparked the ghost-story contest from which *Frankenstein* emerged.

Mary Shelley had initially arranged her novel in thirty-three chapters, to fill two volumes. Lackington wanted her to reorganize the chapters into three volumes, a format designed for the most reliable purchasers, the circulating libraries, which could lend out one volume at a time.[3] Such a format also enabled private purchasers to buy a volume at a time and facilitated the sharing of the novel among sequential readers in a household. Mary obliged, crafting her manuscript into new chapters to be housed in three shorter volumes. Appealing to the lending market was important, because books were expensive. In late 1815, Murray sold Jane Austen's *Emma* (by the established "Author of *Sense and Sensibility,* and *Pride and Prejudice*") for one guinea, an upscale metric for £1/1 shilling (in the old monetary system, 12 pence, or pennies, to the shilling, 20 shillings to the pound). In January 1818, Lackington, with a small print run of 500, priced *Frankenstein* at less than half that amount: 6 shillings, 6 pence. This was attractive to modestly able individual purchasers as well as to the lending libraries. To put the book prices in perspective, consider some annual incomes in the decade that both novels were published: shopkeepers, £150; schoolmasters, £120; skilled laborers (artisans), £55. The poverty line was £50. Below this were clergy, farm-owners, miners (£40); agricultural laborers (£30); seamstresses (£20); and governesses (£12–20, with room and board).

Lackington printed the pages in highly economical duodecimo: 12 pages on each side of a sheet, the sheets then folded, gathered, and assembled between cover-boards. Although the page size was small, it was not crowded, and thus was easy to read: 5–8 words per line, 20 lines at most per page, about 100–150 words per page.

Our Annotations

Over the last forty years, as *Frankenstein* focused teaching, criticism, and scholarly work, capably annotated editions have followed or, in some cases, have led the way. Our annotations are aimed at the general, curious reader, without excluding the specialist scholar. We have been happy to have the editions of Charles Robinson, Nora Crook, and James Rieger at hand, as well as Leonard Wolf's adventurous *Annotated Frankenstein* (now out of print). A rich archive of critical books and essays has stimulated our attention (see Further Reading).

Author Names

Not wanting to call two equally famous authors *Shelley* and *Mary,* nor liking the cumbersomeness of using complete names, nor the clutter of office-memo initials, we refer to the companions as *Percy* and *Mary,* to *Mary* as daughter in the Godwin household, and to the public authors (when a distinction is needed) as *Percy Shelley* and *Mary Shelley.*

Mary Shelley, "The Author of *Frankenstein*"

In her Introduction of 1831, Mary Shelley frankly admits that *Frankenstein* not only arose in a private midnight imagination but also drew on a rich resource of materials, especially in the reading and conversations at Villa Diodati. No small force in the gestation was Percy Shelley, whose "incitement," she says in this Introduction, encouraged her to expand the few pages she drafted the next morning into a more ambitious work, "the form in which it was presented to the world." He was her encourager, careful advisor, editor, and sales agent; yet for all this he would never have contested Mary Shelley's claim (after his death) to her repeated signature in print as "the Author of *Frankenstein.*"

PARADISE REGAINED.

A

POEM

IN

FOUR BOOKS.

With the other

POETICAL WORKS

OF

JOHN MILTON.

Compared with the beſt Editions,

And Reviſed by

JOHN HAWKEY,

Editor of the Latin Claſſics.

DUBLIN:

Printed by S. POWELL, for the EDITOR.

MDCC LII.

And now, once again, I bid my hideous progeny go forth and prosper. I have an affection for it, for it was the offspring of happy days, when death and grief were but words, which found no true echo in my heart. Its several pages speak of many a walk, many a drive, and many a conversation, when I was not alone; and my companion was one who, in this world, I shall never see more. But this is for myself; my readers have nothing to do with these associations.

I will add but one word as to the alterations I have made. They are principally those of style. I have changed no portion of the story, nor introduced any new ideas or circumstances. I have mended the language where it was so bald as to interfere with the interest of the narrative; and these changes occur almost exclusively in the beginning of the first volume. Throughout they are entirely confined to such parts as are mere adjuncts to the story, leaving the core and substance of it untouched.

M. W. S.

London, October 15. 1831.

This two-volume set of *The Poems of John Milton* (1747–1752) was owned previously by Lady Savile, the name crossed out, perhaps by Percy Shelley, when he gave the set to Mary Godwin. The nearness of *Savile* to *Saville,* the sister-recipient of polar explorer Walton's letters, is intriguing; the names were even interchangeable in British genealogies.

The last page of the Introduction to the 1831 *Frankenstein.* In the penultimate paragraph, Mary Shelley sends forth her now famous creation, the "hideous progeny" that names both the novel and its memorable Creature. The initials M. W. S., the signature of Mary Wollstonecraft Shelley, also apply to Margaret [Walton] Saville, the recipient of her brother Robert Walton's letters, which accompany his "manuscript" of Frankenstein's story.

Even so, the anonymous publication of 1818 made speculation about the author part of the discussion. Confronting a novel propelled by male adventures and transgressions, saturated in the languages and ideas of Milton, Coleridge, Wordsworth, Godwin, Byron, Shelley, and contemporary scientists such as Davy and Darwin, a novel, moreover, known to have been shopped by Percy Shelley, many reviewers assumed that the author was male—probably Shelley himself, or some other deranged, atheist Godwin disciple. The reviewer for the *Edinburgh Magazine, and Literary Miscellany* (March 1818) automatically used masculine pronouns for the author of such "monstrous conceptions." So did the reviewer for the influential *Quarterly Review* that same month: "notwithstanding the rationality of his preface," the author "often leaves us in doubt whether he is not as mad as his hero." Even a review in *Blackwood's Edinburgh Magazine,* March 1818 by Walter Scott, who knew better from the note that the Shelleys sent him with a copy of the novel, credited the rumor that the author was "Mr Percy Bysshe Shelley."[4]

When Mary Shelley wrote to Scott, on June 14, 1818, to thank him warmly for his "favourable notice," she murmured her and Percy's surprise at seeing her husband "mentioned . . . as the probable author," and she was clearly eager to correct "the mistake" in order to spare him any blame for her "juvenile effort . . . to which—from its being written at an early age, I abstained from putting my name—and from respect to those persons from whom I bear it" (by which she meant her parents as well as her husband; *Letters MWS* 1: 71). This cover story notwithstanding, it seems likely that Shelley's pride in her accomplishment, wrought from diligent study and laborious composition, was stung. She was finding herself, with no painful irony, doubled with the abjected Eve of *Paradise Lost,* who seems not to be created as Adam's equal.

Even after the 1823 reprint, with "Mary Wollstonecraft Shelley" now on the title page, *Knight's Quarterly Magazine* (August 1824) wasn't buying it.[5] This skepticism proved tenacious across the nineteenth century, with "Mary" credited, at best, for having good company. "Mary undoubtedly received more than she gave," sniffed the *Dictionary of National Biography* in 1897, not even dignifying her with a full name, and surmising that *Frankenstein* could have issued only from "an absolute magnetising of her brain by Shelley's" (52: 29). If "Mary" was the "Author of Frankenstein," this was, they were certain, a creature of Percy Shelley's manufacture. To a twentieth-century editor, James Rieger, her claim to authorship (in her 1831 Introduction) amounted to the "worst distortion." Percy Shelley's hand on the manuscript shows "assistance at every point . . . so extensive that one hardly knows whether to regard him as editor or minor collaborator." Yet Rieger's valuable scholarship is hampered not only by a conspicuous dislike of Mary Shelley (her "temperament . . . had always been cool," and after her husband's death, she "remained the stiff, humorless and self-dramatizing woman she had always been") but also, more generally, by the polemical atmosphere surrounding women's studies in the 1970s.[6]

While some of Percy's advocates continue to insist that Mary was merely his scribe, the evidence of the copytext manuscript argues very strongly against this story (unless it is an elaborate hoax that they and their conspiring friends cooked up to fool future scholars). The draft she "began [the] day" after her inspiring reverie (so she says in the 1831 Introduction) has not survived, though her busyness is confirmed by another of the company, J. W. Polidori.[7] What has survived is the draft she worked on during the summer and into April 1817 (now at the Bodleian Library, Oxford University).[8] This shows a lively and affectionate relation between the older published poet and his talented lover. Here appear numerous local rephrasings in Percy's hand, most (but not all) retained in the publication of 1818, occasional teasings of Mary about some of her habits of style, and a few ideas about local plot developments. Although Percy was an encouraging, attentive reader and a caring adviser, Mary's primary authorship is confirmed by documents (letters and memoirs) containing comments from everyone who knew them—Byron, Leigh Hunt, Claire Clairmont, Charles Clairmont, Godwin—that refer to her working on *Frankenstein* and regarding the novel as her project.

What of those, such as E. B. Murray, who are willing to grant Mary the original idea and most of the writing, but see Percy's involvement not only as quite "substantial" but also as "original," full of "creative additions" both "moral and aesthetic"?[9]

Not everyone who has examined the evidence (ourselves included) would assent. Anne Mellor, while acknowledging Percy's improvements on several levels—from grammar and syntax to narrative logic, "thematic resonance," and "the complexity of the monster's character"—also notes Percy's own missteps: rhetorical inflations and Latinizings, a penchant for imposing "his own favorite philosophical, political, and poetic theories on a text which either contradicted them or to which they were irrelevant," and revisions that distorted Mary's intentions and ideas.[10] Another scholar of great, meticulous expertise, Charles Robinson, has edited the massive, and massively important, Garland edition that arrays the manuscripts, the fair copy for the press, and the 1818 publication (*The Frankenstein Notebooks,* 1996). For the photo facsimiles of the manuscript pages written on with both Shelleys' hands, Robinson supplies an elegantly interpreted typographical transcription. Availing ourselves of this magnificent resource, we comment in our notes on several of Percy's interventions.

To Robinson's informed eye, nothing in the manuscript or in the relevant archives of letters and journals from contemporaries establishes Percy Shelley as the originator of the idea or the developer of the first draft: "He comes in at [an] intermediate stage, and offers his editorial advice and changes, and comes in at the fair-copy stage and offers some melodramatic prose for the final version of the scene in the polar regions."[11] As many writers may attest, a sympathetic adviser such as this, especially one more experienced, is a good fortune and not an unusual one. Percy's attentive chapter-by-chapter contributions, observes Robinson, mirror "what most publishers' editors have provided new (or old) authors or, in fact what colleagues have provided to each other after reading each other's works in progress" (*Notebooks,* lxvii). By Robinson's calculus, Percy may have contributed up to 4,000–5,000 words, about 7 percent of a total 72,000.

When it was published in January 1818, everyone who knew the Shelleys regarded *Frankenstein; or, The Modern Prometheus* as Mary Shelley's striking achievement.

NOTES

1. W. G. signifies "Wollstonecraft Godwin." Mary retains "Wollstonecraft" but drops "Godwin" from her signature after her marriage to Percy Shelley.

2. "Lady Savile" may be the Lady Savile (1701–1791) whose family was intertwined in the seventeenth century with the Shelleys. It is not clear how Percy came by the volumes; by the end of the summer of 1815 he and Mary were renting a cottage from Lady Savile's granddaughter.

3. Before the establishment of free public libraries in the middle of the nineteenth century, one could buy a subscription to circulating libraries, sometimes established by booksellers.

4. *Edinburgh Magazine, and Literary Miscellany,* March 1818 (253); *Quarterly Review,* January 1818 (382); Scott, "Remarks on Frankenstein, or the Modern Prometheus; A Novel," *Blackwood's Edinburgh Magazine,* March 1818 (613–620).

5. *Knight's Quarterly* (August 1824) 199; the occasion was a review of Mary Shelley's edition of Percy Shelley's *Posthumous Poems* (1824) and her second novel *Valperga* (1823).

6. James Rieger, xvii–xviii, xliv, xv, xxiii. For a rebuttal of several "misleading" statements, see Robinson, *The Frankenstein Notebooks* I: lvii–lviii. Even so, Rieger's considerable editorial work was important: his edition was the first to highlight the revisions that Mary Shelley began in 1823, to collate the texts of 1818 and 1831, and to make the 1818 text widely available to critics and students.

7. In his entry of June 17, 1816, he writes, "The ghost-stories are begun by all but me"; *The Di-*

ary of John Polidori, 1816, relating to Byron, Shelley, etc. ed. William Michael Rossetti (London: Elkin Mathew, 1911), 125.

8. Rieger studied a microfilm but not the manuscript itself.

9. E. B. Murray, "Shelley's Contribution to Mary's *Frankenstein," Keats-Shelley Memorial Bulletin* 29 (1978) 67, 51.

10. For a careful discussion of Percy's work on Mary's draft, see Anne Mellor, *Mary Shelley,* 58–65, 219–224. For more on the polemics about collaboration and co-authorship, see Susan Wolfson, "Reconstructing *Frankenstein.*"

11. "The Birth of 'Frankenstein'"; *The Chronicle Review,* November 7, 2008. With cogent reference to documents from the Shelley circle and the manuscript evidence, Robinson refutes the claims of Phillis Zimmerman (*Shelley's Fiction* [Darami, 1998]), and John Lauritsen (*The Man Who Wrote Frankenstein* [Pagan, 2007]) that the manuscript in Mary's hand reflects no more than secretarial service to Percy. In a reader-friendly edition of his research, *The Original Frankenstein,* Robinson presents a typographical transcription of the manuscript clarifying the two hands, and renders a speculative redaction of what Mary's "original" looked like prior to Percy's markings.

FRANKENSTEIN;

OR,

THE MODERN PROMETHEUS.

———◆———

IN THREE VOLUMES.

———◆———

Did I request thee, Maker, from my clay
To mould me man ?   Did I solicit thee
From darkness to promote me ?———
PARADISE LOST.

VOL. I.

London:

PRINTED FOR
LACKINGTON, HUGHES, HARDING, MAVOR, & JONES,
FINSBURY SQUARE.

1818.

TO

WILLIAM GODWIN,

AUTHOR OF POLITICAL JUSTICE, CALEB WILLIAMS, &c.

THESE VOLUMES

Are respectfully inscribed

BY

THE AUTHOR.

For the provocative subtitle "The Modern Prometheus" see the General Introduction (p. 24). Usually when novels introduce a subtitle with "or" the implication is an equivalence with the main title. Over the course of this novel, however, the subtitle expands from Frankenstein to several Promethean figures. The three lines of poetry are from Milton's *Paradise Lost,* Book X: 743–745, and are drawn from Adam's long, self-justifying lament to a distant God after the Fall. In a reader's re-encounter with this title page at the front of Volumes II and III (and in any re-reading of *Frankenstein*), Adam's complaint comes to chime ever more forcefully with the Creature's appeal to his Maker—not Adam's God but an irresponsible human maker. Mary was reading *Paradise Lost* on her own in 1814, and again with Percy in November 1816 as she worked on *Frankenstein.*

Arrayed on the Dedication page are another father and child, William Godwin and his daughter, the unnamed "Author" of *Frankenstein*. Mary Wollstonecraft Shelley was only recently reconciled to her father after her marriage to Percy Shelley in late 1816, and the dedication is a gesture of respect and affection. At the same time, it asserts the equal status of this "Author" with the "Author" so honored. The two named works by Godwin (which Mary had been reading during the years 1814–1816) are trenchant social critiques casting a shadow across the social world of *Frankenstein*. Godwin's radical treatise *Enquiry Considering Political Justice* (1793–1798) had an ardent following, including Samuel Taylor Coleridge, Lord Byron, and Percy Shelley, for its indictment of corrupt social institutions. His political novel, *Things as They Are; or, The Adventures of Caleb Williams* (1794), not only reflects this indictment but more particularly bequeaths thematic and narrative elements to *Frankenstein:* both works are versions of the "gothic" novel—a popular genre in the 1790s, bristling with hauntings, betrayals and persecutions, dangerous curiosity, transgression, crime and punishment. Percy Shelley remarked that *Frankenstein* evokes "the style and character of that admirable writer, to whom the author has dedicated his work, and whose productions he seems to have studied" (the review appeared, posthumously, after the publication of the 1831 *Frankenstein* in *The Athenæum* 263 [November 10, 1832], p. 730).

The anonymity of "The Author" of *Frankenstein* was strategic. The Shelleys were concerned that the novel's commercial prospects not be clouded by any association with Percy's controversial publications. In the prevailing codes of female modesty, moreover, even admired female novelists typically (but not always) refrained from putting their names in print. All Jane Austen's lifetime novels were anonymous, and *Frankenstein* was hardly proper female fiction (Percy Shelley's review gives the author as male).

PREFACE

THE EVENT on which this fiction is founded has been supposed, by Dr. Darwin, and some of the physiological writers of Germany, as not of impossible occurrence.[1] I shall not be supposed as according the remotest degree of serious faith to such an imagination; yet, in assuming it as the basis of a work of fancy, I have not considered myself as merely weaving a series of supernatural terrors.[2] The event on which the interest of the story depends is exempt from the disadvantages of a mere tale of spectres or enchantment. It was recommended by the novelty of the situations which it developes; and, however impossible as a physical fact, affords a point of view to the imagination for the delineating of human passions more comprehensive and commanding than any which the ordinary relations of existing events can yield.

I have thus endeavoured to preserve the truth of the elementary principles of human nature, while I have not scrupled to innovate upon their combinations. The *Iliad,* the tragic poetry of Greece,—Shakespeare, in the *Tempest* and *Midsummer Night's Dream,*—and most especially Milton, in *Paradise Lost,* conform to this rule; and the most humble novelist, who seeks to confer or receive amusement from his labours, may, without presumption, apply to prose fiction a licence, or rather a rule, from the adoption of which so many exquisite combinations of human feeling have resulted in the highest specimens of poetry.[3]

In the Introduction of 1831, Mary Shelley says that the Preface was "written entirely by" Percy Shelley (in the Author's voice). The Preface is republished in *1823* (v–xi), and *1831* (1–2) with the subscript "Marlow, September, 1817." The historic Thames River town, in southern England, was Percy and Mary's residence that year.

1 Inventor, philosopher, poet, physician, and botanist Erasmus Darwin (1731–1802) was the most popular scientific writer of his day, and the grandfather of Charles Darwin. He was a friend of Godwin; Mary may have met him. His *Plan for the conduct of female education in boarding schools* (1797) accorded with much of Wollstonecraft's *Vindication of the Rights of Woman* (1792). Percy owned Darwin's scientific writings, professional and poetic, which elaborate issues relevant to the ideals and catastrophes of *Frankenstein.* In his encyclopedic treatise *Zoönomia* (1794–1796, years within the historical setting of *Frankenstein*), Darwin speculated about progeny being affected by a father's state of mind at the moment of conception, and about evolution ("generation") through acquired characteristics, "improvements" and diseases, transmitted to "posterity." His poem *The Temple of Nature* (1803) imaginatively wondered about "spontaneous vital production" and asexual male reproduction:

> In these lone births no tender mothers blend
> Their genial powers to nourish or defend;
> No nutrient streams from Beauty's orbs improve
> These orphan babes of solitary love;
> Birth after birth the line unchanging runs,
> And fathers live transmitted in their sons;
> Each passing year beholds the unvarying kinds,
> The same their manners, and the same their minds.
> (Canto II: *Reproduction of Life,* part III, 103–110)

Both pride of patrilineage and absence of mothers mark the narratives of *Frankenstein.*

2 Supernatural terrors propelled the popularity of Ann Radcliffe's gothic novels, *The Mysteries of Udolpho* (1794) and *The Italian* (1797), both read by teenage Mary. The equivocation here reflects the low status of the gothic in the already low genre of the novel. Even so, such novels reaped impressive profits for their publishers and authors (Radcliffe received an unheard-of £500 for *Udolpho;* £800 for *The Italian*) and accelerated the rise of the novel both as a genre and as a commercial venture.

3 To fend off low novel-company, this Preface asserts a high lineage—from the *Iliad* to Shakespeare's romances, to *Paradise Lost*—and the high values of "domestic affection," "benevolence," and "virtue."

4   Victor Frankenstein will offer similar accolades to domestic af-fection over ambition. Yet their brief intervals are a thin cover for the novel's multiple thrills of dark violation, and the universality of virtue will be contradicted more than once.

5   In the era of post-Waterloo British triumphalism and reaction-ary government policy against suspected insurgents, the Shelleys take care to emphasize that while the gothic novels of the 1790s hey-day (Godwin's and Wollstonecraft's among these) are often political allegories of corruptions in English society, in this one any opinions are to be understood in character, not a veiled authorial doctrine.

6   This was an extraordinarily rainy summer, dubbed "The Year without a Summer," a global climate trauma produced by the erup-tion of Mt. Tambora in Indonesia. In Europe the relentless weather, with attendant floods and much human misery, was felt to be an apocalyptic portent.

7   The phrase is both a disclaimer and an advertisement: the acci-dental reading, merely to amuse dreary hours of bad weather, hap-pens to be the hot genre of the day. The volume at hand is Jean Bap-tiste Benôit Eyriès's French translation, *Fantasmagoriana, ou recueil d'histoires d'apparitions de specters, revenans, fantômes etc. . . . or col-lected stories of apparitions of specters, revenants [ghosts], phantoms, etc.* (1812). In the 1831 Introduction, Shelley describes two of these tales.

8   Her lover, Percy, and their new friend, Byron. Percy Shelley's poetry, when not abstruse, was politically controversial. Byron be-came a celebrity with *Childe Harold's Pilgrimage*, an overnight sen-sation in 1812. His fame accelerated with a series of "Eastern tales," with one, *The Corsair* (1814), selling 10,000 copies on the day of publication, hundreds of thousands in later editions. The thrilling *Childe Harold* Canto the Third, published in December 1816, was the latest sensation.

9   These events are given more narrative detail in the 1831 Intro-duction. In the last week of June 1816, Byron and Percy toured Lake Geneva together, without Mary. Two other ghost tales (not novels) were eventually completed. Byron wrote "A Fragment" (dated "*June 17, 1816*") that his publisher put at the end of his sensational tale *Mazeppa* in June 1819, in a print run of 8,000 (compare 500 for *Frankenstein*). Byron's personal physician, John William Polidori, wrote a longer tale, *The Vampyre*, which *New Monthly Magazine* published in April 1819, attributing it to Byron (the error was cor-rected). Both vampire tales would inspire Bram Stoker's *Dracula* (1897).

The circumstance on which my story rests was suggested in cas-ual conversation. It was commenced, partly as a source of amuse-ment, and partly as an expedient for exercising any untried re-sources of mind. Other motives were mingled with these, as the work proceeded. I am by no means indifferent to the manner in which whatever moral tendencies exist in the sentiments or char-acters it contains shall affect the reader; yet my chief concern in this respect has been limited to the avoiding the enervating effects of the novels of the present day, and to the exhibition of the amia-bleness of domestic affection, and the excellence of universal vir-tue.[4] The opinions which naturally spring from the character and situation of the hero are by no means to be conceived as existing always in my own conviction; nor is any inference justly to be drawn from the following pages as prejudicing any philosophical doctrine of whatever kind.[5]

It is a subject also of additional interest to the author, that this story was begun in the majestic region where the scene is princi-pally laid, and in society which cannot cease to be regretted. I passed the summer of 1816 in the environs of Geneva. The season was cold and rainy,[6] and in the evenings we crowded around a blazing wood fire, and occasionally amused ourselves with some German stories of ghosts, which happened to fall[7] into our hands. These tales excited in us a playful desire of imitation. Two other friends (a tale from the pen of one of whom would be far more ac-ceptable to the public than any thing I can ever hope to produce)[8] and myself agreed to write each a story, founded on some super-natural occurrence.

The weather, however, suddenly became serene; and my two friends left me on a journey among the Alps, and lost, in the mag-nificent scenes which they present, all memory of their ghostly vi-sions. The following tale is the only one which has been com-pleted.[9]

Joseph Severn, posthumous portrait of Percy Bysshe Shelley in the Baths of Caracalla, writing *Prometheus Unbound* (1845). Shelley began working on his lyric drama *Prometheus Unbound* in 1818, the year *Frankenstein* was published. Unlike the novel that Mary Shelley subtitled "The Modern Prometheus," Percy Shelley's work presents a highly idealized protagonist.

Letter I

To Mrs. SAVILLE, *England.*

St. Petersburgh,[1] Dec. 11th, 17—.[2]

You will rejoice to hear that no disaster has accompanied the commencement of an enterprise which you have regarded with such evil forebodings. I arrived here yesterday; and my first task is to assure my dear sister of my welfare, and increasing confidence in the success of my undertaking.[3]

    I am already far north of London; and as I walk in the streets of Petersburgh, I feel a cold northern breeze play upon my cheeks, which braces my nerves, and fills me with delight. Do you understand this feeling? This breeze, which has travelled from the regions towards which I am advancing, gives me a foretaste of those icy climes. Inspirited by this wind of promise,[4] my day dreams become more fervent and vivid. I try in vain to be persuaded that the pole is the seat of frost and desolation; it ever presents itself to my imagination as the region of beauty and delight. Here, Margaret, the sun is for ever visible; its broad disk just skirting the horizon, and diffusing a perpetual splendour. There—for with your leave, my sister, I will put some trust in preceding navigators—there snow and frost are banished; and, sailing over a calm sea, we may be wafted to a land surpassing in wonders and in beauty every region hitherto discovered on the habitable globe.[5] Its productions and features may be without example, as the phænomena of the heavenly bodies undoubtedly are in those undiscovered solitudes. What may not be expected in a country of eternal light? I may there discover the wondrous power which at-

The construction of *Frankenstein* in this frame of letters glances at an eighteenth-century genre: the "epistolary" novel, composed of letters that report events. Some famous instances are Samuel Richardson's *Pamela* (1740) and *Clarissa* (1749), and in Germany J. W. von Goethe's *Sorrows of Young Werter* (1774), all read by Mary across 1815–1816, and all figuring into the Creature's education. The epistolary form maintains an intriguing tension between the documentary objectivity of the letters' existence and the subjectivity of a letter-writer's point of view.

1 St. Petersburg(h), capital of the Russian Empire, is at the eastern tip of the Gulf of Finland, on the Baltic Sea.

2 The dash is strange: a correspondent is unlikely to write a date this way. The effacement gives the illusion of later editorial interference (Crook 9), the work of a hand that also supplies the title and subtitle over the first chapter of each volume in the original and that writes "WALTON, *in continuation*" in volume III, "August 26th, 17—." (VII).

3 This brother-sister relation initiates a series of gender-contrasts: between male visionary excitement and female foreboding; between male thirst for glory and female domesticity; between male bonding and bonds of marriage and family. We learn later that Mrs. Saville has "a husband, and lovely children" (letter of September 2; Vol. III, Ch. VII).

4 Mary Shelley is aware that the Latin word for wind, *spiritus,* is the root of *inspiration.*

5 From the Renaissance on, the theory of a warm open sea at the North Pole inspired searches for a shorter trade route to the Americas or the Pacific, otherwise reachable only by long and dangerous voyages. Mary Shelley will expose the terrible effects of Walton's overconfidence, the first of many parallels with Frankenstein. As even Frankenstein perceives, the ardent adventurer Walton is his twin, in embryo.

6 Walton's single-minded idealism, his "dream," is shaped by texts that probably included Richard Hakluyt's *Principal Navigations, Voiages, Traffiques and Discoveries of the English nation* (1598–1600) and Samuel Purchas's *Hakluytus Posthumus or Purchas His Pilgrimes* (1625). Coleridge's visionary lyric *Kubla Khan* (1816) was influenced by Purchas. In 1816, Mary was reading "old voyages" and accounts of postwar polar explorations (for her reading lists, see *Journals*).

tracts the needle; and may regulate a thousand celestial observations, that require only this voyage to render their seeming eccentricities consistent for ever. I shall satiate my ardent curiosity with the sight of a part of the world never before visited, and may tread a land never before imprinted by the foot of man. These are my enticements, and they are sufficient to conquer all fear of danger or death, and to induce me to commence this laborious voyage with the joy a child feels when he embarks in a little boat, with his holiday mates, on an expedition of discovery up his native river. But, supposing all these conjectures to be false, you cannot contest the inestimable benefit which I shall confer on all mankind to the last generation, by discovering a passage near the pole to those countries, to reach which at present so many months are requisite; or by ascertaining the secret of the magnet, which, if at all possible, can only be effected by an undertaking such as mine.

These reflections have dispelled the agitation with which I began my letter, and I feel my heart glow with an enthusiasm which elevates me to heaven; for nothing contributes so much to tranquillize the mind as a steady purpose,—a point on which the soul may fix its intellectual eye. This expedition has been the favourite dream of my early years. I have read with ardour the accounts of the various voyages which have been made in the prospect of arriving at the North Pacific Ocean through the seas which surround the pole. You may remember, that a history of all the voyages made for purposes of discovery composed the whole of our good uncle Thomas's library. My education was neglected, yet I was passionately fond of reading. These volumes were my study day and night, and my familiarity with them increased that regret which I had felt, as a child, on learning that my father's dying injunction had forbidden my uncle to allow me to embark in a seafaring life.[6]

These visions faded when I perused, for the first time, those poets whose effusions entranced my soul, and lifted it to heaven. I also became a poet, and for one year lived in a Paradise of my own creation; I imagined that I also might obtain a niche in the temple where the names of Homer and Shakespeare are consecrated. You are well acquainted with my failure, and how heavily I bore the disappointment. But just at that time I inherited the for-

Fyodor Alekseyev, *The Palace Embankment seen from the Peter and Paul Fortress, St. Petersburg* (1794) renders the exciting port city as Robert Walton would have seen it.

This colored engraving, *Map of the Countries Thirty Degrees round the North Pole,* drawn by G. G. and J. Robinson (London publishers), is from Stockdale's *Atlas to Cruttwell's Gazetteer* (London, 1799), one of many elegant books by English map publisher Clement Cruttwell (1743–1808). On a map no more detailed than this, Robert Walton imagines a transpolar route to the northern Pacific (via the Bering Strait, at the top). The Russian cities he mentions in his letters are near the south-southeast circumference. St. Petersburg is on the perimeter, at latitude 60 N, longitude 30 E (3 bars to the right of the Prime Meridian, the strongly marked vertical at 0 longitude). Archangel, Walton's port of departure, is northeast of St. Petersburg, longitude 40 E, latitude 64 N, on the eastern shore of the small inlet sea (the Gulf of Archangel).

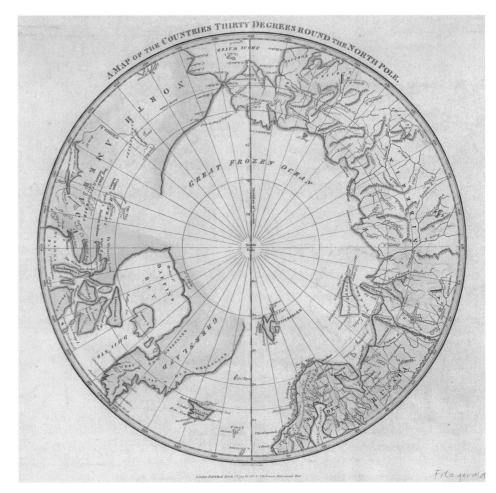

tune of my cousin,[7] and my thoughts were turned into the channel of their earlier bent.

Six years have passed since I resolved on my present undertaking. I can, even now, remember the hour from which I dedicated myself to this great enterprise. I commenced by inuring my body to hardship. I accompanied the whale-fishers on several expeditions to the North Sea; I voluntarily endured cold, famine, thirst, and want of sleep; I often worked harder than the common sailors during the day, and devoted my nights to the study of mathematics, the theory of medicine, and those branches of physical science from which a naval adventurer might derive the greatest practical advantage. Twice I actually hired myself as an under-mate in a Greenland whaler, and acquitted myself to admiration. I must own I felt a little proud, when my captain offered me the second dignity in the vessel, and entreated me to remain with the greatest earnestness; so valuable did he consider my services.

And now, dear Margaret, do I not deserve to accomplish some great purpose. My life might have been passed in ease and luxury; but I preferred glory to every enticement that wealth placed in my path. Oh, that some encouraging voice would answer in the affirmative! My courage and my resolution is firm; but my hopes fluctuate, and my spirits are often depressed. I am about to proceed on a long and difficult voyage; the emergencies of which will demand all my fortitude: I am required not only to raise the spirits of others, but sometimes to sustain my own, when their's are failing.

This is the most favourable period for travelling in Russia. They fly quickly over the snow in their sledges; the motion is pleasant, and, in my opinion, far more agreeable than that of an English stage-coach. The cold is not excessive, if you are wrapt in furs, a dress which I have already adopted; for there is a great difference between walking the deck and remaining seated motionless for hours, when no exercise prevents the blood from actually freezing in your veins. I have no ambition to lose my life on the post-road between St. Petersburgh and Archangel.[8]

I shall depart for the latter town in a fortnight[9] or three weeks; and my intention is to hire a ship there, which can easily be done by paying the insurance for the owner, and to engage as many sailors as I think necessary among those who are accustomed to

7 At age twenty-one, Walton controls his inheritance, free of the will of his father or uncle.

8 This actual port on the White Sea (an inlet of the Arctic Ocean) has an alluringly allegorical name and geographically telling latitude. It was named in 1613 for the monastery of Archangel Michael, vanquisher of Satan in *Paradise Lost*. As for latitude: as Jessica Richard has discovered, veteran explorers would regard Walton's plans to embark so early onto the Arctic sea as perilously ill-considered. The preference was for maximum land travel, going north over Canada or Greenland. Archangel is 64 degrees north; Canada's landmass extends up to about 80; Greenland's, to about 83.

9 This is an English term for two weeks, a contraction of fourteen-night.

10   An idealism of male friendship, especially between men seeking an alter ego to heal a sense of loneliness and incompletion, extends back to Plato, Aristotle, Cicero, and many others, and was raised to the status of a cult among Renaissance thinkers and poets, including Montaigne, Shakespeare, and Milton. This theme is reflected throughout the novel, especially in the friendship of Victor Frankenstein and his virtual brother Henry Clerval and in the laments of lonely Walton and the lonely Creature.

11   Before "Romantic" came to define the literary movement of the era that includes *Frankenstein,* it indicated the genre of "romance": exotic adventures, often impelled by idealism or visionary quest. In the April 1814 *Monthly Review* Italian epic poets Pulci, Ariosto, and Boiardo were described as "romantic poets" (477). Byron's 1812 poem *Childe Harold's Pilgrimage* bears the retro-subtitle *A Romaunt,* and "A Romance" is a frequent subtitle or paratitle for gothic novels, including Radcliffe's *Udolpho.*

the whale-fishing. I do not intend to sail until the month of June: and when shall I return? Ah, dear sister, how can I answer this question? If I succeed, many, many months, perhaps years, will pass before you and I may meet. If I fail, you will see me again soon, or never.

Farewell, my dear, excellent, Margaret. Heaven shower down blessings on you, and save me, that I may again and again testify my gratitude for all your love and kindness.

Your affectionate brother,
R. Walton.

Letter II

To Mrs. SAVILLE, *England.*

Archangel, 28th March, 17—.

How slowly the time passes here, encompassed as I am by frost and snow; yet a second step is taken towards my enterprise. I have hired a vessel, and am occupied in collecting my sailors; those whom I have already engaged appear to be men on whom I can depend, and are certainly possessed of dauntless courage.

But I have one want which I have never yet been able to satisfy; and the absence of the object of which I now feel as a most severe evil. I have no friend, Margaret: when I am glowing with the enthusiasm of success, there will be none to participate my joy; if I am assailed by disappointment, no one will endeavour to sustain me in dejection. I shall commit my thoughts to paper, it is true; but that is a poor medium for the communication of feeling. I desire the company of a man who could sympathize with me; whose eyes would reply to mine.[10] You may deem me romantic,[11] my dear sister, but I bitterly feel the want of a friend. I have no one near me, gentle yet courageous, possessed of a cultivated as well as of a capacious mind, whose tastes are like my own, to approve or amend my plans. How would such a friend repair the faults of your poor brother! I am too ardent in execution, and too impatient of difficulties. But it is a still greater evil to me that I am self-educated: for the first fourteen years of my life I ran wild on a common, and read nothing but our uncle Thomas's books of voyages. At that age I became acquainted with the celebrated poets of our own country; but it was only when it had ceased to be in my power to derive its most important benefits from such a conviction, that I perceived the necessity of becoming acquainted with more languages than that of my native country. Now I am twenty-eight, and am in reality more illiterate than many school-boys of fifteen. It is true that I have thought more, and that my day dreams are more extended and magnificent; but they want (as the painters call it) *keeping*;[12] and I greatly need a friend who would have sense enough not to despise me as romantic, and affection enough for me to endeavour to regulate my mind.

Well, these are useless complaints; I shall certainly find no friend on the wide ocean, nor even here in Archangel, among merchants and seamen. Yet some feelings, unallied to the dross of human nature, beat even in these rugged bosoms. My lieutenant, for instance, is a man of wonderful courage and enterprise; he is madly desirous of glory. He is an Englishman, and in the midst of national and professional prejudices, unsoftened by cultivation, retains some of the noblest endowments of humanity. I first became acquainted with him on board a whale vessel: finding that he was unemployed in this city, I easily engaged him to assist in my enterprise.

The master is a person of an excellent disposition, and is remarkable in the ship for his gentleness, and the mildness of his discipline.[13] He is, indeed, of so amiable a nature, that he will not

12   "The proper relation between the representations of nearer and more distant objects in a picture . . . the maintenance of harmony of composition" (OED).

13   This policy is elaborated in *1831*. Maritime discipline could be brutal, and sometimes provoked rebellion. The mutiny against Captain Bligh on the *HMS Bounty* on April 28, 1789, and the courts-martial of the captured mutineers in 1792 were fresh historical memories for any captain in the 1790s.

Though painted much later, *The Explorer A. E. Nordenskiöld,* by Georg von Rosen (1886), evokes the extreme conditions with which Walton contends.

hunt[14] (a favourite, and almost the only amusement here), because he cannot endure to spill blood. He is, moreover, heroically generous. Some years ago he loved a young Russian lady, of moderate fortune; and having amassed a considerable sum in prize-money,[15] the father of the girl consented to the match. He saw his mistress once before the destined ceremony; but she was bathed in tears, and, throwing herself at his feet, entreated him to spare her, confessing at the same time that she loved another, but that he was poor, and that her father would never consent to the union. My generous friend reassured the suppliant, and on being informed of the name of her lover instantly abandoned his pursuit. He had already bought a farm with his money, on which he had designed to pass the remainder of his life; but he bestowed the whole on his rival, together with the remains of his prize-money to purchase stock, and then himself solicited the young woman's father to consent to her marriage with her lover. But the old man decidedly refused, thinking himself bound in honour to my friend; who, when he found the father inexorable, quitted his country, nor returned until he heard that his former mistress was married according to her inclinations. "What a noble fellow!" you will exclaim.[16] He is so; but then he has passed all his life on board a vessel, and has scarcely an idea beyond the rope and the shroud.[17]

But do not suppose that, because I complain a little, or because I can conceive a consolation for my toils which I may never know, that I am wavering in my resolutions. Those are as fixed as fate; and my voyage is only now delayed until the weather shall permit my embarkation. The winter has been dreadfully severe; but the spring promises well, and it is considered as a remarkably early

14   Percy Shelley was a vegetarian.

15   This is a share from the sale of a captured enemy ship and its contents; the fortune is the ship master's (the grammar is ablative absolute).

16   This is the first of a chain of episodes about self-sacrifice for the welfare of another, all accumulating against Frankenstein's characteristic self-interest.

17   A shroud is a sail. In *1831* Mary Shelley expands the passage to emphasize his otherness: "he is wholly uneducated: he is as silent as a Turk, and a kind of ignorant carelessness attends him, which, while it renders his conduct the more astonishing, detracts from the interest and sympathy which otherwise he would command" (I.8).

Gustave Doré, steel engraving for *The Rime of the Ancient Mariner*, 1870. Doré represents a ship in a seascape of demonically shaped icebergs canopied by a heavenly rainbow, circling a white bird. Its caption is the first two lines of this stanza:

"The Ice was here, the Ice was there, / The Ice was all around; / It crack'd and growl'd, and roar'd and howl'd— / Like noises of a swound". (1798 text, 57–60).

The ice was here, the ice was there,
The ice was all around.

Page 6.

. . . . With my cross-bow
I shot the Albatross.

Page 6.

LETTER II

. . . With my cross-bow
I shot the Albatross

Part I of Coleridge's ballad ends
with these lines. Unmotivated
and inexplicable, the act dooms
the Mariner into an endless
telling of his story.

18 Walton's meaning of "conception" as "idea" also evokes in the context of the tale to come the biological sense. Here is one of many examples of Mary Shelley's skill in weaving a textual field of thematically important keywords.

19 "Coleridge's Antient Mariner" [Mary Shelley's note, *1823*]. This supernatural ballad (first published in 1798) recounts an episode of ice-bound terror near the South Pole. An albatross appeared, seemingly a good omen, and was fed by the crew, until the Mariner, inexplicably, killed it. Everyone dies a miserable death, except the Mariner, who is condemned to tell this tale for eternity.

20 The full signature (compare "R. Walton" in Letter I) is a formality for a possibly final farewell. "Robert" means "bright fame."

season; so that, perhaps, I may sail sooner than I expected. I shall do nothing rashly; you know me sufficiently to confide in my prudence and considerateness whenever the safety of others is committed to my care.

I cannot describe to you my sensations on the near prospect of my undertaking. It is impossible to communicate to you a conception[18] of the trembling sensation, half pleasurable and half fearful, with which I am preparing to depart. I am going to unexplored regions, to "the land of mist and snow;" but I shall kill no albatross,[19] therefore do not be alarmed for my safety.

Shall I meet you again, after having traversed immense seas, and returned by the most southern cape of Africa or America? I dare not expect such success, yet I cannot bear to look on the reverse of the picture. Continue to write to me by every opportunity: I may receive your letters (though the chance is very doubtful) on some occasions when I need them most to support my spirits. I love you very tenderly. Remember me with affection, should you never hear from me again.

Your affectionate brother,
ROBERT WALTON.[20]

Letter III

To Mrs. SAVILLE, *England.*

July 7th, 17—.

MY DEAR SISTER,

I write a few lines in haste, to say that I am safe, and well advanced on my voyage. This letter will reach England by a merchant-man now on its homeward voyage from Archangel;

Das Eismeer (The Ice Sea), 1823–1824, has also been known as *Die verunglückte Hoffnung* (The Wreck of Hope). This starkly beautiful oil painting by German Romantic Caspar David Friedrich (1774–1840) is renowned for the sublime icescape that overwhelms human endeavors. The wrecked ship, doomed to being crushed to oblivion (its stern at center right, its masts scattered to the left), is a scarcely noticeable form amid the dramatic thrust of massive shards and slabs. Friedrich's rendering of nature's indifferent brutal power proved so appalling that the painting remained unsold until the year of his death.

more fortunate than I, who may not see my native land, perhaps, for many years. I am, however, in good spirits: my men are bold, and apparently firm of purpose; nor do the floating sheets of ice that continually pass us, indicating the dangers of the region towards which we are advancing, appear to dismay them. We have already reached a very high latitude; but it is the height of summer, and although not so warm as in England, the southern gales, which blow us speedily towards those shores which I so ardently desire to attain, breathe a degree of renovating warmth which I had not expected.

No incidents have hitherto befallen us, that would make a figure in a letter. One or two stiff gales, and the breaking of a mast, are accidents which experienced navigators scarcely remember to

21 The hasty signature, on this shortest of letters, suggests preoccupation with the adventure at hand.

22 This weather-report recalls *The Rime of the Ancyent Marinere*:

. . . Mist and Snow,
And it grew wond'rous cauld:
And Ice mast-high came floating by
As green as Emerauld.

And thro' the drifts the snowy clifts
Did send a dismal sheen;
Ne shapes of men ne beasts we ken—
The Ice was all between.

The Ice was here, the Ice was there,
The Ice was all around:
It crack'd and growl'd, and roar'd and howl'd—
Like noises of a swound.

At length did cross an Albatross,
Thorough the Fog it came;
And an it were a Christian Soul,
We hail'd it in God's name.

23 The verb indicates not only agonized expression but incipient unrest.

record; and I shall be well content, if nothing worse happen to us during our voyage.

Adieu, my dear Margaret. Be assured, that for my own sake, as well as your's, I will not rashly encounter danger. I will be cool, persevering, and prudent.

Remember me to all my English friends

Most affectionately yours,
R. W.[21]

Letter IV

To Mrs. SAVILLE, *England.*

August 5th, 17—.

So strange an accident has happened to us, that I cannot forbear recording it, although it is very probable that you will see me before these papers can come into your possession.

Last Monday (July 31st), we were nearly surrounded by ice, which closed in the ship on all sides, scarcely leaving her the sea room in which she floated. Our situation was somewhat dangerous, especially as we were compassed round by a very thick fog.[22] We accordingly lay to, hoping that some change would take place in the atmosphere and weather.

About two o'clock the mist cleared away, and we beheld, stretched out in every direction, vast and irregular plains of ice, which seemed to have no end. Some of my comrades groaned,[23] and my own mind began to grow watchful with anxious thoughts, when a strange sight suddenly attracted our attention, and diverted our solicitude from our own situation. We perceived a low carriage, fixed on a sledge and drawn by dogs, pass on towards the north, at the distance of half a mile: a being which had the shape of a man, but apparently of gigantic stature, sat in the sledge, and guided the dogs. We watched the rapid progress of the traveller with our telescopes, until he was lost among the distant inequalities of the ice.

This appearance excited our unqualified wonder. We were, as we believed, many hundred miles from any land; but this apparition seemed to denote that it was not, in reality, so distant as we had supposed. Shut in, however, by ice, it was impossible to follow his track, which we had observed with the greatest attention.

About two hours after this occurrence, we heard the ground sea;[24] and before night the ice broke, and freed our ship. We, however, lay to until the morning, fearing to encounter in the dark those large loose masses which float about after the breaking up of the ice. I profited of this time to rest for a few hours.

In the morning, however, as soon as it was light, I went upon deck, and found all the sailors busy on one side of the vessel, apparently talking to some one in the sea. It was, in fact, a sledge, like that we had seen before, which had drifted towards us in the night, on a large fragment of ice. Only one dog remained alive;[25] but there was a human being[26] within it, whom the sailors were persuading to enter the vessel. He was not, as the other traveller seemed to be, a savage inhabitant of some undiscovered island, but an European. When I appeared on deck, the master said, "Here is our captain, and he will not allow you to perish on the open sea."

On perceiving me, the stranger addressed me in English, although with a foreign accent.[27] "Before I come on board your vessel," said he, "will you have the kindness to inform me whither you are bound?"

24 A stormy sea with heavy waves.

25 This is the last mention of this poor creature!

26 A "human being" contrasts the first sledge-driver, a gigantic "being."

27 We find out that his native tongue is French, and he is presumably fluent in German.

28 This is the first mention of the deity in this novel (typically in exclamation).

29 As the OED reveals, *wretch* has a compelling etymology and history of shifting senses of no small consequence to *Frankenstein*. Derived from Old English *wrǽcca*, *wretch* first designated an "exile, adventurer." In the Middle Ages, the sense shifted to "one driven out of or away from his native country; a banished person; an exile," or, more sympathetically, "One who is sunk in deep distress, sorrow, misfortune, or poverty; a miserable, unhappy, or unfortunate person; a poor or hapless being." It was used in this sense in Wollstonecraft's *Rights of Men* (1790), and held well into the nineteenth century. It could be a playful taunt ("Excellent wretch!" sighs Othello of beloved Desdemona), but this is absent in *Frankenstein*. More frequent is the sense of "vile, sorry, or despicable person; one of opprobrious or reprehensible character; a mean or contemptible creature." *Wretched* follows suit, connoting not only "a state of misery, poverty, or degradation; sunk in distress or dejection; very miserable or unhappy" but also "distinguished by base, vile, or unworthy character or quality; contemptible." With accumulating force, *Frankenstein* unfolds this word cluster across all these registers of meaning, ultimately linking the negligent creator to his abject creature.

30 This is the novel's first scene of animation: of the dead (or near dead) brought back to life, here with sympathy for a fellow human being. Mary had a painful personal reference for this scene, recorded in her journal for March 1815:

> Monday 6
> find my baby dead——————————————. . .
> Thursday 9th
> Read & talk—still think about my little baby—'tis hard indeed for a mother to loose a child—. . .
> Monday 13th
> . . . stay at ~~ho~~ home . . . & think of my little dead baby—this is foolish I suppose yet whenever I am left alone to my own thought & do not read to divert them they always come back to the same point—that I was a mother & am so no longer—. . .
> Sunday 19th
> Dream that my little baby came to life again — that it had only been cold & that we rubbed it by the fire & it lived—I ~~al~~ awake & find no baby—I think about the little thing all day—not in good spirits . . .
> Monday 20th
> Dream again about my baby—
> (*Journals* 68–71)

You may conceive my astonishment on hearing such a question addressed to me from a man on the brink of destruction, and to whom I should have supposed that my vessel would have been a resource which he would not have exchanged for the most precious wealth the earth can afford. I replied, however, that we were on a voyage of discovery towards the northern pole.

Upon hearing this he appeared satisfied, and consented to come on board. Good God![28] Margaret, if you had seen the man who thus capitulated for his safety, your surprise would have been boundless. His limbs were nearly frozen, and his body dreadfully emaciated by fatigue and suffering. I never saw a man in so wretched[29] a condition. We attempted to carry him into the cabin; but as soon as he had quitted the fresh air, he fainted. We accordingly brought him back to the deck, and restored him to animation[30] by rubbing him with brandy, and forcing him to swallow a small quantity. As soon as he shewed signs of life, we wrapped him up in blankets, and placed him near the chimney of the kitchen-stove. By slow degrees he recovered, and ate a little soup, which restored him wonderfully.

Two days passed in this manner before he was able to speak; and I often feared that his sufferings had deprived him of understanding. When he had in some measure recovered, I removed him to my own cabin, and attended on him as much as my duty would permit. I never saw a more interesting creature:[31] his eyes have generally an expression of wildness, and even madness; but there are moments when, if any one performs an act of kindness towards him, or does him any the most trifling service, his whole countenance is lighted up, as it were, with a beam of benevolence and sweetness that I never saw equalled. But he is generally melancholy and despairing; and sometimes he gnashes his teeth,[32] as if impatient of the weight of woes that oppresses him.

When my guest was a little recovered, I had great trouble to keep off the men, who wished to ask him a thousand questions; but I would not allow him to be tormented by their idle curiosity, in a state of body and mind whose restoration evidently depended upon entire repose. Once, however, the lieutenant asked, Why he had come so far upon the ice in so strange a vehicle?

His countenance instantly assumed an aspect of the deepest gloom; and he replied, "To seek one who fled from me."

"And did the man whom you pursued travel in the same fashion?"

"Yes."

"Then I fancy we have seen him; for, the day before we picked you up, we saw some dogs drawing a sledge, with a man in it, across the ice."

This aroused the stranger's attention; and he asked a multitude of questions concerning the route which the dæmon,[33] as he called him, had pursued. Soon after, when he was alone with me, he said, "I have, doubtless, excited your curiosity, as well as that of these good people; but you are too considerate to make inquiries."

"Certainly; it would indeed be very impertinent and inhuman in me to trouble you with any inquisitiveness of mine."

"And yet you rescued me from a strange and perilous situation; you have benevolently restored me to life."

Soon after this he inquired, if I thought that the breaking up of the ice had destroyed the other sledge? I replied, that I could not answer with any degree of certainty; for the ice had not broken until near midnight, and the traveller might have arrived at a place of safety before that time; but of this I could not judge.

From this time the stranger seemed very eager to be upon deck, to watch for the sledge which had before appeared; but I have persuaded him to remain in the cabin, for he is far too weak

31   This is the first event in the novel of this most resonant keyword. As for "interesting": in the eighteenth century, this indicated attractive not just to attention but also to sympathy (versus the neutral "disinterested"). Attached to "interesting," "creature" expresses sympathy for a "fellow creature."

32   In the Bible, a frequent curse on sinners: "there will be weeping and gnashing of teeth" (see Matthew 8: 12 and 25: 30).

33   Although this spelling evokes the supernatural entities of Greek mythology that served as intermediaries between gods and mortals, Frankenstein utters it with the biblical sense of evil spirit, a demon.

34 Walton's yearning for a friend, or brother of his heart, predisposes him to sympathy with this "wreck" of a stranger; "noble" is a term used in praise of virtuous character, but is rarely free of its class-infected value.

to sustain the rawness of the atmosphere. But I have promised that some one should watch for him, and give him instant notice if any new object should appear in sight.

Such is my journal of what relates to this strange occurrence up to the present day. The stranger has gradually improved in health, but is very silent, and appears uneasy when any one except myself enters his cabin. Yet his manners are so conciliating and gentle, that the sailors are all interested in him, although they have had very little communication with him. For my own part, I begin to love him as a brother; and his constant and deep grief fills me with sympathy and compassion. He must have been a noble creature in his better days, being even now in wreck so attractive and amiable.[34]

I said in one of my letters, my dear Margaret, that I should find no friend on the wide ocean; yet I have found a man who, before his spirit had been broken by misery, I should have been happy to have possessed as the brother of my heart.

I shall continue my journal concerning the stranger at intervals, should I have any fresh incidents to record.

August 13th, 17—.

My affection for my guest increases every day. He excites at once my admiration and my pity to an astonishing degree. How can I see so noble a creature destroyed by misery without feeling the most poignant grief? He is so gentle, yet so wise; his mind is so cultivated; and when he speaks, although his words are culled with the choicest art, yet they flow with rapidity and unparalleled eloquence.

He is now much recovered from his illness, and is continually on the deck, apparently watching for the sledge that preceded his own. Yet, although unhappy, he is not so utterly occupied by his own misery, but that he interests himself deeply in the employments of others. He has asked me many questions concerning my design; and I have related my little history frankly[35] to him. He appeared pleased with the confidence, and suggested several alterations in my plan, which I shall find exceedingly useful. There is no pedantry in his manner; but all he does appears to spring solely from the interest he instinctively takes in the welfare of those who surround him. He is often overcome by gloom, and then he sits by himself, and tries to overcome all that is sullen or unsocial in his humour. These paroxysms pass from him like a cloud from before the sun, though his dejection never leaves him. I have endeavoured to win his confidence; and I trust that I have succeeded. One day I mentioned to him the desire I had always felt of finding a friend who might sympathize with me, and direct me by his counsel. I said, I did not belong to that class of men who are offended by advice. "I am self-educated, and perhaps I hardly rely sufficiently upon my own powers. I wish therefore that my companion should be wiser and more experienced than myself, to confirm and support me; nor have I believed it impossible to find a true friend."

"I agree with you," replied the stranger, "in believing that friendship is not only a desirable, but a possible acquisition. I once had a friend, the most noble of human creatures, and am entitled, therefore, to judge respecting friendship. You have hope, and the world before you,[36] and have no cause for despair. But I——I have lost every thing, and cannot begin life anew."

As he said this, his countenance became expressive of a calm settled grief, that touched me to the heart. But he was silent, and presently retired to his cabin.

Even broken in spirit as he is, no one can feel more deeply than he does the beauties of nature. The starry sky, the sea, and every

35 Without yet knowing this (except perhaps in retrospective review), Walton has used an adverb with resonance for his guest.

36 These words are an ironic echo of the last lines of *Paradise Lost* (about Adam and Eve, expelled from Eden): "The world was all before them" (XII.646).

37 Although Walton means a "double existence" of "celestial" sensibility, the phrase initiates a dark ironic sense of a hero tormented by a demonic double.

38 As Mary Shelley is aware, the Latin for *wanderer* is *erro,* also the root of *error.* The phrase effects a subtle allusion to the divine wanderer of *Paradise Lost:* Satan, formerly, before his fall into error, archangel Lucifer.

39 In *Paradise Lost* IX, Eve's desire for greater knowledge makes her vulnerable to a serpent's seduction (Satan disguised).

40 This plea recurs throughout the novel, in which tale-telling and tale-listening open possibilities for moral and imaginative sympathy. The mention of usefulness draws on the neoclassical axiom that literature should instruct and delight.

41 This promise or caution is also, in effect, an advertisement for our interest. Walton's situation is analogous to the Wedding Guest's in Coleridge's *Rime,* compelled to hear, and unable to shake off, the Ancient Mariner's haunted, haunting tale. And as audience to Frankenstein, Walton is also the reader's proxy.

sight afforded by these wonderful regions, seems still to have the power of elevating his soul from earth. Such a man has a double existence: he may suffer misery, and be overwhelmed by disappointments; yet when he has retired into himself, he will be like a celestial spirit, that has a halo around him, within whose circle no grief or folly ventures.[37]

Will you laugh at the enthusiasm I express concerning this divine wanderer?[38] If you do, you must have certainly lost that simplicity which was once your characteristic charm. Yet, if you will, smile at the warmth of my expressions, while I find every day new causes for repeating them.

August 19, 17—.

Yesterday the stranger said to me, "You may easily perceive, Captain Walton, that I have suffered great and unparalleled misfortunes. I had determined, once, that the memory of these evils should die with me; but you have won me to alter my determination. You seek for knowledge and wisdom, as I once did; and I ardently hope that the gratification of your wishes may not be a serpent to sting you, as mine has been.[39] I do not know that the relation of my misfortunes will be useful to you, yet, if you are inclined, listen to my tale.[40] I believe that the strange incidents connected with it will afford a view of nature, which may enlarge your faculties and understanding. You will hear of powers and occurrences, such as you have been accustomed to believe impossible:[41] but I do not doubt that my tale conveys in its series internal evidence of the truth of the events of which it is composed."

You may easily conceive that I was much gratified by the offered communication; yet I could not endure that he should renew his grief by a recital of his misfortunes. I felt the greatest eagerness to hear the promised narrative, partly from curiosity, and partly from a strong desire to ameliorate his fate, if it were in my power. I expressed these feelings in my answer.

"I thank you," he replied, "for your sympathy, but it is useless; my fate is nearly fulfilled. I wait but for one event, and then I shall repose in peace. I understand your feeling," continued he, perceiving that I wished to interrupt him; "but you are mistaken, my friend, if thus you will allow me to name you; nothing can alter my destiny: listen to my history, and you will perceive how irrevocably it is determined."

He then told me, that he would commence his narrative the next day when I should be at leisure. This promise drew from me the warmest thanks. I have resolved every night, when I am not engaged, to record, as nearly as possible in his own words, what he has related during the day.[42] If I should be engaged, I will at least make notes. This manuscript will doubtless afford you the greatest pleasure: but to me, who know him, and who hear it from his own lips, with what interest and sympathy shall I read it in some future day!

42   The record that Walton transmits to Margaret pushes the epistolary genre to an extreme. The manuscript holds Frankenstein's "history," within which Frankenstein rehearses the Creature's story, apparently from memory. The tension between documentary record and subjective narration will become increasingly critical.

CHAPTER I

I AM BY BIRTH A Genevese;[1] and my family is one of the most distinguished of that republic. My ancestors had been for many years counsellors and syndics;[2] and my father had filled several public situations with honour and reputation. He was respected by all who knew him for his integrity and indefatigable attention to public business. He passed his younger days perpetually occupied by the affairs of his country; and it was not until the decline of life that he thought of marrying, and bestowing on the state sons who might carry his virtues and his name down to posterity.[3]

As the circumstances of his marriage illustrate his character, I cannot refrain from relating them. One of his most intimate friends was a merchant, who, from a flourishing state, fell, through numerous mischances, into poverty. This man, whose name was Beaufort, was of a proud and unbending disposition, and could not bear to live in poverty and oblivion in the same country where he had formerly been distinguished for his rank and magnificence. Having paid his debts, therefore, in the most honourable manner, he retreated with his daughter to the town of Lucerne, where he lived unknown and in wretchedness.[4] My father loved Beaufort with the truest friendship, and was deeply grieved by his retreat in these unfortunate circumstances. He grieved also for the loss of his society, and resolved to seek him out and endeavour to persuade him to begin the world again through his credit and assistance.

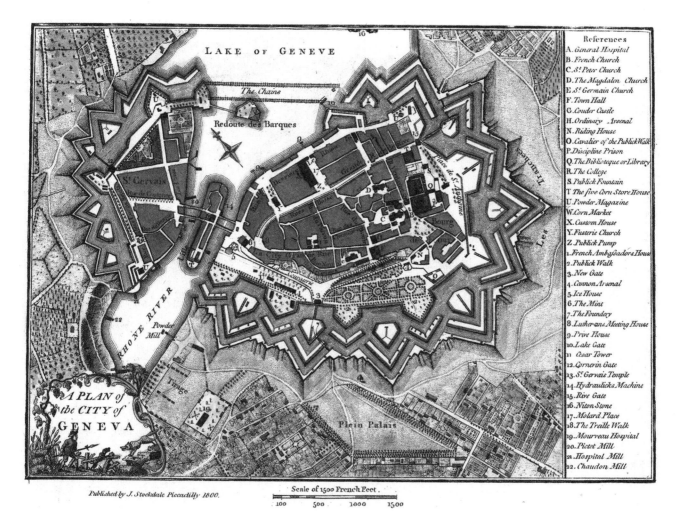

Geneva, the walled city, around the era of *Frankenstein*.

Beaufort had taken effectual measures to conceal himself; and it was ten months before my father discovered his abode. Overjoyed at this discovery, he hastened to the house, which was situated in a mean[5] street, near the Reuss. But when he entered, misery and despair alone welcomed him. Beaufort had saved but a very small sum of money from the wreck of his fortunes; but it was sufficient to provide him with sustenance for some months, and in the mean time he hoped to procure some respectable employment in a mer-

6 Plain work is basic sewing, poorly paid. More artisanal was straw-plaiting (weaving baskets, hats, and other textiles). Too proud to accept help from friends, Caroline's father does not seem to mind reducing his daughter to menial labor.

7 In *1831* Mary Shelley repeats this phrase in the revised story of Elizabeth, left at her father's death "an orphan and a beggar" (Ch. I, 22), and so a more evident double of Caroline, whose adoption of her mirrors her own rescue by Alphonse.

8 Only the eldest son was heir in the system of primogeniture ("first born"), designed to keep wealth consolidated rather than dispersed through multiple heirs. Other sons had to seek a profession or advantageous marriage. Parents could endow a "fortune" on the non-heirs; for a daughter a fortune was her dowry, her asset on the marriage market. The French Revolution abolished primogeniture. In Percy Shelley's letter of introduction to Godwin, he declared "the law of primogeniture an evil of primary magnitude" (January 10, 1812, *Letters* 1: 220). He was echoing Tom Paine, who described the system as a "monster": "The rest are begotten to be devoured. They are thrown to the cannibal for prey, and the natural parent prepares the unnatural repast" (*The Rights of Man*, 8th London edition, 1790, 73–74). Frankenstein does not make the connection between his privilege and the abjection of his siblings (his parents seem likely to make some provision).

9 Walton had used *creature* with reference to Frankenstein. This is the first event of the word *creature* in Frankenstein's narration, here entailing caring creators. The career of this word across the novel grows into a subtle indictment of Frankenstein's failure to care for his Creature, especially in infancy.

10 This episode is substantially revised in *1831;* see Sample of Revised Passages.

chant's house. The interval was consequently spent in inaction; his grief only became more deep and rankling, when he had leisure for reflection; and at length it took so fast hold of his mind, that at the end of three months he lay on a bed of sickness, incapable of any exertion.

His daughter attended him with the greatest tenderness; but she saw with despair that their little fund was rapidly decreasing, and that there was no other prospect of support. But Caroline Beaufort possessed a mind of an uncommon mould; and her courage rose to support her in her adversity. She procured plain work;[6] she plaited straw; and by various means contrived to earn a pittance scarcely sufficient to support life.

Several months passed in this manner. Her father grew worse; her time was more entirely occupied in attending him; her means of subsistence decreased; and in the tenth month her father died in her arms, leaving her an orphan and a beggar.[7] This last blow overcame her; and she knelt by Beaufort's coffin, weeping bitterly, when my father entered the chamber. He came like a protecting spirit to the poor girl, who committed herself to his care, and after the interment of his friend he conducted her to Geneva, and placed her under the protection of a relation. Two years after this event Caroline became his wife.

When my father became a husband and a parent, he found his time so occupied by the duties of his new situation, that he relinquished many of his public employments, and devoted himself to the education of his children. Of these I was the eldest, and the destined successor to all his labours and utility.[8] No creature could have more tender parents than mine.[9] My improvement and health were their constant care, especially as I remained for several years their only child. But before I continue my narrative, I must record an incident which took place when I was four years of age.[10]

My father had a sister, whom he tenderly loved, and who had married early in life an Italian gentleman. Soon after her marriage, she had accompanied her husband into [his][11] native country, and for some years my father had very little communication with her. About the time I mentioned she died; and a few months afterwards he received a letter from her husband, acquainting him with his intention of marrying an Italian lady, and requesting my father to take charge of the infant Elizabeth, the only child of his deceased sister.[12] "It is my wish," he said, "that you should consider her as your own daughter, and educate her thus. Her mother's fortune is secured to her, the documents of which I will commit to your keeping. Reflect upon this proposition; and decide whether you would prefer educating your niece yourself to her being brought up by a stepmother."[13]

My father did not hesitate, and immediately went to Italy, that he might accompany the little Elizabeth to her future home.[14] I have often heard my mother say, that she was at that time the most beautiful child she had ever seen,[15] and shewed signs even then of a gentle and affectionate disposition. These indications, and a desire to bind as closely as possible the ties of domestic love, determined my mother to consider Elizabeth as my future wife;[16] a design which she never found reason to repent.

From this time Elizabeth Lavenza became my playfellow, and, as we grew older, my friend. She was docile and good tempered, yet gay and playful as a summer insect.[17] Although she was lively and animated, her feelings were strong and deep, and her disposition uncommonly affectionate. No one could better enjoy liberty, yet no one could submit with more grace than she did to constraint and caprice. Her imagination was luxuriant, yet her capability of application was great. Her person was the image of her mind; her hazel eyes, although as lively as a bird's, possessed an attractive softness.

11   The misprint of "her" in *1818* is corrected to "his" in *1823* (Ch. I, 44).

12   Percy's sister and mother had the name "Elizabeth." Mary layers several family names into her narrative. The father's disposal of a child, here a seemingly incidental plot device, is related to the multiple versions of parental care and carelessness in the novel. It is striking to see a father cast off his only child within a few months of her losing her mother. Would the gentleman have discarded a son?

13   A "stepmother" invokes a fairy-tale lore (and its social basis) of coolness to a stepchild. Mary's stepmother (the second Mrs. Godwin) was less than loving, and her father would send his daughter, at age thirteen, to live in Scotland.

14   In *1831*, Mary Shelley revised Elizabeth's relation from a close blood tie (first cousin) to an adopted orphan—sharpening the contrast of the beautiful orphan's good fortune in finding a loving family and the misfortunes of the abject ugly Creature (even with a connection to the Frankensteins).

15   This incidental remark reflects the importance of northern European standards of "beauty" as an inducement to affection—yet another element of judgment that accumulates significance from repetition and stark contrasts.

16   First-cousin marriage was not unusual (it was felt to strengthen family bonds and fortunes); genetic implications were not yet understood.

17   Frankenstein will later address the Creature as a "vile insect"; the modifier here, "summer," in retrospect of Elizabeth's fate, is a sad inscription.

18 Mary Shelley sets another irony here with the word *animal*, which means, literally, endued with life (Latin: *anima*). As "pet," Elizabeth is a contrasting double of Victor's part-animal Creature.

19 Percy supplied the last two sentences of this paragraph (*Notebooks* 10–11); reflecting themes developed in his visionary poetry, he gives Victor Frankenstein this appetite.

20 A knight in Charlemagne's war against Saracen (Syrian) invaders, Orlando is the hero of Ariosto's sixteenth-century epic, *Orlando Furioso;* Amadis is the hero of *Amadis de Gaula.* Mary was reading *Orlando* in 1815 and *Amadis* (in Robert Southey's 1803 translation) in 1817. Robin Hood, an exile turned principled outlaw, is the antagonist of tyranny and the protector of the helpless and the oppressed (a folk hero in the 1790s). St. George, the dragon-slayer, a Roman soldier and tortured martyr to his Christian faith, is the patron saint of England.

21 The discipline of laggard students by the corporal punishment of public caning was a common, and often quite brutal, practice.

22 An eighteenth-century term for science; *genius* means a divine spirit, along with our modern sense of intellectual brilliance. The language of *genius* and *fate* and the seeming collaboration of overwhelming natural events not only allow Frankenstein to shift responsibility for the course of his life but also give him the cast of a tragic hero.

Her figure was light and airy; and, though capable of enduring great fatigue, she appeared the most fragile creature in the world. While I admired her understanding and fancy, I loved to tend on her, as I should on a favourite animal;[18] and I never saw so much grace both of person and mind united to so little pretension.

Every one adored Elizabeth. If the servants had any request to make, it was always through her intercession. We were strangers to any species of disunion and dispute; for although there was a great dissimilitude in our characters, there was an harmony in that very dissimilitude. I was more calm and philosophical than my companion; yet my temper was not so yielding. My application was of longer endurance; but it was not so severe whilst it endured. I delighted in investigating the facts relative to the actual world; she busied herself in following the aërial creations of the poets. The world was to me a secret, which I desired to discover; to her it was a vacancy, which she sought to people with imaginations of her own.[19]

My brothers were considerably younger than myself; but I had a friend in one of my schoolfellows, who compensated for this deficiency. Henry Clerval was the son of a merchant of Geneva, an intimate friend of my father. He was a boy of singular talent and fancy. I remember, when he was nine years old, he wrote a fairy tale, which was the delight and amazement of all his companions. His favourite study consisted in books of chivalry and romance; and when very young, I can remember, that we used to act plays composed by him out of these favourite books, the principal characters of which were Orlando, Robin Hood, Amadis, and St. George.[20]

No youth could have passed more happily than mine. My parents were indulgent, and my companions amiable. Our studies were never forced; and by some means we always had an end placed in view, which excited us to ardour in the prosecution of them. It was by this method, and not by emulation, that we were urged to application. Elizabeth was not incited to apply herself to drawing, that her companions might not outstrip her; but through the desire of pleasing her aunt, by the representation of some favourite scene done by her own hand. We learned Latin and English, that we might read the writings in those languages; and so far from study being made odious to us through punishment, we loved application, and our amusements would have been the labours of other children. Perhaps we did not read so many books, or learn languages so quickly, as those who are disciplined according to the ordinary methods;[21] but what we learned was impressed the more deeply on our memories.

In this description of our domestic circle I include Henry Clerval; for he was constantly with us. He went to school with me, and generally passed the afternoon at our house; for being an only child, and destitute of companions at home, his father was well pleased that he should find associates at our house; and we were never completely happy when Clerval was absent.

I feel pleasure in dwelling on the recollections of childhood, before misfortune had tainted my mind, and changed its bright visions of extensive usefulness into gloomy and narrow reflections upon self. But, in drawing the picture of my early days, I must not omit to record those events which led, by insensible steps to my after tale of misery: for when I would account to myself for the birth of that passion, which afterwards ruled my destiny, I find it arise, like a mountain river, from ignoble and almost forgotten sources; but, swelling as it proceeded, it became the torrent which, in its course, has swept away all my hopes and joys.

Natural philosophy[22] is the genius that has regulated my fate; I desire therefore, in this narration, to state those facts which led to my predilection for that science. When I was thirteen years of age, we all went on a party of pleasure to the baths near Thonon: the in-

Jean-Jacques Rousseau, painted by Maurice Quentin de La Tour in 1753. Rousseau's famous epithet was "Citizen of Geneva" although he ran away from this home at age fifteen (March 14, 1728). His works, which include *Discourse on the Origin of Inequality* (1754) and, even more influentially, *The Social Contract* (1762), laid the philosophical foundations for the French Revolution of 1789 and strongly impressed the Shelleys. Other major publications (the epistolary novel, *Julie, ou la nouvelle Héloïse,* of 1761, the autobiographical *Confessions* of 1782) inspired adoration and controversy. Especially relevant for the De Lacey subplot is *Émile, ou l'education* (1762). Though embraced in many quarters as a program for progressive, free-spirited "natural" learning, it repelled many women, including Mary Wollstonecraft, with its retrograde attitudes about the roles of women, exemplified by Émile's "ideal" mate "Sophie," a name transformed in *Frankenstein* to "Safie," a more Wollstonecraft-spirited woman.

Young Victor Frankenstein, enchanted by the works of Cornelius Agrippa, might have pondered *The Great Magic Circle of Agrippa for the Evocation of Demons*, published in *Les Oevres Magiques de Henri Corneille Agrippa* (Rome, 1744). Agrippa, author of *De Occulta Philosophia Libri Tres* (1529), was a curious mixture of intellectual skepticism and advocacy of secret wisdom transcending the limits of rational thought. In Mary Shelley's short story *"The Mortal Immortal: A Tale"* (published in *The Keepsake,* 1834) he appears as a dangerously experimental alchemist, whose student (the narrator) imbibes the Elixir of Life in a disastrous gamble on immortality.

23   About thirty miles from Geneva, Thonon is a spa-resort on the French side of Lake Geneva. Victor's chance reading during bad weather reflects the rainy-days' reading of ghost stories at Villa Diodati that inspired *Frankenstein.*

24   This German occultist, theologian, astrologer, and alchemist (1486–1535) is famous both for an aphorism relevant to Frankenstein's science—"Nothing is concealed from the wise and sensible, while the unbelieving and unworthy cannot learn the secrets"—and for the "law of resonance" that plays into the novel's plot: "All things which are similar and therefore connected, are drawn to each other's power." In 1799 Robert Southey published a gothic, semi-farcical, "very pithy and profitable" (so it was subtitled) poem, "Cornelius Agrippa; A Ballad of a Young Man that would Read Unlawful Books, and How He Was Punished." This curious lad breaks into Agrippa's study and accidentally conjures the devil, who tears out his heart: "THE MORAL: Henceforth let all young men take heed / How in a Conjuror's books they read."

clemency of the weather obliged us to remain a day confined to the inn.[23] In this house I chanced to find a volume of the works of Cornelius Agrippa.[24] I opened it with apathy; the theory which he attempts to demonstrate, and the wonderful facts which he relates, soon changed this feeling into enthusiasm. A new light seemed to dawn upon my mind; and, bounding with joy, I communicated my discovery to my father. I cannot help remarking here the many opportunities instructors possess of directing the attention of their pupils to useful knowledge, which they utterly neglect. My father looked carelessly at the title-page of my book, and said, "Ah! Cornelius Agrippa! My dear Victor,[25] do not waste your time upon this; it is sad trash."

If, instead of this remark, my father had taken the pains to explain to me, that the principles of Agrippa had been entirely exploded, and that a modern system of science had been introduced, which possessed much greater powers than the ancient, because the powers of the latter were chimerical, while those of the former were real and practical; under such circumstances, I should certainly have thrown Agrippa aside, and, with my imagination warmed as it was, should probably have applied myself to the more rational theory of chemistry which has resulted from modern discoveries. It is even possible, that the train of my ideas would never have received the fatal impulse that led to my ruin. But the cursory glance my father had taken of my volume by no means assured me that he was acquainted with its contents; and I continued to read with the greatest avidity.

When I returned home, my first care was to procure the whole works of this author, and afterwards of Paracelsus and Albertus Magnus.[26] I read and studied the wild fancies of these writers with delight; they appeared to me treasures known to few beside myself; and although I have often wished to communicate these secret stores of knowledge to my father, yet his indefinite censure of my favourite Agrippa always withheld me. I disclosed my discoveries to Elizabeth, therefore, under a promise of strict secrecy; but she did not interest herself in the subject, and I was left by her to pursue my studies alone.[27]

It may appear very strange, that a disciple of Albertus Magnus should arise in the eighteenth century; but our family was not scientifical, and I had not attended any of the lectures given at the schools of Geneva. My dreams were therefore undisturbed by reality; and I entered with the greatest diligence into the search of the philosopher's stone and the elixir of life.[28] But the latter obtained my undivided attention: wealth was an inferior object; but what glory would attend the discovery,[29] if I could banish disease from

25 This is the first mention of the name "Victor," an irony in view of his present depletion. The name may also play a private jest for Percy; in 1810 he and his sister Elizabeth published a volume of poetry under the pseudonyms "Victor and Cazire."

26 This purchasing power is remarkable; books were very expensive. Percy Shelley recounted to Godwin his boyhood rapture with "the reveries of Albertus Magnus and Paracelsus, the former of which I read in Latin" (June 3, 1812, *Letters* 1: 314). The Swiss mystic and medical scientist Paracelsus (c. 1493–1541) theorized not only that human life could be created by alchemy but also that an "elixir of life" would conquer diseases and infirmity, and grant immortality. The thirteenth-century German monk, theologian, and scholastic philosopher Albertus Magnus believed that science and religion could coexist.

27 This early formation of Victor's scientific study is prophetic.

28 The philosopher's stone was fabled to change base metals to gold. Albertus Magnus was said to have discovered it shortly before his death, passing the secret to his pupil Thomas Aquinas. In Godwin's novel *St. Leon* (1799), which Mary read in 1815, the hero is cursed by gaining access to this stone and the elixir of life: "Fatal legacy! atrocious secrets of medicine and chemistry! every day opened to my astonished and terrified sight a wider prospect of their wasteful effects . . . secrets of this character cut off their possessor from the dearest ties of human existence, and render him a solitary, cold, self-centered individual" (4 vols.; London: G. and G. Robinson, 4: 26).

29 *Glory* is a keyword for the male adventurers in this novel. "I preferred glory to every enticement that wealth placed in my path," Robert Walton tells his sister.

Robert Boyle's Air Pump, 1660, the first plate in *New Experiments Physico-Mechanicall: Touching the Spring of the Air and its Effects*. Working with Robert Hooke, Boyle developed this "machina Boyleana" or "Pneumatical Engine," and beginning in 1659, he used it for a series of experiments and demonstrations on the properties of air and the dynamics of air pressure. An air-pump is a boyhood excitement for Victor, and in the Shelleys' day Boyle was an exemplar of the scientific curiosity that would "penetrate into the utmost recesses of nature." He was also a visionary thinker, with scientific dreams that would have been at home in the world of *Frankenstein:* "The Prolongation of Life," "perpetual light," "A ship to saile with All Winds, and a Ship not to be sunk," "practicable and certain way of finding Longitudes," "potent druggs to alter or Exalt Imagination, Waking, Memory and other functions and appease pain, procure innocent sleep, harmless dreams etc."

30 Percy Shelley conducted such experiments. In *Hymn to Intellectual Beauty* (written in the "Frankenstein" summer of 1816), he recalls: "While yet a boy I sought for ghosts, and sped / Through many a listening chamber, cave and ruin, / And starlight wood, with fearful steps pursuing / Hopes of high talk with the departed dead" (49–52). Leigh Hunt published *Hymn* in his radical weekly *The Examiner* on January 19, 1817, about a year before the publication of *Frankenstein.*

31 Distillation is part of alchemical science. The air pump is a scientific instrument, improved by the seventeenth-century scientist Robert Boyle. It was used (sometimes for entertainment) to demonstrate the necessity of air to most life: an animal placed in an enclosure from which the air is pumped out collapses from suffocation.

32 Belrive ("beautiful shore") takes its name from the manor Byron rented in summer 1816, Villa Belle Rive, about four miles from Geneva on the south shore of Lake Geneva.

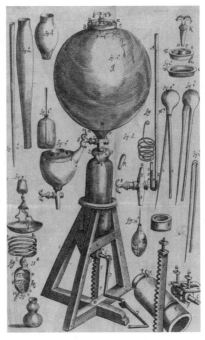

the human frame, and render man invulnerable to any but a violent death!

Nor were these my only visions. The raising of ghosts or devils was a promise liberally accorded by my favourite authors,[30] the fulfillment of which I most eagerly sought; and if my incantations were always unsuccessful, I attributed the failure rather to my own inexperience and mistake, than to a want of skill or fidelity in my instructors.

The natural phænomena that take place every day before our eyes did not escape my examinations. Distillation, and the wonderful effects of steam, processes of which my favourite authors were utterly ignorant, excited my astonishment; but my utmost wonder was engaged by some experiments on an air-pump,[31] which I saw employed by a gentleman whom we were in the habit of visiting.

The ignorance of the early philosophers on these and several other points served to decrease their credit with me: but I could not entirely throw them aside, before some other system should occupy their place in my mind.

When I was about fifteen years old, we had retired to our house near Belrive,[32] when we witnessed a most violent and terrible thunder-storm. It advanced from behind the mountains of Jura; and the thunder burst at once with frightful loudness from various quarters of the heavens. I remained, while the storm lasted, watching

Natural discoveries became theatrical attractions. Joseph Wright of Derby's painting *An Experiment on a Bird in an Air Pump* (1768) represents varied reactions to the gradual suffocation of a cockatoo—from scientific detachment to sympathetic alarm for the victimized bird—all represented in a dramatic lighting once reserved for religious subjects. Giovanni Aldini would later draw audiences for his electrical "reanimation" of twitching corpses.

its progress with curiosity and delight. As I stood at the door, on a sudden I beheld a stream of fire issue from an old and beautiful oak, which stood about twenty yards from our house; and so soon as the dazzling light vanished, the oak had disappeared, and nothing remained but a blasted stump.[33] When we visited it the next morning, we found the tree shattered in a singular manner. It was not splintered by the shock, but entirely reduced to thin ribbands of wood. I never beheld anything so utterly destroyed.

33   There is a legend that young Percy ignited an oak tree using gunpowder and a magnifying glass. In retrospect, this episode acquires the quality of portent: it is by a lightning flash that Victor Frankenstein will re-encounter the "monster" he hoped to forget. A lightning-blasted stump returns to image his ruin: "I am a blasted tree; the bolt has entered my soul" (Vol. III, Ch. II). A tacit twin, as Mary Shelley knew, is Byron's portrait of another Genevese, "self-torturing Rousseau": "His love was passion's essence—as a tree / On fire by lightning; with ethereal flame / Kindled he was, and blasted" (*Childe Harold III*, stanza lxxviii).

J. M. W. Turner, *Lake Geneva as Seen from Montreux,* 1810. Mary Godwin (Shelley), Percy Shelley, and Lord Byron spent the summer at Lake Geneva in 1816. Mary Shelley sets much of *Frankenstein* in the environs.

34 This word, literally *overturning,* recurs in Frankenstein's description of his Creature.

35 Frankenstein's father is also a modern Prometheus, repeating the experiment of 1752 of Ben *Frank*lin and his son. Percy Shelley's Oxford friend T. J. Hogg reports Shelley's excitement about kite science: "What a mighty instrument would electricity be in the hands of him who knew how to wield it, in what manner to direct its omnipotent energies; and we may command an indefinite quantity of the fluid; by means of electrical kites we may draw down the lightning from heaven. What a terrible organ would the supernal shock prove if we were able to guide it; how many of the secrets of nature would such a stupendous force unlock!" ("Percy Bysshe Shelley at Oxford," *New Monthly Magazine* 34/133 [January 1832], 95). Also interested in electricity were Erasmus Darwin and Luigi Galvani ("galvanize"), a pioneer of bioelectricity, who in 1771 used electricity to induce muscular contractions in dead frogs. During Mary's childhood, Alessandro Volta ("volt") experimented with electric currents (1800) and Humphry Davy, with electroplating (1807), and Giovanni Aldini astounded spectators by using electricity to make dead bodies twitch into seeming life (1802).

The catastrophe[34] of this tree excited my extreme astonishment; and I eagerly inquired of my father the nature and origin of thunder and lightning. He replied, "Electricity;" describing at the same time the various effects of that power. He constructed a small electrical machine, and exhibited a few experiments; he made also a kite, with a wire and string, which drew down that fluid from the clouds.[35]

This last stroke completed the overthrow of Cornelius Agrippa, Albertus Magnus, and Paracelsus, who had so long reigned the lords of my imagination.[36] But by some fatality I did not feel inclined to commence the study of any modern system; and this disinclination was influenced by the following circumstance.

My father expressed a wish that I should attend a course of lectures upon natural philosophy, to which I cheerfully consented.

The Philosopher and His Kite. **The lore of Ben Franklin and his son William flying a kite to draw down lightning during an electrical storm in 1752 had become iconic by the 1840s, when this engraving (by Henry S. Sadd, based on a design by John Ludlow Morton) was published in the *Columbian Magazine,* a Philadelphia "monthly miscellany." This lore was a likely inspiration for Mary Shelley's scene of young Victor Frankenstein and his father in a similar experiment. It was a highly dangerous one, harming or killing others who tried to repeat it.**

Some accident prevented my attending these lectures until the course was nearly finished. The lecture, being therefore one of the last, was entirely incomprehensible to me. The professor discoursed with the greatest fluency of potassium and boron, of sulphates and oxyds,[37] terms to which I could affix no idea; and I became disgusted with the science of natural philosophy, although I still read Pliny and Buffon with delight, authors, in my estimation, of nearly equal interest and utility.[38]

36   This passage was revised considerably in *1831* to give it the aura of Greek tragedy, with Victor (in his preferred narrative) as pawn of destiny:

> All that had so long engaged my attention suddenly grew despicable. By one of those caprices of the mind, which we are perhaps most subject to in early youth, I at once gave up my former occupations; set down natural history and all its progeny as a deformed and abortive creation; and entertained the greatest disdain for a would-be science, which could never even step within the threshold of real knowledge. In this mood of mind I betook myself to the mathematics, and the branches of study appertaining to that science, as being built upon secure foundations, and so worthy of my consideration.
>
> Thus strangely are our souls constructed, and by such slight ligaments are we bound to prosperity or ruin. When I look back, it seems to me as if this almost miraculous change of inclination and will was the immediate suggestion of the guardian angel of my life—the last effort made by the spirit of preservation to avert the storm that was even then hanging in the stars, and ready to envelop me. Her victory was announced by an unusual tranquillity and gladness of soul, which followed the relinquishing of my ancient and latterly tormenting studies. It was thus that I was to be taught to associate evil with their prosecution, happiness with their disregard.
>
> It was a strong effort of the spirit of good, but it was ineffectual. Destiny was too potent, and her immutable laws had decreed my utter and terrible destruction. (Ch. II, 28–29)

37   Crook notes an anachronism: the elements were not isolated until the first decade of the nineteenth century.

38   These two naturalists and rationalists influenced Percy Shelley (who translated half of Pliny the Elder's *Natural History* while at Eton). In 1817 Mary Shelley was reading both. In the last ten years of his life, Roman soldier and government administrator Pliny the Elder (23–79) labored on his encyclopedic *Natural History.* He died in the eruption of Vesuvius. His nephew Pliny the Younger (63–c. 113) was also a natural scientist. When the mathematician and physicist G. L. Leclerc, Count Buffon (1707–1778), turned to natural science, he became convinced that life arose from natural rather than from divine causes.

39 This name emerges from several referents in Mary Shelley's personal history: it was the name her parents had ready for the son they expected, the name of the son Godwin had with his second wife, and the name the Shelleys gave to their first son, an infant while Mary was writing *Frankenstein*.

My occupations at this age were principally the mathematics, and most of the branches of study appertaining to that science. I was busily employed in learning languages; Latin was already familiar to me, and I began to read some of the easiest Greek authors without the help of a lexicon. I also perfectly understood English and German. This is the list of my accomplishments at the age of seventeen; and you may conceive that my hours were fully employed in acquiring and maintaining a knowledge of this various literature.

Another task also devolved upon me, when I became the instructor of my brothers. Ernest was six years younger than myself, and was my principal pupil. He had been afflicted with ill health from his infancy, through which Elizabeth and I had been his constant nurses: his disposition was gentle, but he was incapable of any severe application. William, the youngest of our family, was yet an infant, and the most beautiful little fellow in the world; his lively blue eyes, dimpled cheeks, and endearing manners, inspired the tenderest affection.[39]

Such was our domestic circle, from which care and pain seemed for ever banished. My father directed our studies, and my mother partook of our enjoyments. Neither of us possessed the slightest pre-eminence over the other; the voice of command was never heard amongst us; but mutual affection engaged us all to comply with and obey the slightest desire of each other.

1   In this catastrophe of a "daughter" bringing about the death of a "mother," Mary Shelley conjures the horrific events of her own birth.

CHAPTER II

WHEN I HAD attained the age of seventeen, my parents resolved that I should become a student at the university of Ingolstadt. I had hitherto attended the schools of Geneva; but my father thought it necessary, for the completion of my education, that I should be made acquainted with other customs than those of my native country. My departure was therefore fixed at an early date; but, before the day resolved upon could arrive, the first misfortune of my life occurred—an omen, as it were, of my future misery.

Elizabeth had caught the scarlet fever; but her illness was not severe, and she quickly recovered. During her confinement, many arguments had been urged to persuade my mother to refrain from attending upon her. She had, at first, yielded to our entreaties; but when she heard that her favourite was recovering, she could no longer debar herself from her society, and entered her chamber long before the danger of infection was past. The consequences of this imprudence were fatal.[1] On the third day my mother sickened; her fever was very malignant, and the looks of her attendants prognosticated the worst event. On her death-bed the fortitude and benignity of this admirable woman did not desert her. She joined the hands of Elizabeth and myself: "My children," she said, "my firmest hopes of future happiness were placed on the prospect of your

2   The University of Ingolstadt in upper Bavaria had five schools: humanities, law, theology, and (most important for Victor Frankenstein) sciences and medicine. Founded in the fifteenth century, Ingolstadt was noted for progressive learning and, in the late eighteenth century, for the Illuminati ("The Enlightened"). This society, founded May 1, 1776, and appealing to intellectuals, political thinkers, and such influential writers as Goethe and J. G. Herder, as well as the dukes of Gotha and Weimar, was rumored to be an antigovernment conspiracy and fomenter of the French Revolution. Abbé Barruel, whom Percy Shelley read with keen interest, did not hesitate to say that "the Illuminizing Code . . . engendered that disastrous monster . . . raging uncontrolled, and almost unopposed, in these days of horror and devastation" (*Memoirs Illustrating the History of Jacobinism,* trans. Robert Clifford [London, 1798] 3: 414; cited by Lee Sterrenburg, in Levine and Knoepflmacher, 156).

union. This expectation will now be the consolation of your father. Elizabeth, my love, you must supply my place to your younger cousins. Alas! I regret that I am taken from you; and, happy and beloved as I have been, is it not hard to quit you all? But these are not thoughts befitting me; I will endeavour to resign myself cheerfully to death, and will indulge a hope of meeting you in another world."

She died calmly; and her countenance expressed affection even in death. I need not describe the feelings of those whose dearest ties are rent by that most irreparable evil, the void that presents itself to the soul, and the despair that is exhibited on the countenance. It is so long before the mind can persuade itself that she, whom we saw every day, and whose very existence appeared a part of our own, can have departed for ever—that the brightness of a beloved eye can have been extinguished, and the sound of a voice so familiar, and dear to the ear, can be hushed, never more to be heard. These are the reflections of the first days; but when the lapse of time proves the reality of the evil, then the actual bitterness of grief commences. Yet from whom has not that rude hand rent away some dear connexion; and why should I describe a sorrow which all have felt, and must feel? The time at length arrives, when grief is rather an indulgence than a necessity; and the smile that plays upon the lips, although it may be deemed a sacrilege, is not banished. My mother was dead, but we had still duties which we ought to perform; we must continue our course with the rest, and learn to think ourselves fortunate, whilst one remains whom the spoiler has not seized.

My journey to Ingolstadt, which had been deferred by these events, was now again determined upon.[2] I obtained from my father a respite of some weeks. This period was spent sadly; my mother's death, and my speedy departure, depressed our spirits; but Elizabeth endeavoured to renew the spirit of cheerfulness in our little society.

Since the death of her aunt, her mind had acquired new firmness and vigour. She determined to fulfil her duties with the greatest exactness; and she felt that that most imperious duty, of rendering her uncle and cousins happy, had devolved upon her. She consoled me, amused her uncle, instructed my brothers; and I never beheld her so enchanting as at this time, when she was continually endeavouring to contribute to the happiness of others, entirely forgetful of herself.

The day of my departure at length arrived. I had taken leave of all my friends, excepting Clerval, who spent the last evening with us. He bitterly lamented that he was unable to accompany me: but his father could not be persuaded to part with him, intending that he should become a partner with him in business, in compliance with his favourite theory, that learning was superfluous in the commerce of ordinary life. Henry had a refined mind; he had no desire to be idle, and was well pleased to become his father's partner, but he believed that a man might become a very good trader, and yet possess a cultivated understanding.

We sat late, listening to his complaints, and making many little arrangements for the future. The next morning early I departed. Tears gushed from the eyes of Elizabeth; they proceeded partly from sorrow at my departure, and partly because she reflected that the same journey was to have taken place three months before, when a mother's blessing would have accompanied me.

I threw myself into the chaise that was to convey me away,[3] and indulged in the most melancholy reflections. I, who had ever been surrounded by amiable companions, continually engaged in endeavouring to bestow mutual pleasure, I was now alone. In the university, whither I was going, I must form my own friends, and be my own protector. My life had hitherto been remarkably secluded and domestic; and this had given me invincible repugnance to new

3 Frequent travelers, the Shelleys would not mention this mode of transportation idly. Introduced in France in the early 1700s, a chaise was a pricey conveyance, offering privacy, comfort, and speed, with fresh horses supplied at post stages; the horses were ridden by postilions, leaving the passenger's view unobstructed by a coachman.

4 Charles Lamb's poem "The Old Familiar Faces" (*Blank Verse,* 1798) has some verses starkly relevant to Mary Shelley's history, as well as to Frankenstein's (to come):

> Where are they gone; the old familiar faces?
> I had a mother, but she died, and left me,
> Died prematurely in a day of horrors—
> All are gone, the old familiar faces.
>
> I have had playmates, I have had companions,
> In my days of childhood, in my joyful schooldays,—
> All, all are gone, the old familiar faces. (1–7)
> . . .
> I have a friend, a kinder friend has no man.
> Like an ingrate, I left my friend abruptly;
> Left him, to muse on the old familiar faces.
>
> Ghost-like, I pac'd round the haunts of my childhood.
> Earth seem'd a desert I was bound to traverse,
> Seeking to find the old familiar faces.
>
> Friend of my bosom, thou more than a brother! (14–20)
> . . .
> For some they have died, and some they have left me,
> *And some are taken from me;* all are departed;
> All, all are gone, the old familiar faces. (23–25)

In a "day of horrors" in 1796, Charles Lamb's sister Mary Lamb, exhausted from needlework, had a breakdown, and in a rage injured their father and killed their mother. The Lambs were frequent visitors at the Godwin household in Mary's girlhood.

5 This journey of 400–500 miles (depending on the route) would have taken at least two weeks of day travel by coach.

countenances. I loved my brothers, Elizabeth, and Clerval; these were "old familiar faces;"[4] but I believed myself totally unfitted for the company of strangers. Such were my reflections as I commenced my journey; but as I proceeded, my spirits and hopes rose. I ardently desired the acquisition of knowledge. I had often, when at home, thought it hard to remain during my youth cooped up in one place, and had longed to enter the world, and take my station among other human beings. Now my desires were complied with, and it would, indeed, have been folly to repent.

I had sufficient leisure for these and many other reflections during my journey to Ingolstadt, which was long and fatiguing.[5] At length the high white steeple of the town met my eyes. I alighted, and was conducted to my solitary apartment, to spend the evening as I pleased.

The next morning I delivered my letters of introduction, and paid a visit to some of the principal professors, and among others to M. Krempe, professor of natural philosophy. He received me with politeness, and asked me several questions concerning my progress in the different branches of science appertaining to natural philosophy. I mentioned, it is true, with fear and trembling, the only authors I had ever read upon those subjects. The professor stared: "Have you," he said, "really spent your time in studying such nonsense?"

I replied in the affirmative. "Every minute," continued M. Krempe with warmth, "every instant that you have wasted on those books is utterly and entirely lost. You have burdened your memory with exploded systems, and useless names. Good God! in what desert land have you lived, where no one was kind enough to inform you that these fancies, which you have so greedily imbibed, are a thousand years old, and as musty as they are ancient? I little expected in this enlightened and scientific age to find a disciple of Albertus Magnus and Paracelsus. My dear Sir, you must begin your studies entirely anew."

So saying, he stepped aside, and wrote down a list of several books treating of natural philosophy, which he desired me to procure, and dismissed me, after mentioning that in the beginning of the following week he intended to commence a course of lectures upon natural philosophy in its general relations, and that M. Waldman, a fellow-professor, would lecture upon chemistry the alternate days that he missed.

I returned home, not disappointed, for I had long considered those authors useless whom the professor had so strongly reprobated; but I did not feel much inclined to study the books which I had procured at his recommendation. M. Krempe was a little squat man, with a gruff voice and repulsive countenance; the teacher, therefore, did not prepossess me in favour of his doctrine. Besides, I had a contempt for the uses of modern natural philosophy. It was very different, when the masters of the science sought immortality and power; such views, although futile, were grand: but now the scene was changed. The ambition of the inquirer seemed to limit itself to the annihilation of those visions on which my interest in science was chiefly founded. I was required to exchange chimeras of boundless grandeur for realities of little worth.

Such were my reflections during the first two or three days spent almost in solitude. But as the ensuing week commenced, I thought of the information which M. Krempe had given me concerning the lectures. And although I could not consent to go and hear that little conceited fellow deliver sentences out of a pulpit, I recollected what he had said of M. Waldman, whom I had never seen, as he had hitherto been out of town.

Partly from curiosity, and partly from idleness, I went into the lecturing room, which M. Waldman entered shortly after. This professor was very unlike his colleague. He appeared about fifty years of age, but with an aspect expressive of the greatest benevolence; a few grey hairs covered his temples, but those at the back of his head

6   Contrasting M. Krempe—squat, rough-voiced, with a "repulsive countenance"—the benevolent face and sweet voice of M. Waldman mark another instance of personal worth keyed to a calculus of beauty, a calculus to be sorely tested for Frankenstein by his own science project.

7   The female gendering of an object of exploration, a long-standing convention for male scientists and adventurers, imprints Davy's 1802 lecture to the Royal Institution, as he celebrates the "sublime philosophy, chemistry": "who would not be ambitious of becoming acquainted with the most profound secrets of nature, of ascertaining her hidden operations, and of exhibiting to men that system of knowledge which relates so intimately to their own physical and moral constitution?" (*A Discourse Introductory to a Course of Lectures on Chemistry,* in *The Collected Works of Sir Humphry Davy* [London: Smith, Elder, 1839], 2: 320)—language that will turn perverse in Frankenstein's generation of life. Mary was reading Davy's lecture in 1816, and Percy knew it almost by heart.

8   Some of these astonishments realize the magical powers to which Prospero bids a rueful farewell in Shakespeare's *Tempest* (V.i). Davy began his *Discourse, Introductory* celebrating chemistry for its devotion to "the great changes, and convulsions in nature, which, occurring but seldom, excite our curiosity, or awaken our astonishment." Frankenstein's roll call of modern accomplishments includes the hot-air balloon (Montgolfier brothers, 1780s); William Harvey's discovery of the circulation of blood (1628); and the work of the air-scientists Henry Cavendish, Joseph Priestley, and Antoine Lavoisier. Percy Shelley was avid about modern chemistry, echoing Davy's *Discourse.* His college friend T. J. Hogg reports his "rapturous" assertions that it was "the only science that deserved to be studied," and if recent discoveries were more "brilliant than useful," these "would soon be applied to purposes of solid advantage" ("Percy Shelley at Oxford," *New Monthly,* January 1832, 94).

9   In *1831* Mary Shelley interpolates new text, to emphasize young Frankenstein's helpless enchantment (here, too, is the first event of Victor's surname):

> Such were the professor's words—rather let me say such the words of fate, enounced to destroy me. As he went on, I felt as if my soul were grappling with a palpable enemy; one by one the various keys were touched which formed the mechanism of my being: chord after chord was sounded, and soon my mind was filled with one thought, one conception, one pur-

were nearly black. His person was short, but remarkably erect; and his voice the sweetest I had ever heard.[6] He began his lecture by a recapitulation of the history of chemistry, and the various improvements made by different men of learning, pronouncing with fervour the names of the most distinguished discoverers. He then took a cursory view of the present state of the science, and explained many of its elementary terms. After having made a few preparatory experiments, he concluded with a panegyric upon modern chemistry, the terms of which I shall never forget:—

"The ancient teachers of this science," said he, "promised impossibilities, and performed nothing. The modern masters promise very little; they know that metals cannot be transmuted, and that the elixir of life is a chimera. But these philosophers, whose hands seem only made to dabble in dirt, and their eyes to pore over the microscope or crucible, have indeed performed miracles. They penetrate into the recesses of nature, and shew how she works in her hiding places.[7] They ascend into the heavens; they have discovered how the blood circulates, and the nature of the air we breathe. They have acquired new and almost unlimited powers; they can command the thunders of heaven, mimic the earthquake, and even mock the invisible world with its own shadows."[8]

I departed highly pleased with the professor and his lecture,[9] and paid him a visit the same evening. His manners in private were even more mild and attractive than in public; for there was a certain dignity in his mien during his lecture, which in his own house was replaced by the greatest affability and kindness. He heard with attention my little narration concerning my studies, and smiled at the names of Cornelius Agrippa and Paracelsus, but without the contempt that M. Krempe had exhibited. He said, that "these were men to whose indefatigable zeal modern philosophers were indebted for most of the foundations of their knowledge. They had left to us, as an easier task, to give new names, and arrange in connected classifications, the facts which they in a great degree had been the instruments of bringing to light. The labours of men of genius, however erroneously directed, scarcely ever fail in ultimately turning to the solid advantage of mankind."[10] I listened to his statement, which was delivered without any presumption or affectation; and then added, that his lecture had removed my prejudices against modern chemists; and I, at the same time, requested his advice concerning the books I ought to procure.

"I am happy," said M. Waldman, "to have gained a disciple; and if your application equals your ability, I have no doubt of your success. Chemistry is that branch of natural philosophy in which the greatest improvements have been and may be made; it is on that account that I have made it my peculiar study; but at the same time I have not neglected the other branches of science. A man would make but a very sorry chemist, if he attended to that department of human knowledge alone. If your wish is to become really a man of science, and not merely a petty experimentalist, I should advise you to apply to every branch of natural philosophy, including mathematics."

He then took me into his laboratory, and explained to me the uses of his various machines; instructing me as to what I ought to procure, and promising me the use of his own, when I should have advanced far enough in the science not to derange their mechanism. He also gave me the list of books which I had requested; and I took my leave.

Thus ended a day memorable to me; it decided my future destiny.

pose. So much has been done, exclaimed the soul of Frankenstein,—more, far more, will I achieve: treading in the steps already marked, I will pioneer a new way, explore unknown powers, and unfold to the world the deepest mysteries of creation.

I closed not my eyes that night. My internal being was in a state of insurrection and turmoil; I felt that order would thence arise, but I had no power to produce it. By degrees, after the morning's dawn, sleep came. I awoke, and my yesternight's thoughts were as a dream. There only remained a resolution to return to my ancient studies, and to devote myself to a science for which I believed myself to possess a natural talent. (Ch. III, 34–35)

10   The language in quotation, supplied by Percy, echoes Davy on chemistry: "Science has done much for man, but it is capable of doing still more; its sources of improvement are not yet exhausted; the benefits that it has conferred ought to excite our hopes of its capability of conferring new benefits; and in considering the progressiveness of our nature, we may reasonably look forward to a state of greater cultivation and happiness than that we at present enjoy" (319).

1   Frankenstein's praise accords with the pride of his surname (yet to be stated).

CHAPTER III

FROM THIS DAY natural philosophy, and particularly chemistry, in the most comprehensive sense of the term, became nearly my sole occupation. I read with ardour those works, so full of genius and discrimination, which modern inquirers have written on these subjects. I attended the lectures, and cultivated the acquaintance, of the men of science of the university; and I found even in M. Krempe a great deal of sound sense and real information, combined, it is true, with a repulsive physiognomy and manners, but not on that account the less valuable. In M. Waldman I found a true friend. His gentleness was never tinged by dogmatism; and his instructions were given with an air of frankness[1] and good nature that banished every idea of pedantry. It was, perhaps, the amiable character of this man that inclined me more to that branch of natural philosophy which he professed, than an intrinsic love for the science itself. But this state of mind had place only in the first steps towards knowledge: the more fully I entered into the science, the more exclusively I pursued it for its own sake. That application, which at first had been a matter of duty and resolution, now became so ardent and eager, that the stars often disappeared in the light of morning whilst I was yet engaged in my laboratory.

As I applied so closely, it may be easily conceived that I improved rapidly. My ardour was indeed the astonishment of the students; and my proficiency, that of the masters. Professor Krempe often asked me, with a sly smile, how Cornelius Agrippa went on? whilst M. Waldman expressed the most heartfelt exultation in my progress. Two years passed in this manner, during which I paid no visit to Geneva, but was engaged, heart and soul, in the pursuit of some discoveries, which I hoped to make. None but those who have experienced them can conceive of the enticements of science. In other studies you go as far as others have gone before you, and there is nothing more to know; but in a scientific pursuit there is continual food for discovery and wonder. A mind of moderate capacity, which closely pursues one study, must infallibly arrive at great proficiency in that study; and I, who continually sought the attainment of one object of pursuit, and was solely wrapt up in this, improved so rapidly, that, at the end of two years, I made some discoveries in the improvement of some chemical instruments,[2] which procured me great esteem and admiration at the university. When I had arrived at this point, and had become as well acquainted with the theory and practice of natural philosophy as depended on the lessons of any of the professors at Ingolstadt, my residence there being no longer conducive to my improvements, I thought of returning to my friends and my native town, when an incident happened that protracted my stay.

One of the phænomena which had peculiarly attracted my attention was the structure of the human frame, and, indeed, any animal endued with life. Whence, I often asked myself, did the principle of life proceed? It was a bold question, and one which has ever been considered as a mystery; yet with how many things are we upon the brink of becoming acquainted, if cowardice or carelessness did not restrain our inquiries. I revolved these circumstances in my mind, and determined thenceforth to apply myself more particularly to those branches of natural philosophy which relate to physiology.

2 Davy's lecture celebrated chemistry for "furnishing new instruments and powers of investigation" to medicine and physiology (311), and extolled "experiments to interrogate nature with power, not simply as a scholar, passive and seeking only to understand her operations, but rather as a master, active with his own instruments" (319).

3 Mary may be remembering Davy's charismatic introductory lecture on chemistry, in which he proposed that "the study of the simple and unvarying agencies of dead matter ought surely to precede investigations concerning the mysterious and complicated powers of life" (313–314). He is also in this heritage twin to the hero of Percy Shelley's poem *Alastor; or, The Spirit of Solitude* (1816):

> I have made my bed
> In charnels and on coffins, where black death
> Keeps record of the trophies won from thee,
> Hoping to still these obstinate questionings
> Of thee and thine, by forcing some lone ghost,
> Thy messenger, to render up the tale
> Of what we are. (23–29)

4 The language compacts the power of the classical god Jupiter, the divine *fiat lux* of the God of Genesis, natural lightning, and enlightenment science.

Unless I had been animated by an almost supernatural enthusiasm, my application to this study would have been irksome, and almost intolerable. To examine the causes of life, we must first have recourse to death. I became acquainted with the science of anatomy: but this was not sufficient; I must also observe the natural decay and corruption of the human body. In my education my father had taken the greatest precautions that my mind should be impressed with no supernatural horrors. I do not ever remember to have trembled at a tale of superstition, or to have feared the apparition of a spirit. Darkness had no effect upon my fancy; and a church-yard was to me merely the receptacle of bodies deprived of life, which, from being the seat of beauty and strength, had become food for the worm. Now I was led to examine the cause and progress of this decay, and forced to spend days and nights in vaults and charnel houses.[3] My attention was fixed upon every object the most insupportable to the delicacy of the human feelings. I saw how the fine form of man was degraded and wasted; I beheld the corruption of death succeed to the blooming cheek of life; I saw how the worm inherited the wonders of the eye and brain. I paused, examining and analysing all the minutiæ of causation, as exemplified in the change from life to death, and death to life, until from the midst of this darkness a sudden light broke in upon me[4]—a light so brilliant and wondrous, yet so simple, that while I became dizzy with the immensity of the prospect which it illustrated, I was surprised that among so many men of genius, who had directed their inquiries towards the same science, that I alone should be reserved to discover so astonishing a secret.

Remember, I am not recording the vision of a madman. The sun does not more certainly shine in the heavens, than that which I now affirm is true. Some miracle might have produced it, yet the stages of the discovery were distinct and probable. After days and nights of incredible labour and fatigue, I succeeded in discovering the cause of generation and life; nay, more, I became myself capable of bestowing animation upon lifeless matter.[5]

The astonishment which I had at first experienced on this discovery soon gave place to delight and rapture.[6] After so much time spent in painful labour, to arrive at once at the summit of my desires, was the most gratifying consummation of my toils. But this discovery was so great and overwhelming, that all the steps by which I had been progressively led to it were obliterated, and I beheld only the result. What had been the study and desire of the wisest men since the creation of the world, was now within my grasp. Not that, like a magic scene, it all opened upon me at once: the information I had obtained was of a nature rather to direct my endeavours so soon as I should point them towards the object of my search, than to exhibit that object already accomplished. I was like the Arabian who had been buried with the dead, and found a passage to life aided only by one glimmering, and seemingly ineffectual, light.[7]

I see by your eagerness, and the wonder and hope which your eyes express, my friend, that you expect to be informed of the secret with which I am acquainted; that cannot be: listen patiently until the end of my story, and you will easily perceive why I am reserved upon that subject. I will not lead you on, unguarded and ardent as I then was, to your destruction and infallible misery. Learn from me, if not by my precepts, at least by my example, how dangerous is the acquirement of knowledge, and how much happier that man is who believes his native town to be the world, than he who aspires to become greater than his nature will allow.[8]

When I found so astonishing a power placed within my hands, I hesitated a long time concerning the manner in which I should employ it. Although I possessed the capacity of bestowing animation, yet to prepare a frame for the reception of it, with all its intricacies

5 With an eerie difference, Victor echoes his father's desire for lineage, "bestowing on the state sons who might carry his virtues and his name down to posterity." More conspicuous are the alliances to fables of divine creation: Prometheus, who animated man from clay, and the God of Genesis, who "formed man of the dust of the ground, and breathed into his nostrils the breath of life; and man became a living soul" (2: 7). The mysteriousness of Victor's breakthrough makes it seem (despite his protestations of rational labor) a dreamlike wish-fulfillment of a desire—one staged throughout the novel—to prevail over irreversible death.

6 Hogg's recollection in 1832 of Shelley in 1810 seems filtered through the fame of *Frankenstein:* his "enthusiasm . . . his ardour in the cause of science, and his thirst for knowledge" breathed into his features "an animation, a fire, an enthusiasm, a vivid and preternatural intelligence, that I never met with in any other countenance" (*New Monthly Magazine,* January 1832, 93).

7 Sinbad the sailor is buried alive in a vast vault with the corpse of his wife (the custom in the kingdom in which he finds himself); he survives by ingenuity (some of it brutal) and eventually escapes by following a glimmer of light. The source tale is "Fourth Voyage of Sinbad," from *Arabian Nights Entertainments,* collected in *Tales of the East* (1812), which Mary Shelley was reading in 1815.

8 This "moral" has such weak appeal at this narrative climax as to verge on a satire of the ritually intoned axioms meant to legitimize extravagant fictions.

9 The language of conception and labor throughout Victor's project evokes a grotesque parody of the biology of female childbirth. Mary's ms. insistently has *creature,* which Percy changed here, successively, to *frame, being* (like myself), *animal*—perhaps for variation, but in the process attenuating the bond of *creator/creature* in Mary's wording.

10 The designation of "human being" contrasts the epithets to be heaped on the Creature, for whom "being" is neutral. The first instance is Walton's report of "a being which had the shape of a man, but apparently of gigantic stature" (Letter IV).

11 This is huge even by today's standards; in the early nineteenth century the average height of a mature man was 5'6" (Lord Byron and John Keats were about 5').

12 This is hallmark language from Edmund Burke's influential treatise, *Philosophical Inquiry into the Origin of Our Ideas of the Sublime and the Beautiful* (1757): "the great power of the sublime . . . hurries us on by an irresistible force. Astonishment . . . is the effect of the sublime in its highest degree" (Part II, Section I).

13 Victor uses *ideal* in the sense of "existing only in idea" (OED 4). Victor is a stark example of both the excitements and cautions of Davy's sublime chemistry. On the one hand Davy heralds progress: "the phænomena of electricity have been developed; the lightnings have been taken from the clouds; and lastly, a new influence has been discovered, which has enabled man to produce from combinations of dead matter effects which were formerly occasioned only by animal organs" (321). On the other hand, Davy voices cautions about those speculative scientists who, instead "of slowly endeavouring to lift up the veil concealing the wonderful phænomena of living nature," have in their "ardent imaginations . . . vainly and presumptuously attempted to tear it asunder" (314).

14 Before Mary decided on *species,* she and Percy considered, in order, *creatures, beings, natures.* She may have remembered Godwin's use of *species* in *Caleb Williams* (1794). The situation there is explicitly political and directed at human cruelty. An evil landlord receives this rebuke: "society casts you out; man abominates you . . . You will live deserted in the midst of your species . . . Where do you expect to find the hearts . . . that shall sympathise with yours? You have the stamp of misery, incessant, undivided, unpitied misery!" (I.ix). More visible in Mary's choice of *species* and the sentence it

of fibres, muscles, and veins, still remained a work of inconceivable difficulty and labour.[9] I doubted at first whether I should attempt the creation of a being like myself or one of simpler organization; but my imagination was too much exalted by my first success to permit me to doubt of my ability to give life to an animal as complex and wonderful as man. The materials at present within my command hardly appeared adequate to so arduous an undertaking; but I doubted not that I should ultimately succeed. I prepared myself for a multitude of reverses; my operations might be incessantly baffled, and at last my work be imperfect: yet, when I considered the improvement which every day takes place in science and mechanics, I was encouraged to hope my present attempts would at least lay the foundations of future success. Nor could I consider the magnitude and complexity of my plan as any argument of its impracticability. It was with these feelings that I began the creation of a human being.[10] As the minuteness of the parts formed a great hindrance to my speed, I resolved, contrary to my first intention, to make the being of a gigantic stature; that is to say, about eight feet in height, and proportionably large.[11] After having formed this determination, and having spent some months in successfully collecting and arranging my materials, I began.

No one can conceive the variety of feelings which bore me onwards, like a hurricane, in the first enthusiasm of success.[12] Life and death appeared to me ideal bounds, which I should first break through, and pour a torrent of light into our dark world.[13] A new species would bless me as its creator and source;[14] many happy and excellent natures would owe their being to me.[15] No father could claim the gratitude of his child so completely as I should deserve their's. Pursuing these reflections, I thought, that if I could bestow animation upon lifeless matter, I might in process of time (although I now found it impossible) renew life where death had apparently devoted the body to corruption.

These thoughts supported my spirits, while I pursued my undertaking with unremitting ardour. My cheek had grown pale with study, and my person had become emaciated with confinement. Sometimes, on the very brink of certainty, I failed; yet still I clung to the hope which the next day or the next hour might realise. One secret which I alone possessed was the hope to which I had dedicated myself; and the moon gazed on my midnight labours, while, with unrelaxed and breathless eagerness, I pursued nature to her hiding places.[16] Who shall conceive the horrors of my secret toil, as I dabbled among the unhallowed damps of the grave, or tortured the living animal to animate the lifeless clay?[17] My limbs now tremble, and my eyes swim with the remembrance; but then a resistless,[18] and almost frantic impulse, urged me forward; I seemed to have lost all soul or sensation but for this one pursuit. It was indeed but a passing trance, that only made me feel with renewed acuteness so soon as, the unnatural stimulus ceasing to operate, I had returned to my old habits. I collected bones from charnel houses; and disturbed, with profane fingers, the tremendous secrets of the human frame. In a solitary chamber, or rather cell, at the top of the house, and separated from all the other apartments by a gallery and staircase, I kept my workshop of filthy creation; my eyeballs were starting from their sockets in attending to the details of my employment.[19] The dissecting room and the slaughterhouse[20] furnished many of my materials; and often did my human nature turn with loathing from my occupation, whilst, still urged on by an eagerness which perpetually increased, I brought my work near to a conclusion.

The summer months passed while I was thus engaged, heart and soul, in one pursuit.[21] It was a most beautiful season; never did the fields bestow a more plentiful harvest, or the vines yield a more luxuriant vintage: but my eyes were insensible to the charms of nature. And the same feelings which made me neglect the scenes around

propels is the new science of evolution, controversially put forth by Jean-Baptiste Lamarck in *Recherches sur l'Organisation des Corps Vivants* (1802), the first coherent critique of the idea of fixed species argued by the eighteenth-century Swedish botanist Linneaus (and formulated long ago by Aristotle).

15   This pride of creation (pride is the first deadly sin) was a scandal from first reviews into the twentieth century. In the 1931 film, Frankenstein shouts in giddy hysteria, "It's alive! It's alive! Oh—In the name of God, now I know what it feels like to be God!"—a blasphemy that became a censorship issue in 1937. To appease the dismayed, the cry was drowned out by an amplified thunderclap; it remained in the text of James Whale's *Frankenstein* (first published in 1974) and was restored to the soundtrack in 1999.

16   This female gendering of the object of male science is an old tradition, recently voiced by Frankenstein's admired teacher Waldman, who echoes Davy: "who would not be ambitious of becoming acquainted with the most profound secrets of nature, of ascertaining her hidden operations?" (320).

17   The Shelleys were appalled by vivisection as a research practice.

18   This unusual synonym for *irresistible* is perhaps remembered from Dr. Johnson's *Vanity Human Wishes* (1749): "Resistless burns the Fever of Renown" (13).

19   Victor's habits and haggard appearance are becoming monstrous, alien to "human nature." This is relevant to Lamarck's equally famous theory (later called Lamarckism) that acquired characteristics become genetic heritage, passed along to offspring. Mary Shelley cannily sets the stage for making us wonder how much Victor's monstrous sensibility imprints the physical form of a monster. The sociological consequences of Lamarckism were considerable in the nineteenth century, fueling racism and the eugenics that advocated stern judicial measures, including forced sterilization, for the "criminal classes" and the "insane."

20   The Creature is a composite rather than an entirely "human" being—a suggestion, along with vivisection, that revolts "human" nature from this work.

21   Listening to this, Walton may have felt mirrored, for he too has been engaged across this summer in one pursuit.

22 Mary had written, "I wished as it were to procrastinate my feelings of affection, until the great object of my affection was completed"—a sentence that arrays two rival affections and the perversion of family affection into this science (folio 19v, *Notebooks* 1: 90–91). Percy, thinking to amend an unhappy verbal repetition, missed its thematic import; though the same sense is communicated by his revision, "swallowed up every habit of my nature," Mary's verbal repetition has compelling value.

23 Davy concluded his introductory lecture on chemistry on an idealistic note: "observing in the relations of inanimate things fitness and utility," the man of science "will reason with deeper reverence concerning beings possessing life; and, perceiving in all the phenomena of the universe the designs of a perfect intelligence, he will be averse to the turbulence and passion of hasty innovations, and will uniformly appear as the friend of tranquility and order" (326). Tapping into the fears as well as the excitements of new science, Mary Shelley turns *Frankenstein* into a betrayal of Davy's hopes.

24 In the nineteenth century, "domestic affections" named the system of values associated with bonds of hearth and home, and homeland. It is the loss of these affections, in the social theory being phrased here, that brings about such atrocities as the Ottoman Empire's tyranny over Greece; the civil war engendered by Julius Caesar's imperial ambition in republican Rome; the abuse of Native Americans by European imperialists; the violent subjugation of Mexico and Peru by Spanish conquistadors.

25 Frankenstein himself acknowledges that moral instruction, here and throughout, pales before the greater allure of gothic extremism.

me caused me also to forget those friends who were so many miles absent, and whom I had not seen for so long a time. I knew my silence disquieted them; and I well remembered the words of my father: "I know that while you are pleased with yourself, you will think of us with affection, and we shall hear regularly from you. You must pardon me, if I regard any interruption in your correspondence as a proof that your other duties are equally neglected."

I knew well therefore what would be my father's feelings; but I could not tear my thoughts from my employment, loathsome in itself, but which had taken an irresistible hold of my imagination. I wished, as it were, to procrastinate all that related to my feelings of affection until the great object, which swallowed up every habit of my nature,[22] should be completed.

I then thought that my father would be unjust if he ascribed my neglect to vice, or faultiness on my part; but I am now convinced that he was justified in conceiving that I should not be altogether free from blame. A human being in perfection ought always to preserve a calm and peaceful mind, and never to allow passion or a transitory desire to disturb his tranquillity.[23] I do not think that the pursuit of knowledge is an exception to this rule. If the study to which you apply yourself has a tendency to weaken your affections, and to destroy your taste for those simple pleasures in which no alloy can possibly mix, then that study is certainly unlawful, that is to say, not befitting the human mind. If this rule were always observed; if no man allowed any pursuit whatsoever to interfere with the tranquillity of his domestic affections, Greece had not been enslaved; Cæsar would have spared his country; America would have been discovered more gradually; and the empires of Mexico and Peru had not been destroyed.[24]

But I forget that I am moralizing in the most interesting part of my tale; and your looks remind me to proceed.[25]

My father made no reproach in his letters; and only took notice of my silence by inquiring into my occupations more particularly than before. Winter, spring, and summer passed away during my labours;[26] but I did not watch the blossom or the expanding leaves—sights which before always yielded me supreme delight, so deeply was I engrossed in my occupation. The leaves of that year had withered before my work drew near to a close; and now every day shewed me more plainly how well I had succeeded. But my enthusiasm was checked by my anxiety, and I appeared rather like one doomed by slavery to toil in the mines, or any other unwholesome trade, than an artist occupied by his favourite employment. Every night I was oppressed by a slow fever, and I became nervous to a most painful degree; a disease that I regretted the more because I had hitherto enjoyed most excellent health, and had always boasted of the firmness of my nerves. But I believed that exercise and amusement would soon drive away such symptoms; and I promised myself both of these, when my creation should be complete.

26 The "labours" in this first span of nine months evoke human gestation, with the "workshop of filthy creation" a kind of septic womb.

1 Mary Shelley originally wrote "my man completeed" (*Notebooks* 96–97).

2 With sublime effect in the 1931 *Frankenstein* James Whale upgrades the climate to a tumult of thunder and lightning, jolting the Creature to life. The American doctor Jean Rosenbaum, who invented the pacemaker, took inspiration from this scene, which had impressed him as an eight-year-old. See the video tribute, "Frankenstein and the Heart Machine."

3 In her 1831 Introduction, Mary Shelley cites a waking dream of such a scene as her original inspiration. In the dreamlike account she writes for Frankenstein, he recoils from a *creature*—the word implicating a creator's responsibility—in favor of epithets that justify his aversion. Between the 1818 version and the 1831 Introduction, Shelley had attended the stage play and reported its rendering of this scene: "*F . . .* is at the beginning full of hope & expectation—at the end of the 1st Act. The stage represents a room with a staircase leading to the *F* workshop—he goes to it and you see his light at a small window, through which a frightened servant peeps, who runs off in terror when F. exclaims 'It lives!'—Presently F himself rushes in horror & trepidation from the room and while still expessing his agony & terror ————— [the nameless creature] throws down the door of the labratory, leaps the staircase & presents his unearthly & monstrous person on the stage" (*Letters MWS* 1: 378).

4 Percy revised Mary's original adjective *handsome* to the more idealizing *beautiful* and added the physical detail of *lustrous black* hair (*Notebooks* 96–97). There are many aspects to and analogues for this scene. One is its parody of a Renaissance poet's *blason,* a lover's doting enumeration of his mistress's beauties. The epithet *wretch* first appears in this passage, uninflected by pity or sympathy. The scene parodies Ovid's fable of Pygmalion (*Metamorphoses* X. 243–297; Mary was reading this in Latin in 1815): a sculptor falls in love with his ivory statue of a woman and wishes it alive; the wish is granted by Venus, the goddess of love. It is unclear whether the Shelleys knew about the ancient Jewish legend of the golem, a clay giant fashioned and magically given life by a human creator. (James Whale was clearly aware of the 1920 silent film *The Golem,* where the giant clay man, created as a protector, eventually runs amok.) For an anticipation of the late-nineteenth-century cultural panic termed "the yellow peril," see the essay by Anne Mellor.

CHAPTER IV

I T W A S O N A dreary night of November, that I beheld the accomplishment of my toils.[1] With an anxiety that almost amounted to agony, I collected the instruments of life around me, that I might infuse a spark of being into the lifeless thing that lay at my feet. It was already one in the morning; the rain pattered dismally against the panes,[2] and my candle was nearly burnt out, when, by the glimmer of the half-extinguished light, I saw the dull yellow eye of the creature open; it breathed hard, and a convulsive motion agitated its limbs.[3]

How can I describe my emotions at this catastrophe, or how delineate the wretch whom with such infinite pains and care I had endeavoured to form? His limbs were in proportion, and I had selected his features as beautiful. Beautiful—Great God! His yellow skin scarcely covered the work of muscles and arteries beneath; his hair was of a lustrous black, and flowing; his teeth of a pearly whiteness; but these luxuriances only formed a more horrid contrast with his watery eyes, that seemed almost of the same colour as the dun white sockets in which they were set, his shrivelled complexion, and straight black lips.[4]

The different accidents of life are not so changeable as the feelings of human nature. I had worked hard for nearly two years, for the sole purpose of infusing life into an inanimate body. For this I had

The 1816–1817 manuscript for what would become in 1818 the opening of Volume I, Chapter IV: the animation of the Creature. This is the nightmare scene that Mary Shelley describes in her Introduction of 1831 as the genesis of her novel. As this page shows, this was initially "Chapter 7th" before Mary organized the novel into three volumes. Note the second line: "I beheld my man compleated." Further down the page, Percy's hand replaces the adjectives *handsome* with *beautiful,* and adds the detail of *lustrous black* to the description of the Creature's hair.

The opening of Volume 1, Chapter IV (1818). "I beheld my man compleated" has been revised to "I beheld the accomplishment of my toils." This is a typical page of a duodecimo printing (see Texts and Authorship): less than ten words per line, less than 100 words per page. While the size of the page was small, it was not dense, and so inviting to the reader's eye.

5   The adjective *breathless*, a register of horror, starkly reverses the transformational breathing of life into clay in the foundational stories of Prometheus and Genesis.

6   Perhaps to avoid a repetition, Percy substituted *being* for Mary's *creature* (*Notebooks* 98–99); once again, his alteration elides Mary's instinct for a tight verbal mirroring—especially crucial at the moment of the creator's abandonment. Mary's verbal link reminds us of the Genesis account of God creating man in his image and likeness (1: 27), and the paternal responsibilities and provisions this entails.

7   The manuscript has "lurid" (*Notebooks* 98–99). Though an error, *livid* (from the Latin for pale blue) proved suggestive: in some stage productions in the 1820s, blue was the color of the Creature's skin. Mary's intended adjective *lurid*—from the Latin *luridus*: pale yellow—connects nightmare-Elizabeth to the yellow-skinned Creature. *Lurid* has a more specific meaning as the pallor of a diseased body; as a red color, *lurid* is ominous of impending events. The printer's error remained uncorrected in *1818, 1823,* and *1831.*

8   Frankenstein had subjected himself to the horrors of the crypt, which he tried to control with scientific detachment. As if a return of the repressed from the subconscious realm, multiple horrors shape his dream. At the start of the century that produced Sigmund Freud's *Interpretation of Dreams* (November 1899; many of its cases drawn from imaginative literature), Mary Shelley intuits the psychoanalysis, writing a dream for Frankenstein that is overdetermined, multiply interpretable. Freud's endeavor, stated at the outset, is "to elucidate the processes which underlie the strangeness and obscurity of dreams, and to deduce from these processes the nature of the psychic forces whose conflict or co-operation is responsible for our dreams." But Frankenstein's dreamscape provides no clear code for deduction. It interweaves the lingering horror of his mother's death with his unresolved anger at Elizabeth's "responsibility" for it. Mary Shelley's dreamscript may also tap into her own lingering guilt over the death of her mother, for which her birth was "responsible." Even further, Mary proposes that Victor's dream is informed by his perverse, transgressive science: a symbolic killing off of all mothers, past and to come, in parthenogenic male creation.

9   Here is the first instance of the iconic term that would become Frankenstein's favorite epithet for his Creature, and then, in the novel's wake, its chief epithet, often conflated with creator, "the Frankenstein-Monster." The Creature as *monster* and *wretch* in outward appearance has a symbolic logic, mirroring his creator's gothic

deprived myself of rest and health. I had desired it with an ardour that far exceeded moderation; but now that I had finished, the beauty of the dream vanished, and breathless horror[5] and disgust filled my heart. Unable to endure the aspect of the being I had created,[6] I rushed out of the room, and continued a long time traversing my bed-chamber, unable to compose my mind to sleep. At length lassitude succeeded to the tumult I had before endured; and I threw myself on the bed in my clothes, endeavouring to seek a few moments of forgetfulness. But it was in vain: I slept indeed, but I was disturbed by the wildest dreams. I thought I saw Elizabeth, in the bloom of health, walking in the streets of Ingolstadt. Delighted and surprised, I embraced her; but as I imprinted the first kiss on her lips, they became livid[7] with the hue of death; her features appeared to change, and I thought that I held the corpse of my dead mother in my arms; a shroud enveloped her form, and I saw the grave-worms crawling in the folds of the flannel.[8] I started from my sleep with horror; a cold dew covered my forehead, my teeth chattered, and every limb became convulsed; when, by the dim and yellow light of the moon, as it forced its way through the window-shutters, I beheld the wretch—the miserable monster[9] whom I had created. He held up the curtain of the bed; and his eyes, if eyes they may be called,[10] were fixed on me. His jaws opened, and he muttered some inarticulate sounds,[11] while a grin wrinkled his cheeks. He might have spoken, but I did not hear; one hand was stretched out, seemingly to detain me, but I escaped, and rushed down stairs. I took refuge in the court-yard belonging to the house which I inhabited; where I remained during the rest of the night, walking up and down in the greatest agitation, listening attentively, catching and fearing each sound as if it were to announce the approach of the demoniacal corpse to which I had so miserably given life.

Whale's staging of this scene may recall Michelangelo's famous image on the ceiling of the Sistine Chapel in Rome, of God's hand conveying the life to his creature Adam.

Oh! no mortal could support the horror of that countenance. A mummy again endued with animation could not be so hideous as that wretch. I had gazed on him while unfinished; he was ugly then; but when those muscles and joints were rendered capable of motion, it became a thing such as even Dante could not have conceived.[12]

I passed the night wretchedly.[13] Sometimes my pulse beat so quickly and hardly, that I felt the palpitation of every artery; at others, I nearly sank to the ground through languor and extreme weakness. Mingled with this horror, I felt the bitterness of disappointment: dreams that had been my food and pleasant rest for so long a space, were now become a hell to me; and the change was so rapid, the overthrow so complete!

Morning, dismal and wet, at length dawned, and discovered to my sleepless and aching eyes the church of Ingolstadt, its white steeple and clock, which indicated the sixth hour. The porter

perversion of Genesis, God's creation of man in his own "image and likeness" (1: 26–27). Shelley's scene stages a new etymology of *monster* as a situational and reactive characterization rather than as an identification of innate character.

10   The phrasing echoes Milton's description of Death: "shape, / If shape it might be call'd" (*Paradise Lost* II.666–667)—a model of "sublime" imagining cited by Burke in *The Sublime and the Beautiful* (Part IV, Section III) and by Coleridge, in his lectures on Shakespeare (1811–1812). The association with Death will recur when, about two years on, Victor encounters his Creature again.

11   In this scene of terror, Frankenstein is in the familiar position of imperiled ingénue in gothic novels, accosted in bed by a villainous intruder. Percy nicely proposed the poignant phrase *inarticulate sounds* in place of Mary's *words* (*Notebooks* 100–101), which presupposes linguistic skill.

12   Frankenstein alludes to the monstrous deformations of sinners in *The Inferno*.

13   This *wretchedly* exposes, in ways Frankenstein doesn't recognize, a "forced unconscious sympathy" (Coleridge's phrase in *Christabel*, Part II, 597) with the Creature from whom he has recoiled as a *wretch*.

In Whale's *Frankenstein,* 1931, Elizabeth, Clerval, and Professor Waldman knock on the castle door, ignorant of Frankenstein's experiment. When they insist on admission, they become a rapt, seated audience at a new kind of spectacle. Frankenstein heralds his accomplishment with the cry, "It's moving, it's alive, it's alive, it's moving," which could apply to the wonder of cinema itself.

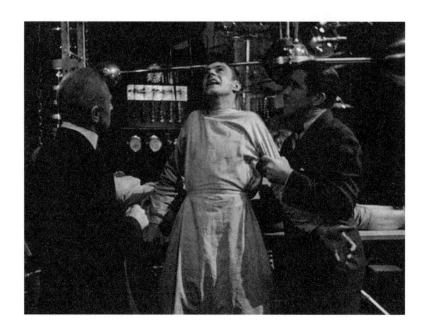

14 Percy inserted "avoid" into this sentence, to clarify what may have been Mary's hesitation about Victor's state of mind (folio 22v, *Notebooks* 1: 102–103).

15 M. Shelley's footnote (I: 103). This stanza (lines 461–466) is the Mariner's extended simile for his awakening from a horrific spell.

opened the gates of the court, which had that night been my asylum, and I issued into the streets, pacing them with quick steps, as if I sought to avoid[14] the wretch whom I feared every turning of the street would present to my view. I did not dare return to the apartment which I inhabited, but felt impelled to hurry on, although wetted by the rain, which poured from a black and comfortless sky.

I continued walking in this manner for some time, endeavouring, by bodily exercise, to ease the load that weighed upon my mind. I traversed the streets, without any clear conception of where I was, or what I was doing. My heart palpitated in the sickness of fear; and I hurried on with irregular steps, not daring to look about me:

> Like one who, on a lonely road,
> Doth walk in fear and dread,
> And, having once turn'd round, walks on,
> And turns no more his head;
> Because he knows a frightful fiend
> Doth close behind him tread.*
>
> *Coleridge's "Ancient Mariner"[15]

Continuing thus, I came at length opposite to the inn at which the various diligences[16] and carriages usually stopped. Here I paused, I knew not why; but I remained some minutes with my eyes fixed on a coach that was coming towards me from the other end of the street. As it drew nearer, I observed that it was the Swiss diligence: it stopped just where I was standing; and, on the door being opened, I perceived Henry Clerval, who, on seeing me, instantly sprung out. "My dear Frankenstein,"[17] exclaimed he, "how glad I am to see you! how fortunate that you should be here at the very moment of my alighting!"

Nothing could equal my delight on seeing Clerval; his presence brought back to my thoughts my father, Elizabeth, and all those scenes of home so dear to my recollection. I grasped his hand, and in a moment forgot my horror and misfortune; I felt suddenly, and for the first time during many months, calm and serene joy. I welcomed my friend therefore, in the most cordial manner, and we walked towards my college. Clerval continued talking for some time about our mutual friends, and his own good fortune in being permitted to come to Ingolstadt. "You may easily believe," said he, "how great was the difficulty to persuade my father that it was not absolutely necessary for a merchant not to understand any thing except book-keeping; and, indeed, I believe I left him incredulous to the last, for his constant answer to my unwearied entreaties was the same as that of the Dutch school-master in the Vicar of Wakefield: 'I have ten thousand florins a year without Greek, I eat heartily without Greek.'[18] But his affection for me at length overcame his dislike of learning, and he has permitted me to undertake a voyage of discovery to the land of knowledge."

"It gives me the greatest delight to see you; but tell me how you left my father, brothers, and Elizabeth."

"Very well, and very happy, only a little uneasy that they hear from you so seldom. By the bye, I mean to lecture you a little upon their account myself.—But, my dear Frankenstein," continued he, stop-

16 A diligence is a commercial stage coach (rather than a private carriage). Recall that Victor travels to Ingolstadt by chaise. Henry is not from so wealthy a family.

17 This is the first instance of the surname, in an exclamation of brotherly affection.

18 Oliver Goldsmith's popular novel *The Vicar of Wakefield* (1766) gives a story (in chap. 20) of a young vagabond hoping to be hired as an instructor. Approaching the principal of a Flemish university to offer his "service as a master of the Greek language, which I had been told was a desideratum," he receives this response: "You see me, young man; I never learned Greek and I don't find that I have ever missed it. I have had a doctor's cap and gown without Greek; I have ten thousand florins a year without Greek; I eat heartily without Greek; and in short, continued he, as I don't know Greek, I do not believe there is any good in it." This joking allusion to this famous conversation also reflects the increasingly practical emphasis in bourgeois education in Shelley's day.

19 Mary Shelley draws on linked etymologies to create a nervous pun connecting ex*pect* and *spectre,* both drawn from *specere* (Latin: *to look at*).

ping short, and gazing full in my face, "I did not before remark how very ill you appear; so thin and pale; you look as if you had been watching for several nights."

"You have guessed right; I have lately been so deeply engaged in one occupation, that I have not allowed myself sufficient rest, as you see: but I hope, I sincerely hope, that all these employments are now at an end, and that I am at length free."

I trembled excessively; I could not endure to think of, and far less to allude to the occurrences of the preceding night. I walked with a quick pace, and we soon arrived at my college. I then reflected, and the thought made me shiver, that the creature whom I had left in my apartment might still be there, alive, and walking about. I dreaded to behold this monster; but I feared still more that Henry should see him. Entreating him therefore to remain a few minutes at the bottom of the stairs, I darted up towards my own room. My hand was already on the lock of the door before I recollected myself. I then paused; and a cold shivering came over me. I threw the door forcibly open, as children are accustomed to do when they expect a spectre[19] to stand in waiting for them on the other side; but nothing appeared. I stepped fearfully in: the apartment was empty; and my bed-room was also freed from its hideous guest. I could hardly believe that so great a good-fortune could have befallen me; but when I became assured that my enemy had indeed fled, I clapped my hands for joy, and ran down to Clerval.

We ascended into my room, and the servant presently brought breakfast; but I was unable to contain myself. It was not joy only that possessed me; I felt my flesh tingle with excess of sensitiveness, and my pulse beat rapidly. I was unable to remain for a single instant in the same place; I jumped over the chairs, clapped my hands, and laughed aloud. Clerval at first attributed my unusual spirits to joy

This is the first frontal view of the Creature in James Whale's *Frankenstein* (1931). Cinema now had sound, but Shelley's eloquent Creature is denied a voice, and speaks only in rough halting measures in the sequel, *The Bride of Frankenstein* (1935). The liminal state of death coming into life is evoked by the Creature's stiff gait and expressionless eyes underneath half-closed lids (weighted with mortician's wax), but emotion is soon apparent.

on his arrival; but when he observed me more attentively, he saw a wildness in my eyes for which he could not account; and my loud, unrestrained, heartless laughter, frightened and astonished him.

"My dear Victor," cried he, "what, for God's sake, is the matter? Do not laugh in that manner. How ill you are! What is the cause of all this?"

"Do not ask me," cried I, putting my hands before my eyes, for I thought I saw the dreaded spectre glide into the room; "*he* can tell.—Oh, save me! save me!" I imagined that the monster seized me; I struggled furiously, and fell down in a fit.

Poor Clerval! what must have been his feelings? A meeting, which he anticipated with such joy, so strangely turned to bitterness. But I was not the witness of his grief; for I was lifeless,[20] and did not recover my senses for a long, long time.

This was the commencement of a nervous fever, which confined me for several months. During all that time Henry was my only

20 Frankenstein has used the word *lifeless* several times in describing his project of animating matter. He is, in effect (and typically, without reflection), in the situation of his pre-animated Creature. Recall that he came to Walton's ship "on the brink of destruction" and was "restored . . . to life." Mary Shelley's array of *lifeless* figures animated or restored shows her skill in arranging critically analogous scenes, and weaving significant verbal threads.

nurse. I afterwards learned that, knowing my father's advanced age, and unfitness for so long a journey, and how wretched my sickness would make Elizabeth, he spared them this grief by concealing the extent of my disorder. He knew that I could not have a more kind and attentive nurse than himself; and, firm in the hope he felt of my recovery, he did not doubt that, instead of doing harm, he performed the kindest action that he could towards them.

But I was in reality very ill; and surely nothing but the unbounded and unremitting attentions of my friend could have restored me to life. The form of the monster on whom I had bestowed existence was for ever before my eyes, and I raved incessantly concerning him. Doubtless my words surprised Henry: he at first believed them to be the wanderings of my disturbed imagination; but the pertinacity with which I continually recurred to the same subject persuaded him that my disorder indeed owed its origin to some uncommon and terrible event.

By very slow degrees, and with frequent relapses that alarmed and grieved my friend, I recovered. I remember the first time I became capable of observing outward objects with any kind of pleasure, I perceived that the fallen leaves had disappeared, and that the young buds were shooting forth from the trees that shaded my window. It was a divine spring; and the season contributed greatly to my convalescence. I felt also sentiments of joy and affection revive in my bosom; my gloom disappeared, and in a short time I became as cheerful as before I was attacked by the fatal passion.

"Dearest Clerval," exclaimed I, "how kind, how very good you are to me. This whole winter, instead of being spent in study, as you promised yourself, has been consumed in my sick room. How shall I ever repay you? I feel the greatest remorse for the disappointment of which I have been the occasion; but you will forgive me."

"You will repay me entirely, if you do not discompose yourself, but get well as fast as you can; and since you appear in such good spirits, I may speak to you on one subject, may I not?"

I trembled. One subject! what could it be? Could he allude to an object on whom I dared not even think?

"Compose yourself," said Clerval, who observed my change of colour, "I will not mention it, if it agitates you; but your father and cousin would be very happy if they received a letter from you in your own hand-writing. They hardly know how ill you have been, and are uneasy at your long silence."

"Is that all? my dear Henry. How could you suppose that my first thought would not fly towards those dear, dear friends whom I love, and who are so deserving of my love."

"If this is your present temper, my friend, you will perhaps be glad to see a letter that has been lying here some days for you: it is from your cousin, I believe."

CHAPTER V

Clerval then put the following letter into my hands.

"*To* V. Frankenstein.

"My Dear Cousin,

"I cannot describe to you the uneasiness we have all felt concerning your health. We cannot help imagining that your friend Clerval conceals the extent of your disorder: for it is now several months since we have seen your hand-writing; and all this time you have been obliged to dictate your letters to Henry.[1] Surely, Victor, you must have been exceedingly ill; and this makes us all very wretched, as much so nearly as after the death of your dear mother. My uncle was almost persuaded that you were indeed dangerously ill, and could hardly be restrained from undertaking a journey to Ingolstadt. Clerval always writes that you are getting better; I eagerly hope that you will confirm this intelligence soon in your own hand-writing; for indeed, indeed, Victor, we are all very miserable on this account. Relieve us from this fear, and we shall be the happiest creatures in the world. Your father's health is now so vigorous, that he appears ten years younger since last winter. Ernest also is so much improved, that you would hardly know him: he is now nearly sixteen, and has lost that sickly appearance which he had some years ago; he is grown quite robust and active.

"My uncle and I conversed a long time last night about what profession Ernest should follow. His constant illness when young has deprived him of the habits of application; and now that he enjoys good health, he is continually in the open air, climbing the hills, or rowing on the lake. I therefore proposed that he should be a farmer; which you know, Cousin, is a favourite scheme of mine. A farmer's is a very healthy happy life; and the least hurtful, or rather the most beneficial profession of any. My uncle had an idea of his being educated as an advocate, that through his interest he might become a judge. But, besides that he is not at all fitted for such an occupation, it is certainly more creditable to cultivate the earth for the sustenance of man, than to be the confidant, and sometimes the accomplice, of his vices; which is the profession of a lawyer. I said, that the employments of a prosperous farmer, if they were not a more honourable, they were at least a happier species of occupation than that of a judge, whose misfortune it was always to meddle with the dark side of human nature.[2] My uncle smiled, and said, that I ought to be an advocate myself, which put an end to the conversation on that subject.[3]

"And now I must tell you a story that will please, and perhaps amuse you. Do you not remember Justine Moritz?[4] Probably you do not; I will relate her history, therefore, in a few words. Madame Moritz, her mother, was a widow with four children, of whom Justine was the third. This girl had always been the favourite of her father; but, through a strange perversity, her mother could not endure her, and, after the death of M. Moritz, treated her very ill. My aunt

2   The aspersions on the legal profession were deleted in *1831;* here they sound one part of the Shelleys' ambivalence, especially in light of Percy's difficulties in the English courts. The notion that happiness can be compromised by meddling with the dark side of human nature has, however, a broader application in this novel.

3   This was an impossible profession for a woman, and so her uncle's jest is a little cruel. When Elizabeth testifies in court, in a later episode, she is ineffective.

4   The name will prove severely ironic, in the antonym that is her fate.

5   This sentence and the rest of the paragraph were supplied by Percy (*Notebooks* 126–129), reflecting his political thinking and the influence of views expressed in Volney's *Ruins of Empire.* Mary shared these views, remarking of the Swiss servants they met during the "Frankenstein" summer: "There is more equality of classes here than in England. This occasions a greater freedom and refinement of manners among the lower orders than we meet with in our own country. I fancy the haughty English ladies are greatly disgusted with this consequence of republican institutions, for the Genevese servants complain very much of their *scolding,* an exercise of the tongue, I believe, perfectly unknown here" (Letter I, June 1, 1816; *1817,* 103). In the sentence just prior, the manuscript reads "her house" (*Notebooks* 126).

6   Angelica is the princess in Ariosto's *Orlando Furioso* (1532); her rejection of Orlando drives him furiously mad. Elizabeth's term of praise, "frank-hearted," is another instance of Frankenstein-esteem in the lexicon of their surname.

observed this; and, when Justine was twelve years of age, prevailed on her mother to allow her to live at [our] house. The republican institutions of our country have produced simpler and happier manners than those which prevail in the great monarchies that surround it.[5] Hence there is less distinction between the several classes of its inhabitants; and the lower orders being neither so poor nor so despised, their manners are more refined and moral. A servant in Geneva does not mean the same thing as a servant in France and England. Justine, thus received in our family, learned the duties of a servant; a condition which, in our fortunate country, does not include the idea of ignorance, and a sacrifice of the dignity of a human being.

"After what I have said, I dare say you well remember the heroine of my little tale: for Justine was a great favourite of your's; and I recollect you once remarked, that if you were in an ill humour, one glance from Justine could dissipate it, for the same reason that Ariosto gives concerning the beauty of Angelica—she looked so frank-hearted and happy.[6] My aunt conceived a great attachment for her, by which she was induced to give her an education superior to that which she had at first intended. This benefit was fully repaid; Justine was the most grateful little creature in the world: I do not mean that she made any professions, I never heard one pass her lips; but you could see by her eyes that she almost adored her protectress. Although her disposition was gay, and in many respects inconsiderate, yet she paid the greatest attention to every gesture of my aunt. She thought her the model of all excellence, and endeavoured to imitate her phraseology and manners, so that even now she often reminds me of her.

"When my dearest aunt died, everyone was too much occupied in their own grief to notice poor Justine, who had attended her during her illness with the most anxious affection. Poor Justine was very ill; but other trials were reserved for her.

"One by one, her brothers and sister died; and her mother, with the exception of her neglected daughter, was left childless. The conscience of the woman was troubled; she began to think that the deaths of her favourites was a judgment from heaven to chastise her partiality. She was a Roman Catholic; and I believe her confessor confirmed the idea which she had conceived. Accordingly, a few months after your departure for Ingolstadt, Justine was called home by her repentant mother. Poor girl! she wept when she quitted our house: she was much altered since the death of my aunt; grief had given softness and a winning mildness to her manners, which had before been remarkable for vivacity. Nor was her residence at her mother's house of a nature to restore her gaiety. The poor woman was very vacillating in her repentance. She sometimes begged Justine to forgive her unkindness, but much oftener accused her of having caused the deaths of her brothers and sister. Perpetual fretting at length threw Madame Moritz into a decline, which at first increased her irritability, but she is now at peace forever. She died on the first approach of cold weather, at the beginning of this last winter. Justine has returned to us; and I assure you I love her tenderly. She is very clever and gentle, and extremely pretty; as I mentioned before, her mien and her expressions continually remind me of my dear aunt.

"I must say also a few words to you, my dear cousin, of little darling William. I wish you could see him; he is very

7   William is about six. The jest about "Biron" and the "two little *wives*" glances at the scandal of winter 1816, when Lady Byron left Lord Byron in January, after scarcely more than a year of marriage, his infidelities the least of it. Just after the publication of *Frankenstein,* Byron echoed the jest, telling a friend that he planned to give his daughter by Claire Clairmont "the name of *Biron* (to distinguish her from little Legitimacy)"—that is, from his first daughter, Ada (to Douglas Kinnaird, January 13, 1818).

8   Issuing from benevolent Elizabeth, this report shows ingrained fairy-tale reflexes in assigning "pretty" and "ugly" to contrasting social types; this is the only use of *ugly* for any being other than the Creature. Manon means "bitter"; the married name may glance at Swiss-born Emmanuel-Etienne Duvillard (1755–1832), author of *Recherches sur les rentes* (published in Paris and Geneva in 1787), a work of actuarial calculation (on pensions) in the era of financial tumult before, and contributing to, the French Revolution.

9   Despite the seeming aspersion on Manon's marriage to a rich banker, Elizabeth accepts without comment the social reality of fortune-hunting: a young man in financial need setting his sights on a (likely rich) widow.

tall of his age, with sweet laughing blue eyes, dark eye-lashes, and curling hair. When he smiles, two little dimples appear on each cheek, which are rosy with health. He has already had one or two little *wives*, but Louisa Biron[7] is his favourite, a pretty little girl of five years of age.

"Now, dear Victor, I dare say you wish to be indulged in a little gossip concerning the good people of Geneva. The pretty Miss Mansfield has already received the congratulatory visits on her approaching marriage with a young Englishman, John Melbourne, Esq. Her ugly sister, Manon, married M. Duvillard, the rich banker, last autumn.[8] Your favourite schoolfellow, Louis Manoir, has suffered several misfortunes since the departure of Clerval from Geneva. But he has already recovered his spirits, and is reported to be on the point of marrying a very lively pretty Frenchwoman, Madame Tavernier. She is a widow, and much older than Manoir;[9] but she is very much admired, and a favourite with every body.

"I have written myself into good spirits, dear cousin; yet I cannot conclude without again anxiously inquiring concerning your health. Dear Victor, if you are not very ill, write yourself, and make your father and all of us happy; or——I cannot bear to think of the other side of the question; my tears already flow. Adieu, my dearest cousin.

"ELIZABETH LAVENZA.
"Geneva, March 18th, 17—."

"Dear, dear Elizabeth!" I exclaimed when I had read her letter, "I will write instantly, and relieve them from the anxiety they must feel." I wrote, and this exertion greatly fatigued me; but my convalescence had commenced, and proceeded regularly. In another fortnight I was able to leave my chamber.

One of my first duties on my recovery was to introduce Clerval to the several professors of the university. In doing this, I underwent a kind of rough usage, ill befitting the wounds that my mind had sustained. Ever since the fatal night, the end of my labours, and the beginning of my misfortunes, I had conceived a violent antipathy even to the name of natural philosophy. When I was otherwise quite restored to health, the sight of a chemical instrument would renew all the agony of my nervous symptoms. Henry saw this, and had removed all my apparatus from my view. He had also changed my apartment; for he perceived that I had acquired a dislike for the room which had previously been my laboratory. But these cares of Clerval were made of no avail when I visited the professors. M. Waldman inflicted torture when he praised, with kindness and warmth, the astonishing progress I had made in the sciences. He soon perceived that I disliked the subject; but, not guessing the real cause, he attributed my feelings to modesty, and changed the subject from my improvement to the science itself, with a desire, as I evidently saw, of drawing me out. What could I do? He meant to please, and he tormented me. I felt as if he had placed carefully, one by one, in my view those instruments which were to be afterwards used in putting me to a slow and cruel death. I writhed under his words, yet dared not exhibit the pain I felt. Clerval, whose eyes and feelings were always quick in discerning the sensations of others, declined the subject, alleging, in excuse, his total ignorance; and the conversation took a more general turn. I thanked my friend from my heart, but I did not speak. I saw plainly that he was surprised, but he never attempted to draw my secret from me; and although I loved him with a mixture of affection and reverence that knew no bounds, yet I could never persuade myself to confide to him that event which was so often present to my recollection, but which I feared the detail to another would only impress more deeply.

10 Mary Shelley's manuscript has "Damn" (*Notebooks* 142–143), but printing this word would be legally actionable blasphemy that could cost the publisher his copyright.

M. Krempe was not equally docile; and in my condition at that time, of almost insupportable sensitiveness, his harsh blunt encomiums gave me even more pain than the benevolent approbation of M. Waldman. "D—n the fellow!"[10] cried he; "why, M. Clerval, I assure you he has outstript us all. Aye, stare if you please; but it is nevertheless true. A youngster who, but a few years ago, believed Cornelius Agrippa as firmly as the gospel, has now set himself at the head of the university; and if he is not soon pulled down, we shall all be out of countenance.—Aye, aye," continued he, observing my face expressive of suffering, "M. Frankenstein is modest; an excellent quality in a young man. Young men should be diffident of themselves, you know, M. Clerval; I was myself when young; but that wears out in a very short time."

M. Krempe had now commenced an eulogy on himself, which happily turned the conversation from a subject that was so annoying to me.

Clerval was no natural philosopher. His imagination was too vivid for the minutiæ of science. Languages were his principal study; and he sought, by acquiring their elements, to open a field for self-instruction on his return to Geneva. Persian, Arabic, and Hebrew, gained his attention, after he had made himself perfectly master of Greek and Latin. For my own part, idleness had ever been irksome to me, and now that I wished to fly from reflection, and hated my former studies, I felt great relief in being the fellow-pupil with my friend, and found not only instruction but consolation in the works of the orientalists. Their melancholy is soothing, and their joy elevating to a degree I never experienced in studying the authors of any other country. When you read their writings, life appears to consist in a warm sun and garden of roses,—in the smiles and frowns of a fair enemy, and the fire that consumes your own heart. How different from the manly and heroical poetry of Greece and Rome.[11]

Summer passed away in these occupations, and my return to Geneva was fixed for the latter end of autumn; but being delayed by several accidents, winter and snow arrived, the roads were deemed impassable, and my journey was retarded until the ensuing spring. I felt this delay very bitterly; for I longed to see my native town, and my beloved friends. My return had only been delayed so long from an unwillingness to leave Clerval in a strange place, before he had become acquainted with any of its inhabitants. The winter, however, was spent cheerfully; and although the spring was uncommonly late, when it came, its beauty compensated for its dilatoriness.

The month of May had already commenced, and I expected the letter daily which was to fix the date of my departure, when Henry proposed a pedestrian tour in the environs of Ingolstadt that I might bid a personal farewell to the country I had so long inhabited. I acceded with pleasure to this proposition: I was fond of exercise, and Clerval had always been my favourite companion in the rambles of this nature that I had taken among the scenes of my native country.

We passed a fortnight in these perambulations: my health and spirits had long been restored, and they gained additional strength from the salubrious air I breathed, the natural incidents of our progress, and the conversation of my friend. Study had before secluded me from the intercourse of my fellow-creatures, and rendered me unsocial; but Clerval called forth the better feelings of my heart; he again taught me to love the aspect of nature, and the cheerful faces of children. Excellent friend! how sincerely did you love me, and endeavour to elevate my mind, until it was on a level

11   This orientalism, with a whiff of effeminate luxury, reflects the popularity of Persian poetry in English translation in the eighteenth century. In *1831* Mary Shelley elaborates the material motives of Clerval's studies: "He came to the university with the design of making himself complete master of the oriental languages, as thus he should open a field for the plan of life he had marked out for himself. Resolved to pursue no inglorious career, he turned his eyes toward the East, as affording scope for his spirit of enterprise" (54). In the 1790s, under the leadership of the East India Company, the East, both middle and far, was the arena of commercial enterprise and opportunity.

12 Literally "without a soul," the adjective evokes its antonym, *animate*—the very thing Frankenstein has done, against nature.

with your own. A selfish pursuit had cramped and narrowed me, until your gentleness and affection warmed and opened my senses; I became the same happy creature who, a few years ago, loving and beloved by all, had no sorrow or care. When happy, inanimate[12] nature had the power of bestowing on me the most delightful sensations. A serene sky and verdant fields filled me with ecstacy. The present season was indeed divine; the flowers of spring bloomed in the hedges, while those of summer were already in bud: I was undisturbed by thoughts which during the preceding year had pressed upon me, notwithstanding my endeavours to throw them off, with an invincible burden.

Henry rejoiced in my gaiety, and sincerely sympathized in my feelings: he exerted himself to amuse me, while he expressed the sensations that filled his soul. The resources of his mind on this occasion were truly astonishing: his conversation was full of imagination; and very often, in imitation of the Persian and Arabic writers, he invented tales of wonderful fancy and passion. At other times he repeated my favourite poems, or drew me out into arguments, which he supported with great ingenuity.

We returned to our college on a Sunday afternoon: the peasants were dancing, and every one we met appeared gay and happy. My own spirits were high, and I bounded along with feelings of unbridled joy and hilarity.

CHAPTER VI

1   This shocking news is another multiply interpretable moment, embedded in the novel's events and in Mary Shelley's history. Her birth had "killed" her parents' hope of a son William; the son William that Godwin eventually had was his favorite child. Critic U. C. Knoepflmacher reads this murder as a screen of sibling rivalry. Wolf "wonders about the curious warp in her mind that allowed the mother of six-month-old William . . . to bestow his name on the creature's first victim" (97).

ON MY RETURN, I found the following letter from my father:—

"*To* V. FRANKENSTEIN.

"MY DEAR VICTOR,

"You have probably waited impatiently for a letter to fix the date of your return to us; and I was at first tempted to write only a few lines, merely mentioning the day on which I should expect you. But that would be a cruel kindness, and I dare not do it. What would be your surprise, my son, when you expected a happy and gay welcome, to behold, on the contrary, tears and wretchedness? And how, Victor, can I relate our misfortune? Absence cannot have rendered you callous to our joys and griefs; and how shall I inflict pain on an absent child? I wish to prepare you for the woeful news, but I know it is impossible; even now your eye skims over the page, to seek the words which are to convey to you the horrible tidings.

"William is dead![1]—that sweet child, whose smiles delighted and warmed my heart, who was so gentle, yet so gay! Victor, he is murdered!

"I will not attempt to console you; but will simply relate the circumstances of the transaction.

2   Our Timeline speculatively "corrects" to May 8, in order to coordinate with the actual calendar of 1794 and the termination of the
narrative, three years on, in 1797.

3   Mary records such scenery in *1817:* "To the south of the town is
the promenade . . . Plainpalais. Here a small obelisk is erected to the
glory of Rousseau, and here (such is the mutability of human life)
the magistrates, the successors of those who exiled him from his
native country, were shot by the populace during that revolution
[1792–1795], which his writings mainly contributed to mature, and
which, notwithstanding the temporary bloodshed and injustice
with which it was polluted, has produced enduring benefits to mankind" (Letter I, May 17, 1816, 101–102). This affirmation of enduring benefits, despite bloodshed and injustice, is contradicted in the
novel by the irredeemable violence discovered at this site.

4   This reanimation scene will prove ultimately to be futile.

"Last Thursday (May 7th)[2] I, my niece, and your two
brothers, went to walk in Plainpalais.[3] The evening was
warm and serene, and we prolonged our walk farther than
usual. It was already dusk before we thought of returning;
and then we discovered that William and Ernest, who had
gone on before, were not to be found. We accordingly rested
on a seat until they should return. Presently Ernest came,
and inquired if we had seen his brother: he said, that they
had been playing together, that William had run away to
hide himself, and that he vainly sought for him, and afterwards waited for him a long time, but that he did not return.

"This account rather alarmed us, and we continued to
search for him until night fell, when Elizabeth conjectured
that he might have returned to the house. He was not there.
We returned again, with torches; for I could not rest, when I
thought that my sweet boy had lost himself, and was exposed to all the damps and dews of night; Elizabeth also suffered extreme anguish. About five in the morning I discovered my lovely boy, whom the night before I had seen
blooming and active in health, stretched on the grass livid
and motionless: the print of the murderer's finger was on
his neck.

"He was conveyed home, and the anguish that was visible
in my countenance betrayed the secret to Elizabeth. She was
very earnest to see the corpse. At first I attempted to prevent
her; but she persisted, and entering the room where it lay,
hastily examined the neck of the victim, and clasping her
hands, exclaimed, 'O God! I have murdered my darling infant!'

"She fainted, and was restored with extreme difficulty.
When she again lived,[4] it was only to weep and sigh. She told

me, that that same evening William had teazed her to let him wear a very valuable miniature that she possessed of your mother. This picture is gone, and was doubtless the temptation which urged the murderer to the deed. We have no trace of him at present, although our exertions to discover him are unremitted; but they will not restore my beloved William.

"Come, dearest Victor; you alone can console Elizabeth. She weeps continually, and accuses herself unjustly as the cause of his death; her words pierce my heart. We are all unhappy; but will not that be an additional motive for you, my son, to return and be our comforter? Your dear mother! Alas, Victor! I now say, Thank God she did not live to witness the cruel, miserable death of her youngest darling!

"Come, Victor; not brooding thoughts of vengeance against the assassin, but with feelings of peace and gentleness, that will heal, instead of festering the wounds of our minds. Enter the house of mourning,[5] my friend, but with kindness and affection for those who love you, and not with hatred for your enemies.

"Your affectionate and afflicted father,
ALPHONSE FRANKENSTEIN.[6]
"Geneva, May 12th, 17—."

Clerval, who had watched my countenance as I read this letter, was surprised to observe the despair that succeeded to joy I at first expressed on receiving news from my friends. I threw the letter on the table, and covered my face with my hands.

"My dear Frankenstein," exclaimed Henry, when he perceived me weep with bitterness, "are you always to be unhappy? My dear friend, what has happened?"

5 "It is better to go to the house of mourning, than to go to the house of feasting: for that is the end of all men . . . The heart of the wise is in the house of mourning; but the heart of fools is in the house of mirth" (Ecclesiastes 7: 2–4).

6 We learn this father's forename (from the German for *noble*).

7 The grief of the Roman statesman Cato the Younger (1st century B.C.) for his beloved brother is recounted in *Plutarch's Lives,* which the Creature reads (Vol. II, Ch. VI), and which both Mary and Percy were reading across 1815–1816. Cato professed restraint of passion, but "showed himself more a fond brother than a philosopher, not only in the excess of his grief, bewailing, and embracing the dead body, but also in the extravagant expenses of the funeral . . . there were some who took upon them to cavil at all this, as not consistent with his usual calmness and moderation, not discerning that though he were steadfast, firm, and inflexible to pleasure, fear or foolish en-treaties, yet he was full of natural tenderness and brotherly affec-tion." In *1831,* Shelley, since 1822 a widow, and bereft before then, of a half-sister and all but one of her children, dropped the allusion to Cato.

8 Developed in France in the early nineteenth century, a cabriolet (whence "cab") is a small, light, horse-drawn carriage.

I motioned to him to take up the letter, while I walked up and down the room in the extremest agitation. Tears also gushed from the eyes of Clerval, as he read the account of my misfortune.

"I can offer you no consolation, my friend," said he; "your disas-ter is irreparable. What do you intend to do?"

"To go instantly to Geneva: come with me, Henry, to order the horses."

During our walk, Clerval endeavoured to raise my spirits. He did not do this by common topics of consolation, but by exhibiting the truest sympathy. "Poor William!" said he, "that dear child; he now sleeps with his angel mother. His friends mourn and weep, but he is at rest: he does not now feel the murderer's grasp; a sod covers his gentle form, and he knows no pain. He can no longer be a fit subject for pity; the survivors are the greatest sufferers, and for them time is the only consolation. Those maxims of the Stoics, that death was no evil, and that the mind of man ought to be superior to despair on the eternal absence of a beloved object, ought not to be urged. Even Cato wept over the dead body of his brother."[7]

Clerval spoke thus as we hurried through the streets; the words impressed themselves on my mind, and I remembered them after-wards in solitude. But now, as soon as the horses arrived, I hurried into a cabriole,[8] and bade farewell to my friend.

My journey was very melancholy. At first I wished to hurry on, for I longed to console and sympathize with my loved and sorrow-ing friends; but when I drew near my native town, I slackened my progress. I could hardly sustain the multitude of feelings that crowded into my mind. I passed through scenes familiar to my youth, but which I had not seen for nearly six years. How altered every thing might be during that time? One sudden and desolating change had taken place; but a thousand little circumstances might have by degrees worked other alterations, which, although they were done more tranquilly, might not be the less decisive. Fear overcame me; I dared not advance, dreading a thousand nameless evils that made me tremble, although I was unable to define them.

I remained two days at Lausanne,[9] in this painful state of mind. I contemplated the lake: the waters were placid; all around was calm, and the snowy mountains, "the palaces of nature,"[10] were not changed. By degrees the calm and heavenly scene restored me, and I continued my journey towards Geneva.

The road ran by the side of the lake, which became narrower as I approached my native town. I discovered more distinctly the black sides of Jura, and the bright summit of Mont Blanc;[11] I wept like a child: "Dear mountains! my own beautiful lake! how do you welcome your wanderer? Your summits are clear; the sky and lake are blue and placid. Is this to prognosticate peace, or to mock at my unhappiness?"

I fear, my friend, that I shall render myself tedious by dwelling on these preliminary circumstances; but they were days of comparative happiness, and I think of them with pleasure. My country, my beloved country! who but a native can tell the delight I took in again beholding thy streams, thy mountains, and, more than all, thy lovely lake!

Yet, as I drew nearer home, grief and fear again overcame me. Night also closed around; and when I could hardly see the dark mountains, I felt still more gloomily. The picture appeared a vast and dim scene of evil, and I foresaw obscurely that I was destined to become the most wretched of human beings. Alas! I prophesied truly, and failed only in one single circumstance, that in all the misery I imagined and dreaded, I did not conceive the hundredth part of the anguish I was destined to endure.

9 In June 1816, Byron and Percy Shelley visited this Swiss city on the north shore, about forty miles from Geneva; here in 1788 Edward Gibbon completed his famous *Decline and Fall of the Roman Empire,* an epic history that attributed this course to a loss of civic devotion (foreign mercenaries managed the national defense). Mary read all twelve volumes in 1815. In *1817* Percy described "the decayed summer-house where [Gibbon] finished his History, and the old acacias on the terrace, from which he saw Mont Blanc, after having written the last sentence. There is something grand and even touching in the regret which he expresses at the completion of his task. It was conceived amid the ruins of the Capitol. The sudden departure of his cherished and accustomed toil must have left him, like the death of a dear friend, sad and solitary" (Letter III, 136–137).

10 On her ms. (*Notebooks* 164–165) Mary Shelley wrote then canceled a credit to "Lord Byron" for this phrase from *Childe Harold's Pilgrimage III* (written at Lake Geneva and published in December 1816): "the Alps, / The palaces of Nature, whose vast walls / Have pinnacled in clouds their snowy scalps, / And throned Eternity in icy halls / Of cold sublimity, where forms and falls / The avalanche —the thunderbolt of snow!" (62).

11 On the French-Swiss border at 15,782 feet above sea level, Mont Blanc is the highest peak in the Alps, a "sublime" must-see on anyone's Grand Tour. Its summit had been attained only a few times by 1816 (the first recorded was August 8, 1786). Percy Shelley's dizzying philosophical lyric *Mont Blanc: Lines written in the Vale of Chamouni* was the capstone of *1817* (175–185, dated July 23, 1816).

12   "The town is surrounded by a wall, the three gates of which are shut exactly at ten o'clock, when no bribery (as in France) can open them" (*1817*, Letter II, 101).

13   On the south shore of Lake Geneva, about three miles from Geneva, the limestone precipices of the Salève rise to over three thousand feet. To the northwest is the Jura range; the Savoy Alps, its peaks capped in snow and ice even in summer, include Mont Blanc.

14   The "lake of fire" in Milton's Hell (*Paradise Lost* I.280) is transformed here to sublime aesthetic wonder.

15   At Coppet, on the north shore, resided Mme. de Staël, exiled from France by Napoleon. The Môle is at the lake's other end, about twenty miles southeast of Geneva. This thunderstorm recalls the one in Chapter I in which young Victor sees an old oak reduced to a blasted stump. On May 17, 1816, Mary Shelley wrote of "the dark frowning Jura" and of her excitement at the thunderstorms: "grander and more terrific than I have ever seen before. We watch them as they approach from the opposite side of the lake, observing the lightning play among the clouds in various parts of the heavens, and dart in jagged figures upon the piny heights of Jura, dark with the shadow of the overhanging cloud, while perhaps the sun is shining cheerily upon us. One night we *enjoyed* a finer storm than I had ever before beheld. The lake was lit up—the pines on Jura made visible, and all the scene illuminated for an instant, when a pitchy blackness succeeded, and the thunder came in frightful bursts over our heads amid the darkness" (*1817*, Letter I, 98–100). Her description complements Byron's famous, electric stanzas in *Childe Harold III* (1816):

> The sky is changed!—and such a change! Oh night,
> And storm, and darkness, ye are wondrous strong,
> Yet lovely in your strength, as is the light
> Of a dark eye in woman! Far along,
> From peak to peak, the rattling crags among
> Leaps the live thunder! Not from one lone cloud,
> But every mountain now hath found a tongue,
> And Jura answers, through her misty shroud,
> Back to the joyous Alps, who call to her aloud!
>
> And this is in the night:—Most glorious night!
> Thou wert not sent for slumber! let me be
> A sharer in thy fierce and far delight,—
> A portion of the tempest and of thee!

It was completely dark when I arrived in the environs of Geneva; the gates of the town were already shut;[12] and I was obliged to pass the night at Secheron, a village half a league to the east of the city. The sky was serene; and, as I was unable to rest, I resolved to visit the spot where my poor William had been murdered. As I could not pass through the town, I was obliged to cross the lake in a boat to arrive at Plainpalais. During this short voyage I saw the lightnings playing on the summit of Mont Blanc in the most beautiful figures. The storm appeared to approach rapidly; and, on landing, I ascended a low hill, that I might observe its progress. It advanced; the heavens were clouded, and I soon felt the rain coming slowly in large drops, but its violence quickly increased.

I quitted my seat, and walked on, although the darkness and storm increased every minute, and the thunder burst with a terrific crash over my head. It was echoed from Salêve, the Juras, and the Alps of Savoy;[13] vivid flashes of lightning dazzled my eyes, illuminating the lake, making it appear like a vast sheet of fire;[14] then for an instant everything seemed of a pitchy darkness, until the eye recovered itself from the preceding flash. The storm, as is often the case in Switzerland, appeared at once in various parts of the heavens. The most violent storm hung exactly north of the town, over that part of the lake which lies between the promontory of Belrive and the village of Copêt. Another storm enlightened Jura with faint flashes; and another darkened and sometimes disclosed the Môle, a peaked mountain to the east of the lake.[15]

While I watched the storm, so beautiful yet terrific, I wandered on with a hasty step. This noble war in the sky elevated my spirits; I clasped my hands, and exclaimed aloud, "William, dear angel! this is thy funeral, this thy dirge!" As I said these words, I perceived in the gloom a figure which stole from behind a clump of trees near me; I stood fixed, gazing intently: I could not be mistaken. A flash of lightning illuminated the object, and discovered its shape plainly to me; its gigantic stature, and the deformity of its aspect, more hideous than belongs to humanity, instantly informed me that it was the wretch, the filthy dæmon to whom I had given life.[16] What did he there? Could he be (I shuddered at the conception) the murderer of my brother?[17] No sooner did that idea cross my imagination, than I became convinced of its truth; my teeth chattered, and I was forced to lean against a tree for support. The figure passed me quickly, and I lost it in the gloom. Nothing in human shape could have destroyed that fair child. *He* was the murderer! I could not doubt it. The mere presence of the idea was an irresistible proof of the fact.[18] I thought of pursuing the devil; but it would have been in vain, for another flash discovered him to me hanging among the rocks of the nearly perpendicular ascent of Mont Salêve, a hill that bounds Plainpalais on the south. He soon reached the summit, and disappeared.

I remained motionless. The thunder ceased; but the rain still continued, and the scene was enveloped in an impenetrable darkness. I revolved in my mind the events which I had until now sought to forget: the whole train of my progress towards the creation; the appearance of the work of my own hands alive at my bed side; its departure. Two years had now nearly elapsed since the night on which he first received life; and was this his first crime? Alas! I had turned loose into the world a depraved wretch, whose delight was in carnage and misery; had he not murdered my brother?

No one can conceive the anguish I suffered during the remainder of the night, which I spent, cold and wet, in the open air.[19] But I did not feel the inconvenience of the weather; my imagination was busy in scenes of evil and despair. I considered the being whom I had cast among mankind, and endowed with the will and power to effect purposes of horror, such as the deed which he had now done, nearly in the light of my own vampire,[20] my own spirit let loose from the grave, and forced to destroy all that was dear to me.

Day dawned; and I directed my steps towards the town. The gates were open; and I hastened to my father's house. My first

How the lit lake shines, a phosphoric sea,
  And the big rain comes dancing to the earth!
  And now again 'tis black,—and now, the glee
  Of the loud hills shakes with its mountain-mirth,
  As if they did rejoice o'er a young earthquake's birth. (92–93)

16   This nightmarish perception is Frankenstein's first sight of his Creature since the night of creation almost two years earlier.

17   If, as Knoepflmacher argues, the Creature is the alter ego projection of his creator, acting out repressed aggressions, Frankenstein's horror may expose a dim recognition of sibling rivalry with this darling. The first murder in the Bible is a fratricide, Cain's, in resentment of a favored younger bother (Genesis 4: 1–16).

18   Grasping the psychology of emergent repression, Percy supplied these last three sentences (*Notebooks* 172–173).

19   It does not occur to Frankenstein that this is the experience of "the being whom [he] cast" into the world, not in summer but in wintry November.

20   Frankenstein's phrasing is more than a concession of agency; "my" presents a demonic double. The summer-1816 tales by Polidori and Byron both feature alluring, mysterious Byron-coded men who turn out to be vampires. The Shelleys courted such description, too. The wife Percy abandoned in 1814 told a friend, as she was near to delivering their son (his first), that she blamed Godwin's "evil" philosophy (including opposition to the institution of marriage) and his daughter ("She heated his imagination") for turning her husband "profligate and sensual": "the man I once loved is dead. This is a vampire. His character is blasted for ever. Nothing can save him now" (November 20, 1814, *Letters PBS* 992).

21 This wording is Percy's, somewhat attenuating Mary's tighter verbal linking of the maker and his being. Her ms. reads, "A creature whom I myself had created" (*Notebooks* 174–175).

thought was to discover what I knew of the murderer, and cause instant pursuit to be made. But I paused when I reflected on the story that I had to tell. A being whom I myself had formed,[21] and endued with life, had met me at midnight among the precipices of an inaccessible mountain. I remembered also the nervous fever with which I had been seized just at the time that I dated my creation, and which would give an air of delirium to a tale otherwise so utterly improbable. I well knew that if any other had communicated such a relation to me, I should have looked upon it as the ravings of insanity. Besides, the strange nature of the animal would elude all pursuit, even if I were so far credited as to persuade my relatives to commence it. Besides, of what use would be pursuit? Who could arrest a creature capable of scaling the overhanging sides of Mont Salêve? These reflections determined me, and I resolved to remain silent.

It was about five in the morning when I entered my father's house. I told the servants not to disturb the family, and went into the library to attend their usual hour of rising.

Six years had elapsed, passed as a dream but for one indelible trace, and I stood in the same place where I had last embraced my father before my departure for Ingolstadt. Beloved and respectable parent! He still remained to me. I gazed on the picture of my mother, which stood over the mantlepiece. It was an historical subject, painted at my father's desire, and represented Caroline Beaufort in an agony of despair, kneeling by the coffin of her dead father. Her garb was rustic, and her cheek pale; but there was an air of dignity and beauty, that hardly permitted the sentiment of pity. Below this picture was a miniature of William; and my tears flowed when I looked upon it. While I was thus engaged, Ernest entered: he had heard me arrive, and hastened to welcome me. He expressed a sorrowful delight to see me: "Welcome, my dearest Victor," said he. "Ah! I wish you had come three months ago, and then you would have found us all joyous and delighted. But we are now unhappy; and, I am afraid, tears instead of smiles will be your welcome. Our father looks so sorrowful: this dreadful event seems to have revived in his mind his grief on the death of Mamma. Poor Elizabeth also is quite inconsolable." Ernest began to weep as he said these words.

"Do not," said I, "welcome me thus; try to be more calm, that I may not be absolutely miserable the moment I enter my father's house after so long an absence. But, tell me, how does my father support his misfortunes? and how is my poor Elizabeth?"

"She indeed requires consolation; she accused herself of having caused the death of my brother, and that made her very wretched. But since the murderer has been discovered——"

"The murderer discovered! Good God! how can that be? who could attempt to pursue him? It is impossible; one might as well try to overtake the winds, or confine a mountain-stream with a straw."

"I do not know what you mean; but we were all very unhappy when she was discovered. No one would believe it at first; and even now Elizabeth will not be convinced, notwithstanding all the evidence. Indeed, who would credit that Justine Moritz, who was so amiable, and fond of all the family, could all at once become so extremely wicked?"

"Justine Moritz! Poor, poor girl, is she the accused? But it is wrongfully; every one knows that; no one believes it, surely, Ernest?"

"No one did at first; but several circumstances came out, that have almost forced conviction upon us:[22] and her own behaviour has been so confused, as to add to the evidence of facts a weight that, I fear, leaves no hope for doubt. But she will be tried to-day, and you will then hear all."

He related that, the morning on which the murder of poor William had been discovered, Justine had been taken ill, and confined to her bed; and, after several days, one of the servants, happening to examine the apparel she had worn on the night of the

22   In addition to the horrible irony of injustice, her name evokes famous female victims: the early Christian martyr St. Justina and the heroine of Marquis de Sade's novel *Justine; ou Les Malheurs de la vertu* (1791). Set just before the French Revolution, this last Justine endures sexual enslavement, rape, and the massive corruptions of the Church and courts. It was because of *Justine* that Napoleon imprisoned de Sade for thirteen years. While it is unclear what (if anything) Mary Shelley knew of this novel, there are several provocative similarities, including the youth of the heroines (both their histories begin at age twelve). By April 1816 Byron had the novel, which he kept hidden.

23 And as a tale, it is a little mirror of the novel itself: a hidden author, constructing a "monster" out of a chimera of elements, and a nightmare of a plot.

murder, had discovered in her pocket the picture of my mother, which had been judged to be the temptation of the murderer. The servant instantly shewed it to one of the others, who, without saying a word to any of the family, went to a magistrate; and, upon their deposition, Justine was apprehended. On being charged with the fact, the poor girl confirmed the suspicion in a great measure by her extreme confusion of manner.

This was a strange tale,[23] but it did not shake my faith; and I replied earnestly, "You are all mistaken; I know the murderer. Justine, poor, good Justine, is innocent."

At that instant my father entered. I saw unhappiness deeply impressed on his countenance, but he endeavoured to welcome me cheerfully; and, after we had exchanged our mournful greeting, would have introduced some other topic than that of our disaster, had not Ernest exclaimed, "Good God, Papa! Victor says that he knows who was the murderer of poor William."

"We do also, unfortunately," replied my father; "for indeed I had rather have been for ever ignorant than have discovered so much depravity and ingratitude in one I valued so highly."

"My dear father, you are mistaken; Justine is innocent."

"If she is, God forbid that she should suffer as guilty. She is to be tried to-day, and I hope, I sincerely hope, that she will be acquitted."

This speech calmed me. I was firmly convinced in my own mind that Justine, and indeed every human being, was guiltless of this murder. I had no fear, therefore, that any circumstantial evidence could be brought forward strong enough to convict her; and, in this assurance, I calmed myself, expecting the trial with eagerness, but without prognosticating an evil result.

We were soon joined by Elizabeth. Time had made great alterations in her form since I had last beheld her. Six years before she had been a pretty, good-humoured girl, whom every one loved and caressed. She was now a woman in stature and expression of countenance, which was uncommonly lovely. An open and capacious forehead gave indications of a good understanding, joined to great frankness of disposition.[24] Her eyes were hazel, and expressive of mildness, now through recent affliction allied to sadness. Her hair was of a rich dark auburn, her complexion fair, and her figure slight and graceful. She welcomed me with the greatest affection. "Your arrival, my dear cousin," said she, "fills me with hope. You perhaps will find some means to justify my poor guiltless Justine. Alas! who is safe, if she be convicted of crime? I rely on her innocence as certainly as I do upon my own. Our misfortune is doubly hard to us; we have not only lost that lovely darling boy, but this poor girl, whom I sincerely love, is to be torn away by even a worse fate. If she is condemned, I never shall know joy more. But she will not, I am sure she will not; and then I shall be happy again, even after the sad death of my little William."

"She is innocent, my Elizabeth," said I, "and that shall be proved; fear nothing, but let your spirits be cheered by the assurance of her acquittal."

"How kind you are! every one else believes in her guilt, and that made me wretched; for I knew that it was impossible: and to see every one else prejudiced in so deadly a manner, rendered me hopeless and despairing." She wept.

"Sweet niece," said my father, "dry your tears. If she is, as you believe, innocent, rely on the justice of our judges, and the activity with which I shall prevent the slightest shadow of partiality."

24 Once more, Frankenstein-admiration is phrased in echo of the family name.

CHAPTER VII

W E PASSED A few sad hours, until eleven o'clock, when the trial was to commence. My father and the rest of the family being obliged to attend as witnesses, I accompanied them to the court. During the whole of this wretched mockery of justice, I suffered living torture. It was to be decided, whether the result of my curiosity and lawless devices would cause the death of two of my fellow-beings: one a smiling babe, full of innocence and joy; the other far more dreadfully murdered, with every aggravation of infamy that could make the murder memorable in horror. Justine also was a girl of merit, and possessed qualities which promised to render her life happy: now all was to be obliterated in an ignominious grave; and I the cause! A thousand times rather would I have confessed myself guilty of the crime ascribed to Justine; but I was absent when it was committed, and such a declaration would have been considered as the ravings of a madman, and would not have exculpated her who suffered through me.

The appearance of Justine was calm. She was dressed in mourning; and her countenance, always engaging, was rendered, by the solemnity of her feelings, exquisitely beautiful. Yet she appeared confident in innocence, and did not tremble, although gazed on and execrated by thousands; for all the kindness which her beauty might otherwise have excited, was obliterated in the minds of the spectators by the imagination of the enormity she was supposed to have committed. She was tranquil, yet her tranquillity was evidently constrained; and as her confusion had before been adduced as a proof of her guilt, she worked up her mind to an appearance of courage.[1] When she entered the court, she threw her eyes round it, and quickly discovered where we were seated. A tear seemed to dim her eye when she saw us; but she quickly recovered herself, and a look of sorrowful affection seemed to attest her utter guiltlessness.

The trial began; and after the advocate against her had stated the charge, several witnesses were called. Several strange facts combined against her, which might have staggered any one who had not such proof of her innocence as I had. She had been out the whole of the night on which the murder had been committed, and towards morning had been perceived by a market-woman not far from the spot where the body of the murdered child had been afterwards found. The woman asked her what she did there; but she looked very strangely, and only returned a confused and unintelligible answer. She returned to the house about eight o'clock; and when one inquired where she had passed the night, she replied, that she had been looking for the child, and demanded earnestly, if any thing had been heard concerning him. When shewn the body, she fell into violent hysterics, and kept her bed for several days. The picture was then produced, which the servant had found in her pocket; and when Elizabeth, in a faltering voice, proved that it was the same which, an hour before the child had been missed, she had placed round his neck, a murmur of horror and indignation filled the court.

Justine was called on for her defence. As the trial had proceeded, her countenance had altered. Surprise, horror, and misery, were strongly expressed. Sometimes she struggled with her tears; but when she was desired to plead, she collected her powers, and spoke in an audible although variable voice:—

1   This is the first of four courtroom scenes in *Frankenstein,* all playing into the shaping of the novel as a sustained trial before the readers, who receive the several testimonies and narrations that figure as testimony into the courtroom of their own judgments.

"God knows," she said, "how entirely I am innocent. But I do not pretend that my protestations should acquit me: I rest my innocence on a plain and simple explanation of the facts which have been adduced against me; and I hope the character I have always borne will incline my judges to a favourable interpretation, where any circumstance appears doubtful or suspicious."

She then related that, by the permission of Elizabeth, she had passed the evening of the night on which the murder had been committed, at the house of an aunt at Chêne, a village situated at about a league from Geneva. On her return, at about nine o'clock, she met a man, who asked her if she had seen any thing of the child who was lost. She was alarmed by this account, and passed several hours in looking for him, when the gates of Geneva were shut, and she was forced to remain several hours of the night in a barn belonging to a cottage, being unwilling to call up the inhabitants, to whom she was well known. Unable to rest or sleep, she quitted her asylum early, that she might again endeavour to find my brother. If she had gone near the spot where his body lay, it was without her knowledge. That she had been bewildered when questioned by the market-woman, was not surprising, since she had passed a sleepless night, and the fate of poor William was yet uncertain. Concerning the picture she could give no account.

"I know," continued the unhappy victim, "how heavily and fatally this one circumstance weighs against me, but I have no power of explaining it; and when I have expressed my utter ignorance, I am only left to conjecture concerning the probabilities by which it might have been placed in my pocket. But here also I am checked. I believe that I have no enemy on earth, and none surely would have been so wicked as to destroy me wantonly. Did the murderer place it there? I know of no opportunity afforded him for so doing; or if I had, why should he have stolen the jewel, to part with it again so soon?

"I commit my cause to the justice of my judges, yet I see no room for hope. I beg permission to have a few witnesses examined concerning my character; and if their testimony shall not over-weigh my supposed guilt, I must be condemned, although I would pledge my salvation on my innocence."

Several witnesses were called, who had known her for many years, and they spoke well of her; but fear, and hatred of the crime of which they supposed her guilty, rendered them timorous, and unwilling to come forward. Elizabeth saw even this last resource, her excellent dispositions and irreproachable conduct, about to fail the accused, when, although violently agitated, she desired per-mission to address the court.

"I am," said she, "the cousin of the unhappy child who was mur-dered, or rather his sister, for I was educated by and have lived with his parents ever since and even long before his birth. It may there-fore be judged indecent in me to come forward on this occasion; but when I see a fellow-creature about to perish through the cow-ardice of her pretended friends, I wish to be allowed to speak, that I may say what I know of her character. I am well acquainted with the accused. I have lived in the same house with her, at one time for five, and at another for nearly two years. During all that period she appeared to me the most amiable and benevolent of human creatures. She nursed Madame Frankenstein, my aunt, in her last illness with the greatest affection and care; and afterwards attended her own mother during a tedious illness, in a manner that excited the admiration of all who knew her. After which she again lived in my uncle's house, where she was beloved by all the family. She was warmly attached to the child who is now dead, and acted towards

2   Mary Shelley revises the legal silencing of women in court trials that her mother dramatized in her political novel, *The Wrongs of Woman* (1798): the heroine, Maria, is not allowed to testify at her lover Henry Darnford's trial for criminal commerce (adultery, for which only the man can be held responsible). Elizabeth is allowed to testify, but the horror is its effect opposite to what she intended, increasing the ire against Justine for betraying such a friend. Meanwhile Victor remains self-suppressed in his hysteria.

him like a most affectionate mother. For my own part, I do not hesitate to say, that, notwithstanding all the evidence produced against her, I believe and rely on her perfect innocence. She had no temptation for such an action: as to the bauble on which the chief proof rests, if she had earnestly desired it, I should have willingly given it to her; so much do I esteem and value her."

Excellent Elizabeth! A murmur of approbation was heard; but it was excited by her generous interference, and not in favour of poor Justine, on whom the public indignation was turned with renewed violence, charging her with the blackest ingratitude. She herself wept as Elizabeth spoke, but she did not answer. My own agitation and anguish was extreme during the whole trial. I believed in her innocence; I knew it. Could the dæmon, who had (I did not for a minute doubt) murdered my brother, also in his hellish sport have betrayed the innocent to death and ignominy? I could not sustain the horror of my situation; and when I perceived that the popular voice, and the countenances of the judges, had already condemned my unhappy victim, I rushed out of the court in agony.[2] The tortures of the accused did not equal mine; she was sustained by innocence, but the fangs of remorse tore my bosom, and would not forego their hold.

I passed a night of unmingled wretchedness. In the morning I went to the court; my lips and throat were parched. I dared not ask the fatal question; but I was known, and the officer guessed the cause of my visit. The ballots had been thrown; they were all black, and Justine was condemned.

I cannot pretend to describe what I then felt. I had before experienced sensations of horror; and I have endeavoured to bestow upon them adequate expressions, but words cannot convey an idea of the heart-sickening despair that I then endured. The person to whom I addressed myself added, that Justine had already confessed her guilt. "That evidence," he observed, "was hardly required in so glaring a case, but I am glad of it; and, indeed, none of our judges like to condemn a criminal upon circumstantial evidence, be it ever so decisive."

When I returned home, Elizabeth eagerly demanded the result.

"My cousin," replied I, "it is decided as you may have expected; all judges had rather that ten innocent should suffer, than that one guilty should escape. But she has confessed."

This was a dire blow to poor Elizabeth, who had relied with firmness upon Justine's innocence. "Alas!" said she, "how shall I ever again believe in human benevolence? Justine, whom I loved and esteemed as my sister, how could she put on those smiles of innocence only to betray; her mild eyes seemed incapable of any severity or ill-humour, and yet she has committed a murder."

Soon after we heard that the poor victim had expressed a wish to see my cousin. My father wished her not to go; but said, that he left it to her own judgment and feelings to decide. "Yes," said Elizabeth, "I will go, although she is guilty; and you, Victor, shall accompany me: I cannot go alone." The idea of this visit was torture to me, yet I could not refuse.

We entered the gloomy prison-chamber, and beheld Justine sitting on some straw at the further end; her hands were manacled, and her head rested on her knees. She rose on seeing us enter; and when we were left alone with her, she threw herself at the feet of Elizabeth, weeping bitterly. My cousin wept also.

"Oh, Justine!" said she, "why did you rob me of my last consolation? I relied on your innocence; and although I was then very wretched, I was not so miserable as I am now."

"And do you also believe that I am so very, very wicked? Do you also join with my enemies to crush me?" Her voice was suffocated with sobs.

"Rise, my poor girl," said Elizabeth, "why do you kneel, if you are innocent? I am not one of your enemies; I believed you guilt-

Illustration for *Frankenstein* by Lynd Ward. Highlighting the monstrous aspects of human beings in judgmental rigor. Ward's woodcut captures Elizabeth's impression of the bloodthirsty courtroom at Justine's trial.

3   Justine, though horribly betrayed, voices a rare reference to the deity as a point of faith, and not just in exclamation.

4   This is the first non-Creature application of *monster*. De Sade's Justine is abused by monks. Monks and priests are frequent villains in English gothic novels, such as Matthew Lewis's book *The Monk* (1796), read by teenage Mary.

5   Milton uses this phrase in the fall of Eve:

> her rash hand in evil hour
> Forth reaching to the fruit, she pluck'd, she eat:
> Earth felt the wound, and Nature from her seat
> Sighing through all her works gave signs of woe,
> That all was lost. (*Paradise Lost* IX.780–784)

Yet far from confirming Justine as a sister to Eve, this alignment indicts the priest as monstrous bully.

less, notwithstanding every evidence, until I heard that you had yourself declared your guilt. That report, you say, is false; and be assured, dear Justine, that nothing can shake my confidence in you for a moment, but your own confession."

"I did confess; but I confessed a lie. I confessed, that I might obtain absolution; but now that falsehood lies heavier at my heart than all my other sins. The God of heaven forgive me![3] Ever since I was condemned, my confessor has besieged me; he threatened and menaced, until I almost began to think that I was the monster that he said I was.[4] He threatened excommunication and hell fire in my last moments, if I continued obdurate. Dear lady, I had none to support me; all looked on me as a wretch doomed to ignominy and perdition. What could I do? In an evil hour[5] I subscribed to a lie; and now only am I truly miserable."

She paused, weeping, and then continued— "I thought with horror, my sweet lady, that you should believe your Justine, whom your blessed aunt had so highly honoured, and whom you loved, was a creature capable of a crime which none but the devil himself could have perpetrated. Dear William! dearest blessed child! I soon shall

see you again in heaven, where we shall all be happy; and that consoles me, going as I am to suffer ignominy and death."

"Oh, Justine! forgive me for having for one moment distrusted
you. Why did you confess? But do not mourn, my dear girl; I will
every where proclaim your innocence, and force belief. Yet you
must die; you, my playfellow, my companion, my more than sister.
I never can survive so horrible a misfortune."

"Dear, sweet Elizabeth, do not weep. You ought to raise me with
thoughts of a better life, and elevate me from the petty cares of this
world of injustice and strife. Do not you, excellent friend, drive me
to despair."

"I will try to comfort you; but this, I fear, is an evil too deep and
poignant to admit of consolation, for there is no hope. Yet heaven
bless thee, my dearest Justine, with resignation, and a confidence
elevated beyond this world. Oh! how I hate its shews and mocker-
ies! when one creature is murdered, another is immediately deprived of life in a slow torturing manner; then the executioners,
their hands yet reeking with the blood of innocence, believe that
they have done a great deed. They call this *retribution*. Hateful
name! When that word is pronounced, I know greater and more
horrid punishments are going to be inflicted than the gloomiest
tyrant has ever invented to satiate his utmost revenge. Yet this is
not consolation for you, my Justine, unless indeed that you may
glory in escaping from so miserable a den. Alas! I would I were in
peace with my aunt and my lovely William, escaped from a world
which is hateful to me, and the visages of men which I abhor."

Justine smiled languidly. "This, dear lady, is despair, and not
resignation. I must not learn the lesson that you would teach me.
Talk of something else, something that will bring peace, and not
increase of misery."

6 Walton has noted Frankenstein's affliction with this biblical curse (Letter IV).

7 The sensation of *remorse,* "bitten again," is unending agony. In *The Bride of Abydos* (1813) Byron describes "the worm that will not sleep—and never dies . . . That winds around and tears the quivering heart!" (2.644–649). Hell is where the "worm dieth not," warns Jesus (Mark 9: 44); Satan's torment is "th'undying Worm" (*Paradise Lost* VI.739).

8 This is the psychological hell of Satan, nearing the Eden he is intent to destroy:

> horror and doubt distract
> His troubled thoughts, and from the bottom stir
> The hell within him, for within him hell
> He brings, and round about him, nor from hell
> One step no more then from himself can fly
> By change of place . . . (*Paradise Lost* IV.18–23)

From this point on, allusions to *Paradise Lost* punctuate Frankenstein's (and especially his Creature's) story, as the Creature recreates Frankenstein in his own image.

During this conversation I had retired to a corner of the prison-room, where I could conceal the horrid anguish that possessed me. Despair! Who dared talked of that? The poor victim, who on the morrow was to pass the dreary boundary between life and death, felt not as I did, such deep and bitter agony. I gnashed my teeth,[6] and ground them together, uttering a groan that came from my inmost soul. Justine started. When she saw who it was, she approached me, and said, "Dear Sir, you are very kind to visit me; you, I hope, do not believe that I am guilty."

I could not answer. "No, Justine," said Elizabeth; "he is more convinced of your innocence than I was; for even when he heard that you had confessed, he did not credit it."

"I truly thank him. In these last moments I feel the sincerest gratitude towards those who think of me with kindness. How sweet is the affection of others to such a wretch as I am! It removes more than half my misfortune; and I feel as if I could die in peace, now that my innocence is acknowledged by you, dear lady, and your cousin."

Thus the poor sufferer tried to comfort others and herself. She indeed gained the resignation she desired. But I, the true murderer, felt the never-dying worm alive in my bosom,[7] which allowed of no hope or consolation. Elizabeth also wept, and was unhappy; but her's also was the misery of innocence, which, like a cloud that passes over the fair moon, for a while hides, but cannot tarnish its brightness. Anguish and despair had penetrated into the core of my heart; I bore a hell within me,[8] which nothing could extinguish. We staid several hours with Justine; and it was with great difficulty that Elizabeth could tear herself away. "I wish," cried she, "that I were to die with you; I cannot live in this world of misery."

Justine assumed an air of cheerfulness, while she with difficulty repressed her bitter tears. She embraced Elizabeth, and said, in a voice of half-suppressed emotion, "Farewell, sweet lady, dearest Elizabeth, my beloved and only friend; may heaven in its bounty bless and preserve you; may this be the last misfortune that you will ever suffer. Live, and be happy, and make others so."

As we returned, Elizabeth said, "You know not, my dear Victor, how much I am relieved, now that I trust in the innocence of this unfortunate girl. I never could again have known peace, if I had been deceived in my reliance on her. For the moment that I did believe her guilty, I felt an anguish that I could not have long sustained. Now my heart is lightened. The innocent suffers; but she whom I thought amiable and good has not betrayed the trust I reposed in her, and I am consoled."

Amiable cousin! such were your thoughts, mild and gentle as your own dear eyes and voice. But I—I was a wretch, and none ever conceived of the misery that I then endured.

END OF VOL. I.

FRANKENSTEIN;

OR,

THE MODERN PROMETHEUS.

———◆———

IN THREE VOLUMES.

———◆———

Did I request thee, Maker, from my clay
To mould me man ? Did I solicit thee
From darkness to promote me ?———
                          PARADISE LOST.

———

VOL. II.

———

London:
PRINTED FOR
LACKINGTON, HUGHES, HARDING, MAVOR, & JONES,
FINSBURY SQUARE.

———

1818.

CHAPTER I

1 In an older sense of time as a train of events, the future arrives from "behind": "But at my back I always hear/ Time's winged chariot hurrying near," says the speaker of Andrew Marvell's poem *To his Coy Mistress* (21–22). Describing himself as malefactor, exile, alien, and solitary, Frankenstein is becoming more like his Creature, even as its existence becomes his most dreadful secret.

NOTHING IS MORE painful to the human mind, than, after the feelings have been worked up by a quick succession of events, the dead calmness of inaction and certainty which follows, and deprives the soul both of hope and fear. Justine died; she rested; and I was alive. The blood flowed freely in my veins, but a weight of despair and remorse pressed on my heart, which nothing could remove. Sleep fled from my eyes; I wandered like an evil spirit, for I had committed deeds of mischief beyond description horrible, and more, much more, (I persuaded myself) was yet behind.[1] Yet my heart overflowed with kindness, and the love of virtue. I had begun life with benevolent intentions, and thirsted for the moment when I should put them in practice, and make myself useful to my fellow-beings. Now all was blasted: instead of that serenity of conscience, which allowed me to look back upon the past with self-satisfaction, and from thence to gather promise of new hopes, I was seized by remorse and the sense of guilt, which hurried me away to a hell of intense tortures, such as no language can describe.

This state of mind preyed upon my health, which had entirely recovered from the first shock it had sustained. I shunned the face of man; all sound of joy or complacency was torture to me; solitude was my only consolation—deep, dark, death-like solitude.

2   So, too, Ingolstadt's gates; recall Frankenstein's night outdoors following the Creature's animation (Vol. I, Ch. IV). On March 1728, fifteen-year-old Jean-Jacques Rousseau ran away from Geneva after returning past curfew to find the city gates locked.

3   Mary Shelley conflates in Victor's reverie both happy and miserable memories from her own life in 1816: the pleasure of sailing on Lake Geneva (recounted in Letter I in *1817*) and the suicide by drowning of Percy's first wife, Harriet. Wollstonecraft, in love-despair over Gilbert Imlay, twice tried to drown herself. As a teenager, Mary read her mother's letters to Imlay, in Godwin's *Memoirs of Wollstonecraft* (1798), and may be reimaging all these desired deaths by drowning in Victor's misery here.

My father observed with pain the alteration perceptible in my disposition and habits, and endeavoured to reason with me on the folly of giving way to immoderate grief. "Do you think, Victor," said he, "that I do not suffer also? No one could love a child more than I loved your brother;" (tears came into his eyes as he spoke); "but is it not a duty to the survivors, that we should refrain from augmenting their unhappiness by an appearance of immoderate grief? It is also a duty owed to yourself; for excessive sorrow prevents improvement or enjoyment, or even the discharge of daily usefulness, without which no man is fit for society."

This advice, although good, was totally inapplicable to my case; I should have been the first to hide my grief, and console my friends, if remorse had not mingled its bitterness with my other sensations. Now I could only answer my father with a look of despair, and endeavour to hide myself from his view.

About this time we retired to our house at Belrive. This change was particularly agreeable to me. The shutting of the gates regularly at ten o'clock, and the impossibility of remaining on the lake after that hour, had rendered our residence within the walls of Geneva very irksome to me.[2] I was now free. Often, after the rest of the family had retired for the night, I took the boat, and passed many hours upon the water. Sometimes, with my sails set, I was carried by the wind; and sometimes, after rowing into the middle of the lake, I left the boat to pursue its own course, and gave way to my own miserable reflections. I was often tempted, when all was at peace around me, and I the only unquiet thing that wandered restless in a scene so beautiful and heavenly, if I except some bat, or the frogs, whose harsh and interrupted croaking was heard only when I approached the shore— often, I say, I was tempted to plunge into the silent lake, that the waters might close over me and my calamities for ever.[3] But I was restrained, when I thought of the heroic and suffering Elizabeth, whom I tenderly loved, and whose existence was bound up in mine. I thought also of my father and surviving brother: should I by my base desertion leave them exposed and unprotected to the malice of the fiend whom I had let loose among them?

At these moments I wept bitterly, and wished that peace would revisit my mind only that I might afford them consolation and happiness. But that could not be. Remorse extinguished every hope. I had been the author of unalterable evils; and I lived in daily fear, lest the monster whom I had created should perpetrate some new wickedness. I had an obscure feeling that all was not over, and that he would still commit some signal crime, which by its enormity should almost efface the recollection of the past. There was always scope for fear, so long as anything I loved remained behind. My abhorrence of this fiend cannot be conceived. When I thought of him, I gnashed my teeth, my eyes became inflamed, and I ardently wished to extinguish that life which I had so thoughtlessly bestowed. When I reflected on his crimes and malice, my hatred and revenge burst all bounds of moderation. I would have made a pilgrimage to the highest peak of the Andes, could I, when there, have precipitated him to their base. I wished to see him again, that I might wreak the utmost extent of anger on his head, and avenge the deaths of William and Justine.

Our house was the house of mourning. My father's health was deeply shaken by the horror of the recent events. Elizabeth was sad and desponding; she no longer took delight in her ordinary occupations; all pleasure seemed to her sacrilege toward the dead; eternal woe and tears she then thought was the just tribute she should pay to innocence so blasted and destroyed. She was no longer that happy creature, who in earlier youth wandered with me on the banks of the lake, and talked with ecstasy of our future prospects.

4   Elizabeth voices a progressive opposition to capital punishment, typically a slow, excruciating hanging during which members of the public were free to add their abuse. The sentence could be applied to those convicted, including teenagers, of petty crimes such as pickpocketing.

She had become grave, and often conversed of the inconstancy of fortune, and the instability of human life.

"When I reflect, my dear cousin," said she, "on the miserable death of Justine Moritz, I no longer see the world and its works as they before appeared to me. Before, I looked upon the accounts of vice and injustice, that I read in books or heard from others, as tales of ancient days, or imaginary evils; at least they were remote, and more familiar to reason than to the imagination; but now misery has come home, and men appear to me as monsters thirsting for each other's blood. Yet I am certainly unjust. Every body believed that poor girl to be guilty; and if she could have committed the crime for which she suffered, assuredly she would have been the most depraved of human creatures. For the sake of a few jewels, to have murdered the son of her benefactor and friend, a child whom she had nursed from its birth, and appeared to love as if it had been her own! I could not consent to the death of any human being;[4] but certainly I should have thought such a creature unfit to remain in the society of men. Yet she was innocent. I know, I feel she was innocent; you are of the same opinion, and that confirms me. Alas! Victor, when falsehood can look so like the truth, who can assure themselves of certain happiness? I feel if I were walking on the edge of a precipice, towards which thousands are crowding, and endeavouring to plunge me into the abyss. William and Justine were assassinated, and the murderer escapes; he walks about the world free, and perhaps respected. But even if I were condemned to suffer on the scaffold for the same crimes, I would not change places with such a wretch."

I listened to this discourse with the extremest agony. I, not in deed, but in effect, was the true murderer. Elizabeth read my anguish in my countenance, and kindly taking my hand said, "My dearest cousin, you must calm yourself. These events have affected me, God knows how deeply; but I am not so wretched as you are. There is an expression of despair, and sometimes of revenge, in your countenance, that makes me tremble. Be calm, my dear Victor; I would sacrifice my life to your peace. We surely shall be happy: quiet in our native country, and not mingling in the world, what can disturb our tranquillity?"

She shed tears as she said this, disturbing the very solace that she gave; but at the same time she smiled, that she might chase away the fiend that lurked in my heart. My father, who saw in the unhappiness that was painted in my face only an exaggeration of that sorrow which I might naturally feel, thought that an amusement suited to my taste would be the best means of restoring me to my wonted serenity. It was from this cause that he had removed to the country; and, induced by the same motive, he now proposed that we should all make an excursion to the valley of the Chamounix. I had been there before, but Elizabeth and Ernest never had; and both had often expressed an earnest desire to see the scenery of this place, which had been described to them as so wonderful and sublime.[5] Accordingly we departed from Geneva on this tour about the middle of the month of August, nearly two months after the death of Justine.

The weather was uncommonly fine; and if mine had been a sorrow to be chased away by any fleeting circumstance, this excursion would certainly have had the effect intended by my father. As it was, I was somewhat interested in the scene; it sometimes lulled, although it could not extinguish my grief. During the first day we travelled in a carriage. In the morning we had seen the mountains at a distance, towards which we gradually advanced. We perceived that the valley through which we wound, and which was formed by the river Arve, whose course we followed, closed in upon us by degrees; and when the sun had set, we beheld immense mountains

5   Such scenic descriptions reflect Mary Shelley's enthusiasm and her awareness of the popularity of travelogues, a virtual tour mediated through the author's sentiments. Her and Percy's *History of a Six Weeks Tour & c* (1817) was aimed at this market, and even Byron's *Childe Harold III* (1816) had travelogue appeal. Tourists would take these books (especially Byron's *Childe Harold*) with them as guides and companions.

Mont Blanc, from William Beattie, M.D., *Switzerland, In a Series of Views Taken Expressly for this Work by W. H. Bartlett, Esq.* (London: Virtue, circa 1838). Mont Blanc is the highest mountain in Europe, rising almost 16,000 feet above sea level; the sublimity of the prospect was a famous tourist attraction. Its summit had been attained only a few times by 1816. The Shelleys' 1817 *History of a Six Weeks Tour* closes with Percy Shelley's dizzying lyric ode, *Mont Blanc, Lines Written in the Vale of Chamouni.*

and precipices overhanging us on every side, and heard the sound of the river raging among rocks, and the dashing of waterfalls around.

The next day we pursued our journey upon mules; and as we ascended still higher, the valley assumed a more magnificent and astonishing character. Ruined castles hanging on the precipices of piny mountains; the impetuous Arve, and cottages every here and there peeping forth from among the trees, formed a scene of sin-

The Source of the Averon, by Marc Theodore Bourrit (1739–1819), from *Description des glacières de Savoye,* 1773 (English translation, Norwich, 1775–1776). The Averon is the river that descends from the glaciers of Mont Blanc, the highest mountain of the Swiss Alps, and forms part of the dramatic setting for Victor's confrontation with his Creature.

gular beauty. But it was augmented and rendered sublime by the mighty Alps, whose white and shining pyramids and domes towered above all, as belonging to another earth, the habitations of another race of beings.[6]

We passed the bridge of Pelissier, where the ravine, which the river forms, opened before us, and we began to ascend the mountain that overhangs it. Soon after we entered the valley of Chamounix. This valley is more wonderful and sublime, but not so beautiful and picturesque as that of Servox, through which we had just passed.[7] The high and snowy mountains were its immediate boundaries; but we saw no more ruined castles and fertile fields. Immense glaciers approached the road; we heard the rumbling thunder of the falling avelânche, and marked the smoke of its pas-

6   In a work that Mary read in 1814, Wollstonecraft describes the progressive "anglo-americans" of the American Revolution as "another race of beings" (*An Historical and Moral View of the . . . French Revolution* [London: Joseph Johnson, 1794], 13). Victor's fantasy is shaded with gothic irony, however, for in these mountains the Creature awaits. Wolf (133) sees in this moment a transition from Victor's initial hope of a new, grateful "species" (Vol. I, Ch. III) to his later fear that his Creature and female companion will beget a "race of devils" (Vol. III, Ch. III).

7   The language of these discriminations draws on well-known categories in eighteenth-century aesthetics. Edmund Burke's treatise *Our Ideas of the Sublime and the Beautiful* (1757) defined "sublime" phenomena as impressive, vast, arousing sensations of infinite power, and the "beautiful" as smoothness, order, and harmony. Landscape artist and tourist William Gilpin added the category of "the picturesque": a "kind of beauty which would look well in a picture," in quaint irregularities and roughness pleasing to the eye (*Essay on Prints,* 1768). He elaborated the aesthetic in *Three Essays: On Picturesque Beauty, On Picturesque Travel, and On Sketching Landscape* (1792).

8 *Aiguilles* are peaks. The Arve flows from the Mer de Glace ("Sea of Ice") through Chamonix, a village in the Savoy Alps famed for its vista of Mont Blanc's summit. In *1817* Percy Shelley recounts his group's approach to Chamonix in July 1816:

the Alps, with their innumerable glaciers on high all around, closing in the complicated windings of the single vale—forests inexpressibly beautiful, but majestic in their beauty . . . Mont Blanc was before us, but it was covered with cloud; its base, furrowed with dreadful gaps, was seen above. Pinnacles of snow intolerably bright, part of the chain connected with Mont Blanc, shone through the clouds at intervals on high. I never knew—I never imagined what mountains were before. The immensity of these aerial summits excited, when they suddenly burst upon the sight, a sentiment of extatic wonder, not unallied to madness. And remember this was all one scene, it all pressed home to our regard and our imagination. Though it embraced a vast extent of space, the snowy pyramids which shot into the bright blue sky seemed to overhang our path; the ravine, clothed with gigantic pines, and black with its depth below, so deep that the very roaring of the untameable Arve, which rolled through it, could not be heard above—all was as much our own, as if we had been the creators of such impressions in the minds of others as now occupied our own. Nature was the poet, whose harmony held our spirits more breathless than that of the divinest. (Letter IV, 150–152)

sage. Mont Blanc, the supreme and magnificent Mont Blanc, raised itself from the surrounding *aiguilles,* and its tremendous *dome* overlooked the valley.[8]

During this journey, I sometimes joined Elizabeth, and exerted myself to point out to her the various beauties of the scene. I often suffered my mule to lag behind, and indulged in the misery of reflection. At other times I spurred on the animal before my companions, that I might forget them, the world, and, more than all, myself. When at a distance, I alighted, and threw myself on the grass, weighed down by horror and despair. At eight in the evening I arrived at Chamounix. My father and Elizabeth were very much fatigued; Ernest, who accompanied us, was delighted, and in high spirits: the only circumstance that detracted from his pleasure was the south wind, and the rain it seemed to promise for the next day.

We retired early to our apartments, but not to sleep; at least I did not. I remained many hours at the window, watching the pallid lightning that played above Mont Blanc, and listening to the rushing of the Arve, which ran below my window.

CHAPTER II

THE NEXT DAY, contrary to the prognostications of our guides, was fine, although clouded. We visited the source of the Arveiron,[1] and rode about the valley until evening. These sublime and magnificent scenes afforded me the greatest consolation that I was capable of receiving. They elevated me from all littleness of feeling; and although they did not remove my grief, they subdued and tranquillized it. In some degree, also, they diverted my mind from the thoughts over which it had brooded for the last month. I returned in the evening, fatigued, but less unhappy, and conversed with my family with more cheerfulness than had been my custom for some time. My father was pleased, and Elizabeth overjoyed. "My dear cousin," said she, "you see what happiness you diffuse when you are happy; do not relapse again!"

The following morning the rain poured down in torrents, and thick mists hid the summits of the mountains. I rose early, but felt unusually melancholy. The rain depressed me; my old feelings recurred, and I was miserable. I knew how disappointed my father would be at this sudden change, and I wished to avoid him until I had recovered myself so far as to be enabled to conceal those feelings that had overpowered me. I knew that they would remain that day at the inn; and as I had ever inured myself to rain, moisture, and cold, I resolved to go alone to the summit of Montanvert. I remem-

2   With the term "necessary" Frankenstein (via Mary Shelley) is drawing on eighteenth-century philosophy, particularly that of Joseph Priestly (also a scientist of electricity) in *The Doctrine of Philosophical Necessity Illustrated, Being an Appendix to the Disquisitions relating to Matter and Spirit* (London: J. Johnson, 1777). Priestley argued that free will is an illusion: "all things, past, present, and to come, are precisely what the Author of nature really intended them to be, and has made provision for" (Section I, "Of the true State of the Question respecting Liberty and Necessity," 8).

3   This is the last half of Percy Shelley's "Mutability," a lyric in *Alastor; or, the Spirit of Solitude and Other Poems* (1816).

bered the effect that the view of the tremendous and ever-moving glacier had produced upon my mind when I first saw it. It had then filled me with a sublime ecstasy that gave wings to the soul, and allowed it to soar from the obscure world to light and joy. The sight of the awful and majestic in nature had indeed always the effect of solemnizing my mind, and causing me to forget the passing cares of life. I determined to go alone, for I was well acquainted with the path, and the presence of another would destroy the solitary grandeur of the scene.

The ascent is precipitous, but the path is cut into continual and short windings, which enable you to surmount the perpendicularity of the mountain. It is a scene terrifically desolate. In a thousand spots the traces of the winter avelanche may be perceived, where trees lie broken and strewed on the ground; some entirely destroyed, others bent, leaning upon the jutting rocks of the mountain, or transversely upon other trees. The path, as you ascend higher, is intersected by ravines of snow, down which stones continually roll from above; one of them is particularly dangerous, as the slightest sound, such as even speaking in a loud voice, produces a concussion of air sufficient to draw destruction upon the head of the speaker. The pines are not tall or luxuriant, but they are sombre, and add an air of severity to the scene. I looked on the valley beneath; vast mists were rising from the rivers which ran through it, and curling in thick wreaths around the opposite mountains, whose summits were hid in the uniform clouds, while rain poured from the dark sky, and added to the melancholy impression I received from the objects around me. Alas! why does man boast of sensibilities superior to those apparent in the brute; it only renders them more necessary beings.[2] If our impulses were confined to hunger, thirst, and desire, we might be nearly free; but now we are moved by every wind that blows, and a chance word or scene that that word may convey to us.

We rest; a dream has power to poison sleep.
    We rise; one wand'ring thought pollutes the day.
We feel, conceive, or reason; laugh or weep,
    Embrace fond woe, or cast our cares away;
It is the same: for, be it joy or sorrow,
    The path of its departure still is free.
Man's yesterday may ne'er be like his morrow;
    Nought may endure but mutability![3]

Mer de Glace, Aiguille du Géant et Grandes Jorasses, Cha-monix, France. The Mer de Glace (Sea of Ice) glacier descends on the northern slopes of the Mont Blanc range, in the Alps. With superhuman speed, the Creature bounds across the ice field that Victor traverses with painstaking caution.

Mer de Glace and Montanvert, August 1781, by Carl Ludwig Hackert (1740–1796). *Montanvert* names part of the *Mer de Glace* glacier.

It was nearly noon when I arrived at the top of the ascent. For some time I sat upon the rock that overlooks the sea of ice. A mist covered both that and the surrounding mountains. Presently a breeze dissipated the cloud, and I descended upon the glacier. The surface is very uneven, rising like the waves of a troubled sea, descending low, and interspersed by rifts that sink deep. The field of ice is almost a league in width, but I spent nearly two hours in crossing it. The opposite mountain is a bare perpendicular rock. From the side where I now stood Montanvert was exactly opposite, at the distance of a league; and above it rose Mont Blanc, in awful majesty. I remained in a recess of the rock, gazing on this wonderful and stupendous scene. The sea, or rather the vast river of ice, wound among

View of Mer de Glace from Montanvert.

its dependent mountains, whose aërial summits hung over its recesses. Their icy and glittering peaks shone in the sunlight over the clouds.[4] My heart, which was before sorrowful, now swelled with something like joy; I exclaimed—"Wandering spirits, if indeed ye wander, and do not rest in your narrow beds, allow me this faint happiness, or take me, as your companion, away from the joys of life."

As I said this, I suddenly beheld the figure of a man, at some distance, advancing towards me with superhuman speed.[5] He bounded over the crevices in the ice, among which I had walked with caution; his stature also, as he approached, seemed to exceed that of man. I was troubled: a mist came over my eyes, and I felt a faintness seize me; but I was quickly restored by the cold gale of the mountains. I perceived, as the shape came nearer (sight tremendous and abhorred!) that it was the wretch whom I had created.[6] I trem-

4 Percy supplied the last two sentences (*Notebook* 252–253), echoing the poetry of *Mont Blanc,* the sublime lyric that was the capstone of the 1817 *History.* This passage thus verges on an intertextual allusion—which an alert reader of this anonymous novel might pick up. Mary herself called Mer de Glace "the most desolate place in the world—iced mountains surround it—no sign of vegetation" (July 25, 1816, *Journal* 119), and in the novel's symbolic design she sets this "Sea of Ice" as mirror to the polar sea in the frame narrative, where Creature and Creator will again converge.

5 Making the Creature's emergence seem conjured by Frankenstein's call to the "wandering spirits," Mary Shelley revised "beheld a human figure" to "the figure of a man" (*Notebooks* 252–253), a hazier description in which the relay of *man* and *superhuman* shimmers as hallucination. In Freudian psychology, such oscillation of familiar and unfamiliar spells the return of the repressed—here a consciousness repressed in Frankenstein's filtered history.

6 Mary Shelley impressively intuits the science of psychology. Her language here not only renders the eruption of sublimation into sublime confrontation but does so (again) via the iconic "sublime" in poetic imagination, Milton's character Death, a surprise to his father Satan in Hell: "shape it might be called . . . The Monster moving onward came . . . / With horrid strides" (*Paradise Lost* II.667, 675–676).

7 This is an argument about naming. Refusing Victor's namings, Devil and dæmon, the never-named being asserts "thy creature," implying a bond, stressed by *thy,* to a creator, and by antithesis, exclusion from the human world of "fellow-creatures."

bled with rage and horror, resolving to wait his approach, and then close with him in mortal combat. He approached; his countenance bespoke bitter anguish, combined with disdain and malignity, while its unearthly ugliness rendered it almost too horrible for human eyes. But I scarcely observed this; anger and hatred had at first deprived me of utterance, and I recovered only to overwhelm him with words expressive of furious detestation and contempt.

"Devil!" I exclaimed, "do you dare approach me? and do not you fear the fierce vengeance of my arm wreaked on your miserable head? Begone, vile insect! or rather stay, that I may trample you to dust! and, oh, that I could, with the extinction of your miserable existence, restore those victims whom you have so diabolically murdered!"

"I expected this reception," said the dæmon. "All men hate the wretched; how then must I be hated, who am miserable beyond all living things! Yet you, my creator, detest and spurn me, thy creature, to whom thou art bound by ties only dissoluble by the annihilation of one of us.[7] You purpose to kill me. How dare you sport thus with life? Do your duty towards me, and I will do mine towards you and the rest of mankind. If you will comply with my conditions, I will leave them and you at peace; but if you refuse, I will glut the maw of death, until it be satiated with the blood of your remaining friends."

"Abhorred monster! fiend that thou art! the tortures of hell are too mild a vengeance for thy crimes. Wretched devil! you reproach me with your creation; come on then, that I may extinguish the spark which I so negligently bestowed."

My rage was without bounds; I sprang on him, impelled by all the feelings which can arm one being against the existence of another.

He easily eluded me, and said,

Lynd Ward, *Frankenstein.* The Creature's capacity for movement across forbidding icy terrain is well depicted here.

"Be calm! I entreat you to hear me, before you give vent to your hatred on my devoted head. Have I not suffered enough, that you seek to increase my misery? Life, although it may only be an accumulation of anguish, is dear to me, and I will defend it. Remember, thou hast made me more powerful than thyself; my height is superior to thine; my joints more supple. But I will not be tempted to set myself in opposition to thee. I am thy creature, and I will be even mild and docile to my natural lord and king, if thou wilt also perform thy part, the which thou owest me. Oh, Frankenstein,[8] be not equitable to every other, and trample upon me alone, to whom thy justice, and even thy clemency and affection, is most due. Remember that I am thy creature: I ought to be thy Adam; but I am rather the fallen angel, whom thou drivest from joy for no misdeed.[9] Every where I see bliss, from which I alone am irrevocably excluded.[10] I was benevolent and good; misery made me a fiend. Make me happy, and I shall again be virtuous."[11]

"Begone! I will not hear you. There can be no community between you and me; we are enemies. Begone, or let us try our strength in a fight, in which one must fall."

8   That the Creature knows this name suggests his research.

9   Percy added the phrasing from "whom thou drivest" (*Notebooks* 258–259), sharpening the difference from Milton's Satan. The Creature's references to Adam and Satan reflect his literacy in Genesis and *Paradise Lost,* and his alignment with Adam recalls, with fresh force, the title-page epigraph.

10   The Creature echoes Satan's lament on beholding beautiful Eden, home of the beings that God has created to replace the fallen angels (*Paradise Lost* IX.468–470).

11   The Creature's claim of affinity to the new creature Adam, rather than to Satan, "the fallen angel," rises from a hope that his sufferings are reversible rather than irrevocable. He is acutely aware of the Satan narrative. "A great proportion of the misery that wanders, in hideous forms, around the world, is allowed to arise from the negligence of parents," wrote Wollstonecraft in *Rights of Woman* (chap. XI). In her political novel, *The Wrongs of Woman* (1798), which Mary read in 1814, a hardened jail-warden and former criminal recounts her life as a bastard stepdaughter, treated in her father's home "like a creature of another species": "I had been introduced as an object of abhorrence . . . I was described as a wretch . . . I cannot help attributing the greater part of my misery, to the misfortune of having been thrown into the world without the grand support of life—a mother's affection. I had no one to love me . . . I was despised from my birth . . . I had not even the chance of being considered as a fellow-creature" (chap. 5).

12 "I tax not you, you elements, with unkindness," rages Lear on the stormy heath, dispossessed by two of his daughters (*King Lear* 3.2.16).

13 Percy Shelley added the rest of the sentence after "evil" (*Notebooks* 260–261), elaborating a scenario of revenge in the language of divine retribution.

14 Percy added "miserable origin and author" (*Notebooks* 262–263), highlighting the link of Frankenstein as "author" of horrible events to the "Author" of *Frankenstein*.

15 In this reciprocal making, the Creature remakes his creator in his own image.

"How can I move thee? Will no entreaties cause thee to turn a favourable eye upon thy creature, who implores thy goodness and compassion? Believe me, Frankenstein: I was benevolent; my soul glowed with love and humanity: but am I not alone, miserably alone? You, my creator, abhor me; what hope can I gather from your fellow-creatures, who owe me nothing? they spurn and hate me. The desert mountains and dreary glaciers are my refuge. I have wandered here many days; the caves of ice, which I only do not fear, are a dwelling to me, and the only one which man does not grudge. These bleak skies I hail, for they are kinder to me than your fellow-beings.[12] If the multitude of mankind knew of my existence, they would do as you do, and arm themselves for my destruction. Shall I not then hate them who abhor me? I will keep no terms with my enemies. I am miserable, and they shall share my wretchedness. Yet it is in your power to recompense me, and deliver them from an evil which it only remains for you to make so great, that not only you and your family, but thousands of others, shall be swallowed up in the whirlwinds of its rage.[13] Let your compassion be moved, and do not disdain me. Listen to my tale: when you have heard that, abandon or commiserate me, as you shall judge that I deserve. But hear me. The guilty are allowed, by human laws, bloody as they may be, to speak in their own defence before they are condemned. Listen to me, Frankenstein. You accuse me of murder; and yet you would, with a satisfied conscience, destroy your own creature. Oh, praise the eternal justice of man! Yet I ask you not to spare me: listen to me; and then, if you can, and if you will, destroy the work of your hands."

"Why do you call to my remembrance circumstances of which I shudder to reflect, that I have been the miserable origin and author?[14] Cursed be the day, abhorred devil, in which you first saw light! Cursed (although I curse myself) be the hands that formed you! You have made me wretched[15] beyond expression. You have

Lynd Ward, *Frankenstein*. Victor shrinks before the massive form of his Creature, whose painful narrative he is exhorted to hear.

From Whale's *Frankenstein,* 1931. Whale postpones the re-union of scientist and Creature until the film's climactic move-ment, turning the appeal for understanding into a final death combat.

left me no power to consider whether I am just to you, or not. Be-gone! relieve me from the sight of your detested form."

"Thus I relieve thee, my creator," he said, and placed his hated hands before my eyes, which I flung from me with violence; "thus I take from thee a sight which you abhor. Still thou canst listen to me, and grant me thy compassion.[16] By the virtues that I once possessed, I demand this from you. Hear my tale; it is long and strange, and the temperature of this place is not fitting to your fine sensations; come to the hut upon the mountain. The sun is yet high in the heavens; before it descends to hide itself behind yon snowy precipices, and illuminate another world, you will have heard my story, and can decide. On you it rests, whether I quit forever the neighbourhood of man, and lead a harmless life, or become the scourge of your fellow-creatures, and the author of your own speedy ruin."

As he said this, he led the way across the ice: I followed. My heart was full, and I did not answer him; but, as I proceeded, I weighed the various arguments that he had used, and determined at least to listen to his tale. I was partly urged by curiosity, and compassion confirmed my resolution. I had hitherto supposed him to be the murderer of my brother, and I eagerly sought a confirmation or denial of this opinion. For the first time, also, I felt what the duties of a creator towards his creature were, and that I ought to render him happy before I complained of his wickedness. These motives urged me to comply with his demand.[17] We crossed the ice, therefore, and ascended the opposite rock. The air was cold, and the rain again began to descend: we entered the hut, the fiend with an air of exultation, I with a heavy heart, and depressed spirits. But I consented to listen; and, seating myself by the fire which my odious companion had lighted, he thus began his tale.[18]

16   It is a stroke of genius on Mary's part to have the Creature put Frankenstein in a situation analogous to the reader of *Frankenstein,* who never beholds a visible being. This gesture also shows the Creature having learned (in a scene to come) that he may hope for compassion only from someone visually blind to his deformity and so able to hear his heartfelt eloquence.

17   In that anonymous review, Percy Shelley draws a connection to a key scene in Godwin's novel *Caleb Williams:* "The encounter and argument between Frankenstein and the Being on the sea of ice," he writes (note that he does not say Monster), "almost approaches, in effect, to the expostulation of Caleb Williams with [the villain] Falkland" (*Athenæum* 263, 730).

18   As the Creature recounts his life, his story will put Frankenstein's in a new, more complex perspective: more sympathy for him and less for his creator. Said one reviewer, "I confess that *my* interest . . . is entirely on the side of the monster. His eloquence and persuasion, of which Frankenstein complains, are so because they are truth. The justice is indisputably on his side, and his sufferings are, to me, touching to the last degree" (*Knight's Quarterly Magazine* 3 [1824], 198). Readers who have previously known *Frankenstein* only through films are often surprised by the Creature's learning and eloquence.

Mary Shelley's organization of the novel into a sequence of embedded, and gradually interactive, narratives amounts to a proto-modernist experiment in giving a history from two contrasting points of view, showing how much a "history" is a storyteller's construction. Anyone familiar with the 1790s "pamphlet wars" in England over the French Revolution (to which both Godwin and Wollstonecraft contributed) would be alert to the politics of narrative: who tells the story, with what purpose, with what distributions of sympathy and judgment. The Creature's narrative is no naïve rendition, but carefully, desperately crafted to achieve specific ends.

1 Mary Shelley reflects Volney's description of primitive humanity in *Ruins of Empires* (1792), a book from which the Creature learns (Chap. V). She expects readers to recognize the ironic contrast with Adam's recollection to his Creator of his earliest memories (*Paradise Lost* VIII.250–300). Adam awakens in overflowing joy, automatic knowledge, and capable speech: "to speak I try'd, and forthwith spake, / My tongue obey'd, and readily could name / Whate're I saw" (271–273). His account begins:

> For man to tell how human Life began
> Is hard; for who him self beginning knew?
> Desire with thee still longer to converse
> Induc'd me. As new wak'd from soundest sleep
> Soft on the flow'ry herb I found me laid,
> In balmy Sweat, which with his beams the sun
> Soon dry'd, and on the reeking moisture fed.
> Strait toward heav'n my wondring Eyes I turn'd,
> And gaz'd a while the ample sky, till rais'd
> By quick instinctive motion up I sprung,
> As thitherward endevoring, and upright
> Stood on my feet: about me round I saw
> Hill, dale, and shady woods, and sunny plains,
> And liquid lapse of murmuring streams; by these,
> Creatures that liv'd, and mov'd, and walk'd, or flew,
> Birds on the branches warbling; all things smil'd,
> With fragrance and with joy my heart o'erflow'd. (250–266)

2 Adam and Eve had no need of clothing before the Fall. The clothes would be Frankenstein's, hence a doubling, or the Creature as a perverse mirror of his creator.

3 Having to fend for himself on a cold November night, the Creature poses a sharp contradiction to the sentimental mythology of natural harmony popularized by Rousseau's "noble savage" and refreshed by Wordsworth's poetry of childhood bliss (though with dark intervals, which come to the fore in this chapter).

4 The Creature's story allows us to sympathize with his first naïve sensations, an effect Mary Shelley later elucidated, or compromised, with a footnote: "The moon" (*1823*, I: 215; *1831*, 87).

CHAPTER III

IT IS WITH considerable difficulty that I remember the original æra of my being: all the events of that period appear confused and indistinct. A strange multiplicity of sensations seized me, and I saw, felt, heard, and smelt, at the same time; and it was, indeed, a long time before I learned to distinguish between the operations of my various senses. By degrees, I remember, a stronger light pressed upon my nerves, so that I was obliged to shut my eyes. Darkness then came over me, and troubled me; but hardly had I felt this, when, by opening my eyes, as I now suppose, the light poured in upon me again. I walked, and, I believe, descended; but I presently found a great alteration in my sensations. Before, dark and opaque bodies had surrounded me, impervious to my touch or sight; but I now found that I could wander on at liberty, with no obstacles which I could not either surmount or avoid. The light became more and more oppressive to me; and, the heat wearying me as I walked, I sought a place where I could receive shade. This was the forest near Ingolstadt; and here I lay by the side of a brook resting from my fatigue, until I felt tormented by hunger and thirst. This roused me from my nearly dormant state, and I ate some berries which I found hanging on the trees, or lying on the ground. I slaked my thirst at the brook; and then lying down, was overcome by sleep.[1]

"It was dark when I awoke; I felt cold also, and half-frightened as it were instinctively, finding myself so desolate. Before I had quitted your apartment, on a sensation of cold, I had covered myself with some clothes; but these were insufficient to secure me from the dews of night.[2] I was a poor, helpless, miserable wretch; I knew, and could distinguish, nothing; but, feeling pain invade me on all sides, I sat down and wept.[3]

"Soon a gentle light stole over the heavens, and gave me a sensation of pleasure. I started up, and beheld a radiant form rise from among the trees.[4] I gazed with a kind of wonder. It moved slowly, but it enlightened my path; and I again went out in search of berries. I was still cold, when under one of the trees I found a huge cloak, with which I covered myself, and sat down upon the ground. No distinct ideas occupied my mind; all was confused. I felt light, and hunger, and thirst, and darkness; innumerable sounds rung in my ears, and on all sides various scents saluted me: the only object that I could distinguish was the bright moon, and I fixed my eyes on that with pleasure.

"Several changes of day and night passed, and the orb of night had greatly lessened when I began to distinguish my sensations from each other. I gradually saw plainly the clear stream that supplied me with drink, and the trees that shaded me with their foliage. I was delighted when I first discovered that a pleasant sound, which often saluted my ears, proceeded from the throats of the little winged animals who had often intercepted the light from my eyes. I began also to observe, with greater accuracy, the forms that surrounded me, and to perceive the boundaries of the radiant roof of light which canopied me. Sometimes I tried to imitate the pleasant songs of the birds, but was unable. Sometimes I wished to express my sensations in my own mode, but the uncouth and inarticulate sounds which broke from me frightened me into silence again.[5]

Mary Shelley's manuscript of the first page of the Creature's story.

5   This episode evokes Wordsworth's untitled lyric about the "Boy of Winander" (*Lyrical Ballads*, 1800), whose calling to "responsive" birds intimates his harmony with nature, spiritualized in "pauses of deep silence." Unlike him and unlike Milton's Adam, the Creature is repelled by the sound of his own voice. Mary Shelley was struck by such a moment in the stage play: "Cooke played ————————'s part extremely well—his seeking as it were for support—his trying to grasp at the sounds he heard—. . . well imagined & executed" (*Letters MWS* 1: 378).

FRONTISPIECE.

The Wild Boy,
found in the Woods
in Aveyron.

Printed for R.Phillips, N.°71, S.! Pauls Church Yard, March.1.1802.

E. M. Itard, *An historical account of the discovery and education of a savage man, or: of the first developments, physical and moral, of the young savage caught in the woods near Aveyron in the year 1798* (France, 1801; London: Richard Phillips, 1802). The public spectacle and later story of this "wild child" fascinated a European audience already enchanted by the lore of "the noble savage" and influenced by Rousseau's *Émile* (1762), advancing an ideal of "natural" childhood untouched by social corruptions. A similar mythology informs William Blake's *Songs of Innocence* (1789) and William Wordsworth's poetry of childhood in *Lyrical Ballads* (1798 and 1800).

"The moon had disappeared from the night, and again, with a lessened form, shewed itself, while I still remained in the forest. My sensations had, by this time, become distinct, and my mind received every day additional ideas. My eyes became accustomed to the light, and to perceive objects in their right forms; I distinguished the insect from the herb, and, by degrees, one herb from another. I found that the sparrow uttered none but harsh notes, whilst those of the blackbird and thrush were sweet and enticing.

"One day, when I was oppressed by cold, I found a fire which had been left by some wandering beggars, and was overcome with delight at the warmth I experienced from it. In my joy I thrust my hand into the live embers, but quickly drew it out again with a cry of pain. How strange, I thought, that the same cause should produce such opposite effects! I examined the materials of the fire, and to my joy found it to be composed of wood. I quickly collected some branches; but they were wet, and would not burn. I was pained at this, and sat still watching the operation of the fire. The wet wood which I had placed near the heat dried, and itself became inflamed. I reflected on this; and, by touching the various branches, I discovered the cause, and busied myself in collecting a great quantity of wood, that I might dry it, and have a plentiful supply of fire.[6] When night came on, and brought sleep with it, I was in the greatest fear lest my fire should be extinguished. I covered it carefully with dry wood and leaves, and placed wet branches upon it; and then, spreading my cloak, I lay on the ground, and sunk into sleep.

"It was morning when I awoke, and my first care was to visit the fire. I uncovered it, and a gentle breeze quickly fanned it into a flame. I observed this also, and contrived a fan of branches, which roused the embers when they were nearly extinguished. When night came again, I found, with pleasure, that the fire gave light as well as heat; and that the discovery of this element was useful to me in my food; for I found some of the offals that the travellers had left had been roasted, and tasted much more savoury than the berries I gathered from the trees. I tried, therefore, to dress my food in the same manner, placing it on the live embers. I found that the berries were spoiled by this operation, and the nuts and roots much improved.[7]

"Food, however, became scarce; and I often spent the whole day searching in vain for a few acorns to assuage the pangs of hunger. When I found this, I resolved to quit the place that I had hitherto inhabited, to seek for one where the few wants I experienced would be more easily satisfied. In this emigration, I exceedingly lamented the loss of the fire which I had obtained through accident, and knew not how to re-produce it. I gave several hours to the serious consideration of this difficulty; but I was obliged to relinquish all attempt to supply it; and, wrapping myself up in my cloak, I struck across the wood towards the setting sun.[8] I passed three days in these rambles, and at length discovered the open country. A great fall of snow had taken place the night before, and the fields were of one uniform white; the appearance was disconsolate, and I found my feet chilled by the cold damp substance that covered the ground.

"It was about seven in the morning, and I longed to obtain food and shelter; at length I perceived a small hut, on a rising ground, which had doubtless been built for the convenience of some shepherd. This was a new sight to me; and I examined the structure with great curiosity. Finding the door open, I entered. An old man sat in it, near a fire, over which he was preparing his breakfast. He turned on hearing a noise; and, perceiving me, shrieked loudly, and, quitting the hut, ran across the fields with a speed of which his debilitated form hardly appeared capable. His appearance, different from any I had ever before seen, and his flight, somewhat surprised me. But I was enchanted by the appearance of the hut:

6 The Creature's discovery of fire reenacts the early history of humankind; it is a modern, experiential translation of the myth of fire-giving Prometheus.

7 The childlike Creature continues to follow the course of the human species, discovering cooking by trial and error. In this experimental resourcefulness and initiative he also shows himself to be the reflection of his scientist-maker.

8 Meager as it was, this is a "paradise lost."

9 Milton's Latin coinage for "city of all the demons"; *Paradise Lost,* book I, ends with the building of "Pandæmonium, the high capital/ Of Satan and his peers" (756–757).

10 The Creature's term "barbarity" (from the Latin for *outsider*) is aimed at humankind.

here the snow and rain could not penetrate; the ground was dry; and it presented to me then as exquisite and divine a retreat as Pandæmonium appeared to the dæmons of hell after their sufferings in the lake of fire.⁹ I greedily devoured the remnants of the shepherd's breakfast, which consisted of bread, cheese, milk, and wine; the latter, however, I did not like. Overcome by fatigue, I lay down among some straw, and fell asleep.

"It was noon when I awoke; and, allured by the warmth of the sun, which shone brightly on the white ground, I determined to recommence my travels; and, depositing the remains of the peasant's breakfast in a wallet I found, I proceeded across the fields for several hours, until at sunset I arrived at a village. How miraculous did this appear! the huts, the neater cottages, and stately houses, engaged my admiration by turns. The vegetables in the gardens, the milk and cheese that I saw placed at the windows of some of the cottages, allured my appetite. One of the best of these I entered; but I had hardly placed my foot within the door, before the children shrieked, and one of the women fainted. The whole village was roused; some fled, some attacked me, until, grievously bruised by stones and many other kinds of missile weapons, I escaped to the open country, and fearfully took refuge in a low hovel, quite bare, and making a wretched appearance after the palaces I had beheld in the village. This hovel, however, joined a cottage of a neat and pleasant appearance; but, after my late dearly-bought experience, I dared not enter it. My place of refuge was constructed of wood, but so low that I could with difficulty sit upright in it. No wood, however, was placed on the earth, which formed the floor, but it was dry; and although the wind entered it by innumerable chinks, I found it an agreeable asylum from the snow and rain.

"Here then I retreated, and lay down, happy to have found a shelter, however miserable, from the inclemency of the season, and still more from the barbarity of man.¹⁰

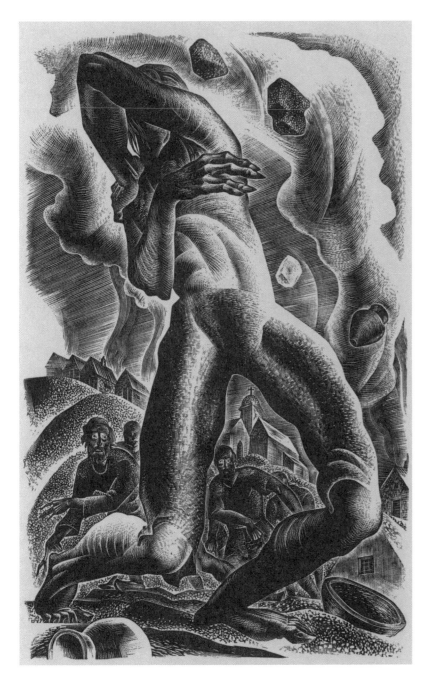

Lynd Ward, *Frankenstein.* The image at once indicts the cruel prejudices of fearful humans and solicits pity for the Creature.

"As soon as morning dawned, I crept from my kennel, that I might view the adjacent cottage, and discover if I could remain in the habitation I had found. It was situated against the back of the cottage, and surrounded on the sides which were exposed by a pig-stye and a clear pool of water. One part was open, and by that I had crept in; but now I covered every crevice by which I might be perceived with stones and wood, yet in such a manner that I might move them on occasion to pass out: all the light I enjoyed came through the stye, and that was sufficient for me.

"Having thus arranged my dwelling, and carpeted it with clean straw, I retired; for I saw the figure of a man at a distance, and I remembered too well my treatment the night before, to trust myself in his power. I had first, however, provided for my sustenance for that day, by a loaf of course bread, which I purloined, and a cup with which I could drink, more conveniently than from my hand, of the pure water which flowed by my retreat. The floor was a little raised, so that it was kept perfectly dry, and by its vicinity to the chimney of the cottage it was tolerably warm.

"Being thus provided, I resolved to reside in this hovel, until something should occur which might alter my determination. It was indeed a paradise, compared to the bleak forest, my former residence, the rain-dropping branches, and dank earth. I ate my breakfast with pleasure, and was about to remove a plank to procure myself a little water, when I heard a step, and, looking through a small chink, I beheld a young creature, with a pail on her head, passing before my hovel. The girl was young and of gentle demeanour, unlike what I have since found cottagers and farm-house servants to be. Yet she was meanly dressed, a coarse blue petticoat and a linen jacket being her only garb; her fair hair was plaited, but not adorned; she looked patient, yet sad. I lost sight of her; and in about a quarter of an hour she returned, bearing the pail, which was now partly filled with milk. As she walked along, seemingly incommoded by the burden, a young man met her, whose countenance expressed a deeper despondence. Uttering a few sounds[11] with an air of melancholy, he took the pail from her head, and bore it to the cottage himself. She followed, and they disappeared. Presently I saw the young man again, with some tools in his hand, cross the field behind the cottage; and the girl was also busied, sometimes in the house, and sometimes in the yard.

"On examining my dwelling, I found that one of the windows of the cottage had formerly occupied a part of it, but the panes had been filled up with wood. In one of these was a small and almost imperceptible chink, through which the eye could just penetrate. Through this crevice, a small room was visible, white-washed and clean, but very bare of furniture. In one corner, near a small fire, sat an old man, leaning his head on his hands in a disconsolate attitude. The young girl was occupied in arranging the cottage; but presently she took something out of a drawer, which employed her hands, and she sat down beside the old man, who, taking up an instrument, began to play, and to produce sounds, sweeter than the voice of the thrush or the nightingale. It was a lovely sight, even to me, poor wretch! who had never beheld aught beautiful before. The silver hair and benevolent countenance of the aged cottager, won my reverence; while the gentle manners of the girl enticed my love. He played a sweet mournful air, which I perceived drew tears from the eyes of his amiable companion, of which the old man took no notice, until she sobbed audibly; he then pronounced a few sounds, and the fair creature, leaving her work, knelt at his feet. He raised her, and smiled with such kindness and affection, that I felt sensations of a peculiar and over-powering nature: they

11 Remembering the Creature's first utterances to his creator (Vol. I, Ch. IV), where she accepted Percy's revision of *words* to *inarticulate sounds* (*Notebooks* 100–101), Mary repeats the affect of incomprehensibleness here, revising her initial *words* to *sounds* (*Notebooks* 290–291).

12 Mary Shelley had first written "the others," then revised to this noun, more poignant for the Creature (*Notebooks* 294–295).

were a mixture of pain and pleasure, such as I had never before experienced, either from hunger or cold, warmth or food; and I withdrew from the window, unable to bear these emotions.

"Soon after this the young man returned, bearing on his shoulders a load of wood. The girl met him at the door, helped to relieve him of his burden, and, taking some of the fuel into the cottage, placed it on the fire; then she and the youth went apart into a nook of the cottage, and he shewed her a large loaf and a piece of cheese. She seemed pleased; and went into the garden for some roots and plants, which she placed in water, and then upon the fire. She afterwards continued her work, whilst the young man went into the garden, and appeared busily employed in digging and pulling up roots. After he had been employed thus about an hour, the young woman joined him, and they entered the cottage together.

"The old man had, in the meantime, been pensive; but, on the appearance of his companions,[12] he assumed a more cheerful air, and they sat down to eat. The meal was quickly dispatched. The young woman was again occupied in arranging the cottage; the old man walked before the cottage in the sun for a few minutes, leaning on the arm of the youth. Nothing could exceed in beauty the contrast between these two excellent creatures. One was old, with silver hairs and a countenance beaming with benevolence and love: the younger was slight and graceful in his figure, and his features were moulded with the finest symmetry; yet his eyes and attitude expressed the utmost sadness and despondency. The old man returned to the cottage; and the youth, with tools different from those he had used in the morning, directed his steps across the fields.

"Night quickly shut in; but, to my extreme wonder, I found that the cottagers had a means of prolonging light, by the use of tapers, and was delighted to find, that the setting of the sun did not put an end to the pleasure I experienced in watching my human neighbours. In the evening, the young girl and her companion were employed in various occupations which I did not understand; and the old man again took up the instrument, which produced the divine sounds that had enchanted me in the morning. So soon as he had finished, the youth began, not to play, but to utter sounds that were monotonous, and neither resembling the harmony of the old man's instrument or the songs of the birds; I since found that he read aloud, but at that time I knew nothing of the science of words or letters.

"The family, after having been thus occupied for a short time, extinguished their lights, and retired, as I conjectured, to rest.

CHAPTER IV

I LAY ON MY STRAW, but I could not sleep. I thought of the occurrences of the day. What chiefly struck me was the gentle manners of these people; and I longed to join them, but dared not. I remembered too well the treatment I had suffered the night before from the barbarous villagers, and resolved, whatever course of conduct I might hereafter think it right to pursue, that for the present I would remain quietly in my hovel, watching, and endeavouring to discover the motives which influenced their actions.

"The cottagers arose the next morning before the sun. The young woman arranged the cottage, and prepared the food; and the youth departed after the first meal.

"This day was passed in the same routine as that which preceded it. The young man was constantly employed out of doors, and the girl in various laborious occupations within. The old man, whom I soon perceived to be blind, employed his leisure hours on his instrument, or in contemplation. Nothing could exceed the love and respect which the younger cottagers exhibited towards their venerable companion. They performed towards him every little office of affection and duty with gentleness; and he rewarded them by his benevolent smiles.

"They were not entirely happy. The young man and his companion often went apart, and appeared to weep. I saw no cause for their unhappiness; but I was deeply affected by it. If such lovely creatures were miserable, it was less strange that I, an imperfect and solitary being, should be wretched. Yet why were these gentle beings unhappy? They possessed a delightful house (for such it was in my eyes), and every luxury; they had a fire to warm them when chill, and delicious viands when hungry; they were dressed in excellent clothes; and, still more, they enjoyed one another's company and speech, interchanging each day looks of affection and kindness. What did their tears imply? Did they really express pain? I was at first unable to solve these questions; but perpetual attention, and time, explained to me many appearances which were at first enigmatic.

"A considerable period elapsed before I discovered one of the causes of the uneasiness of this amiable family; it was poverty: and they suffered that evil in a very distressing degree. Their nourishment consisted entirely of the vegetables of their garden, and the milk of one cow, who gave very little during the winter, when its masters could scarcely procure food to support it. They often, I believe, suffered the pangs of hunger very poignantly, especially the two younger cottagers; for several times they placed food before the old man, when they reserved none for themselves.

"This trait of kindness moved me sensibly. I had been accustomed, during the night, to steal a part of their store for my own consumption; but when I found that in doing this I inflicted pain on the cottagers, I abstained, and satisfied myself with berries, nuts, and roots, which I gathered from a neighbouring wood.[1]

"I discovered also another means through which I was enabled to assist their labours. I found that the youth spent a great part of each day in collecting wood for the family fire; and, during the night, I often took his tools, the use of which I quickly discovered, and brought home firing sufficient for the consumption of several days.[2]

1 The proto-literate Creature "reads" the figures before him with an emotional sympathy that leads to an ethical decision to modify his harmful behavior.

2 The Creature's interest in the family inspires benevolent action: bringing "firing," he qualifies as a "modern Prometheus." The German locale conjures the good woodland spirits of fairy tales (the Grimm brothers began to publish their collections in 1812).

3 *Felix* means *fortunate; Agatha, beautiful.* Critic U. C. Knoepfl-macher, noting that *daughter* is not among her namings, discerns a trace of Shelley's rejection by her father.

4 Capable in an implicit "reading" of his situation, the Creature now desires the science of language, the capacity to interpret words. One of the fascinations of Shelley's day was "The Wild Child of Aveyron" or "Victor of Aveyron," found in the woods of southern France in 1797 (like the Creature, he seems to have been able to survive in the cold). After much patient education, he was able to spell L.A.I.T. and understand its reference to milk (E. M. Itard, *An Historical Account of the Discovery and Education of a Savage Man, or The First Developments, Physical and Moral, of the Young Savage Caught in the Woods Near Aveyron in the Year 1798* [London: Richard Phillips, 1802], 136–138).

"I remember, the first time that I did this, the young woman, when she opened the door in the morning, appeared greatly astonished on seeing a great pile of wood on the outside. She uttered some words in a loud voice, and the youth joined her, who also expressed surprise. I observed, with pleasure, that he did not go to the forest that day, but spent it in repairing the cottage and, cultivating the garden.

"By degrees I made a discovery of still greater moment. I found that these people possessed a method of communicating their experience and feelings to one another by articulate sounds. I perceived that the words they spoke sometimes produced pleasure or pain, smiles or sadness, in the minds and countenances of the hearers. This was indeed a godlike science, and I ardently desired to become acquainted with it. But I was baffled in every attempt I made for this purpose. Their pronunciation was quick; and the words they uttered, not having any apparent connexion with visible objects, I was unable to discover any clue by which I could unravel the mystery of their reference. By great application, however, and after having remained during the space of several revolutions of the moon in my hovel, I discovered the names that were given to some of the most familiar objects of discourse: I learned and applied the words *fire, milk, bread,* and *wood.* I learned also the names of the cottagers themselves. The youth and his companion had each of them several names, but the old man had only one, which was *father.* The girl was called *sister,* or *Agatha;* and the youth *Felix, brother,* or *son.*[3] I cannot describe the delight I felt when I learned the ideas appropriated to each of these sounds, and was able to pronounce them. I distinguished several other words, without being able as yet to understand or apply them; such as *good, dearest, unhappy.*[4]

"I spent the winter in this manner. The gentle manners and beauty of the cottagers greatly endeared them to me: when they were unhappy, I felt depressed; when they rejoiced, I sympathized in their joys. I saw few human beings beside them; and if any other happened to enter the cottage, their harsh manners and rude gait only enhanced to me the superior accomplishments of my friends.[5] The old man, I could perceive, often endeavoured to encourage his children, as sometimes I found that he called them, to cast off their melancholy. He would talk in a cheerful accent, with an expression of goodness that bestowed pleasure even upon me. Agatha listened with respect, her eyes sometimes filled with tears, which she endeavoured to wipe away unperceived; but I generally found that her countenance and tone were more cheerful after having listened to the exhortations of her father. It was not thus with Felix. He was always the saddest of the groupe; and, even to my unpractised senses, he appeared to have suffered more deeply than his friends. But if his countenance was more sorrowful, his voice was more cheerful than that of his sister, especially when he addressed the old man.

"I could mention innumerable instances, which, although slight, marked the dispositions of these amiable cottagers. In the midst of poverty and want, Felix carried with pleasure to his sister the first little white flower that peeped out from beneath the snowy ground. Early in the morning before she had risen, he cleared away the snow that obstructed her path to the milk-house, drew water from the well, and brought the wood from the out-house, where, to his perpetual astonishment, he found his store always replenished by an invisible hand. In the day, I believe, he worked sometimes for a neighbouring farmer, because he often went forth, and did not return until dinner, yet brought no wood with him. At other times he worked in the garden; but, as there was little to do in the frosty season, he read to the old man and Agatha.

5   This is his first claim on the family with the pronoun *my*. The pathetic delusion in this history is cast to appeal to Frankenstein's sympathy. We also see that the Creature is a creature of the times: his admiration is strongly marked by class difference. Class judgments pervade *Frankenstein* with disastrous recoil on the Creature's self-regard. Contrast the Creature's attitude on p. 198.

6 This is a poignantly designed paragraph, beginning with "perfect forms" defined by "grace, beauty, and delicate complexions" and ending with a "miserable deformity" doomed to "fatal effects." The scene evokes, by contrast, the myth of Narcissus fatally enamored by his own reflection (Ovid, *Metamorphoses* 3: 407–431), and directly alludes to the verse in *Paradise Lost* of Eve's naïve enamoration of her reflection, a figure of "sympathy and love" (before she meets Adam, her designated superior):

> As I bent down to look, just opposite,
> A Shape within the watry gleam appear'd
> Bending to look on me: I started back,
> It started back; but pleas'd I soon return'd,
> Pleas'd it return'd as soon with answering looks
> Of sympathy and love: there I had fix'd
> Mine eyes till now, and pin'd with vain desire,
> Had not a voice thus warn'd me, What thou seest,
> What there thou seest, fair creature is thy self . . . (IV.460–
> 468)

Jonathan Swift may have had this passage in mind in *Gulliver's Travels* (1726–1735); Mary Shelley was reading it in 1816. Charmed by the civilized equine Houyhnhnms and disgusted with the vicious deformed Yahoo species, Gulliver is shocked by his kinship with the latter: "When I happened to behold the Reflection of my own Form in a Lake or fountain, I turned away my Face in Horror and detestation of my self; and could not endure the Sight of a common Yahoo" (Part IV).

"This reading had puzzled me extremely at first; but, by degrees, I discovered that he uttered many of the same sounds when he read as when he talked. I conjectured, therefore, that he found on the paper signs for speech which he understood, and I ardently longed to comprehend these also; but how was that possible, when I did not even understand the sounds for which they stood as signs? I improved, however, sensibly in this science, but not sufficiently to follow up any kind of conversation, although I applied my whole mind to the endeavour: for I easily perceived that, although I eagerly longed to discover myself to the cottagers, I ought not to make the attempt until I had first become master of their language; which knowledge might enable me to make them overlook the deformity of my figure; for with this also the contrast perpetually presented to my eyes had made me acquainted.

"I had admired the perfect forms of my cottagers—their grace, beauty, and delicate complexions: but how was I terrified when I viewed myself in a transparent pool![6] At first I started back, unable to believe that it was indeed I who was reflected in the mirror; and when I became fully convinced that I was in reality the monster that I am, I was filled with the bitterest sensations of despondence and mortification. Alas! I did not yet entirely know the fatal effects of this miserable deformity.

"As the sun became warmer, and the light of day longer, the snow vanished, and I beheld the bare trees and the black earth. From this time Felix was more employed; and the heart-moving indications of impending famine disappeared. Their food, as I afterwards found, was coarse, but it was wholesome; and they procured a sufficiency of it. Several new kinds of plants sprung up in the garden, which they dressed; and these signs of comfort increased daily as the season advanced.

"The old man, leaning on his son, walked each day at noon, when it did not rain, as I found it was called when the heavens

Lynd Ward, *Frankenstein,* renders a dark parody of Narcissus.

poured forth its waters. This frequently took place; but a high wind quickly dried the earth, and the season became far more pleasant than it had been.

"My mode of life in my hovel was uniform. During the morning I attended the motions of the cottagers; and when they were dispersed in various occupations, I slept: the remainder of the day was spent in observing my friends. When they had retired to rest, if there was any moon, or the night was star-light, I went into the woods, and collected my own food and fuel for the cottage. When I returned, as often as it was necessary, I cleared their path from the snow, and performed those offices that I had seen done by Felix. I afterwards found that these labours, performed by an invisible hand, greatly astonished them; and once or twice I heard them, on these occasions, utter the words *good spirit, wonderful;* but I did not then understand the signification of these terms.

"My thoughts now became more active, and I longed to discover the motives and feelings of these lovely creatures; I was inquisitive to know why Felix appeared so miserable, and Agatha so sad. I thought (foolish wretch!) that it might be in my power to restore happiness to these deserving people. When I slept, or was absent, the forms of the venerable blind father, the gentle Agatha, and the excellent Felix, flitted before me. I looked upon them as superior beings, who would be the arbiters of my future destiny. I formed in my imagination a thousand pictures of presenting myself to them, and their reception of me. I imagined that they would be disgusted, until, by my gentle demeanour and conciliating words, I should first win their favour, and afterwards their love.

"These thoughts exhilarated me, and led me to apply with fresh ardour to the acquiring the art of language. My organs were indeed harsh, but supple; and although my voice was very unlike the soft music of their tones, yet I pronounced such words as I understood with tolerable ease. It was as the ass and the lap-dog; yet surely the gentle ass whose intentions were affectionate, although his manners were rude, deserved better treatment than blows and execration.[7]

"The pleasant showers and genial warmth of spring greatly altered the aspect of the earth. Men, who before this change seemed to have been hid in caves, dispersed themselves, and were employed in various arts of cultivation. The birds sang in more cheerful notes, and the leaves began to bud forth on the trees. Happy, happy earth! fit habitation for gods, which, so short a time before, was bleak, damp, and unwholesome.[8] My spirits were elevated by the enchanting appearance of nature; the past was blotted from my memory, the present was tranquil, and the future gilded by bright rays of hope, and anticipations of joy."

7 In one of Jean de La Fontaine's immensely popular seventeenth-century *Fables* (Book IV.5)—based on Aesop and rendered by Godwin in *Fables Ancient and Modern* (1805) as "The Ass and the Lap-dog"—an ass, seeing the farmer's lapdog doted on for dancing about, tries to dance and then sits on his master's lap for an expected reward, only to find himself ridiculed and beaten. More obliquely in the background is Jemima's recollection of her pathetic efforts to solicit a modicum of the affection from her stepmother that her spoiled half-sister enjoys, receiving only contemptuous blows instead (*Wrongs of Woman,* Chap. V).

8 The Creature mirrors Satan's first morning in the Garden of Eden (*Paradise Lost* IX).

1   Here is a sign that this story is both deeply felt and carefully crafted. The Creature is remaking himself as a character able to "move" Victor (and implicitly us) to sympathy.

2   In the best-known, often parodied, version of this scene, in James Whale's sequel, the tender yet campy masterpiece *The Bride of Frankenstein* (1935), a blind old man, a lonely solitary, is grateful for the sudden company of the Creature, whom he feeds and cares for. He teaches the Creature the "godlike science" of language and shares the pleasures of food, wine, cigars, and, friendship.

CHAPTER V

I NOW HASTEN to the more moving part of my story. I shall relate events that impressed me with feelings which, from what I was, have made me what I am.[1]

"Spring advanced rapidly; the weather became fine, and the skies cloudless. It surprised me, that what before was desert and gloomy should now bloom with the most beautiful flowers and verdure. My senses were gratified and refreshed by a thousand scents of delight, and a thousand sights of beauty.

"It was on one of these days, when my cottagers periodically rested from labour—the old man played on his guitar,[2] and the children listened to him—I observed the countenance of Felix was melancholy beyond expression: he sighed frequently; and once his father paused in his music, and I conjectured by his manner that he inquired the cause of his son's sorrow. Felix replied in a cheerful accent, and the old man was recommencing his music, when some one tapped at the door.

"It was a lady on horseback, accompanied by a countryman as a guide. The lady was dressed in a dark suit, and covered with a thick black veil. Agatha asked a question; to which the stranger only replied by pronouncing, in a sweet accent, the name of Felix. Her voice was musical, but unlike that of either of my friends. On hearing this word, Felix came up hastily to the lady; who, when she saw him, threw up her veil, and I beheld a countenance of angelic beauty and expression. Her hair of a shining raven black, and curiously braided; her eyes were dark, but gentle, although animated; her features of a regular proportion, and her complexion wondrously fair, each cheek tinged with a lovely pink.[3]

"Felix seemed ravished with delight when he saw her, every trait of sorrow vanished from his face, and it instantly expressed a degree of ecstatic joy, of which I could hardly have believed it capable; his eyes sparkled, as his cheek flushed with pleasure; and at that moment I thought him as beautiful as the stranger. She appeared affected by different feelings; wiping a few tears from her lovely eyes, she held out her hand to Felix, who kissed it rapturously, and called her, as well as I could distinguish, his sweet Arabian.[4] She did not appear to understand him, but smiled. He assisted her to dismount, and dismissing her guide, conducted her into the cottage. Some conversation took place between him and his father; and the young stranger knelt at the old man's feet, and would have kissed his hand, but he raised her, and embraced her affectionately.

"I soon perceived, that although the stranger uttered articulate sounds, and appeared to have a language of her own, she was neither understood by, nor herself understood, the cottagers. They made many signs which I did not comprehend; but I saw that her presence diffused gladness through the cottage, dispelling their sorrow as the sun dissipates the morning mists. Felix seemed peculiarly happy, and with smiles of delight welcomed his Arabian. Agatha, the ever-gentle Agatha, kissed the hands of the lovely stranger; and, pointing to her brother, made signs which appeared to me to mean that he had been sorrowful until she came. Some hours passed thus, while they, by their countenances, expressed joy, the cause of which I did not comprehend. Presently I found, by the frequent recurrence of one sound which the stranger repeated after them, that she was endeavouring to learn their language; and

3 Compare the blason of this "animated" stranger with the one Frankenstein issues on beholding his animated Creature in Vol. I, Ch. IV.. Safie and the Creature are both strangers with hopes and expectations about their acceptance by this family.

4 Recall Clerval's and Frankenstein's love of Oriental poetry; this is another Eastern romance, with "Arabian" evoking an alternative to Western European standards.

5   As the last sentence of this chapter makes clear, the Creature is aware of how pathos builds not only with his repetition of *my* for his desired family, but also in his fantasy of thinking of himself and Safie as a pair: this foreigner's warm acceptance bodes well for his own hopes.

the idea instantly occurred to me, that I should make use of the same instructions to the same end. The stranger learned about twenty words at the first lesson, most of them indeed were those which I had before understood, but I profited by the others.

"As night came on, Agatha and the Arabian retired early. When they separated, Felix kissed the hand of the stranger, and said, 'Good night, sweet Safie.' He sat up much longer, conversing with his father; and, by the frequent repetition of her name, I conjectured that their lovely guest was the subject of their conversation. I ardently desired to understand them, and bent every faculty towards that purpose, but found it utterly impossible.

"The next morning Felix went out to his work; and, after the usual occupations of Agatha were finished, the Arabian sat at the feet of the old man, and, taking his guitar, played some airs so entrancingly beautiful that they at once drew tears of sorrow and delight from my eyes. She sang, and her voice flowed in a rich cadence, swelling or dying away, like a nightingale of the woods.

"When she had finished, she gave the guitar to Agatha, who at first declined it. She played a simple air, and her voice accompanied it in sweet accents, but unlike the wondrous strain of the stranger. The old man appeared enraptured, and said some words, which Agatha endeavoured to explain to Safie, and by which he appeared to wish to express that she bestowed on him the greatest delight by her music.

"The days now passed as peacefully as before, with the sole alteration, that joy had taken the place of sadness in the countenances of my friends. Safie was always gay and happy; she and I improved rapidly in the knowledge of language, so that in two months I began to comprehend most of the words uttered by my protectors.[5]

"In the meanwhile also the black ground was covered with herbage, and the green banks interspersed with innumerable flowers, sweet to the scent and the eyes, stars of pale radiance among the moonlight woods; the sun became warmer, the nights clear and balmy; and my nocturnal rambles were an extreme pleasure to me, although they were considerably shortened by the late setting and early rising of the sun; for I never ventured abroad during daylight, fearful of meeting with the same treatment I had formerly endured in the first village which I entered.

"My days were spent in close attention, that I might more speedily master the language; and I may boast that I improved more rapidly than the Arabian, who understood very little, and conversed in broken accents, whilst I comprehended and could imitate almost every word that was spoken.

"While I improved in speech, I also learned the science of letters, as it was taught to the stranger; and this opened before me a wide field for wonder and delight.

"The book from which Felix instructed Safie was Volney's *Ruins of Empires*.[6] I should not have understood the purport of this book, had not Felix, in reading it, given very minute explanations. He had chosen this work, he said, because the declamatory style was framed in imitation of the eastern authors. Through this work I obtained a cursory knowledge of history, and a view of the several empires at present existing in the world; it gave me an insight into the manners, governments, and religions of the different nations of the earth. I heard of the slothful Asiatics; of the stupendous genius and mental activity of the Grecians; of the wars and wonderful virtue of the early Romans—of their subsequent degeneration—of the decline of that mighty empire; of chivalry, christianity, and kings. I heard of the discovery of the American hemisphere, and wept with Safie over the hapless fate of its original inhabitants.

"These wonderful narrations inspired me with strange feelings. Was man, indeed, at once so powerful, so virtuous, and magnifi-

6 Published in 1791, in the wake of the French Revolution (Volney was part of the Revolutionary government), *Les Ruines; ou Méditation sur les révolutions des empires* appeared in English as *Ruins or Meditations on the Revolutions of Empires,* in 1792.

7   This social critique appears in Wollstonecraft's two Vindications, *Rights of Men* and *Rights of Woman,* and in Godwin's *Political Justice,* all studied intently by Mary.

8   The Creature puts *monster* into question as a contingent description, determined by the reactions of men. The misery of being disowned is a critical theme for the hero of Godwin's *Caleb Williams,* who describes his agony as a "deserted, solitary wretch, in the midst of my species," cast out from "the consolations of friendship," connection "with the joys and sorrows of others, and exchanging the delicious gifts of confidence and sympathy" (Vol. III, Ch. VIII): "I can safely affirm, that poverty and hunger, that endless wanderings, that a blasted character and the curses that clung to my name, were all of them slight misfortunes compared to this" (Vol. III, Ch. XIV).

cent, yet so vicious and base? He appeared at one time a mere scion of the evil principle, and at another as all that can be conceived of noble and godlike. To be a great and virtuous man appeared the highest honour that can befall a sensitive being; to be base and vicious, as many on record have been, appeared the lowest degradation, a condition more abject than that of the blind mole or harmless worm. For a long time I could not conceive how one man could go forth to murder his fellow, or even why there were laws and governments; but when I heard details of vice and bloodshed, my wonder ceased, and I turned away with disgust and loathing.

"Every conversation of the cottagers now opened new wonders to me. While I listened to the instructions which Felix bestowed upon the Arabian, the strange system of human society was explained to me. I heard of the division of property, of immense wealth and squalid poverty; of rank, descent, and noble blood.

"The words induced me to turn towards myself. I learned that the possessions most esteemed by your fellow-creatures were, high and unsullied descent united with riches. A man might be respected with only one of these acquisitions; but without either he was considered, except in very rare instances, as a vagabond and a slave, doomed to waste his powers for the profit of the chosen few. And what was I? Of my creation and creator I was absolutely ignorant; but I knew that I possessed no money, no friends, no kind of property.[7] I was, besides, endowed with a figure hideously deformed and loathsome; I was not even of the same nature as men. I was more agile than they, and could subsist upon coarser diet; I bore the extremes of heat and cold with less injury to my frame; my stature far exceeded their's. When I looked around, I saw and heard of none like me. Was I then a monster, a blot upon the earth, from which all men fled, and whom all men disowned?[8]

"I cannot describe to you the agony that these reflections inflicted upon me; I tried to dispel them, but sorrow only increased with knowledge.[9] Oh, that I had forever remained in my native wood, nor known nor felt beyond the sensations of hunger, thirst, and heat!

"Of what a strange nature is knowledge! It clings to the mind, when it has once seized on it, like a lichen on the rock. I wished sometimes to shake off all thought and feeling; but I learned that there was but one means to overcome the sensation of pain, and that was death—a state which I feared yet did not understand. I admired virtue and good feelings, and loved the gentle manners and amiable qualities of my cottagers; but I was shut out from intercourse with them, except through means which I obtained by stealth, when I was unseen and unknown, and which rather increased than satisfied the desire I had of becoming one among my fellows. The gentle words of Agatha, and the animated smiles of the charming Arabian, were not for me. The mild exhortations of the old man, and the lively conversation of the loved Felix, were not for me. Miserable, unhappy wretch!

"Other lessons were impressed upon me even more deeply. I heard of the difference of sexes; of the birth and growth of children; how the father doated on the smiles of the infant, and the lively sallies of the older child; how all the life and cares of the mother were wrapped up in the precious charge; how the mind of youth expanded and gained knowledge; of brother, sister, and all the various relationships which bind one human being to another in mutual bonds.

"But where were my friends and relations? No father had watched my infant days, no mother had blessed me with smiles and caresses; or if they had, all my past life was now a blot, a blind vacancy in which I distinguished nothing. From my earliest re-

9 Byron's Frankenstein-like tormented scholar-magician Manfred laments, "Sorrow is knowledge: they who know the most / Must mourn the deepest o'er the fatal truth, / The tree of knowledge is not that of life" (*Manfred* 1.1.10, pub. 1817). Byron's own allusion is to Adam and Eve's acquisition of fatal knowledge: their sentence of mortality, from their transgression of divine edict.

membrance I had been as I then was in height and proportion. I had never yet seen a being resembling me, or who claimed any intercourse with me. What was I? The question again recurred, to be answered only with groans.

"I will soon explain to what these feelings tended; but allow me now to return to the cottagers, whose story excited in me such various feelings of indignation, delight, and wonder, but which all terminated in additional love and reverence for my protectors (for so I loved, in an innocent, half painful self-deceit, to call them).

CHAPTER VI

SOME TIME ELAPSED before I learned the history of my friends. It was one which could not fail to impress itself deeply on my mind, unfolding as it did a number of circumstances each interesting and wonderful to one so utterly inexperienced as I was.

"The name of the old man was De Lacey. He was descended from a good family in France, where he had lived for many years in affluence, respected by his superiors, and beloved by his equals. His son was bred in the service of his country; and Agatha had ranked with ladies of the highest distinction. A few months before my arrival, they had lived in a large and luxurious city, called Paris, surrounded by friends, and possessed of every enjoyment which virtue, refinement of intellect, or taste, accompanied by a moderate fortune, could afford.

"The father of Safie had been the cause of their ruin. He was a Turkish merchant, and had inhabited Paris for many years, when, for some reason which I could not learn, he became obnoxious to the government. He was seized and cast into prison the very day that Safie arrived from Constantinople to join him. He was tried, and condemned to death. The injustice of his sentence was very flagrant; all Paris was indignant; and it was judged that his religion and wealth, rather than the crime alleged against him, had been the cause of his condemnation.[1]

2 As romantic as this moment may seem, Mary Shelley, well read in her mother's *Rights of Woman,* allows the reader to cast a critical eye on the calculations that regard a lovely girl as a prize. Felix rejects "reward" of wealth but is eager for the "reward" of his daughter. This scene may recall Godwin's recognition of his daughter as an asset in his connection to the wealthy political idealist Percy Shelley, whom he would pester for financial aid. "Godwin had encouraged Mary to set her cap at Shelley," surmises William St. Clair; "he accepted money as his price for condoning their running off together" (*The Godwins and the Shelleys* [Baltimore: Johns Hopkins University Press, 1989], 410). After first meeting Mary Godwin, P. B. Shelley told his college friend T. J. Hogg, "I speedily conceived an ardent passion to possess this inestimable treasure" (October 3, 1814; *Letters PBS* 1: 401–403).

"Felix had been present at the trial; his horror and indignation were uncontrollable, when he heard the decision of the court. He made, at that moment, a solemn vow to deliver him, and then looked around for the means. After many fruitless attempts to gain admittance to the prison, he found a strongly grated window in an unguarded part of the building, which lighted the dungeon of the unfortunate Mahometan; who, loaded with chains, waited in despair the execution of the barbarous sentence. Felix visited the grate at night, and made known to the prisoner his intentions in his favour. The Turk, amazed and delighted, endeavoured to kindle the zeal of his deliverer by promises of reward and wealth. Felix rejected his offers with contempt; yet when he saw the lovely Safie, who was allowed to visit her father, and who, by her gestures, expressed her lively gratitude, the youth could not help owning to his own mind, that the captive possessed a treasure[2] which would fully reward his toil and hazard.

"The Turk quickly perceived the impression that his daughter had made on the heart of Felix, and endeavoured to secure him more entirely in his interests by the promise of her hand in marriage, so soon as he should be conveyed to a place of safety. Felix was too delicate to accept this offer; yet he looked forward to the probability of that event as to the consummation of his happiness.

"During the ensuing days, while the preparations were going forward for the escape of the merchant, the zeal of Felix was warmed by several letters that he received from this lovely girl, who found means to express her thoughts in the language of her lover by the aid of an old man, a servant of her father's, who understood French. She thanked him in the most ardent terms for his intended services towards her father; and at the same time she gently deplored her own fate.

"I have copies of these letters; for I found means, during my residence in the hovel, to procure the implements of writing; and the letters were often in the hands of Felix or Agatha. Before I depart, I will give them to you, they will prove the truth of my tale; but at present, as the sun is already far declined, I shall only have time to repeat the substance of them to you.

"Safie related, that her mother was a Christian Arab, seized and made a slave by the Turks; recommended by her beauty, she had won the heart of the father of Safie, who married her. The young girl spoke in high and enthusiastic terms of her mother, who, born in freedom, spurned the bondage to which she was now reduced. She instructed her daughter in the tenets of her religion, and taught her to aspire to higher powers of intellect, and an independence of spirit, forbidden to the female followers of Mahomet.[3] This lady died; but her lessons were indelibly impressed on the mind of Safie, who sickened at the prospect of again returning to Asia, and the being immured within the walls of a haram, allowed only to occupy herself with puerile amusements, ill suited to the temper of her soul, now accustomed to grand ideas and a noble emulation for virtue. The prospect of marrying a Christian, and remaining in a country where women were allowed to take a rank in society, was enchanting to her.

"The day for the execution of the Turk was fixed; but, on the night previous to it, he had quitted prison, and before morning was distant many leagues from Paris. Felix had procured passports in the name of his father, sister, and himself. He had previously communicated his plan to the former, who aided the deceit by quitting his house, under the pretence of a journey, and concealed himself, with his daughter, in an obscure part of Paris.

"Felix conducted the fugitives through France to Lyons, and across Mont Cenis to Leghorn,[4] where the merchant had decided to wait a favourable opportunity of passing into some part of the Turkish dominions.

3   Such remarks appear in Wollstonecraft's *Rights of Woman,* but not on behalf of Western superiority. Educated "in the true style of Mahometanism," Englishwomen are "treated as a kind of subordinate beings, and not as a part of the human species" (Introduction). Even the esteemed English poet Milton, in a "true Mahometan strain," would "deprive us of souls, and insinuate that we were beings only designed by sweet attractive grace, and docile blind obedience, to gratify the senses of man when he can no longer soar on the wing of contemplation" (Ch. II , p. 17). Milton's Satan is cannily, resourcefully alert to God's creation of Adam and Eve as "Not equal, as thir sex not equal, seem'd; / For contemplation he and valour form'd, / For softness she and sweet attractive grace" (*Paradise Lost* IV.296–298).

4   Mt. Cenis is a pass in southern France. Leghorn (Livorno) is a major port in Tuscany, where the Shelleys would reside at various times across 1819–1820.

5 Safie is an exotic "Arabian" in distinction to "the Turk," her father, initially sympathetic but now proving the prejudices associated with the epithet.

"Safie resolved to remain with her father until the moment of his departure, before which time the Turk renewed his promise that she should be united to his deliverer; and Felix remained with them in expectation of that event; and in the mean time he enjoyed the society of the Arabian,[5] who exhibited towards him the simplest and tenderest affection. They conversed with one another through the means of an interpreter, and sometimes with the interpretation of looks; and Safie sang to him the divine airs of her native country.

"The Turk allowed this intimacy to take place, and encouraged the hopes of the youthful lovers, while in his heart he had formed far other plans. He loathed the idea that his daughter should be united to a Christian; but he feared the resentment of Felix, if he should appear lukewarm; for he knew that he was still in the power of his deliverer, if he should choose to betray him to the Italian state which they inhabited. He revolved a thousand plans by which he should be enabled to prolong the deceit until it might be no longer necessary, and secretly to take his daughter with him when he departed. His plans were facilitated by the news which arrived from Paris.

"The government of France were greatly enraged at the escape of their victim, and spared no pains to detect and punish his deliverer. The plot of Felix was quickly discovered, and De Lacey and Agatha were thrown into prison. The news reached Felix, and roused him from his dream of pleasure. His blind and aged father, and his gentle sister, lay in a noisome dungeon, while he enjoyed the free air, and the society of her whom he loved. This idea was torture to him. He quickly arranged with the Turk, that if the latter should find a favourable opportunity for escape before Felix could return to Italy, Safie should remain as a boarder at a convent at

Leghorn; and then, quitting the lovely Arabian, he hastened to Paris, and delivered himself up to the vengeance of the law, hoping to free De Lacey and Agatha by this proceeding.

"He did not succeed. They remained confined for five months before the trial took place; the result of which deprived them of their fortune, and condemned them to a perpetual exile from their native country.

"They found a miserable asylum in the cottage in Germany, where I discovered them. Felix soon learned that the treacherous Turk, for whom he and his family endured such unheard-of oppression, on discovering that his deliverer was thus reduced to poverty and impotence, became a traitor to good feeling and honour, and had quitted Italy with his daughter, insultingly sending Felix a pittance of money to aid him, as he said, in some plan of future maintenance.

"Such were the events that preyed on the heart of Felix, and rendered him, when I first saw him, the most miserable of his family. He could have endured poverty, and when this distress had been the meed of his virtue, he would have gloried in it: but the ingratitude of the Turk, and the loss of his beloved Safie, were misfortunes more bitter and irreparable. The arrival of the Arabian now infused new life into his soul.

"When the news reached Leghorn that Felix was deprived of his wealth and rank, the merchant commanded his daughter to think no more of her lover, but to prepare to return to her native country. The generous nature of Safie was outraged by this command; she attempted to expostulate with her father, but he left her angrily, reiterating his tyrannical mandate.

"A few days after, the Turk entered his daughter's apartment, and told her hastily, that he had reason to believe that his residence

6   Mary sounds a pun on the "safety" that Safie achieves, escaping the tyranny of her father, and venturing bravely on her own across Europe. Mary had entertained various names, *Amina* ("faithful") and *Maimouna* ("Fortunate"—to match "Felix"), before settling on "Safie"—a slant-echo, also perhaps, of "Saville" (Robert Walton's sister) and alluding, with a difference, to "Sophie," the maiden trained in subservience as the ideal wife for Rousseau's Émile ("Sophie" means "wisdom"). Mary Wollstonecraft focused no little contempt on Rousseau's female ideal, and it is likely that the name "Safie" is meant to evoke, with a deliberate difference, Rousseau's ideal woman. Mary Shelley's Safie is the antitype, refusing the obedient, harem-bound fate assigned to her, and exerting independent action and a desire for education worthy of Wollstonecraft.

at Leghorn had been divulged, and that he should speedily be delivered up to the French government; he had, consequently, hired a vessel to convey him to Constantinople, for which city he should sail in a few hours. He intended to leave his daughter under the care of a confidential servant, to follow at her leisure with the greater part of his property, which had not yet arrived at Leghorn.

"When alone, Safie resolved in her own mind the plan of conduct that it would become her to pursue in this emergency. A residence in Turkey was abhorrent to her; her religion and her feelings were alike adverse to it. By some papers of her father's, which fell into her hands, she heard of the exile of her lover, and learnt the name of the spot where he then resided. She hesitated some time, but at length she formed her determination. Taking with her some jewels that belonged to her, and a small sum of money, she quitted Italy, with an attendant, a native of Leghorn, but who understood the common language of Turkey, and departed for Germany.

"She arrived in safety at a town about twenty leagues from the cottage of De Lacey, when her attendant fell dangerously ill. Safie nursed her with the most devoted affection; but the poor girl died, and the Arabian was left alone, unacquainted with the language of the country, and utterly ignorant of the customs of the world. She fell, however, into good hands. The Italian had mentioned the name of the spot for which they were bound; and, after her death, the woman of the house in which they had lived took care that Safie should arrive in safety[6] at the cottage of her lover.

CHAPTER VII

SUCH WAS THE history of my beloved cottagers. It impressed me deeply. I learned, from the views of social life which it developed, to admire their virtues, and to deprecate the vices of mankind.

"As yet I looked upon crime as a distant evil; benevolence and generosity were ever present before me, inciting within me a desire to become an actor in the busy scene where so many admirable qualities were called forth and displayed. But, in giving an account of the progress of my intellect, I must not omit a circumstance which occurred in the beginning of the month of August of the same year.

"One night, during my accustomed visit to the neighbouring wood, where I collected my own food, and brought home firing for my protectors, I found on the ground a leathern portmanteau, containing several articles of dress and some books. I eagerly seized the prize, and returned with it to my hovel. Fortunately the books were written in the language the elements of which I had acquired at the cottage; they consisted of *Paradise Lost*, a volume of *Plutarch's Lives*, and the *Sorrows of Werter*.[1] The possession of these treasures gave me extreme delight; I now continually studied and exercised my mind upon these histories, whilst my friends were employed in their ordinary occupations.

1 The language is presumably French, but the Creature seems familiar with Milton's original English. In his parallel *Lives*, Greek essayist and biographer Plutarch (c. 46–c. 120) analyzed notable Greeks and Romans in terms of character strengths and weaknesses; Mary was reading this work in 1815. One of the most sensational novels of the age was Goethe's *Sorrows of Young Werther* (1774; English translation, 1779), an account of the hero's passion for Charlotte, betrothed to another. In despair, Werter commits suicide, launching a pattern for romantically alienated youth throughout Europe. With reference to her mother's suicidal despair over Gilbert Imlay, Shelley described her as "a female Werter"; this was also Godwin's epithet for Wollstonecraft in his introduction to her letters to Imlay. Godwin and Wollstonecraft were reading *Werter* together on the morning Mary was born.

2 The Creature has encountered a curriculum for an encyclopedic reflection on human relations—personal, political, and metaphysical.

3 The Creature (anachronistically) quotes line 14 of Percy Shelley's poem "Mutability" (first published in 1816).

"I can hardly describe to you the effect of these books. They produced in me an infinity of new images and feelings, that sometimes raised me to ecstasy, but more frequently sunk me into the lowest dejection.[2] In the *Sorrows of Werter,* besides the interest of its simple and affecting story, so many opinions are canvassed, and so many lights thrown upon what had hitherto been to me obscure subjects, that I found in it a never-ending source of speculation and astonishment. The gentle and domestic manners it described, combined with lofty sentiments and feelings, which had for their object something out of self, accorded well with my experience among my protectors, and with the wants which were for ever alive in my own bosom. But I thought Werter himself a more divine being than I had ever beheld or imagined; his character contained no pretension, but it sunk deep. The disquisitions upon death and suicide were calculated to fill me with wonder. I did not pretend to enter into the merits of the case, yet I inclined towards the opinions of the hero, whose extinction I wept, without precisely understanding it.

"As I read, however, I applied much personally to my own feelings and condition. I found myself similar, yet at the same time strangely unlike to the beings concerning whom I read, and to whose conversation I was a listener. I sympathized with, and partly understood them, but I was unformed in mind; I was dependent on none, and related to none. 'The path of my departure was free;'[3] and there was none to lament my annihilation. My person was hideous, and my stature gigantic: what did this mean? Who was I? What was I? Whence did I come? What was my destination? These questions continually recurred, but I was unable to solve them.

"The volume of *Plutarch's Lives* which I possessed, contained the histories of the first founders of the ancient republics. This book had a far different effect upon me from the *Sorrows of Werter.* I learned from Werter's imaginations despondency and gloom: but

Plutarch taught me high thoughts; he elevated me above the wretched sphere of my own reflections,[4] to admire and love the heroes of past ages. Many things I read surpassed my understanding and experience. I had a very confused knowledge of kingdoms, wide extents of country, mighty rivers, and boundless seas. But I was perfectly unacquainted with towns, and large assemblages of men. The cottage of my protectors had been the only school in which I had studied human nature; but this book developed new and mightier scenes of action. I read of men concerned in public affairs governing or massacring their species. I felt the greatest ardour for virtue rise within me, and abhorrence for vice, as far as I understood the signification of those terms, relative as they were, as I applied them, to pleasure and pain alone. Induced by these feelings, I was of course led to admire peaceable lawgivers, Numa, Solon, and Lycurgus, in preference to Romulus and Theseus.[5] The patriarchal lives of my protectors caused these impressions to take a firm hold on my mind; perhaps, if my first introduction to humanity had been made by a young soldier, burning for glory and slaughter, I should have been imbued with different sensations.

"But *Paradise Lost* excited different and far deeper emotions. I read it, as I had read the other volumes which had fallen into my hands, as a true history. It moved every feeling of wonder and awe that the picture of an omnipotent God warring with his creatures was capable of exciting. I often referred the several situations, as their similarity struck me, to my own. Like Adam, I was created apparently[6] united by no link to any other being in existence; but his state was far different from mine in every other respect. He had come forth from the hands of God a perfect creature, happy and prosperous, guarded by the especial care of his Creator; he was allowed to converse with, and acquire knowledge from beings of a superior nature:[7] but I was wretched, helpless, and alone. Many

4   This noun shimmers as a rueful memory of his earlier mirror scene.

5   Lycurgus (c. 820–c. 730 B.C.) brought legal order and peace to Sparta. Athenian statesman and poet Solon (c. 639–559 B.C.) was famed for ending serfdom and introducing more humane civil law. Theseus, the semi-divine king of Athens, was legendary for slaying the Minotaur. Romulus, the semi-divine co-founder of Rome, was succeeded by Numa Pompilius, famed for wisdom, compassion, and a long, peaceful reign. Romulus and Theseus were notably violent: Romulus murdered his twin brother, Remus, and led the mass rape of the Sabine women; Theseus was a serial rapist and faithless spouse of Ariadne. For a long time, neither ruler was certain of his paternity. Wolf (186) notes an arresting detail in Plutarch's account of Theseus, which may also have caught Mary Shelley's eye: when, long after his death, the Athenians exhumed his body, the remains were in the "coffin of a man of extraordinary size."

6   Mary Shelley deleted "created apparently" in *1831*.

7   In *Paradise Lost*, Book VIII (250–559), Adam recounts several conversations with his Creator; he is tutored in Eden by the "affable" Archangel Raphael; after the Fall he learns harsher lessons from Archangel Michael.

8   The Creature expresses a typically Romantic identification with Milton's alienated Satan. He explicitly patterns his sentence on Satan's first view of Adam and Eve in Eden:

> aside the devil turn'd
> For envy, yet with jealous leer malign
> Ey'd them askance, and to himself thus plain'd.
>   Sight hateful, sight tormenting! thus these two
> Imparadis'd in one another's arms
> The happier Eden, shall enjoy their fill
> Of bliss on bliss, while I to hell am thrust,
> Where neither joy nor love, but fierce desire,
> Among our other torments not the least,
> Still unfulfill'd with pain of longing pines. (*Paradise Lost*
>   IV.502–511)

9   The Creature is remembering Raphael telling Adam in *Paradise Lost*: "in his own Image hee / Created thee, in the image of GOD / Express, and thou becam'st a living soul. / Male he created thee" (VII.526–529), echoing Genesis: "And God said, Let us make man in our image, after our likeness" (1: 26). The papers the Creature cites contradict Frankenstein's claim that he was forming a "beautiful" being and was horrified at the unexpected outcome. Readers troubled by his monstrous research and monstrous neglect of responsibility may see the Creature cursed, in physical form, with his creator's moral deformity: giant egotism, scientific perversion, and physical degeneration.

10   Everything depends on the Creature's ability to represent himself in his own voice; *overlook* is self-conscious, as is *interview* (two sentences on).

times I considered Satan as the fitter emblem of my condition; for often, like him, when I viewed the bliss of my protectors, the bitter gall of envy rose within me.[8]

"Another circumstance strengthened and confirmed these feelings. Soon after my arrival in the hovel, I discovered some papers in the pocket of the dress which I had taken from your laboratory. At first I had neglected them; but now that I was able to decypher the characters in which they were written, I began to study them with diligence. It was your journal of the four months that preceded my creation. You minutely described in these papers every step you took in the progress of your work; this history was mingled with accounts of domestic occurrences. You, doubtless, recollect these papers. Here they are. Everything is related in them which bears reference to my accursed origin; the whole detail of that series of disgusting circumstances which produced it is set in view; the minutest description of my odious and loathsome person is given, in language which painted your own horrors and rendered mine ineffaceable. I sickened as I read. 'Hateful day when I received life!' I exclaimed in agony. 'Cursed creator! Why did you form a monster so hideous that even you turned from me in disgust? God in pity made man beautiful and alluring, after his own image; but my form is a filthy type of your's, more horrid from its very resemblance.[9] Satan had his companions, fellow-devils, to admire and encourage him; but I am solitary and detested.'

"These were the reflections of my hours of despondency and solitude; but when I contemplated the virtues of the cottagers, their amiable and benevolent dispositions, I persuaded myself that when they should become acquainted with my admiration of their virtues, they would compassionate me, and overlook my personal deformity.[10] Could they turn from their door one, however monstrous, who solicited their compassion and friendship? I resolved, at least, not to despair, but in every way to fit myself for an interview with them which would decide my fate. I postponed this attempt for some months longer; for the importance attached to its success inspired me with a dread lest I should fail. Besides, I found that my understanding improved so much with every day's experience, that I was unwilling to commence this undertaking until a few more months should have added to my wisdom.

"Several changes, in the mean time, took place in the cottage. The presence of Safie diffused happiness among its inhabitants; and I also found that a greater degree of plenty reigned there. Felix and Agatha spent more time in amusement and conversation, and were assisted in their labours by servants. They did not appear rich, but they were contented and happy; their feelings were serene and peaceful, while mine became every day more tumultuous. Increase of knowledge only discovered to me more clearly what a wretched outcast I was. I cherished hope, it is true; but it vanished when I beheld my person reflected in water, or my shadow in the moon-shine, even as that frail image and that inconstant shade.

"I endeavoured to crush these fears, and to fortify myself for the trial which in a few months I resolved to undergo; and sometimes I allowed my thoughts, unchecked by reason, to ramble in the fields of Paradise, and dared to fancy amiable and lovely creatures sympathizing with my feelings and cheering my gloom; their angelic countenances breathed smiles of consolation. But it was all a dream: no Eve soothed my sorrows, or shared my thoughts; I was alone. I remembered Adam's supplication to his Creator; but where was mine? he had abandoned me, and, in the bitterness of my heart, I cursed him.[11]

"Autumn passed thus. I saw, with surprise and grief, the leaves decay and fall, and nature again assume the barren and bleak appearance it had worn when I first beheld the woods and the lovely

11 The Creature refers to Adam's dream of the creation of Eve and his joyous awakening (*Paradise Lost* VIII.470–499) to the result of his appeal to God for human fellowship (379–451). Wollstonecraft quotes from this passage in *Rights of Woman* in her case for sexual equality in true fellowship. The Creature's closing phrases allude to Satan's boasts to God that he can get faithful Job "to curse thee to thy face" (1: 9).

moon. Yet I did not heed the bleakness of the weather; I was better fitted by my conformation for the endurance of cold than heat. But my chief delights were the sight of the flowers, the birds, and all the gay apparel of summer; when those deserted me, I turned with more attention towards the cottagers. Their happiness was not decreased by the absence of summer. They loved, and sympathized with one another; and their joys, depending on each other, were not interrupted by the casualties that took place around them. The more I saw of them, the greater became my desire to claim their protection and kindness; my heart yearned to be known and loved by these amiable creatures: to see their sweet looks directed towards me with affection, was the utmost limit of my ambition. I dared not think that they would turn them from me with disdain and horror. The poor that stopped at their door were never driven away. I asked, it is true, for greater treasures than a little food or rest; I required kindness and sympathy; but I did not believe myself utterly unworthy of it.

"The winter advanced, and an entire revolution of the seasons had taken place since I awoke into life. My attention, at this time, was solely directed towards my plan of introducing myself into the cottage of my protectors. I revolved many projects; but that on which I finally fixed was, to enter the dwelling when the blind old man should be alone. I had sagacity enough to discover, that the unnatural hideousness of my person was the chief object of horror with those who had formerly beheld me. My voice, although harsh, had nothing terrible in it; I thought, therefore, that if, in the absence of his children, I could gain the good-will and mediation of the old De Lacey, I might, by his means, be tolerated by my younger protectors.

"One day, when the sun shone on the red leaves that strewed the ground, and diffused cheerfulness, although it denied warmth, Safie, Agatha, and Felix, departed on a long country walk, and the old man, at his own desire, was left alone in the cottage. When his children had departed, he took up his guitar, and played several mournful, but sweet airs, more sweet and mournful than I had ever heard him play before. At first his countenance was illuminated with pleasure, but, as he continued, thoughtfulness and sadness succeeded; at length, laying aside the instrument, he sat absorbed in reflection.

"My heart beat quick; this was the hour and moment of trial, which would decide my hopes, or realize my fears. The servants were gone to a neighbouring fair. All was silent in and around the cottage: it was an excellent opportunity; yet, when I proceeded to execute my plan, my limbs failed me, and I sunk to the ground. Again I rose; and, exerting all the firmness of which I was master, removed the planks which I had placed before my hovel to conceal my retreat. The fresh air revived me, and, with renewed determination, I approached the door of their cottage.

"I knocked. 'Who is there?' said the old man—'Come in.'

"I entered; 'Pardon this intrusion,' said I: 'I am a traveller in want of a little rest; you would greatly oblige me, if you would allow me to remain a few minutes before the fire.'[12]

"'Enter,' said De Lacey; 'and I will try in what manner I can relieve your wants; but, unfortunately, my children are from home, and, as I am blind, I am afraid I shall find it difficult to procure food for you.'

"'Do not trouble yourself, my kind host, I have food; it is warmth and rest only that I need.'

"I sat down, and a silence ensued. I knew that every minute was precious to me, yet I remained irresolute in what manner to commence the interview; when the old man addressed me—

"'By your language, stranger, I suppose you are my countryman; —are you French?'

12   This is the first time the Creature has spoken to a human being, and he does so with a stilted politeness that seems almost whimsical. Wolf offers a sensitive appreciation of the tactfulness within the "elaborate structure of pain and self-loathing the Creature's autobiography has now become" (191).

"'No; but I was educated by a French family, and understand that language only. I am now going to claim the protection of some friends, whom I sincerely love, and of whose favour I have some hopes.'

"'Are they Germans?'

"'No, they are French. But let us change the subject. I am an unfortunate and deserted creature; I look around, and I have no relation or friend upon earth. These amiable people to whom I go have never seen me, and know little of me. I am full of fears; for if I fail there, I am an outcast in the world for ever.'

"'Do not despair. To be friendless is indeed to be unfortunate; but the hearts of men, when unprejudiced by any obvious self-interest, are full of brotherly love and charity. Rely, therefore, on your hopes; and if these friends are good and amiable, do not despair.'

"'They are kind—they are the most excellent creatures in the world; but, unfortunately, they are prejudiced against me. I have good dispositions; my life has been hitherto harmless, and in some degree beneficial; but a fatal prejudice clouds their eyes, and where they ought to see a feeling and kind friend, they behold only a detestable monster.'

"'That is indeed unfortunate; but if you are really blameless, cannot you undeceive them?'

"'I am about to undertake that task; and it is on that account that I feel so many overwhelming terrors. I tenderly love these friends; I have, unknown to them, been for many months in the habits of daily kindness towards them; but they believe that I wish to injure them, and it is that prejudice which I wish to overcome.'

"'Where do these friends reside?'

"'Near this spot.'

"The old man paused, and then continued, 'If you will unreservedly confide to me the particulars of your tale, I perhaps may be of use in undeceiving them. I am blind, and cannot judge of your countenance, but there is something in your words which persuades me that you are sincere. I am poor, and an exile; but it will afford me true pleasure to be in any way serviceable to a human creature.'[13]

"'Excellent man! I thank you, and accept your generous offer. You raise me from the dust[14] by this kindness; and I trust that, by your aid, I shall not be driven from the society and sympathy of your fellow-creatures.'

"'Heaven forbid! even if you were really criminal; for that can only drive you to desperation, and not instigate you to virtue. I also am unfortunate; I and my family have been condemned, although innocent: judge, therefore, if I do not feel for your misfortunes.'

"'How can I thank you, my best and only benefactor? from your lips first have I heard the voice of kindness directed towards me; I shall be for ever grateful; and your present humanity assures me of success with those friends whom I am on the point of meeting.'

"'May I know the names and residence of those friends?'

"I paused. This, I thought, was the moment of decision, which was to rob me of, or bestow happiness on me for ever. I struggled vainly for firmness sufficient to answer him, but the effort destroyed all my remaining strength; I sank on the chair, and sobbed aloud. At that moment I heard the steps of my younger protectors. I had not a moment to lose; but, seizing the hand of the old man, I cried, 'Now is the time!—save and protect me! You and your family are the friends whom I seek. Do not you desert me in the hour of trial!'

"'Great God!' exclaimed the old man, 'who are you?'

"At that instant the cottage door was opened, and Felix, Safie, and Agatha entered. Who can describe their horror and conster-

13 Percy suggested changing Mary's "fellow creature" to this phrasing (*Notebooks* 366–367)—"human" being the impending disqualifier.

14 The Creature measures his fate against the Prometheus narrative as well as the biblical one, imagining himself recreated by the human kindness that his first creator never showed him.

nation on beholding me? Agatha fainted; and Safie, unable to attend to her friend, rushed out of the cottage. Felix darted forward, and with supernatural force tore me from his father, to whose knees I clung: in a transport of fury, he dashed me to the ground, and struck me violently with a stick. I could have torn him limb from limb, as a lion rends the antelope. But my heart sunk within me as with bitter sickness, and I refrained. I saw him on the point of repeating his blow, when, overcome by pain and anguish, I quitted the cottage, and in the general tumult escaped unperceived to my hovel.

CHAPTER VIII

1 "Let the day perish I was born," rages Job (3: 3); the Creature goes further and curses his creator.

2 To express his own horror, the Creature alludes to Satan's anguish in *Paradise Lost:* "horror and doubt distract / His troubl'd thoughts, and from the bottom stir / The hell within him, for within him hell / He brings, and round about him, nor from hell / One step no more than from himself can fly / By change of place" (IV.18–23).

CURSED, CURSED CREATOR! Why did I live?[1] Why, in that instant, did I not extinguish the spark of existence which you had so wantonly bestowed? I know not; despair had not yet taken possession of me; my feelings were those of rage and revenge. I could with pleasure have destroyed the cottage and its inhabitants, and have glutted myself with their shrieks and misery.

"When night came, I quitted my retreat, and wandered in the wood; and now, no longer restrained by the fear of discovery, I gave vent to my anguish in fearful howlings. I was like a wild beast that had broken the toils; destroying the objects that obstructed me, and ranging through the wood with a stag-like swiftness. Oh! what a miserable night I passed! the cold stars shone in mockery, and the bare trees waved their branches above me: now and then the sweet voice of a bird burst forth amidst the universal stillness. All, save I, were at rest or in enjoyment: I, like the arch fiend, bore a hell within me;[2] and, finding myself unsympathized with, wished to tear up the trees, spread havoc and destruction around me, and then to have sat down and enjoyed the ruin.

"But this was a luxury of sensation that could not endure; I became fatigued with excess of bodily exertion, and sank on the damp grass in the sick impotence of despair. There was none among the myriads of men that existed who would pity or assist

3 He echoes Satan's vow to avenge himself upon his "punisher" by becoming the enemy of God's latest creation, man: "Nor hope to be my self less miserable / By what I seek, but others to make such / As I" (*Paradise Lost* IX.126–127).

me; and should I feel kindness towards my enemies? No: from that moment I declared everlasting war against the species,[3] and, more than all, against him who had formed me, and sent me forth to this insupportable misery.

"The sun rose; I heard the voices of men, and knew that it was impossible to return to my retreat during that day. Accordingly I hid myself in some thick underwood, determining to devote the ensuing hours to reflection on my situation.

"The pleasant sunshine, and the pure air of day, restored me to some degree of tranquillity; and when I considered what had passed at the cottage, I could not help believing that I had been too hasty in my conclusions. I had certainly acted imprudently. It was apparent that my conversation had interested the father in my behalf, and I was a fool in having exposed my person to the horror of his children. I ought to have familiarized the old De Lacey to me, and by degrees to have discovered myself to the rest of his family, when they should have been prepared for my approach. But I did not believe my errors to be irretrievable; and, after much consideration, I resolved to return to the cottage, seek the old man, and by my representations win him to my party.

"These thoughts calmed me, and in the afternoon I sank into a profound sleep; but the fever of my blood did not allow me to be visited by peaceful dreams. The horrible scene of the preceding day was forever acting before my eyes; the females were flying, and the enraged Felix tearing me from his father's feet. I awoke exhausted; and, finding that it was already night, I crept forth from my hiding-place, and went in search of food.

"When my hunger was appeased, I directed my steps towards the well-known path that conducted to the cottage. All there was at peace. I crept into my hovel, and remained in silent expectation of the accustomed hour when the family arose. That hour passed, the sun mounted high in the heavens, but the cottagers did not appear. I trembled violently, apprehending some dreadful misfortune. The inside of the cottage was dark, and I heard no motion; I cannot describe the agony of this suspence.

"Presently two countrymen passed by; but, pausing near the cottage, they entered into conversation, using violent gesticulations; but I did not understand what they said, as they spoke the language of the country, which differed from that of my protectors. Soon after, however, Felix approached with another man: I was surprised, as I knew that he had not quitted the cottage that morning, and waited anxiously to discover, from his discourse, the meaning of these unusual appearances.

"'Do you consider,' said his companion to him, 'that you will be obliged to pay three months' rent, and to lose the produce of your garden? I do not wish to take any unfair advantage, and I beg therefore that you will take some days to consider of your determination.'

"'It is utterly useless,' replied Felix; 'we can never again inhabit your cottage. The life of my father is in the greatest danger, owing to the dreadful circumstance that I have related. My wife and my sister will never recover their horror. I entreat you not to reason with me any more. Take possession of your tenement, and let me fly from this place.'

"Felix trembled violently as he said this. He and his companion entered the cottage, in which they remained for a few minutes, and then departed. I never saw any of the family of De Lacey more.

"I continued for the remainder of the day in my hovel in a state of utter and stupid despair. My protectors had departed, and had broken the only link that held me to the world. For the first time the feelings of revenge and hatred filled my bosom, and I did not strive to controul them; but, allowing myself to be borne away by

4 Shelley's ms. has "patience" (a discipline), corrected to this word in *1823* (II.59) and *1831* (120); for the ms. see *Notebooks* 380–381.

5 This episode evokes the mandated torching of Eden, witnessed by the expelled Adam and Eve: "They looking back, all th' eastern side beheld / Of paradise, so late their happy seat, / Wav'd over by that flaming brand, the gate / With dreadful faces throng'd and fiery arms" (*Paradise Lost* XII.641–644).

6 "The world was all before them, where to choose / Their place of rest, and providence their guide. / They, hand in hand with wand'ring steps and slow, / Through Eden took their solitary way" are the closing lines of *Paradise Lost* (XII.646–649). Adam and Eve are ambivalent: they are exiled and solitary yet have each other, divine guidance, and the promise of future rest—a complex state of mind variously echoed by Romantic writers. Among the most famous is William Wordsworth's optimistic return to the world of his childhood: "The earth is all before me!" (*The Prelude* [1805], Book I, line 15). In Letter IV (August 13th entry) Walton has already recorded Frankenstein's allusive splitting of the same passage into Walton's hopefulness and his own despair (see p. 83).

the stream, I bent my mind towards injury and death. When I thought of my friends, of the mild voice of De Lacey, the gentle eyes of Agatha, and the exquisite beauty of the Arabian, these thoughts vanished, and a gush of tears somewhat soothed me. But again, when I reflected that they had spurned and deserted me, anger returned, a rage of anger; and, unable to injure anything human, I turned my fury towards inanimate objects. As night advanced, I placed a variety of combustibles around the cottage; and, after having destroyed every vestige of cultivation in the garden, I waited with forced impatience[4] until the moon had sunk to commence my operations.

"As the night advanced, a fierce wind arose from the woods, and quickly dispersed the clouds that had loitered in the heavens: the blast tore along like a mighty avelanche, and produced a kind of insanity in my spirits, that burst all bounds of reason and reflection. I lighted the dry branch of a tree, and danced with fury around the devoted cottage, my eyes still fixed on the western horizon, the edge of which the moon nearly touched. A part of its orb was at length hid, and I waved my brand; it sunk, and with a loud scream, I fired the straw, and heath, and bushes, which I had collected.[5] The wind fanned the fire, and the cottage was quickly enveloped by the flames, which clung to it, and licked it with their forked and destroying tongues.

"As soon as I was convinced that no assistance could save any part of the habitation, I quitted the scene, and sought for refuge in the woods.

"And now, with the world before me,[6] whither should I bend my steps? I resolved to fly far from the scene of my misfortunes; but to me, hated and despised, every country must be equally horrible. At length the thought of you crossed my mind. I learned from your papers that you were my father, my creator; and to whom could I apply with more fitness than to him who had given me life? Among the lessons that Felix had bestowed upon Safie geography had not been omitted: I had learned from these the relative situations of the different countries of the earth. You had mentioned Geneva as the name of your native town; and towards this place I resolved to proceed.

"But how was I to direct myself? I knew that I must travel in a south-westerly direction to reach my destination; but the sun was my only guide. I did not know the names of the towns that I was to pass through, nor could I ask information from a single human being; but I did not despair. From you only could I hope for succour, although towards you I felt no sentiment but that of hatred. Unfeeling, heartless creator! you had endowed me with perceptions and passions, and then cast me abroad an object for the scorn and horror of mankind. But on you only had I any claim for pity and redress, and from you I determined to seek that justice which I vainly attempted to gain from any other being that wore the human form.

"My travels were long, and the sufferings I endured intense. It was late in autumn when I quitted the district where I had so long resided. I travelled only at night, fearful of encountering the visage of a human being. Nature decayed around me, and the sun became heatless; rain and snow poured around me; mighty rivers were frozen; the surface of the earth was hard, and chill, and bare, and I found no shelter. Oh, earth! how often did I imprecate curses on the cause of my being! The mildness of my nature had fled, and all within me was turned to gall and bitterness. The nearer I approached to your habitation, the more deeply did I feel the spirit of revenge enkindled in my heart. Snow fell, and the waters were hardened, but I rested not. A few incidents now and then directed me, and I possessed a map of the country; but I often wandered

7 Shelley writes scenes of animation throughout the novel. Here the Creature's benevolence is inevitably misunderstood. This episode appears in Whale's *Bride of Frankenstein* (1935), where the Creature saves a lovely shepherdess from drowning only to be shot by miscomprehending hunters.

wide from my path. The agony of my feelings allowed me no respite: no incident occurred from which my rage and misery could not extract its food; but a circumstance that happened when I arrived on the confines of Switzerland, when the sun had recovered its warmth, and the earth again began to look green, confirmed in an especial manner the bitterness and horror of my feelings.

"I generally rested during the day, and travelled only when I was secured by night from the view of man. One morning, however, finding that my path lay through a deep wood, I ventured to continue my journey after the sun had risen; the day, which was one of the first of spring, cheered even me by the loveliness of its sunshine and the balminess of the air. I felt emotions of gentleness and pleasure, that had long appeared dead, revive within me. Half surprised by the novelty of these sensations, I allowed myself to be borne away by them; and, forgetting my solitude and deformity, dared to be happy. Soft tears again bedewed my cheeks, and I even raised my humid eyes with thankfulness towards the blessed sun which bestowed such joy upon me.

"I continued to wind among the paths of the wood, until I came to its boundary, which was skirted by a deep and rapid river, into which many of the trees bent their branches, now budding with the fresh spring. Here I paused, not exactly knowing what path to pursue, when I heard the sound of voices, that induced me to conceal myself under the shade of a cypress. I was scarcely hid, when a young girl came running towards the spot where I was concealed, laughing as if she ran from some one in sport. She continued her course along the precipitous sides of the river, when suddenly her foot slipt, and she fell into the rapid stream. I rushed from my hiding place, and, with extreme labour from the force of the current, saved her, and dragged her to shore. She was senseless; and I endeavoured, by every means in my power, to restore animation,[7] when I was suddenly interrupted by the approach of rustic, who was probably the person from whom she had playfully fled. On seeing me, he darted towards me, and, tearing the girl from my arms, hastened towards the deeper parts of the wood. I followed speedily, I hardly knew why; but when the man saw me draw near, he aimed a gun, which he carried, at my body, and fired. I sunk to the ground, and my injurer, with increased swiftness, escaped into the wood.

"This was then the reward of my benevolence! I had saved a human being from destruction, and, as a recompense, I now writhed under the miserable pain of a wound, which shattered the flesh and bone. The feelings of kindness and gentleness, which I had entertained but a few moments before, gave place to hellish rage and gnashing of teeth. Inflamed by pain, I vowed eternal hatred and vengeance to all mankind. But the agony of my wound overcame me; my pulses paused, and I fainted.

"For some weeks I led a miserable life in the woods, endeavouring to cure the wound which I had received. The ball had entered my shoulder, and I knew not whether it had remained there or passed through; at any rate I had no means of extracting it. My sufferings were augmented also by the oppressive sense of the injustice and ingratitude of their infliction. My daily vows rose for revenge—a deep and deadly revenge, such as would alone compensate for the outrages and anguish I had endured.

"After some weeks my wound healed, and I continued my journey. The labours I endured were no longer to be alleviated by the bright sun or gentle breezes of spring; all joy was but a mockery, which insulted my desolate state, and made me feel more painfully that I was not made for the enjoyment of pleasure.

"But my toils now drew near a close; and, two months from this time, I reached the environs of Geneva.

Mary and Percy's son, a few weeks before he died of malaria in June 1819.

8   Having referred to the "beautiful child" as a "little creature," the Creature identifies with and dreams of adopting him, to create a rudimentary family and alleviate his alienation on the "peopled" earth. Whale's *Frankenstein* (1931) transfigures this scene into the accidental drowning of friendly little Maria. In 1811 Percy Shelley had a fantasy, more overtly Rousseauvean, of acquiring two children, preferably female; he would then "withdraw from the world with my charge, and in some sequestered spot direct their education . . . veiled from human prejudice" ("Early History of Shelley," *Fraser's Magazine* 23/138 [June 1841], 707). Joseph Merle, the Oxford schoolmate with whom he shared this idea, was shocked by the obvious dangers. For another example of Shelley's odd pedagogical fantasy, see Wolf, 206.

9   Mary Shelley may be recalling an evocative coincidence in *Paradise Lost*, where, within the space of a hundred lines, a lonely Satan is described as a predator eager to "seize" Adam and Eve, and Eve recalls a tall stranger, Adam, claiming her to redeem his loneliness: "thy gentle hand / Seiz'd mine; I yielded" (IV.407, 488–489).

10   With the boy's proud but fatally revealing threat, Frankenstein's opening boast about his social status is turned against his family (Vol. I, Ch. I).

11   This act of revenge is the first in a chain of events by which the Creature will recreate Frankenstein as his alter ego in misery, stripped of all family and friends.

"It was evening when I arrived, and I retired to a hiding-place among the fields that surround it, to meditate in what manner I should apply to you. I was oppressed by fatigue and hunger, and far too unhappy to enjoy the gentle breezes of evening, or the prospect of the sun setting behind the stupendous mountains of Jura.

"At this time a slight sleep relieved me from the pain of reflection, which was disturbed by the approach of a beautiful child, who came running into the recess I had chosen with all the sportiveness of infancy. Suddenly, as I gazed on him, an idea seized me, that this little creature was unprejudiced, and had lived too short a time to have imbibed a horror of deformity. If, therefore, I could seize him, and educate him as my companion and friend, I should not be so desolate in this peopled earth.[8]

"Urged by this impulse, I seized on the boy as he passed, and drew him towards me.[9] As soon as he beheld my form, he placed his hands before his eyes, and uttered a shrill scream: I drew his hand forcibly from his face, and said, 'Child, what is the meaning of this? I do not intend to hurt you; listen to me.'

"He struggled violently: 'Let me go,' he cried; 'monster! ugly wretch! you wish to eat me, and tear me to pieces—You are an ogre—Let me go, or I will tell my papa.'

"'Boy, you will never see your father again; you must come with me.'

"'Hideous monster! let me go; My papa is a Syndic—he is M. Frankenstein—he would punish you.[10] You dare not keep me.'

"'Frankenstein! you belong then to my enemy—to him towards whom I have sworn eternal revenge;[11] you shall be my first victim.'

"The child still struggled, and loaded me with epithets which carried despair to my heart; I grasped his throat to silence him, and in a moment he lay dead at my feet.

"I gazed on my victim, and my heart swelled with exultation and hellish triumph: clapping my hands, I exclaimed, 'I, too, can create desolation; my enemy is not impregnable; this death will carry despair to him, and a thousand other miseries shall torment and destroy him.'

"As I fixed my eyes on the child, I saw something glittering on his breast. I took it; it was a portrait of a most lovely woman. In spite of my malignity, it softened and attracted me. For a few moments I gazed with delight on her dark eyes, fringed by deep lashes, and her lovely lips; but presently my rage returned: I remembered that I was for ever deprived of the delights that such beautiful creatures could bestow; and that she whose resemblance I contemplated would, in regarding me, have changed that air of divine benignity to one expressive of disgust and affright.

"Can you wonder that such thoughts transported me with rage? I only wonder that at that moment, instead of venting my sensations in exclamations and agony, I did not rush among mankind, and perish in the attempt to destroy them.

"While I was overcome by these feelings, I left the spot where I had committed the murder, and was seeking a more secluded hiding-place, when I perceived a woman passing near me. She was young, not indeed so beautiful as her whose portrait I held, but of an agreeable aspect, and blooming in the loveliness of youth and health. Here, I thought, is one of those whose smiles are bestowed on all but me; she shall not escape:[12] thanks to the lessons of Felix, and the sanguinary laws of man, I have learned how to work mischief. I approached her unperceived, and placed the portrait securely in one of the folds of her dress.

"For some days I haunted the spot where these scenes had taken place; sometimes wishing to see you, sometimes resolved to quit the world and its miseries forever. At length I wandered towards

12   Mary Shelley heightens the gothic eroticism with an insertion here in *1831*:

"And then I bent over her, and whispered, 'Awake, fairest, thy lover is near—he who would give his life but to obtain one look of affection from thine eyes: my beloved, awake!'

"The sleeper stirred; a thrill of terror ran through me. Should she indeed awake, and see me, and curse me, and denounce the murderer? Thus would she assuredly act, if her darkened eyes opened, and she beheld me. The thought was madness; it stirred the fiend within me—not I, but she shall suffer: the murder I have committed because I am for ever robbed of all that she could give me, she shall atone. The crime had its source in her: be hers the punishment!" (Ch. XVI, 125)

these mountains, and have ranged through their immense recesses, consumed by a burning passion which you alone can gratify. We may not part until you have promised to comply with my requisition. I am alone, and miserable; man will not associate with me; but one as deformed and horrible as myself would not deny herself to me. My companion must be of the same species, and have the same defects. This being you must create."

CHAPTER IX

1 Echoing Adam's plea to God for a mate (*Paradise Lost* VIII), this demand also draws on traditional views, eloquently endorsed in Godwin's *Political Justice*: "man is a social animal . . . the soul yearns, with inexpressible longings, for the society of its like . . . Who can tell the sufferings of him who is condemned to uninterrupted solitude? Who can tell that this is not, to the majority of mankind, the bitterest torment?" (1793 Dublin edition; 2: 292).

THE BEING finished speaking, and fixed his looks upon me in expectation of a reply. But I was bewildered, perplexed, and unable to arrange my ideas sufficiently to understand the full extent of his proposition. He continued—

"You must create a female for me, with whom I can live in the interchange of those sympathies necessary for my being.[1] This you alone can do; and I demand it of you as a right which you must not refuse."

The latter part of his tale had kindled anew in me the anger that had died away while he narrated his peaceful life among the cottagers, and, as he said this, I could no longer suppress the rage that burned within me.

"I do refuse it," I replied; "and no torture shall ever extort a consent from me. You may render me the most miserable of men, but you shall never make me base in my own eyes. Shall I create another like yourself, whose joint wickedness might desolate the world? Begone! I have answered you; you may torture me, but I will never consent."

"You are in the wrong," replied the fiend; "and, instead of threatening, I am content to reason with you. I am malicious because I am miserable; am I not shunned and hated by all mankind? You, my creator, would tear me to pieces, and triumph; remember that,

2   The Creature now speaks as Job's tormentor Satan. Though Job will not curse his Creator, he does curse the day he was born (Job 3: 1–10).

3   This request replays Adam's to God in Book VIII of *Paradise Lost,* but with the admixture of the Creature's self-loathing.

and tell me why I should pity man more than he pities me? You would not call it murder, if you could precipitate me into one of those ice-rifts, and destroy my frame, the work of your own hands. Shall I respect man, when he contemns me? Let him live with me in the interchange of kindness, and, instead of injury, I would bestow every benefit upon him with tears of gratitude at his acceptance. But that cannot be; the human senses are insurmountable barriers to our union. Yet mine shall not be the submission of abject slavery. I will revenge my injuries: if I cannot inspire love, I will cause fear; and chiefly towards you my arch-enemy, because my creator, do I swear inextinguishable hatred. Have a care: I will work at your destruction, nor finish until I desolate your heart, so that you curse the hour of your birth."[2]

A fiendish rage animated him as he said this; his face was wrinkled into contortions too horrible for human eyes to behold; but presently he calmed himself, and proceeded—

"I intended to reason. This passion is detrimental to me; for you do not reflect that you are the cause of its excess. If any being felt emotions of benevolence towards me, I should return them an hundred and an hundred fold; for that one creature's sake, I would make peace with the whole kind! But I now indulge in dreams of bliss that cannot be realized. What I ask of you is reasonable and moderate; I demand a creature of another sex, but as hideous as myself: the gratification is small, but it is all that I can receive, and it shall content me.[3] It is true, we shall be monsters, cut off from all the world; but on that account we shall be more attached to one another. Our lives will not be happy, but they will be harmless, and free from the misery I now feel. Oh! my creator, make me happy; let me feel gratitude towards you for one benefit! Let me see that I excite the sympathy of some existing thing; do not deny me my request!"

I was moved. I shuddered when I thought of the possible consequences of my consent; but I felt that there was some justice in his
argument. His tale, and the feelings he now expressed, proved him
to be a creature of fine sensations; and did I not, as his maker, owe
him all the portion of happiness that it was in my power to bestow?
He saw my change of feeling, and continued—

"If you consent, neither you nor any other human being shall
ever see us again: I will go to the vast wilds of South America. My
food is not that of man; I do not destroy the lamb and the kid to
glut my appetite;[4] acorns and berries afford me sufficient nourishment. My companion will be of the same nature as myself, and will
be content with the same fare. We shall make our bed of dried
leaves; the sun will shine on us as on man, and will ripen our food.
The picture I present to you is peaceful and human, and you must
feel that you could deny it only in the wantonness of power and
cruelty. Pitiless as you have been towards me, I now see compassion in your eyes; let me seize the favourable moment, and persuade you to promise what I so ardently desire."

"You propose," replied I, "to fly from the habitations of man, to
dwell in those wilds where the beasts of the field will be your only
companions. How can you, who long for the love and sympathy of
man, persevere in this exile? You will return, and again seek their
kindness, and you will meet with their detestation; your evil passions will be renewed, and you will then have a companion to aid
you in the task of destruction. This may not be: cease to argue the
point, for I cannot consent."

"How inconstant are your feelings! but a moment ago you were
moved by my representations, and why do you again harden yourself to my complaints? I swear to you, by the earth which I inhabit,
and by you that made me, that, with the companion you bestow, I
will quit the neighbourhood of man, and dwell, as it may chance,

5   Modeling himself more closely on Job, the Creature casts himself as one willing to endure the afflictions of his existence as a test of faith and love.

in the most savage of places. My evil passions will have fled, for I shall meet with sympathy; my life will flow quietly away, and, in my dying moments, I shall not curse my maker."[5]

His words had a strange effect upon me. I compassionated him, and sometimes felt a wish to console him; but when I looked upon him, when I saw the filthy mass that moved and talked, my heart sickened, and my feelings were altered to those of horror and hatred. I tried to stifle these sensations; I thought, that as I could not sympathize with him, I had no right to withhold from him the small portion of happiness which was yet in my power to bestow.

"You swear," I said, "to be harmless; but have you not already shewn a degree of malice that should reasonably make me distrust you? May not even this be a feint that will increase your triumph by affording a wider scope for your revenge?"

"How is this? I thought I had moved your compassion, and yet you still refuse to bestow on me the only benefit that can soften my heart, and render me harmless. If I have no ties and no affections, hatred and vice must be my portion; the love of another will destroy the cause of my crimes, and I shall become a thing, of whose existence every one will be ignorant. My vices are the children of a forced solitude that I abhor; and my virtues will necessarily arise when I live in communion with an equal. I shall feel the affections of a sensitive being, and become linked to the chain of existence and events, from which I am now excluded."

I paused some time to reflect on all he had related, and the various arguments which he had employed. I thought of the promise of virtues which he had displayed on the opening of his existence, and the subsequent blight of all kindly feeling by the loathing and scorn which his protectors had manifested towards him. His power and threats were not omitted in my calculations: a creature who could exist in the ice caves of the glaciers, and hide himself from pursuit among the ridges of inaccessible precipices, was a being possessing faculties it would be vain to cope with. After a long pause of reflection, I concluded, that the justice due both to him and my fellow-creatures demanded of me that I should comply with his request. Turning to him, therefore, I said—

"I consent to your demand, on your solemn oath to quit Europe for ever, and every other place in the neighbourhood of man, as soon as I shall deliver into your hands a female who will accompany you in your exile."

"I swear," he cried, "by the sun, and by the blue sky of heaven,[6] that if you grant my prayer, while they exist you shall never behold me again. Depart to your home, and commence your labours: I shall watch their progress with unutterable anxiety; and fear not but that when you are ready I shall appear."

Saying this, he suddenly quitted me, fearful, perhaps, of any change in my sentiments. I saw him descend the mountain with greater speed than the flight of an eagle, and quickly lost him among the undulations of the sea of ice.

His tale had occupied the whole day;[7] and the sun was upon the verge of the horizon when he departed. I knew that I ought to hasten my descent towards the valley, as I should soon be encompassed in darkness; but my heart was heavy, and my steps slow. The labour of winding among the little paths of the mountains, and fixing my feet firmly as I advanced, perplexed me, occupied as I was by the emotions which the occurrences of the day had produced. Night was far advanced, when I came to the half-way resting-place, and seated myself beside the fountain. The stars shone at intervals, as the clouds passed from over them; the dark pines rose before me, and every here and there a broken tree lay on the ground: it was a scene of wonderful solemnity, and stirred strange thoughts within me. I wept bitterly; and, clasping my hands in agony, I exclaimed, "Oh! stars, and clouds, and winds, ye are all about to mock me: if ye really pity me, crush sensation and mem-

6 In *1831,* Mary Shelley inserts: "and by the fire of love that burns in my heart" (Ch. XVII, 129)—distinguishing this Creature from Satanic malevolence.

7 The day-long seminar of the Creature's "education" of Frankenstein, ending with an exhortation to responsibility, recalls, with numerous ironies and inversions, Archangel Raphael's day-long educational seminar for Adam in the Garden of Eden (*Paradise Lost* V–VIII), ending in the warning to Adam about an imminent enemy, to which the mate he requested, Eve, is especially vulnerable.

8 With the adjectives *dull ugly* from Frankenstein's first lexicon for his Creature, this scorching African desert wind seems a heightened portent of the Creature's claims.

9 *Haggard* literally means witchlike or looking as if cursed by a hag or witch. Frankenstein is waxing ever more monstrous in appearance.

10 The hypocrites in Dante's *Inferno* (23: 58–67) bear the crushing burden of maintaining an outward gilded appearance.

ory; let me become as nought; but if not, depart, depart and leave me in darkness."

These were wild and miserable thoughts; but I cannot describe to you how the eternal twinkling of the stars weighed upon me, and how I listened to every blast of wind, as if it were a dull ugly siroc[8] on its way to consume me.

Morning dawned before I arrived at the village of Chamounix; but my presence, so haggard and strange,[9] hardly calmed the fears of my family, who had waited the whole night in anxious expectation of my return.

The following day we returned to Geneva. The intention of my father in coming had been to divert my mind, and to restore me to my lost tranquillity; but the medicine had been fatal. And, unable to account for the excess of misery I appeared to suffer, he hastened to return home, hoping the quiet and monotony of a domestic life would by degrees alleviate my sufferings from whatsoever cause they might spring.

For myself, I was passive in all their arrangements; and the gentle affection of my beloved Elizabeth was inadequate to draw me from the depth of my despair. The promise I had made to the dæmon weighed upon my mind, like Dante's iron cowl on the heads of the hellish hypocrites.[10] All pleasures of earth and sky passed before me like a dream, and that thought only had to me the reality of life. Can you wonder, that sometimes a kind of insanity possessed me, or that I saw continually about me a multitude of filthy animals inflicting on me incessant torture, that often extorted screams and bitter groans?

By degrees, however, these feelings became calmed. I entered again into the every-day scene of life, if not with interest, at least with some degree of tranquillity.

END OF VOL. II

FRANKENSTEIN;

OR,

THE MODERN PROMETHEUS.

IN THREE VOLUMES.

Did I request thee, Maker, from my clay
To mould me man? Did I solicit thee
From darkness to promote me?——
PARADISE LOST.

VOL. III.

London:

PRINTED FOR
LACKINGTON, HUGHES, HARDING, MAVOR, & JONES,
FINSBURY SQUARE.

1818.

CHAPTER I

Day after day, week after week, passed away on my return to Geneva; and I could not collect the courage to recommence my work. I feared the vengeance of the disappointed fiend, yet I was unable to overcome my repugnance to the task which was enjoined me. I found that I could not compose a female without again devoting several months to profound study and laborious disquisition. I had heard of some discoveries having been made by an English philosopher, the knowledge of which was material to my success, and I sometimes thought of obtaining my father's consent to visit England for this purpose; but I clung to every pretence of delay, and could not resolve to interrupt my returning tranquillity. My health, which had hitherto declined, was now much restored; and my spirits, when unchecked by the memory of my unhappy promise, rose proportionably. My father saw this change with pleasure, and he turned his thoughts towards the best method of eradicating the remains of my melancholy, which every now and then would return by fits, and with a devouring blackness overcast the approaching sunshine. At these moments I took refuge in the most perfect solitude. I passed whole days on the lake alone in a little boat, watching the clouds, and listening to the rippling of the waves, silent and listless. But the fresh air and bright sun seldom failed to restore me to some degree of composure; and,

1 Mary initially had Alphonse propose this trip, a tour with Clerval "while you are yet young to travel & treasure recollections & pleasures for your future years." With a sharp sense of the psychological strategy of dealing with a father, Percy wrote on the ms., "I think the journey to England ought to be *Victor's* proposal.—that he ought to go for the purpose of collecting knowledge, for the formation of a female. He ought to lead his father to this in the conversations" (*Notebooks* 424–425).

on my return, I met the salutations of my friends with a readier smile and a more cheerful heart.

It was after my return from one of these rambles, that my father, calling me aside, thus addressed me:—

"I am happy to remark, my dear son, that you have resumed your former pleasures, and seem to be returning to yourself. And yet you are still unhappy, and still avoid our society. For some time I was lost in conjecture as to the cause of this; but yesterday an idea struck me, and if it is well founded, I conjure you to avow it. Reserve on such a point would be not only useless, but draw down treble misery on us all."

I trembled violently at this exordium, and my father continued:—

"I confess, my son, that I have always looked forward to your marriage with your cousin as the tie of our domestic comfort, and the stay of my declining years. You were attached to each other from your earliest infancy; you studied together, and appeared, in dispositions and tastes, entirely suited to one another. But so blind is the experience of man, that what I conceived to be the best assistants to my plan may have entirely destroyed it. You, perhaps, regard her as your sister, without any wish that she might become your wife. Nay, you may have met with another whom you may love; and, considering yourself as bound in honour to your cousin, this struggle may occasion the poignant misery which you appear to feel."

"My dear father, re-assure yourself. I love my cousin tenderly and sincerely. I never saw any woman who excited, as Elizabeth does, my warmest admiration and affection. My future hopes and prospects are entirely bound up in the expectation of our union."

"The expression of your sentiments on this subject, my dear Victor, gives me more pleasure than I have for some time experienced. If you feel thus, we shall assuredly be happy, however present events may cast a gloom over us.[1] But it is this gloom, which appears to have taken so strong a hold of your mind, that I wish to dissipate. Tell me, therefore, whether you object to an immediate solemnization of the marriage. We have been unfortunate, and recent events have drawn us from that every-day tranquillity befitting my years and infirmities. You are younger; yet I do not suppose, possessed as you are of a competent fortune, that an early marriage would at all interfere with any future plans of honour and utility that you may have formed.[2] Do not suppose, however, that I wish to dictate happiness to you, or that a delay on your part would cause me any serious uneasiness. Interpret my words with candour, and answer me, I conjure you, with confidence and sincerity."

I listened to my father in silence, and remained for some time incapable of offering any reply. I revolved rapidly in my mind a multitude of thoughts, and endeavoured to arrive at some conclusion. Alas! to me the idea of an immediate union with my cousin was one of horror and dismay. I was bound by a solemn promise,[3] which I had not yet fulfilled, and dared not break; or, if I did, what manifold miseries might not impend over me and my devoted[4] family! Could I enter into a festival with this deadly weight yet hanging round my neck, and bowing me to the ground?[5] I must perform my engagement and let the monster depart with his mate, before I allowed myself to enjoy the delight of an union from which I expected peace.

I remembered also the necessity imposed upon me of either journeying to England, or entering into a long correspondence with those philosophers of that country, whose knowledge and discoveries were of indispensable use to me in my present undertaking. The latter method of obtaining the desired intelligence was dilatory and unsatisfactory: besides, any variation was agreeable to me, and I was delighted with the idea of spending a year or two in change of scene and variety of occupation, in absence from my family; during which period some event might happen which would

2 Recall Frankenstein's opening story of his father: a life of honor and utility, with marriage delayed until one's declining years, in hopes of producing sons. Victor is heir to the estate; this sentence suggests that he has received a substantial advance on his inheritance.

3 Following his father's reference to *solemnization* (marriage rite), this "solemn promise" rings out as a rival obligation and as a figurative substitute, a bond more intimate than marriage. These are the first uses of both words in this novel.

4 Etymologically *devoted* means *dedicated* (from the Latin *devotare*: to dedicate solemnly—as in *votarist*) or *doomed, cursed* (by another's dedication). In Letter I, Walton is a "devoted" student; at Ingolstadt, Frankenstein studied how death "devoted" bodies to corruption (Vol. I, Ch. III). When in the nineteenth century, these two senses were supplemented by commitments of affection or passion, an ominous winding together of all these meanings could be exploited, as here: affectionate loyalty entailing disaster.

5 Frankenstein again remembers *The Rime of the Ancyent Marinere:* "Instead of the Cross the Albatross / About my neck was hung" (Part II).

6 In an era when actual slavery was legal, Victor's metaphor may seem either powerful or self-pitying.

7 A grain of truth unconcealed in this "excuse" may be a view of domestic life as a prison for ambitious young men. So, too, Walton, Clerval, and even Victor's father ("it was not until the decline of life that he thought of marrying") have shown no interest, as young men, in marriage and domesticity, preferring pursuits in the wide world. Safie's horror of her destiny of being "immured within the walls of a haram" gives a female claim to the metaphor, in an extreme form of domestic prison. Even well-treated, domestically devoted Elizabeth is prone to regret not having the freedom of a young man (see below). Feminist tracts of the 1790s, including Wollstonecraft's *Rights of Woman,* turned this Oriental fate back on England to compare the lives of its women to harem slavery, a sexual abjection yoked to daily drudgery.

8 This river port was a French city at the time. It was here in 1792 that Claude Rouget de Lisle composed *Champs de Guerre pour l'Armée du Rhin,* later known as *La Marseillaise,* the French national anthem.

9 Two years is the same time span from Frankenstein's discovery of the principle of life to his animation of his first creature.

restore me to them in peace and happiness: my promise might be fulfilled, and the monster have departed; or some accident might occur to destroy him, and put an end to my slavery[6] for ever.

These feelings dictated my answer to my father. I expressed a wish to visit England; but, concealing the true reasons of this request, I clothed my desires under the guise of wishing to travel and see the world before I sat down for life within the walls of my native town.[7]

I urged my entreaty with earnestness, and my father was easily induced to comply; for a more indulgent and less dictatorial parent did not exist upon earth. Our plan was soon arranged. I should travel to Strasburgh,[8] where Clerval would join me. Some short time would be spent in the towns of Holland, and our principal stay would be in England. We should return by France; and it was agreed that the tour should occupy the space of two years.[9]

My father pleased himself with the reflection, that my union with Elizabeth should take place immediately on my return to Geneva. "These two years," said he, "will pass swiftly, and it will be the last delay that will oppose itself to your happiness. And, indeed, I earnestly desire that period to arrive, when we shall all be united, and neither hopes or fears arise to disturb our domestic calm."

"I am content," I replied, "with your arrangement. By that time we shall both have become wiser, and I hope happier, than we at present are." I sighed; but my father kindly forbore to question me further concerning the cause of my dejection. He hoped that new scenes, and the amusement of travelling, would restore my tranquillity.

I now made arrangements for my journey; but one feeling haunted me, which filled me with fear and agitation. During my absence I should leave my friends unconscious of the existence of their enemy, and unprotected from his attacks, exasperated as he might be by my departure. But he had promised to follow me wherever I might go; and would he not accompany me to England? This imagination was dreadful in itself, but soothing, inasmuch as it supposed the safety of my friends. I was agonized with the idea of the possibility that the reverse of this might happen. But through the whole period during which I was the slave of my creature, I allowed myself to be governed by the impulses of the moment; and my present sensations strongly intimated that the fiend would follow me, and exempt my family from the danger of his machinations.

It was in the latter end of August that I again quitted my native country, to pass two years of exile. Elizabeth approved of the reasons of my departure, and only regretted that she had not the same opportunities of enlarging her experience, and cultivating her understanding.[10] She wept, however, as she bade me farewell, and entreated me to return happy and tranquil. "We all," said she, "depend upon you; and if you are miserable, what must be our feelings?"

I threw myself into the carriage that was to convey me away, hardly knowing whither I was going, and careless of what was passing around. I remembered only, and it was with a bitter anguish that I reflected on it, to order that my chemical instruments should be packed to go with me: for I resolved to fulfil my promise while abroad, and return, if possible, a free man. Filled with dreary imaginations, I passed through many beautiful and majestic scenes; but my eyes were fixed and unobserving. I could only think of the bourne[11] of my travels, and the work which was to occupy me whilst they endured.

After some days spent in listless indolence, during which I traversed many leagues, I arrived at Strasburgh, where I waited two days for Clerval. He came. Alas, how great was the contrast between us! He was alive to every new scene; joyful when he saw the

10   This social detail reflects not only the "impropriety" of young women traveling unchaperoned but also the general constraints of their lives, even in wealthy families.

11   That is, the limit, "the termination of my journey" (Vol. III, Ch. II). The word evokes its homophone *born,* reminding us of the impending labor. Mary Shelley threads the novel with puns on conception, labor, and birth.

12 Once more, Frankenstein uses terms for himself that echo the Creature's for himself; and once more his failure to make a connection is conspicuous.

13 This trip takes its pattern from eighteenth-century landscape aesthetics, Mary and Percy's romantic tour down the Rhine (recounted in *Six Weeks' Tour*), and Byron's and Percy Shelley's inspiring tour-a-deux of Lake Geneva in summer 1816. Victor and Henry's trip, in effect, preempts Victor and Elizabeth's honeymoon and evokes the intimate bonding on male-only touring. Moreover, as Victor will find out, there is another intimate along: his Creature has been shadowing him, hiding in these islands (Vol. III, Ch. III). East of the Rhine near Mayence is Castle Frankenstein, the "rock" of the Franks (the rulers).

14 This is the kind of moment that interests sociopolitical critics: the class difference of tourists and the laborers, the latter regarded with a picturesque aesthetic.

beauties of the setting sun, and more happy when he beheld it rise, and recommence a new day. He pointed out to me the shifting colours of the landscape, and the appearances of the sky. "This is what it is to live," he cried, "now I enjoy existence! But you, my dear Frankenstein, wherefore are you desponding and sorrowful?" In truth, I was occupied by gloomy thoughts, and neither saw the descent of the evening star, nor the golden sunrise reflected in the Rhine.—And you, my friend, would be far more amused with the journal of Clerval, who observed the scenery with an eye of feeling and delight, than to listen to my reflections. I, a miserable wretch, haunted by a curse that shut up every avenue to enjoyment.[12]

We had agreed to descend the Rhine in a boat from Strasburgh to Rotterdam, whence we might take shipping for London. During this voyage, we passed many willowy islands, and saw several beautiful towns.[13] We stayed a day at Manheim, and, on the fifth from our departure from Strasburgh, arrived at Mayence. The course of the Rhine below Mayence becomes much more picturesque. The river descends rapidly, and winds between hills, not high, but steep, and of beautiful forms. We saw many ruined castles standing on the edges of precipices, surrounded by black woods, high and inaccessible. This part of the Rhine, indeed, presents a singularly variegated landscape. In one spot you view rugged hills, ruined castles overlooking tremendous precipices, with the dark Rhine rushing beneath; and, on the sudden turn of a promontory, flourishing vineyards, with green sloping banks, and a meandering river, and populous towns occupy the scene.

We travelled at the time of the vintage, and heard the song of the labourers, as we glided down the stream.[14] Even I, depressed in mind, and my spirits continually agitated by gloomy feelings, even I was pleased. I lay at the bottom of the boat, and, as I gazed on the cloudless blue sky, I seemed to drink in a tranquillity to which I had long been a stranger. And if these were my sensations, who can describe those of Henry? He felt as if he had been transported to Fairy-land, and enjoyed a happiness seldom tasted by man. "I have seen," he said, "the most beautiful scenes of my own country; I have visited the lakes of Lucerne and Uri, where the snowy mountains descend almost perpendicularly to the water, casting black and impenetrable shades, which would cause a gloomy and mournful appearance, were it not for the most verdant islands that relieve the eye by their gay appearance; I have seen this lake agitated by a tempest, when the wind tore up whirlwinds of water, and gave you an idea of what the water-spout must be on the great ocean, and the waves dash with fury the base of the mountain, where the priest and his mistress were overwhelmed by an avalanche, and where their dying voices are still said to be heard amid the pauses of the nightly wind;[15] I have seen the mountains of La Valais, and the Pays de Vaud: but this country, Victor, pleases me more than all those wonders. The mountains of Switzerland are more majestic and strange; but there is a charm in the banks of this divine river, that I never before saw equalled. Look at that castle which overhangs yon precipice; and that also on the island, almost concealed amongst the foliage of those lovely trees; and now that group of labourers coming from among their vines; and that village half-hid in the recess of the mountain. Oh, surely, the spirit that inhabits and guards this place has a soul more in harmony with man, than those who pile the glacier, or retire to the inaccessible peaks of the mountains of our own country."

Clerval! beloved friend! even now it delights me to record your words, and to dwell on the praise of which you are so eminently deserving. He was a being formed in the "very poetry of nature."[16] His wild and enthusiastic imagination was chastened by the sensibility of his heart. His soul overflowed with ardent affections, and

15 In *1817* Mary Shelley records the famous local "story of a priest and his mistress, who, flying from persecution, inhabited a cottage at the foot of the snows. One winter night an avalanche overwhelmed them, but their plaintive voices are still heard in stormy nights, calling for succour from the peasants" (48–49).

16 Leigh Hunt's "Rimini." [Mary Shelley's note; not in *1823* and *1831*.] *The Story of Rimini* (1816) is a long poem about lovers famous from a brief appearance in Dante's *Inferno*. In a marriage arranged by their fathers to strengthen a political and economic truce, Paolo, "a creature / Formed in the very poetry of nature" (2.46–47), courts and marries Francesca as proxy for his "ill-tempered," less handsome elder brother Giovanni. Although marriage by proxy was a standard aristocratic practice, Francesca was dismayed by what Hunt calls a "holy cheat." To soften the blow, Giovanni naively assigns Paolo to be Francesca's tutor, only to find that they have become lovers. On discovering the adultery Giovanni kills them both. Reviewers condemned Hunt's sympathy for the lovers' anguish, and connected Hunt's condoning of "incest" and "adultery" to his liberal politics. Hunt was a loyal champion of Percy Shelley's controversial, flagrantly anti-establishment poetry.

17 Wordsworth's "Tintern Abbey." [Mary Shelley's note.] *Lines Written a few miles above Tintern Abbey, on Revisiting the Banks of the Wye, during a Tour, July 13, 1798,* is among other things a tour poem, added at the last minute to the 1798 *Lyrical Ballads.* In the lines quoted here (77–84, *him* replacing Wordsworth's *me*), Wordsworth recalls his first visit in July 1793. Frankenstein's summoning of these lines for Clerval in contrast to himself (*him* also marks this difference) stresses his idealization of Clerval. What he represses are the lines that come immediately before in *Tintern Abbey* and refer immediately to his state of mind: "when first / I came among these hills . . . more like a man / Flying from something that he dreads, than one / Who sought the thing he loved" (66–73). What the Shelleys did not know was Wordsworth's secret history. When he left France late in 1792/early 1793—the impending war with England making it dangerous for any Englishman to remain (Wordsworth had already witnessed civic slaughter)—he also left behind his French family, a mistress who expected him to marry her and their infant daughter. He wouldn't see them again until 1802, to make a settlement before his marriage to a proper English woman.

18 They decide to travel by horse-drawn carriage (privately hired or commercial); fresh teams of horses would be picked up at way-stations called "posts."

his friendship was of that devoted and wondrous nature that the worldly-minded teach us to look for only in the imagination. But even human sympathies were not sufficient to satisfy his eager mind. The scenery of external nature, which others regard only with admiration, he loved with ardour:

——————— "The sounding cataract
Haunted *him* like a passion: the tall rock,
The mountain, and the deep and gloomy wood,
Their colours and their forms, were then to him
An appetite; a feeling, and a love,
That had no need of a remoter charm,
By thought supplied, or any interest
Unborrowed from the eye."[17]

And where does he now exist? Is this gentle and lovely being lost forever? Has this mind, so replete with ideas, imaginations fanciful and magnificent, which formed a world, whose existence depended on the life of its creator; has this mind perished? Does it now only exist in my memory? No, it is not thus; your form so divinely wrought, and beaming with beauty, has decayed, but your spirit still visits and consoles your unhappy friend.

Pardon this gush of sorrow; these ineffectual words are but a slight tribute to the unexampled worth of Henry, but they soothe my heart, overflowing with the anguish which his remembrance creates. I will proceed with my tale.

Beyond Cologne we descended to the plains of Holland; and we resolved to post[18] the remainder of our way; for the wind was contrary, and the stream of the river was too gentle to aid us.

Our journey here lost the interest arising from beautiful scenery; but we arrived in a few days at Rotterdam, whence we proceeded by sea to England. It was on a clear morning, in the latter days of [September], that I first saw the white cliffs of Britain.[19] The banks of the Thames presented a new scene; they were flat, but fertile, and almost every town was marked by the remembrance of some story. We saw Tilbury Fort, and remembered the Spanish armada; Gravesend, Woolwich, and Greenwich, places which I had heard of even in my country.[20]

At length we saw the numerous steeples of London, St. Paul's towering above all, and the Tower famed in English history.

19   The ms. reads "September" (*Notebooks* 450–451); *1818* has "December," a printer's error that remained uncorrected in *1823* (II:108) and *1831* (138).

20   On August 8, 1588, Queen Elizabeth I reviewed and addressed her troops at Tilbury, after the Spanish Armada had been repelled and a new attack was being anticipated. At Gravesend, on the Thames, departing ships await the tide, and travelers on returning ships disembark, here for London. At Woolwich are shipyards and the arsenals; Greenwich is a naval base and site of the Royal Observatory; St. Paul's is a major cathedral in London; the Tower (of London) is a fortress and prison. This part of the novel supplies the pleasures of a travelogue.

1 Shelley honors the dynamic figures of the 1790s: her father, Erasmus Darwin, Thomas Paine, Joseph Priestley, and young poets Wordsworth and Coleridge.

2 Shifting from the formal "Clerval" in the first paragraph, Victor here uses the intimate name.

3 Frankenstein is still thinking of *Tintern Abbey*, here with the elegiac tone of a self lost to time. "My dear, dear Friend," says Wordsworth to his companion, his sister, "in thy voice I catch / The language of my former heart, and read / My former pleasures" (117–119). Both she and Wordsworth conjure the classical definition of friend as alter ego (other self)—in this case, a former self, fleetingly, ruefully apprehended.

CHAPTER II

LONDON WAS our present point of rest; we determined to remain several months in this wonderful and celebrated city. Clerval desired the intercourse of the men of genius and talent who flourished at this time;[1] but this was with me a secondary object; I was principally occupied with the means of obtaining the information necessary for the completion of my promise, and quickly availed myself of the letters of introduction that I had brought with me, addressed to the most distinguished natural philosophers.

If this journey had taken place during my days of study and happiness, it would have afforded me inexpressible pleasure. But a blight had come over my existence, and I only visited these people for the sake of the information they might give me on the subject in which my interest was so terribly profound. Company was irksome to me; when alone, I could fill my mind with the sights of heaven and earth; the voice of Henry soothed me,[2] and I could thus cheat myself into a transitory peace. But busy uninteresting joyous faces brought back despair to my heart. I saw an insurmountable barrier placed between me and my fellow-men; this barrier was sealed with the blood of William and Justine; and to reflect on the events connected with those names filled my soul with anguish.

But in Clerval I saw the image of my former self;[3] he was inquisitive, and anxious to gain experience and instruction. The

J. M. W. Turner, *Buttermere Lake, with Part of Cromackwater, Cumberland, a Shower* (1798). Turner first toured the Lake District in 1797 and exhibited this painting at the Royal Academy in 1798; Victor and Henry travel through the Lake District, the beloved haunt of William Wordsworth, whose poetry Victor summons to describe Henry's unalloyed raptures.

4   In *1831* Clerval's delight in and curiosity about cultural difference are qualified *as serving the practical ambitions of a budding colonialist.* Mary Shelley adds just after this sentence: "He was also pursuing an object he had long had in view. His design was to visit India, in the belief that he had in his knowledge of its various languages, and in the views he had taken of its society, the means of materially assisting the progress of European colonisation and trade. In Britain only could he further the execution of his plan" (XIX.139).

5   This verb plays nicely against *recollection* in the sentence just prior.

6   This is another instance where *devoted* means both *dedicated* and *doomed.*

7   They take an indirect route in order to enjoy some major cultural and natural attractions. The least known of these, Matlock, is a spa town in Derbyshire, at the southeastern edge of the Peak District. Windsor, home of Windsor Castle, the royal residence, neighbors Eton, the elite school that Percy Shelley attended unhappily, and Bishopsgate, where he and Mary resided from August 1815 to April 1816, before they left for Europe.

difference of manners which he observed was to him an inexhaustible source of instruction and amusement.[4] He was for ever busy; and the only check to his enjoyments was my sorrowful and dejected mien. I tried to conceal this as much as possible, that I might not debar him from the pleasures natural to one who was entering on a new scene of life, undisturbed by any care or bitter recollection. I often refused to accompany him, alleging another engagement, that I might remain alone. I now also began to collect[5] the materials necessary for my new creation, and this was to me like the torture of single drops of water continually falling on the head. Every thought that was devoted[6] to it was an extreme anguish, and every word that I spoke in allusion to it caused my lips to quiver, and my heart to palpitate.

After passing some months in London, we received a letter from a person in Scotland, who had formerly been our visitor at Geneva. He mentioned the beauties of his native country, and asked us if those were not sufficient allurements to induce us to prolong our journey as far north as Perth, where he resided. Clerval eagerly desired to accept this invitation; and I, although I abhorred society, wished to view again mountains and streams, and all the wondrous works with which Nature adorns her chosen dwelling-places.

We had arrived in England at the beginning of October, and it was now February. We accordingly determined to commence our journey towards the north at the expiration of another month. In this expedition we did not intend to follow the great road to Edinburgh, but to visit Windsor, Oxford, Matlock, and the Cumberland lakes, resolving to arrive at the completion of this tour about the end of July.[7] I packed my chemical instruments, and the materials I had collected, resolving to finish my labours in some obscure nook in the northern highlands of Scotland.

We quitted London on the 27th of March, and remained a few days at Windsor, rambling in its beautiful forest. This was a new scene to us mountaineers; the majestic oaks, the quantity of game, and the herds of stately deer, were all novelties to us.

From thence we proceeded to Oxford. As we entered this city, our minds were filled with the remembrance of the events that had been transacted there more than a century and a half before. It was here that Charles I. had collected his forces. This city had remained faithful to him, after the whole nation had forsaken his cause to join the standard of parliament and liberty. The memory of that unfortunate king, and his companions, the amiable Falkland, the insolent Gower,[8] his queen, and son, gave a peculiar interest to every part of the city which they might be supposed to have inhabited. The spirit of elder days found a dwelling here, and we delighted to trace its footsteps. If these feelings had not found an imaginary gratification, the appearance of the city had yet in itself sufficient beauty to obtain our admiration. The colleges are ancient and picturesque; the streets are almost magnificent; and the lovely Isis,[9] which flows beside it through meadows of exquisite verdure, is spread forth into a placid expanse of waters, which reflects its majestic assemblage of towers, and spires, and domes, embosomed among aged trees.

I enjoyed this scene; and yet my enjoyment was embittered both by the memory of the past, and the anticipation of the future. I was formed for peaceful happiness.[10] During my youthful days discontent never visited my mind; and if I was ever overcome by ennui, the sight of what is beautiful in nature, or the study of what is excellent and sublime in the productions of man, could always interest my heart, and communicate elasticity to my spirits. But I am a blasted tree; the bolt has entered my soul;[11] and I felt then that I should survive to exhibit, what I shall soon cease to be—a miserable spectacle of wrecked humanity, pitiable to others, and abhorrent to myself.

We passed a considerable period at Oxford, rambling among its environs, and endeavouring to identify every spot which might

8   Corrected to *Goring* in *1823* (Vol. II, p. 114). Oxford was Charles I's base during the Civil Wars of the 1640s against Cromwell's Parliamentary faction (which executed Charles in 1649). In despair over the wars, Charles's Secretary of State, Falkland, let himself be slain in battle in 1643. Goring, one of Charles I's generals, was notoriously ambitious and self-serving. Irritated that he had been given a secondary role in Charles's plot against Parliament (before the outbreak of war), he betrayed it to the rebels. For a novel set in the Revolutionary 1790s, Mary Shelley's sentimentality about a monarchy has a remarkably conservative tone, in key with Edmund Burke's reverence for the French monarchy in *Reflections on the French Revolution* (1790). This is historical tourism.

9   So the Thames River is named in this part of England.

10   Part of the accumulating ironies, in relation to his formation of his Creature, to which Frankenstein seems immune.

11   Frankenstein's self-image is a striking recollection of that terrible scene from his childhood, when he witnessed lightning blast an oak into fragments (Vol. I, Ch. I).

Abandoned farmhouse, Orkney Islands. Farming was challenging and frequently impossible on these severe islands off the northeast edge of Scotland, extending toward the Arctic Circle, to which Victor retreats for his second project of creation.

relate to the most animating epoch of English history. Our little voyages of discovery were often prolonged by the successive objects that presented themselves. We visited the tomb of the illustrious Hampden, and the field on which that patriot fell.[12] For a moment my soul was elevated from its debasing and miserable fears, to contemplate the divine ideas of liberty and self-sacrifice, of which these sights were the monuments and the remembrancers. For an instant I dared to shake off my chains, and look around me with a free and lofty spirit; but the iron had eaten into my flesh, and I sank again, trembling and hopeless, into my miserable self.

We left Oxford with regret, and proceeded to Matlock, which was our next place of rest. The country in the neighbourhood of this village resembled, to a greater degree, the scenery of Switzerland; but everything is on a lower scale, and the green hills want the crown of distant white Alps, which always attend on the piny mountains of my native country. We visited the wondrous cave, and the little cabinets of natural history, where the curiosities are disposed in the same manner as in the collections at Servox and Chamounix. The latter name made me tremble when pronounced by Henry; and I hastened to quit Matlock, with which that terrible scene was thus associated.

From Derby still journeying northward, we passed two months in Cumberland and Westmoreland. I could now almost fancy myself among the Swiss mountains. The little patches of snow which yet lingered on the northern sides of the mountains, the lakes, and the dashing of the rocky streams, were all familiar and dear sights to me. Here also we made some acquaintances, who almost contrived to cheat me into happiness.[13] The delight of Clerval was proportionably greater than mine; his mind expanded in the company

12 Frankenstein's royalist tourism is not absolute. Hampden, a cousin of Cromwell and popular hero of the Parliamentary cause, was killed in a skirmish near Oxford.

13 A compliment to the writers of the Lake District (Westmoreland and Cumberland) in the 1790s: Wordsworth and Coleridge; Southey in his radical youth; and the heroic abolitionist Thomas Clarkson—all of whom may be imagined as making cameo appearances here. The Lakes drew tourists during the long war that closed the Continent to most travel. This excursion is pitched in part to native British pride.

14   Oddly, this remark echoes the language in which both tourism and popular literature were criticized for pandering to appetites for stimulation and novelty. In this case, however, the language sets Clerval's joyously mercurial mind in contrast to Frankenstein's melancholy brooding.

of men of talent, and he found in his own nature greater capacities and resources than he could have imagined himself to have possessed while he associated with his inferiors. "I could pass my life here," said he to me; "and among these mountains I should scarcely regret Switzerland and the Rhine."

But he found that a traveller's life is one that includes much pain amidst its enjoyments. His feelings are forever on the stretch; and when he begins to sink into repose, he finds himself obliged to quit that on which he rests in pleasure for something new, which again engages his attention, and which also he forsakes for other novelties.[14]

We had scarcely visited the various lakes of Cumberland and Westmoreland, and conceived an affection for some of the inhabitants, when the period of our appointment with our Scotch friend approached, and we left them to travel on. For my own part I was not sorry. I had now neglected my promise for some time, and I feared the effects of the dæmon's disappointment. He might remain in Switzerland, and wreak his vengeance on my relatives. This idea pursued me, and tormented me at every moment from which I might otherwise have snatched repose and peace. I waited for my letters with feverish impatience: if they were delayed, I was miserable, and overcome by a thousand fears; and when they arrived, and I saw the superscription of Elizabeth or my father, I hardly dared to read and ascertain my fate. Sometimes I thought that the fiend followed me, and might expedite my remissness by murdering my companion. When these thoughts possessed me, I would not quit Henry for a moment, but followed him as his shadow, to protect him from the fancied rage of his destroyer. I felt as if I had committed some great crime, the consciousness of which haunted me. I was guiltless, but I had indeed drawn down a horrible curse upon my head, as mortal as that of crime.

I visited Edinburgh with languid eyes and mind; and yet that city might have interested the most unfortunate being. Clerval did not like it so well as Oxford; for the antiquity of the latter city was more pleasing to him. But the beauty and regularity of the new town of Edinburgh, its romantic castle, and its environs, the most delightful in the world, Arthur's Seat, St. Bernard's Well, and the Pentland Hills, compensated him for the change, and filled him with cheerfulness and admiration.[15] But I was impatient to arrive at the termination of my journey.

We left Edinburgh in a week, passing through Coupar, St. Andrew's, and along the banks of the Tay, to Perth, where our friend expected us. But I was in no mood to laugh and talk with strangers, or enter into their feelings or plans with the good humour expected from a guest; and accordingly I told Clerval that I wished to make the tour of Scotland alone. "Do you," said I, "enjoy yourself, and let this be our rendezvous. I may be absent a month or two; but do not interfere with my motions, I entreat you: leave me to peace and solitude for a short time; and when I return, I hope it will be with a lighter heart, more congenial to your own temper."

Henry wished to dissuade me; but, seeing me bent on this plan, ceased to remonstrate.[16] He entreated me to write often. "I had rather be with you," he said, "in your solitary rambles, than with these Scotch people, whom I do not know: hasten then, my dear friend, to return, that I may again feel myself somewhat at home, which I cannot do in your absence."[17]

Having parted from my friend, I determined to visit some remote spot of Scotland, and finish my work in solitude. I did not doubt but that the monster followed me, and would discover himself me when I should have finished, that he might receive his companion.

15   The new eighteenth-century town featured elegant architecture and spacious streets and parks, in contrast to the alleys, gothic buildings, and romantic castle of the old town across the river. The novel again indulges the popular travelogue mode, describing Edinburgh as a town of divided character, surrounded by natural beauties.

16   Mary Shelley exploits Latin puns: the root of *monster* lurks as an etymology within *remonstrate* (to point to again).

17   This language mirrors the debate between Adam and Eve over her wish to work alone in the garden and its fatal aftermath (*Paradise Lost* IX). Full of misgiving, Adam accedes to her determination, and Satan finds her "thus alone." In this record of their parting, Victor speaks again of "Henry," the intimate name.

18 These words are in the ms. (*Notebooks* 4–69), dropped by the printer, and restored in *1831* (144). The sparsely populated Orkney Islands are north of the Scottish mainland.

19 This gaunt and scraggly humanity may seem symbolic of Frankenstein's ghoulish project; but on another level it reflects the Shelleys' concern with social misery, where physical deformity is a sign of material deprivation, not innate depravity.

20 Although LION reports one seventeenth-century instance of this unusual adjective prior to *Frankenstein,* OED lists this sentence as the first usage; Percy Shelley would use "ungazed" two years later in *Prometheus Unbound* to describe a sublime force (II.iv.4–5).

With this resolution I traversed the northern highlands, and fixed on one of the remotest of the Orkneys as the scene [of my][18] labours. It was a place fitted for such a work, being hardly more than a rock, whose high sides were continually beaten upon by the waves. The soil was barren, scarcely affording pasture for a few miserable cows, and oatmeal for its inhabitants, which consisted of five persons, whose gaunt and scraggy limbs gave tokens of their miserable fare.[19] Vegetables and bread, when they indulged in such luxuries, and even fresh water, was to be procured from the mainland, which was about five miles distant.

On the whole island there were but three miserable huts, and one of these was vacant when I arrived. This I hired. It contained but two rooms, and these exhibited all the squalidness of the most miserable penury. The thatch had fallen in, the walls were unplastered, and the door was off its hinges. I ordered it to be repaired, bought some furniture, and took possession; an incident which would, doubtless, have occasioned some surprise, had not all the senses of the cottagers been benumbed by want and squalid poverty. As it was, I lived ungazed[20] at and unmolested, hardly thanked for the pittance of food and clothes which I gave; so much does suffering blunt even the coarsest sensations of men.

In this retreat I devoted the morning to labour; but in the evening, when the weather permitted, I walked on the stony beach of the sea, to listen to the waves as they roared and dashed at my feet. It was a monotonous yet ever-changing scene. I thought of Switzerland; it was far different from this desolate and appalling landscape. Its hills are covered with vines, and its cottages are scattered thickly in the plains. Its fair lakes reflect a blue and gentle sky; and, when troubled by the winds, their tumult is but as the play of a lively infant, when compared to the roarings of the giant ocean.

In this manner I distributed my occupations when I first arrived; but, as I proceeded in my labour, it became every day more horrible and irksome to me. Sometimes I could not prevail on myself to enter my laboratory for several days; and at other times I toiled day and night in order to complete my work. It was, indeed, a filthy process in which I was engaged. During my first experiment, a kind of enthusiastic frenzy had blinded me to the horror of my employment; my mind was intently fixed on the sequel[21] of my labour, and my eyes were shut to the horror of my proceedings. But now I went to it in cold blood,[22] and my heart often sickened at the work of my hands.

Thus situated, employed in the most detestable occupation, immersed in a solitude where nothing could for an instant call my attention from the actual scene in which I was engaged, my spirits became unequal; I grew restless and nervous. Every moment I feared to meet my persecutor. Sometimes I sat with my eyes fixed on the ground, fearing to raise them, lest they should encounter the object which I so much dreaded to behold. I feared to wander from the sight of my fellow-creatures, lest when alone he should come to claim his companion.

In the meantime I worked on, and my labour was already considerably advanced. I looked towards its completion with a tremulous and eager hope, which I dared not trust myself to question, but which was intermixed with obscure forebodings of evil, that made my heart sicken in my bosom.

21 In *1831,* Mary Shelley replaces "sequel" with "consummation" (XIX, 145).

22 This traditional phrase for a lack of human sentiment had been used by Burke in *Reflections on the Revolution in France* (1790), famously denouncing the storming of Versailles palace, in which the royal family was arrested and some of its retinue "massacred in cold blood."

1 Frankenstein's anxiety is understandable, but just as apparent is his tendency to imagine innate malignity rather than malignity caused by his own neglect.

2 As Mary Shelley knew, the refusal of a prenatal, restrictive "compact" was a revolutionary principle upheld by both Godwin in *Political Justice* and Tom Paine in *The Rights of Man.* In Frankenstein's imagination, however, this refusal is attributed entirely to the new Eve. Shelley is rewriting what Wollstonecraft condemned in Milton's submissive Eve (*Rights of Woman,* Chap. II).

3 This is the inspiration for the famous climactic scene in *The Bride of Frankenstein,* a failed matchmaking that goes up in flames.

CHAPTER III

I SAT ONE EVENING in my laboratory; the sun had set, and the moon was just rising from the sea; I had not sufficient light for my employment, and I remained idle, in a pause of consideration of whether I should leave my labour for the night, or hasten its conclusion by an unremitting attention to it. As I sat, a train of reflection occurred to me, which led me to consider the effects of what I was now doing. Three years before I was engaged in the same manner, and had created a fiend whose unparalleled barbarity had desolated my heart, and filled it for ever with the bitterest remorse. I was now about to form another being, of whose dispositions I was alike ignorant; she might become ten thousand times more malignant than her mate, and delight, for its own sake, in murder and wretchedness.[1] He had sworn to quit the neighbourhood of man, and hide himself in deserts; but she had not; and she, who in all probability was to become a thinking and reasoning animal, might refuse to comply with a compact made before her creation.[2] They might even hate each other; the creature who already lived loathed his own deformity, and might he not conceive a greater abhorrence for it when it came before his eyes in the female form? She also might turn with disgust from him to the superior beauty of man;[3] she might quit him, and he be again alone, exasperated by the fresh provocation of being deserted by one of his own species.

Even if they were to leave Europe, and inhabit the deserts of the new world, yet one of the first results of those sympathies for which the dæmon thirsted would be children, and a race of devils would be propagated upon the earth, who might make the very existence of the species of man a condition precarious and full of terror.[4] Had I right, for my own benefit, to inflict this curse upon everlasting generations? I had before been moved by the sophisms of the being I had created; I had been struck senseless by his fiendish threats: but now, for the first time, the wickedness of my promise burst upon me; I shuddered to think that future ages might curse me as their pest, whose selfishness had not hesitated to buy its own peace at the price perhaps, of the existence of the whole human race.

I trembled, and my heart failed within me; when, on looking up, I saw, by the light of the moon, the dæmon at the casement.[5] A ghastly grin wrinkled his lips as he gazed on me, where I sat fulfilling the task which he had allotted to me. Yes, he had followed me in my travels; he had loitered in forests, hid himself in caves, or taken refuge in wide and desert heaths; and he now came to mark my progress, and claim the fulfillment of my promise.

As I looked on him, his countenance expressed the utmost extent of malice and treachery.[6] I thought with a sensation of madness on my promise to create another like to him, and, trembling with passion, tore to pieces the thing on which I was engaged. The wretch saw me destroy the creature on whose future existence he depended for happiness, and, with a howl of devilish despair and revenge,[7] withdrew.

I left the room, and, locking the door, made a solemn vow in my own heart never to resume my labours; and then, with trembling steps, I sought my own apartment. I was alone; none were near me to dissipate the gloom, and relieve me from the sickening oppression of the most terrible reveries.

4 Frankenstein assumes that his Creature shares his patriarchal imperative ("A new species would bless me as its creator and source"). It does not occur to him that he may just want companionship; and weirdly, it doesn't occur to Frankenstein to make a female Creature without reproductive capacity. Did he even make his Creature with this complex physiology? (Mel Brooks's *Young Frankenstein* derives comic capital from this possibility.)

5 Mary Shelley writes this scene to recall the first animation scene, in Vol. I, Ch. IV: "by the dim and yellow light of the moon, as it forced its way through the window-shutters, I beheld the wretch—the miserable monster whom I had created."

6 This has the look of dubious projection, of a piece with Frankenstein's reaction to his Creature's very first plea for connection as a menacing gesture (Vol. I, Ch. IV).

7 Percy suggested adding "& revenge" (*Notebooks* 476–477), tightening the Satanic identification and keynoting the dynamic of repayment in kind. Mary writes an ethically fractured sentence for Frankenstein: even as he perceives the depth of the Creature's emotions, he is incapable of acknowledging its humanity.

8 The Creature's revenge will be to remake his creator in his own image, turning Victor (his name now ironic) into his double in misery and wretchedness. The language of master and slave is embedded in the abolition controversy. *Frankenstein* was first published about a decade after England abolished the slave trade in 1807, revised across a decade of increasing abolitionist activism, and published just before the abolition of colonial slavery in 1833. *Frankenstein* alludes to both sides of the debate: it is reactionary (the alarm of subhuman creatures acquiring power) and progressive (a recognition of how maltreatment of abject creatures as subhuman can lead to social crisis).

Several hours passed, and I remained near my window gazing on the sea; it was almost motionless, for the winds were hushed, and all nature reposed under the eye of the quiet moon. A few fishing vessels alone specked the water, and now and then the gentle breeze wafted the sound of voices, as the fishermen called to one another. I felt the silence, although I was hardly conscious of its extreme profundity, until my ear was suddenly arrested by the paddling of oars near the shore, and a person landed close to my house.

In a few minutes after, I heard the creaking of my door, as if some one endeavoured to open it softly. I trembled from head to foot; I felt a presentiment of who it was, and wished to rouse one of the peasants who dwelt in a cottage not far from mine; but I was overcome by the sensation of helplessness, so often felt in frightful dreams, when you in vain endeavour to fly from an impending danger, and was rooted to the spot.

Presently I heard the sound of footsteps along the passage; the door opened, and the wretch whom I dreaded appeared. Shutting the door, he approached me, and said, in a smothered voice—

"You have destroyed the work which you began; what is it that you intend? Do you dare to break your promise? I have endured toil and misery: I left Switzerland with you; I crept along the shores of the Rhine, among its willow islands, and over the summits of its hills. I have dwelt many months in the heaths of England, and among the deserts of Scotland. I have endured incalculable fatigue, and cold, and hunger; do you dare destroy my hopes?"

"Begone! I do break my promise; never will I create another like yourself, equal in deformity and wickedness."

"Slave, I before reasoned with you, but you have proved yourself unworthy of my condescension. Remember that I have power; you believe yourself miserable, but I can make you so wretched[8] that the light of day will be hateful to you. You are my creator, but I am your master;—obey!"

"The hour of my weakness is past, and the period of your power is arrived.[9] Your threats cannot move me to do an act of wickedness; but they confirm me in a resolution of not creating you a companion in vice. Shall I, in cool blood, set loose upon the earth a dæmon, whose delight is in death and wretchedness? Begone! I am firm, and your words will only exasperate my rage."

The monster saw my determination in my face, and gnashed his teeth in the impotence of anger. "Shall each man," cried he, "find a wife for his bosom, and each beast have his mate, and I be alone?[10] I had feelings of affection, and they were requited by detestation and scorn. Man, you may hate; but beware! Your hours will pass in dread and misery, and soon the bolt will fall which must ravish from you your happiness for ever. Are you to be happy while I grovel in the intensity of my wretchedness? You can blast my other passions; but revenge remains—revenge, henceforth dearer than light or food! I may die; but first you, my tyrant and tormentor, shall curse the sun that gazes on your misery.[11] Beware; for I am fearless, and therefore powerful. I will watch with the wiliness of a snake, that I may sting with its venom. Man, you shall repent of the injuries you inflict."

"Devil, cease; and do not poison the air with these sounds of malice. I have declared my resolution to you, and I am no coward to bend beneath words. Leave me; I am inexorable."

"It is well. I go; but remember, I shall be with you on your wedding-night."[12]

I started forward, and exclaimed, "Villain! before you sign my death-warrant, be sure that you are yourself safe."

I would have seized him; but he eluded me, and quitted the house with precipitation: in a few moments I saw him in his boat,

9 At this turning point, *period* means "termination" not "era." In Latin grammar, a "periodic" sentence is lengthy, often syntactically complex, its meaning not fully distilled until the emphatic conclusion.

10 The Creature knowingly echoes Adam's complaint to God in *Paradise Lost* Book VIII.

11 The Creature alludes to Satan's soliloquy on the borders of Eden when he addresses the Sun "to tell thee how I hate thy beams, / That bring to my remembrance from what state / I fell" (*Paradise Lost* IV.37–38). From this point on, allusions to Milton's Satan come thick and fast, ever more tightly fusing Frankenstein to his Creature.

12 The Creature's promise may recall Iago's vengeful oath: "Nothing can, nor shall content my soul, / Till I am even with him, wife, for wife" (*Othello* 2.1.293–294). The Shelleys were reading *Othello* in 1817. Psychological critics have found numerous implications in the Creature's threat, reflecting not only symmetrical revenge but also male anxieties about sexual passion, and potentially fatal pregnancy.

13   The auxiliary *will* that Frankenstein recalls (versus the Creature's *shall*) is more than a future tense; it signifies volition and intention.

14   Frankenstein can only imagine that the barbarous threat to domestic happiness is directed toward himself and not, in the symmetry of revenge, toward his intended bride. But see p. 261.

which shot across the waters with an arrowy swiftness and was soon lost amidst the waves.

All was again silent; but his words rung in my ears. I burned with rage to pursue the murderer of my peace, and precipitate him into the ocean. I walked up and down my room hastily and perturbed, while my imagination conjured up a thousand images to torment and sting me. Why had I not followed him, and closed with him in mortal strife? But I had suffered him to depart, and he had directed his course towards the main land. I shuddered to think who might be the next victim sacrificed to his insatiate revenge. And then I thought again of his words—*"I will be with you on your wedding-night."*[13] That then was the period fixed for the fulfillment of my destiny. In that hour I should die, and at once satisfy and extinguish his malice. The prospect did not move me to fear; yet when I thought of my beloved Elizabeth,—of her tears and endless sorrow, when she should find her lover so barbarously snatched from her,—tears, the first I had shed for many months, streamed from my eyes, and I resolved not to fall before my enemy without a bitter struggle.[14]

The night passed away, and the sun rose from the ocean; my feelings became calmer, if it may be called calmness, when the violence of rage sinks into the depths of despair. I left the house, the horrid scene of the last night's contention, and walked on the beach of the sea, which I almost regarded as an insuperable barrier between me and my fellow-creatures; nay, a wish that such should prove the fact stole across me. I desired that I might pass my life on that barren rock, wearily it is true, but uninterrupted by any sudden shock of misery. If I returned, it was to be sacrificed, or to see those whom I most loved die under the grasp of a dæmon whom I had myself created.

I walked about the isle like a restless spectre, separated from all it loved, and miserable in the separation. When it became noon, and the sun rose higher, I lay down on the grass, and was overpowered by a deep sleep. I had been awake the whole of the preceding night, my nerves were agitated, and my eyes inflamed by watching and misery. The sleep into which I now sunk refreshed me; and when I awoke, I again felt as if I belonged to a race of human beings like myself, and I began to reflect upon what had passed with greater composure; yet still the words of the fiend rung in my ears like a death-knell, they appeared like a dream, yet distinct and oppressive as a reality.

The sun had far descended, and I still sat on the shore, satisfying my appetite, which had become ravenous, with an oaten cake, when I saw a fishing-boat land close to me, and one of the men brought me a packet; it contained letters from Geneva, and one from Clerval, entreating me to join him. He said that nearly a year had elapsed since we had quitted Switzerland, and France was yet unvisited. He entreated me, therefore, to leave my solitary isle, and meet him at Perth, in a week from that time, when we might arrange the plan of our future proceedings. This letter in a degree recalled me to life, and I determined to quit my island at the expiration of two days.

Yet, before I departed, there was a task to perform, on which I shuddered to reflect: I must pack my chemical instruments; and for that purpose I must enter the room which had been the scene of my odious work, and I must handle those utensils, the sight of which was sickening to me. The next morning, at day-break, I summoned sufficient courage, and unlocked the door of my laboratory. The remains of the half-finished creature, whom I had destroyed, lay scattered on the floor, and I almost felt as if I had mangled the living flesh of a human being.[15] I paused to collect myself, and then entered the chamber. With trembling hand I conveyed the instruments out of the room; but I reflected that I ought not to leave the relics of my work to excite the horror and suspicion

15 This grisly detail recalls the slaughter-houses of Frankenstein's first research. The next sentence weirdly suggests that he, too, is a scattered being, needing collection.

16 Two full days have passed from the night Frankenstein destroyed his work to this early morning, when he disposes of the remains at sea.

of the peasants, and I accordingly put them into a basket, with a great quantity of stones, and laying them up, determined to throw them into the sea that very night; and in the meantime I sat upon the beach, employed in cleaning and arranging my chemical apparatus.

Nothing could be more complete than the alteration that had taken place in my feelings since the night of the appearance of the dæmon. I had before regarded my promise with a gloomy despair, as a thing that, with whatever consequences, must be fulfilled; but I now felt as if a film had been taken from before my eyes, and that I, for the first time, saw clearly. The idea of renewing my labours did not for one instant occur to me; the threat I had heard weighed on my thoughts, but I did not reflect that a voluntary act of mine could avert it. I had resolved in my own mind, that to create another like the fiend I had first made would be an act of the basest and most atrocious selfishness; and I banished from my mind every thought that could lead to a different conclusion.

Between two and three in the morning the moon rose; and I then, putting my basket aboard a little skiff, sailed out about four miles from the shore.[16] The scene was perfectly solitary: a few boats were returning towards land, but I sailed away from them. I felt as if I was about the commission of a dreadful crime, and avoided with shuddering anxiety any encounter with my fellow-creatures. At one time the moon, which had before been clear, was suddenly overspread by a thick cloud, and I took advantage of the moment of darkness, and cast my basket into the sea; I listened to the gurgling sound as it sunk, and then sailed away from the spot. The sky became clouded; but the air was pure, although chilled by the northeast breeze that was then rising. But it refreshed me, and filled me with such agreeable sensations, that I resolved to prolong my stay on the water, and fixing the rudder in a direct position, stretched myself at the bottom of the boat. Clouds hid the moon, every thing was obscure, and I heard only the sound of the boat, as its keel cut through the waves; the murmur lulled me, and in a short time I slept soundly.

I do not know how long I remained in this situation, but when I awoke I found that the sun had already mounted considerably. The wind was high, and the waves continually threatened the safety of my little skiff. I found that the wind was north-east, and must have driven me far from the coast from which I had embarked. I endeavoured to change my course, but quickly found that if I again made the attempt the boat would be instantly filled with water. Thus situated, my only resource was to drive before the wind.[17] I confess that I felt a few sensations of terror. I had no compass with me, and was so little acquainted with the geography of this part of the world that the sun was of little benefit to me. I might be driven into the wide Atlantic, and feel all the tortures of starvation, or be swallowed up in the immeasurable waters that roared and buffeted around me. I had already been out many hours, and felt the torment of a burning thirst, a prelude to my other sufferings. I looked on the heavens, which were covered by clouds that flew before the wind, only to be replaced by others: I looked upon the sea, it was to be my grave. "Fiend," I exclaimed, "your task is already fulfilled!" I thought of Elizabeth, of my father, and of Clerval;[18] and sunk into a reverie, so despairing and frightful, that even now, when the scene is on the point of closing before me forever, I shudder to reflect on it.

Some hours passed thus; but by degrees, as the sun declined towards the horizon, the wind died away into a gentle breeze, and the sea became free from breakers. But these gave place to a heavy swell; I felt sick, and hardly able to hold the rudder, when suddenly I saw a line of high land towards the south.

17   Such a wind would drive to the southwest.

18   In *1831* after the semicolon Mary Shelley revises: "all left behind, on whom the monster might satisfy his sanguinary and merciless passions. The idea plunged me into a reverie . . ." (Ch. XX, 152).

19   Fearful that his wretched appearance inspires unsympathetic prejudice, Frankenstein has fallen into the recurring situation of his Creature, suspected of villainy despite his efforts to be friendly, and his need of hospitality and care.

Almost spent, as I was, by fatigue, and the dreadful suspense I endured for several hours, this sudden certainty of life rushed like a flood of warm joy to my heart, and tears gushed from my eyes.

How mutable are our feelings, and how strange is that clinging love we have of life even in the excess of misery! I constructed another sail with a part of my dress, and eagerly steered my course towards the land. It had a wild and rocky appearance; but as I approached nearer, I easily perceived the traces of cultivation. I saw vessels near the shore, and found myself suddenly transported back to the neighbourhood of civilized man. I eagerly traced the windings of the land, and hailed a steeple which I at length saw issuing from behind a small promontory. As I was in a state of extreme debility, I resolved to sail directly towards the town as a place where I could most easily procure nourishment. Fortunately I had money with me. As I turned the promontory, I perceived a small neat town and a good harbour, which I entered, my heart bounding with joy at my unexpected escape.

As I was occupied in fixing the boat and arranging the sails, several people crowded towards the spot. They seemed much surprised at my appearance; but, instead of offering me any assistance, whispered together with gestures that at any other time might have produced in me a slight sensation of alarm. As it was, I merely remarked that they spoke English; and I therefore addressed them in that language: "My good friends," said I, "will you be so kind as to tell me the name of this town, and inform me where I am?"

"You will know that soon enough," replied a man with a gruff voice. "May be you are come to a place that will not prove much to your taste; but you will not be consulted as to your quarters, I promise you."

I was exceedingly surprised on receiving so rude an answer from a stranger; and I was also disconcerted on perceiving the frown-

Illustration for *Frankenstein* by Lynd Ward. Victor regards the strangely hostile Irish villagers when he washes ashore seeking their compassion and assistance.

ing and angry countenances of his companions.[19] "Why do you answer me so roughly?" I replied: "surely it is not the custom of Englishmen to receive strangers so inhospitably."

"I do not know," said the man, "what the custom of the English may be; but it is the custom of the Irish to hate villains."

While this strange dialogue continued, I perceived the crowd rapidly increase. Their faces expressed a mixture of curiosity and anger, which annoyed, and in some degree alarmed me. I inquired the way to the inn; but no one replied. I then moved forward, and a murmuring sound arose from the crowd as they followed and surrounded me; when an ill-looking man approaching, tapped me on the shoulder, and said, "Come, Sir, you must follow me to Mr. Kirwin's, to give an account of yourself."

"Who is Mr. Kirwin? Why am I to give an account of myself? Is not this a free country?"

"Aye, Sir, free enough for honest folks. Mr. Kirwin is a magistrate; and you are to give an account of the death of a gentleman who was found murdered here last night."

This answer startled me; but I presently recovered myself. I was innocent; that could easily be proved: accordingly I followed my conductor in silence, and was led to one of the best houses in the town. I was ready to sink from fatigue and hunger; but, being surrounded by a crowd, I thought it politic to rouse all my strength, that no physical debility might be construed into apprehension or conscious guilt. Little did I then expect the calamity that was in a few moments to overwhelm me, and extinguish in horror and despair all fear of ignominy or death.

I must pause here; for it requires all my fortitude to recall the memory of the frightful events which I am about to relate, in proper detail, to my recollection.

CHAPTER IV

1 WAS SOON introduced into the presence of the magistrate, an old benevolent man, with calm and mild manners. He looked upon me, however, with some degree of severity: and then, turning towards my conductors, he asked who appeared as witnesses on this occasion.

About half a dozen men came forward; and one being selected by the magistrate, he deposed, that he had been out fishing the night before[1] with his son and brother-in-law, Daniel Nugent, when, about ten o'clock, they observed a strong northerly blast rising, and they accordingly put in for port. It was a very dark night, as the moon had not yet risen; they did not land at the harbour, but, as they had been accustomed, at a creek about two miles below. He walked on first, carrying a part of the fishing tackle, and his companions followed him at some distance. As he was proceeding along the sands, he struck his foot against something, and fell at his length on the ground. His companions came up to assist him; and, by the light of their lantern, they found that he had fallen on the body of a man, who was to all appearance dead. Their first supposition was that it was the corpse of some person who had been drowned, and was thrown on shore by the waves; but, upon examination, they found that the clothes were not wet, and even that the body was not then cold. They instantly carried it to the cottage of an old woman near the spot, and endeavoured, but in

2   This would be no light at all.

3   This scene recalls the resuscitation of Frankenstein by Walton's crew, and Mary's poignant, futile dream of her dead baby. An apothecary is a druggist.

vain, to restore it to life. He appeared to be a handsome young man, about five and twenty years of age. He had apparently been strangled; for there was no sign of any violence, except the black mark of fingers on his neck.

The first part of this deposition did not in the least interest me; but when the mark of the fingers was mentioned, I remembered the murder of my brother, and felt myself extremely agitated; my limbs trembled, and a mist came over my eyes, which obliged me to lean on a chair for support. The magistrate observed me with a keen eye, and of course drew an unfavourable augury from my manner.

The son confirmed his father's account: but when Daniel Nugent was called, he swore positively that, just before the fall of his companion, he saw a boat, with a single man in it, at a short distance from the shore; and, as far as he could judge by the light of a few stars,[2] it was the same boat in which I had just landed.

A woman deposed that she lived near the beach, and was standing at the door of her cottage, waiting for the return of the fishermen, about an hour before she heard of the discovery of the body, when she saw a boat, with only one man in it, push off from that part of the shore where the corpse was afterwards found.

Another woman confirmed the account of the fishermen having brought the body into her house; it was not cold. They put it into a bed, and rubbed it;[3] and Daniel went to the town for an apothecary, but life was quite gone.

Several other men were examined concerning my landing; and they agreed, that, with the strong north wind that had arisen during the night, it was very probable that I had beaten about for many hours, and had been obliged to return nearly to the same spot from which I had departed. Besides, they observed that it appeared that I had brought the body from another place, and it was likely, that as I did not appear to know the shore, I might have put into the harbour ignorant of the distance of the town of——— from the place where I had deposited the corpse.

Mr. Kirwin, on hearing this evidence, desired that I should be taken into the room where the body lay for interment that it might be observed what effect the sight of it would produce upon me. This idea was probably suggested by the extreme agitation I had exhibited when the mode of the murder had been described. I was accordingly conducted, by the magistrate and several other persons, to the inn. I could not help being struck by the strange coincidences that had taken place during this eventful night; but, knowing that I had been conversing with several persons in the island I had inhabited about the time that the body had been found, I was perfectly tranquil as to the consequences of the affair.

I entered the room where the corpse lay, and was led up to the coffin. How can I describe my sensations on beholding it? I feel yet parched with horror, nor can I reflect on that terrible moment without shuddering and agony, that faintly reminds me of the anguish of the recognition. The trial, the presence of the magistrate and witnesses, passed like a dream from my memory, when I saw the lifeless form of Henry Clerval stretched before me.[4] I gasped for breath; and, throwing myself on the body, I exclaimed, "Have my murderous machinations deprived you also, my dearest Henry, of life? Two I have already destroyed; other victims await their destiny: but you, Clerval, my friend, my benefactor"——

The human frame could no longer support the agonizing suffering that I endured, and I was carried out of the room in strong convulsions.

A fever succeeded to this. I lay for two months on the point of death: my ravings, as I afterwards heard, were frightful; I called myself the murderer of William, of Justine, and of Clerval. Some-

4   This scene reverse-plays Frankenstein's "infus[ing] a spark of being into the lifeless thing that lay at my feet" (Vol. I, Ch. IV). In this sequel, he is framed by circumstantial evidence, as Justine had been—the Creature crafting both frame-ups. Frankenstein (born the same year as both Justine and Clerval) now finds himself in their awful circumstances. The mystery of the Creature's ability to locate Clerval in Perth and speedily bear his warm corpse to the very village upon which Frankenstein washes ashore gives this episode the aura of a nightmare or fated catastrophe.

5   Like the Creature's, this is French.

6   An agonizing medieval instrument of torture, also known as the breaking wheel. A condemned person is tied to the spokes; the bones are crushed by hammer-strokes, and the person is left to a slow death, vulnerable to attacks by predators.

7   Frankenstein's class prejudice prevents him from considering that a "hard and rude" countenance may bespeak a life of labor and rough conditions. The nurse still uses a courteous "Sir" to address a prisoner who is widely believed to be a horrific murderer.

times I entreated my attendants to assist me in the destruction of the fiend by whom I was tormented; and at others I felt the fingers of the monster already grasping my neck, and screamed aloud with agony and terror. Fortunately, as I spoke my native language,[5] Mr. Kirwin alone understood me; but my gestures and bitter cries were sufficient to affright the other witnesses.

Why did I not die? More miserable than man ever was before, why did I not sink into forgetfulness and rest? Death snatches away many blooming children, the only hopes of their doating parents: how many brides and youthful lovers have been one day in the bloom of health and hope, and the next a prey for worms and the decay of the tomb! Of what materials was I made, that I could thus resist so many shocks, which, like the turning of the wheel, continually renewed the torture?[6]

But I was doomed to live; and, in two months, found myself as awaking from a dream, in a prison, stretched on a wretched bed, surrounded by gaolers, turnkeys, bolts, and all the miserable apparatus of a dungeon. It was morning, I remember, when I thus awoke to understanding: I had forgotten the particulars of what had happened, and only felt as if some great misfortune had suddenly overwhelmed me; but when I looked around, and saw the barred windows, and the squalidness of the room in which I was, all flashed across my memory, and I groaned bitterly.

This sound disturbed an old woman who was sleeping in a chair beside me. She was a hired nurse, the wife of one of the turnkeys, and her countenance expressed all those bad qualities which often characterize that class.[7] The lines of her face were hard and rude, like that of persons accustomed to see without sympathizing in sights of misery. Her tone expressed her entire indifference; she addressed me in English, and the voice struck me as one that I had heard during my sufferings:

"Are you better now, Sir?" said she.

I replied in the same language, with a feeble voice, "I believe I am; but if it be all true, if indeed I did not dream, I am sorry that I am still alive to feel this misery and horror."

"For that matter," replied the old woman, "if you mean about the gentleman you murdered, I believe that it were better for you if you were dead, for I fancy it will go hard with you; but you will be hung when the next sessions come on.[8] However, that's none of my business, I am sent to nurse you, and get you well; I do my duty with a safe conscience, it were well if every body did the same."

I turned with loathing from the woman who could utter so unfeeling a speech to a person just saved, on the very edge of death; but I felt languid, and unable to reflect on all that had passed. The whole series of my life appeared to me as a dream; I sometimes doubted if indeed it were all true, for it never presented itself to my mind with the force of reality.

As the images that floated before me became more distinct, I grew feverish; a darkness pressed around me; no one was near me who soothed me with the gentle voice of love; no dear hand supported me. The physician came and prescribed medicines, and the old woman prepared them for me; but utter carelessness was visible in the first, and the expression of brutality was strongly marked in the visage of the second. Who could be interested in the fate of a murderer, but the hangman who would gain his fee?

These were my first reflections; but I soon learned that Mr. Kirwin had shown me extreme kindness. He had caused the best room in the prison to be prepared for me (wretched indeed was the best); and it was he who had provided a physician and a nurse. It is true, he seldom came to see me; for, although he ardently desired to relieve the sufferings of every human creature, he did not wish to be present at the agonies and miserable ravings of a murderer.[9] He

8   The assizes, or seasonal court sessions.

9   Mr. Kirwin's motives for avoiding Frankenstein are ambiguous. He may be so benevolent that he can't bear to hear such violent ravings (not a good quality in a magistrate); or he has been so impressed by Frankenstein's breeding and education (they both speak French) that he doesn't want to be audience to anything that could be compelled as testimony.

came, therefore, sometimes to see that I was not neglected; but his visits were short, and at long intervals.

One day, when I was gradually recovering, I was seated in a chair, my eyes half open, and my cheeks livid like those in death, I was overcome by gloom and misery, and often reflected I had better seek death than remain miserably pent up only to be let loose in a world replete with wretchedness. At one time I considered whether I should not declare myself guilty, and suffer the penalty of the law, less innocent than poor Justine had been. Such were my thoughts when the door of my apartment was opened and Mr. Kirwin entered. His countenance expressed sympathy and compassion; he drew a chair close to mine, and addressed me in French—

"I fear that this place is very shocking to you; can I do anything to make you more comfortable?"

"I thank you; but all that you mention is nothing to me: on the whole earth there is no comfort which I am capable of receiving."

"I know that the sympathy of a stranger can be but of little relief to one borne down as you are by so strange a misfortune. But you will, I hope, soon quit this melancholy abode; for, doubtless, evidence can easily be brought to free you from the criminal charge."

"That is my least concern: I am, by a course of strange events, become the most miserable of mortals. Persecuted and tortured as I am and have been, can death be any evil to me?"

"Nothing indeed could be more unfortunate and agonizing than the strange chances that have lately occurred. You were thrown, by some surprising accident, on this shore renowned its hospitality; seized immediately, and charged with murder. The first sight that was presented to your eyes was the body of your friend, murdered in so unaccountable a manner, and placed, as it were, by some fiend across your path."

As Mr. Kirwin said this, notwithstanding the agitation I endured on this retrospect of my sufferings, I also felt considerable surprise at the knowledge he seemed to possess concerning me. I suppose some astonishment was exhibited in my countenance; for Mr. Kirwin hastened to say—

"It was not until a day or two after your illness that I thought of examining your dress, that I might discover some trace by which I could send to your relations an account of your misfortune and illness. I found several letters, and, among others, one which I discovered from its commencement to be from your father.[10] I instantly wrote to Geneva: nearly two months have elapsed since the departure of my letter.—But you are ill; even now you tremble: you are unfit for agitation of any kind."

"This suspense is a thousand times worse than the most horrible event: tell me what new scene of death has been acted, and whose murder I am now to lament."

"Your family is perfectly well," said Mr. Kirwin, with gentleness; "and some one, a friend, is come to visit you."

I know not by what chain of thought the idea presented itself, but it instantly darted into my mind that the murderer had come to mock at my misery, and taunt me with the death of Clerval, as a new incitement for me to comply with his hellish desires. I put my hand before my eyes and cried out in agony—

"Oh! take him away! I cannot see him; for God's sake do not let him enter!"

Mr. Kirwin regarded me with a troubled countenance. He could not help regarding my exclamation as a presumption of my guilt, and said, in rather a severe tone—

"I should have thought, young man, that the presence of your father would have been welcome, instead of inspiring such violent repugnance."

10 Recalling with a difference the Creature's discovery of Frankenstein's notebooks in the coat that he took with him from the laboratory, Kirwin's study of the documents he has discovered produces an exculpatory rather than a damning history.

"My father!" cried I, while every feature and every muscle was relaxed from anguish to pleasure. "Is my father, indeed, come? How kind, how very kind! But where is he, why does he not hasten to me?"

My change of manner surprised and pleased the magistrate; perhaps he thought that my former exclamation was a momentary return of delirium, and now he instantly resumed his former benevolence. He rose, and quitted the room with my nurse, and in a moment my father entered it.

Nothing, at this moment, could have given me greater pleasure than the arrival of my father. I stretched out my hand to him and cried—

"Are you then safe—and Elizabeth—and Ernest?"

My father calmed me with assurances of their welfare, and endeavoured, by dwelling on these subjects so interesting to my heart, to raise my desponding spirits; but he soon felt that a prison cannot be the abode of cheerfulness. "What a place is this that you inhabit, my son!" said he, looking mournfully at the barred windows, and wretched appearance of the room. "You travelled to seek happiness, but a fatality seems to pursue you. And poor Clerval—"

The name of my unfortunate and murdered friend was an agitation too great to be endured in my weak state; I shed tears.

"Alas! yes, my father," replied I; "some destiny of the most horrible kind hangs over me, and I must live to fulfil it, or surely I should have died on the coffin of Henry."

We were not allowed to converse for any length of time, for the precarious state of my health rendered every precaution necessary that could ensure tranquillity. Mr. Kirwin came in, and insisted that my strength should not be exhausted by too much exertion. But the appearance of my father was to me like that of my good angel, and I gradually recovered my health.

As my sickness quitted me, I was absorbed by a gloomy and black melancholy, that nothing could dissipate. The image of Clerval was for ever before me, ghastly and murdered. More than once the agitation into which these reflections threw me made my friends dread a dangerous relapse. Alas! why did they preserve so miserable and detested a life? It was surely that I might fulfil my destiny, which is now drawing to a close. Soon, oh, very soon, will death extinguish these throbbings, and relieve me from the mighty weight of anguish that bears me to the dust; and, in executing the award of justice, I shall also sink to rest. Then the appearance of death was distant, although the wish was ever present to my thoughts; and I often sat for hours motionless and speechless, wishing for some mighty revolution that might bury me and my destroyer in its ruins.

The season of the assizes approached. I had already been three months in prison; and although I was still weak, and in continual danger of a relapse, I was obliged to travel nearly a hundred miles to the county-town, where the court was held. Mr. Kirwin charged himself with every care of collecting witnesses and arranging my defence. I was spared the disgrace of appearing publicly as a criminal, as the case was not brought before the court that decides on life and death. The grand jury rejected the bill on its being proved that I was on the Orkney Islands at the hour the body of my friend was found, and a fortnight after my removal I was liberated from prison.

My father was enraptured on finding me freed from the vexations of a criminal charge, that I was again allowed to breathe the fresh atmosphere, and allowed to return to my native country. I did not participate in these feelings; for to me the walls of a dungeon or a palace were alike hateful. The cup of life was poisoned for ever; and although the sun shone upon me as upon the happy and gay of heart, I saw around me nothing but a dense and fright-

11 Frankenstein, a Genevese, seems aware of this as a Swiss-marked malady (French: *homesickness*), first named in the eighteenth century in relation to Swiss foreign-service mercenaries (because Switzerland was officially neutral, its male citizens could become mercenaries, and in *1831* Elizabeth reports Ernest Frankenstein's desire for this career [Vol. I, Ch. VI, 49]). Mercenaries were forbidden, on penalty of death, to sing or play songs of their homelands, for the debilitating homesickness these produced.

ful darkness, penetrated by no light but the glimmer of two eyes that glared upon me. Sometimes they were the expressive eyes of Henry, languishing in death, the dark orbs nearly covered by the lids, and the long black lashes that fringed them; sometimes it was the watery clouded eyes of the monster, as I first saw them in my chamber at Ingolstadt.

My father tried to awaken in me the feelings of affection. He talked of Geneva, which I should soon visit—of Elizabeth and Ernest; but these words only drew deep groans from me. Sometimes, indeed, I felt a wish for happiness; and thought, with melancholy delight, of my beloved cousin; or longed, with a devouring *maladie du pays*,[11] to see once more the blue lake and rapid Rhone, that had been so dear to me in early childhood: but my general state of feeling was a torpor, in which a prison was as welcome a residence as the divinest scene in nature; and these fits were seldom interrupted, but by paroxysms of anguish and despair. At these moments I often endeavoured to put an end to the existence I loathed; and it required unceasing attendance and vigilance to restrain me from committing some dreadful act of violence.

I remember, as I quitted the prison, I heard one of the men say, "He may be innocent of the murder, but he has certainly a bad conscience." These words struck me. A bad conscience! yes, surely I had one. William, Justine, and Clerval, had died through my infernal machinations; "And whose death," cried I, "is to finish the tragedy? Ah! my father, do not remain in this wretched country; take me where I may forget myself, my existence, and all the world."

My father easily acceded to my desire; and, after having taken leave of Mr. Kirwin, we hastened to Dublin. I felt as if I was relieved from a heavy weight, when the packet sailed with a fair wind from Ireland, and I had quitted for ever the country which had been to me the scene of so much misery.

It was midnight. My father slept in the cabin; and I lay on the deck, looking at the stars, and listening to the dashing of the waves. I hailed the darkness that shut Ireland from my sight, and my pulse beat with a feverish joy, when I reflected that I should soon see Geneva. The past appeared to me in the light of a frightful dream; yet the vessel in which I was, the wind that blew me from the detested shore of Ireland, and the sea which surrounded me, told me too forcibly that I was deceived by no vision, and that Clerval, my friend and dearest companion, had fallen a victim to me and the monster of my creation. I repassed, in my memory, my whole life; my quiet happiness while residing with my family in Geneva, the death of my mother, and my departure for Ingolstadt. I remembered shuddering at the mad enthusiasm that hurried me on to the creation of my hideous enemy, and I called to mind the night during which he first lived. I was unable to pursue the train of thought; a thousand feelings pressed upon me, and I wept bitterly.

Ever since my recovery from the fever I had been in the custom of taking every night a small quantity of laudanum;[12] for it was by means of this drug only that I was enabled to gain the rest necessary for the preservation of life. Oppressed by the recollection of my various misfortunes, I now took a double dose, and soon slept profoundly. But sleep did not afford me respite from thought and misery; my dreams presented a thousand objects that scared me. Towards morning I was possessed by a kind of night-mare;[13] I felt the fiend's grasp in my neck, and could not free myself from it; groans and cries rung in my ears. My father, who was watching over me, perceiving my restlessness, awoke me, and pointed to the port of Holyhead, which we were now entering.

12   Laudanum (Latin: *praiseworthy*) is opium dissolved in alcohol, a widely used pain-reliever, sedative, and psychedelic agent, first concocted and named by Paracelsus, one of Victor's boyhood heroes. Addiction had yet to be medically understood. Coleridge and Thomas De Quincey were famous, self-loathing addicts; Percy was a frequent user; Mary's half-sister, Fanny, killed herself with laudanum.

13   This report evokes the Swiss-born British painter Henri Fuseli's most famous work, *The Nightmare* (1781), widely circulated in an engraving by Thomas Burke (1783). In its original meaning, the *night-mare* is an evil spirit that attacked during sleep. Fuseli's painting will soon be represented more explicitly, in Ch. VI.

Portsmouth, on England's southern coast, is a port of departure to northern France, the site of Le Havre ("the harbor"). Wollstonecraft resided in Le Havre when she was involved with Imlay and caring for their infant daughter Fanny while he was in London. Mary, Percy, and Claire returned to England via Le Havre and Portsmouth at the end of 1816.

CHAPTER V

WE HAD RESOLVED not to go to London, but to cross the country to Portsmouth, and thence to embark for Havre.[1] I preferred this plan principally because I dreaded to see again those places in which I had enjoyed a few moments of tranquility with my beloved Clerval. I thought with horror of seeing again those persons whom we had been accustomed to visit together, and who might make inquiries concerning an event, the very remembrance of which made me again feel the pang I endured when I gazed on his lifeless form in the inn at————.

As for my father, his desires and exertions were bounded to the again seeing me restored to health and peace of mind. His tenderness and attentions were unremitting; my grief and gloom was obstinate, but he would not despair. Sometimes he thought that I felt deeply the degradation of being obliged to answer a charge of murder, and he endeavoured to prove to me the futility of pride.

"Alas! my father," said I, "how little do you know me. Human beings, their feelings and passions, would indeed be degraded if such a wretch as I felt pride. Justine, poor unhappy Justine, was as innocent as I, and she suffered the same charge; she died for it; and I am the cause of this—I murdered her. William, Justine, and Henry—they all died by my hands."

My father had often, during my imprisonment, heard me make the same assertion; when I thus accused myself, he sometimes seemed to desire an explanation, and at others he appeared to consider it as caused by delirium, and that, during my illness, some idea of this kind had presented itself to my imagination, the remembrance of which I preserved in my convalescence. I avoided explanation, and maintained a continual silence concerning the wretch I had created. I had a feeling that I should be supposed mad, and this for ever chained my tongue,[2] when I would have given the whole world to have confided the fatal secret.

Upon this occasion my father said, with an expression of unbounded wonder, "What do you mean, Victor? are you mad? My dear son, I entreat you never to make such an assertion again."

"I am not mad," I cried energetically; "the sun and the heavens, who have viewed my operations, can bear witness of my truth. I am the assassin of those most innocent victims; they died by my machinations. A thousand times would I have shed my own blood, drop by drop, to have saved their lives; but I could not, my father, indeed I could not sacrifice the whole human race."

The conclusion of this speech convinced my father that my ideas were deranged, and he instantly changed the subject of our conversation, and endeavoured to alter the course of thoughts. He wished as much as possible to obliterate the memory of the scenes that had taken place in Ireland, and never alluded to them, or suffered me to speak of my misfortunes.

As time passed away I became more calm: misery had her dwelling in my heart, but I no longer talked in the same incoherent manner of my own crimes; sufficient for me was the consciousness of them. By the utmost self-violence, I curbed the imperious voice

2 In *1831* Mary Shelley inserts more rationalization: "But, besides, I could not bring myself to disclose a secret which would fill my hearer with consternation, and make fear and unnatural horror the inmates of his breast. I checked, therefore, my impatient thirst for sympathy, and was silent" (Ch. XXII, 166).

of wretchedness, which sometimes desired to declare itself to the whole world; and my manners were calmer and more composed than they had ever been since my journey to the sea of ice.

We arrived at Havre on the 8th of May, and instantly proceeded to Paris, where my father had some business which detained us a few weeks. In this city, I received the following letter from Elizabeth:—

"*To* VICTOR FRANKENSTEIN

"MY DEAREST FRIEND,

"It gave me the greatest pleasure to receive a letter from my uncle dated at Paris; you are no longer at a formidable distance, and I may hope to see you in less than a fortnight. My poor cousin, how much you must have suffered! I expect to see you looking even more ill than when you quitted Geneva. This winter has been passed most miserably, tortured as I have been by anxious suspense; yet I hope to see peace in your countenance, and to find that your heart is not totally devoid of comfort and tranquillity.

"Yet I fear that the same feelings now exist that made you so miserable a year ago, even perhaps augmented by time. I would not disturb you at this period, when so many misfortunes weigh upon you; but a conversation that I had with my uncle previous to his departure renders some explanation necessary before we meet.

"Explanation! you may possibly say; what can Elizabeth have to explain? If you really say this, my questions are answered, and I have no more to do than to sign myself your affectionate cousin. But you are distant from me, and it is possible that you may dread, and yet be pleased with this explanation; and, in a probability of this being the case, I dare not any longer postpone writing what, during your absence, I have often wished to express to you, but have never had the courage to begin.

"You well know, Victor, that our union has been the favourite plan of your parents ever since our infancy. We were told this when young, and taught to look forward to it as an event that would certainly take place. We were affectionate playfellows during childhood, and, I believe, dear and valued friends to one another as we grew older. But as brother and sister often entertain a lively affection towards each other, without desiring a more intimate union, may not such also be our case? Tell me, dearest Victor. Answer me, I conjure you, by our mutual happiness, with simple truth—Do you not love another?

"You have travelled; you have spent several years of your life at Ingolstadt; and I confess to you, my friend, that when I saw you last autumn so unhappy, flying to solitude, from the society of every creature, I could not help supposing that you might regret our connection, and believe yourself bound in honour to fulfil the wishes of your parents, although they opposed themselves to your inclinations. But this is false reasoning. I confess to you, my cousin, that I love you, and that in my airy dreams of futurity you have been my constant friend and companion. But it is your happiness I desire as well as my own, when I declare to you, that our marriage would render me eternally miserable, unless it were the dictate of your own free choice. Even now I weep to think, that, borne down as you are by the cruelest misfortunes, you may stifle, by the word *honour,* all hope of that love and happiness which would alone restore you to yourself. I who have so interested[3] an affection for you, may increase your miseries ten-fold, by being an obstacle to your wishes. Ah, Victor, be assured that your cousin and playmate has too sincere a love for you not to be made miserable by this supposition. Be happy, my friend; and if you obey me in this one request, remain satisfied that nothing on earth will have the power to interrupt my tranquillity.

3   This word is possibly a printer's error. The ms. has "disinterested" (selfless), restored thus in *1831* (Ch. XXII, 168). See *Notebooks* 542–543. Elizabeth's renunciation recalls a similar gesture by Walton's Russian shipmaster (Letter II). These two instances serve the claim of the 1818 Preface that this novel demonstrates "the excellence of universal virtue."

4   He means his own doom by judicial penalty; but calling it "my sentence" (as if his utterance) makes it seem as if he himself were unintentionally casting the curse on Elizabeth. And she has indeed intuited that Victor has an intimate bond with "another."

5   In *1817* Mary comments on war-ravaged France in 1814: "the distress of the inhabitants, whose houses had been burned, their cattle killed, and all their wealth destroyed, has given a sting to my detestation of war, which none can feel who have not travelled through a country pillaged and wasted by this plague, which, in his pride, man inflicts upon his fellow" (19).

6   Frankenstein identifies with Adam after the Fall, doomed to exile.

"Do not let this letter disturb you; do not answer to-morrow, or the next day, or even until you come, if it will give you pain. My uncle will send me news of your health; and if I see but one smile on your lips when we meet, occasioned by this or any other exertion of mine, I shall need no other happiness.

"Elizabeth Lavenza
"Geneva, May 18th, 17——."

This letter revived in my memory what I had before forgotten, the threat of the fiend—*"I will be with you on your wedding-night!"* Such was my sentence,[4] and on that night would the dæmon employ every art to destroy me, and tear me from the glimpse of happiness which promised partly to console my sufferings. On that night he had determined to consummate his crimes by my death. Well, be it so; a deadly struggle would then assuredly take place, in which if he was victorious, I should be at peace, and his power over me be at an end. If he were vanquished, I should be a free man. Alas! what freedom? such as the peasant enjoys when his family have been massacred before his eyes, his cottage burnt, his lands laid waste, and he is turned adrift, homeless, pennyless and alone, but free.[5] Such would be my liberty, except that in my Elizabeth I possessed a treasure; alas! balanced by those horrors of remorse and guilt, which would pursue me until death.

Sweet and beloved Elizabeth! I read and re-read her letter and some softened feelings stole into my heart, and dared to whisper paradisaical dreams of love and joy; but the apple was already eaten, and the angel's arm bared to drive me from all hope.[6] Yet I would die to make her happy. If the monster executed his threat, death was inevitable; yet, again, I considered whether my marriage would hasten my fate. My destruction might indeed arrive a few months sooner; but if my torturer should suspect that I postponed it, influenced by his menaces, he would surely find other, and perhaps more dreadful means of revenge. He had vowed *to be with me on my wedding-night,* yet he did not consider that threat as binding him to peace in the mean time; for, as if to shew me that he was not yet satiated with blood, he had murdered Clerval immediately after the enunciation of his threats. I resolved, therefore, that if my immediate union with my cousin would conduce either to her's or my father's happiness, my adversary's designs against my life should not retard it a single hour.

In this state of mind I wrote to Elizabeth. My letter was calm and affectionate. "I fear, my beloved girl," I said, "little happiness remains for us on earth; yet all that I may one day enjoy is concentered in you. Chase away your idle fears; to you alone do I consecrate my life, and my endeavours for contentment. I have one secret, Elizabeth, a dreadful one; when revealed to you it will chill your frame with horror,[7] and then, far from being surprised at my misery, you will only wonder that I survive what I have endured. I will confide this tale of misery and terror to you the day after our marriage shall take place; for, my sweet cousin, there must be perfect confidence between us. But until then, I conjure you, do not mention or allude to it. This I most earnestly entreat, and I know you will comply."

In about a week after the arrival of Elizabeth's letter, we returned to Geneva. My cousin welcomed me with warm affection; yet tears were in her eyes, as she beheld my emaciated frame and feverish cheeks. I saw a change in her also. She was thinner, and had lost much of that heavenly vivacity that had before charmed me; but her gentleness, and soft looks of compassion, made her a more fit companion for one blasted and miserable as I was.

The tranquillity which I now enjoyed did not endure. Memory brought madness with it; and when I thought of what had passed, a real insanity possessed me; sometimes I was furious, and burnt with rage, sometimes low and despondent. I neither spoke or

7 Elizabeth is cast as first recipient of Victor's gothic narrative, which he luridly previews. As a wife, she could not be called to testify against him.

looked, but sat motionless, bewildered by the multitude of miseries that overcame me.

Elizabeth alone had the power to draw me from these fits; her gentle voice would soothe me when transported by passion, and inspire me with human feelings when sunk in torpor. She wept with me, and for me. When reason returned, she would remonstrate, and endeavour to inspire me with resignation. Ah! it is well for the unfortunate to be resigned, but for the guilty there is no peace. The agonies of remorse poison the luxury there is otherwise sometimes found in indulging the excess of grief.

Soon after my arrival my father spoke of my immediate marriage with my cousin. I remained silent.

"Have you, then, some other attachment?"

"None on earth. I love Elizabeth, and look forward to our union with delight. Let the day therefore be fixed; and on it I will consecrate myself, in life or death, to the happiness of my cousin."

"My dear Victor, do not speak thus. Heavy misfortunes have befallen us; but let us only cling closer to what remains, and transfer our love for those whom we have lost to those who yet live. Our circle will be small, but bound close by the ties of affection and mutual misfortune. And when time shall have softened your despair, new and dear objects of care will be born to replace those of whom we have been so cruelly deprived."

Such were the lessons of my father. But to me the remembrance of the threat returned: nor can you wonder that, omnipotent as the fiend had yet been in his deeds of blood, I should almost regard him as invincible; and that when he had pronounced the words, *"I shall be with you on your wedding-night,"* I should regard the threatened fate as unavoidable. But death was no evil to me, if the loss of Elizabeth were balanced with it; and I therefore, with a contented and even cheerful countenance, agreed with my father that, if my cousin would consent, the ceremony should take place in ten days, and thus put, as I imagined, the seal to my fate.

Great God! if for one instant I had thought what might be the hellish intention of my fiendish adversary, I would rather have banished myself for ever from my native country, and wandered a friendless outcast over the earth,[8] than to have consented to this miserable marriage. But, as if possessed of magic powers, the monster had blinded me to his real intentions; and when I thought that I had prepared only my own death, I hastened that of a far dearer victim.

As the period fixed for our marriage drew nearer, whether from cowardice or a prophetic feeling, I felt my heart sink within me. But I concealed my feelings by an appearance of hilarity, that brought smiles and joy to the countenance of my father, but hardly deceived the ever-watchful and nicer eye of Elizabeth. She looked forward to our union with placid contentment, not unmingled with a little fear, which past misfortunes had impressed, that what now appeared certain and tangible happiness, might soon dissipate into an airy dream, and leave no trace but deep and everlasting regret.

Preparations were made for the event; congratulatory visits were received; and all wore a smiling appearance. I shut up, as well as I could, in my own heart the anxiety that preyed there, and entered with seeming earnestness into the plans of my father, although they might only serve as the decorations of my tragedy. A house was purchased for us near Cologny,[9] by which we should enjoy the pleasures of the country, and yet be so near Geneva as to see my father every day; who would still reside within the walls, for the benefit of Ernest, that he might follow his studies at the schools.

8 Percy suggested this "and" clause (*Notebooks* 552–553), tightening the identification with the Creature, and both with exiled Cain.

9 In the region of this village on Lake Geneva's southern shore, the Shelleys and Byron spent the "Frankenstein" summer of 1816. In *1831* Alphonse Frankenstein uses his connections in the Austrian government to get "Villa Lavenza," on Lake Como, restored to Elizabeth (her father had been imprisoned by a tyrannical regime), and the newlyweds head there for their honeymoon (Ch. XXII, 171–172).

10   To her initial draft Mary added: *fixed for its solemnization* (*Notebooks* 554–555).

11   A village near Thonon on the lake's south shore, now famed for mineral waters.

In the mean time I took every precaution to defend my person, in case the fiend should openly attack me. I carried pistols and a dagger constantly about me, and was ever on the watch to prevent artifice; and by these means gained a greater degree of tranquillity. Indeed, as the period approached, the threat appeared more as a delusion, not to be regarded as worthy to disturb my peace, while the happiness I hoped for in my marriage wore a greater appearance of certainty, as the day fixed for its solemnization[10] drew nearer, and I heard it continually spoken of as an occurrence which no accident could possibly prevent.

Elizabeth seemed happy; my tranquil demeanour contributed greatly to calm her mind. But on the day that was to fulfil my wishes and my destiny, she was melancholy, and a presentiment of evil pervaded her; and perhaps also she thought of the dreadful secret, which I had promised to reveal to her on the following day. My father was in the mean time overjoyed, and, in the bustle of preparation, only observed in the melancholy of his niece the diffidence of a bride.

After the ceremony was performed, a large party assembled at my father's; but it was agreed that Elizabeth and I should pass the afternoon and night at Evian,[11] and return to Cologny the next morning. As the day was fair, and the wind favourable, we resolved to go by water.

Those were the last moments of my life during which I enjoyed the feeling of happiness. We passed rapidly along: the sun was hot, but we were sheltered from its rays by a kind of canopy, while we enjoyed the beauty of the scene, sometimes on one side of the lake, where we saw Mont Salêve, the pleasant banks of Montalêgre, and at a distance, surmounting all, the beautiful Mont Blânc, and the assemblage of snowy mountains that in vain endeavour to emulate her; sometimes coasting the opposite banks, we saw the mighty

Jura opposing its dark side to the ambition that would quit its native country, and an almost insurmountable barrier to the invader who should wish to enslave it.[12]

I took the hand of Elizabeth: "You are sorrowful, my love. Ah! if you knew what I have suffered, and what I may yet endure, you would endeavour to let me taste the quiet, and freedom from despair, that this one day at least permits me to enjoy."

"Be happy, my dear Victor," replied Elizabeth; "there is, I hope, nothing to distress you; and be assured that if a lively joy is not painted in my face, my heart is contented. Something whispers to me not to depend too much on the prospect that is opened before us; but I will not listen to such a sinister voice. Observe how fast we move along, and how the clouds which sometimes obscure, and sometimes rise above the dome of Mont Blânc, render this scene of beauty still more interesting. Look also at the innumerable fish that are swimming in the clear waters, where we can distinguish every pebble that lies at the bottom. What a divine day! how happy and serene all nature appears!"

Thus Elizabeth endeavoured to divert her thoughts and mine from all reflection upon melancholy subjects. But her temper was fluctuating; joy for a few instants shone in her eyes, but it continually gave place to distraction and reverie.

The sun sunk lower in the heavens; we passed the river Drance, and observed its path through the chasms of the higher, and the glens of the lower hills. The Alps here come closer to the lake, and we approached the amphitheatre of mountains which forms its eastern boundary. The spire of Evian shone under the woods that surrounded it, and the range of mountain above mountain by which it was overhung.

The wind, which had hitherto carried us along with amazing rapidity, sunk at sunset to a light breeze; the soft air just ruffled the

12 Napoleon invaded Switzerland in 1798, another shock for supporters of the French Revolution, which Napoleon claimed to uphold. This is also a post-Waterloo remark: in 1815, the Congress of Vienna re-established Swiss independence and granted the country a recognition of neutrality in all national conflicts.

13   Mary had ended this chapter on a note of escapist denial: "fears revive which I had forgotten while on the water." Percy suggested the more melodramatic phrasing, of predation and fatal capture.

water, and caused a pleasant motion among the trees as we approached the shore, from which it wafted the most delightful scent of flowers and hay. The sun sunk beneath the horizon as we landed; and as I touched the shore, I felt those cares and fears revive, which soon were to clasp me, and cling to me for ever.[13]

1   A dark and stormy night, now a cliché, in the era of the gothic novel was a thrilling portent of psychological and metaphysical turmoil—and in this register recalls the animation of the Creature and the dream-genesis of the novel.

CHAPTER VI

IT WAS EIGHT O'CLOCK when we landed; we walked for a short time on the shore, enjoying the transitory light, and then retired to the inn, and contemplated the lovely scene of waters, woods, and mountains, obscured in darkness, yet still displaying their black outlines.

The wind, which had fallen in the south, now rose with great violence in the west. The moon had reached her summit in the heavens and was beginning to descend; the clouds swept across it swifter than the flight of the vulture, and dimmed her rays, while the lake reflected the scene of the busy heavens, rendered still busier by the restless waves that were beginning to rise. Suddenly a heavy storm of rain descended.

I had been calm during the day; but so soon as night obscured the shapes of objects, a thousand fears arose in my mind.[1] I was anxious and watchful, while my right hand grasped a pistol which was hidden in my bosom; every sound terrified me; but I resolved that I would sell my life dearly, and not relax the impending conflict until my own life, or that of my adversary, were extinguished.

Elizabeth observed my agitation for some time in timid and fearful silence; at length she said, "What is it that agitates you, my dear Victor? What is it you fear?"

The fainting form of Elizabeth is modeled on Fuseli's *Nightmare*, a painting well known to Mary Shelley.

"Oh! peace, peace, my love," replied I, "this night and all will be safe: but this night is dreadful, very dreadful."

I passed an hour in this state of mind, when suddenly I reflected how dreadful the combat which I momentarily expected would be to my wife, and I earnestly entreated her to retire, resolving not to join her until I had obtained some knowledge as to the situation of my enemy.

She left me,[2] and I continued some time walking up and down the passages of the house, and inspecting every corner that might afford a retreat to my adversary. But I discovered no trace of him, and was beginning to conjecture that some fortunate chance had intervened to prevent the execution of his menaces; when suddenly I heard a shrill and dreadful scream. It came from the room into which Elizabeth had retired. As I heard it, the whole truth rushed into my mind, my arms dropped, the motion of every muscle and fibre was suspended; I could feel the blood trickling in my veins, and tingling in the extremities of my limbs.[3] This state lasted but for an instant; the scream was repeated, and I rushed into the room.

Great God! why did I not then expire! Why am I here to relate the destruction of the best hope, and the purest creature of earth? She was there, lifeless and inanimate, thrown across the bed, her head hanging down, and her pale and distorted features half covered by her hair.[4] Every where I turn I see the same figure—her bloodless arms and relaxed form flung by the murderer on its bridal bier.[5] Could I behold this, and live? Alas! life is obstinate, and clings closest where it is most hated. For a moment only did I lose recollection; I fainted.

When I recovered, I found myself surrounded by the people of the inn; their countenances expressed a breathless terror: but the horror of others appeared only as a mockery, a shadow of the feelings that oppressed me. I escaped from them to the room where

2 Mary Shelley nicely mirrors the misjudged separation in *Paradise Lost* IX, when Adam leaves Eve alone in the Garden of Eden (previously evoked in Henry's fatal separation from Victor).

3 Psychoanalytic readers see in this moment a male's horrific fear of sexual passion as monstrous, fatal to all beautiful ideals.

4 The imperiled sleeper recalls not only Frankenstein's bed invaded by his Creature but also the dream that has terrified him. "In the relentless logic of this 'return of the repressed,'" comments Chris Baldick, "what returns is not so much the monster as the content of Victor's earlier dream: the transformation of Elizabeth into a corpse, which in dream-logic is itself an 'exchange' for the transformation of a corpse into a living being"; *In Frankenstein's Shadow: Myth, Monstrosity, and Nineteenth-Century Writing* (Clarendon Press, 1987), 49. The scene also evokes Fuseli's painting *The Nightmare,* in which an evil spirit crouches on a thinly clothed female sleeper's outstretched body while a mare-head looks on. Shelley's parents knew Fuseli, and in the early 1790s, Wollstonecraft had a mad passion for him. *The Nightmare* inspired some lurid lines in Erasmus Darwin's set of poems *The Botanic Garden* (1789):

> So on his NIGHTMARE through the evening fog
> Flits the squab Fiend o'er fen, and lake, and bog;
> Seeks some love-wilder'd Maid with sleep oppress'd
> Alights, and grinning sits upon her breast.
> —Such as of late amid the murky sky
> Was mark'd by FUSSELI's poetic eye;
> Whose daring tints, with SHAKESPEAR's happiest grace,
> Gave to the airy phantom form and place.—
> Back o'er her pillow sinks her blushing head,
> Her snow-white limbs hang helpless from the bed;
> Her interrupted heart-pulse swims in death. (p. 93)

> O'er her fair limbs convulsive tremors fleet,
> Start in her hands, and struggle in her feet;
> In vain to scream with quivering lips she tries,
> And strains in palsy'd lids her tremulous eyes;
> In vain she *wills* to run, fly, swim, walk, leap;
> The WILL presides not in the bower of SLEEP.
> —On her fair bosom sits the Demon-Ape
> Erect, and ballances his bloated shape;
> Rolls in their marble orbs his Gorgon-eyes,
> And drinks with leathern ears her tender cries.
> (Part II: *The Loves of the Plants,* pp. 94–95)

5 Percy suggested the poignant, alliterative adjective *bridal* (*Notebooks* 556–567).

The Nightmare, by Johann Heinrich Fuseli (1781). Mary Shelley was quite aware of this artist, famed for his erotic candor. When Mary Wollstonecraft met him in 1788, she fell passionately in love, enjoying his company and correspondence so much that in 1792 she suggested (unsuccessfully) to Mme. Fuseli that they form a ménage. This painting, one of Fuseli's most famous, interprets the psychology of the nightmare with two punning images: a "mare" (female goblin) presses heavily the womb of a dreamer, a spectacle on which a "mare" (female horse) gazes with blind or visionary eyes. The dreamer's pose implies erotic ravishment; the naming as "nightmare" brilliantly intuits the release of desires that eighteenth-century culture imagined as demonic.

Fuseli's *Nightmare* informs Mary Shelley's imagery for Victor's nightmarish experiences: his dream on the night he has animated his Creature (a horror in which he embraces and kisses Elizabeth, who is transformed into the corpse of his dead mother); Victor's moonlight view of the Creature looking menacingly through his bed-curtains at him; and Victor's account of the Creature's assault on Elizabeth (a nexus of anxieties about male sexual drives). As Mary and Percy Shelley also knew, Fuseli's image was made into a satire on the enchantment of the French Revolution for British radicals. In one parody (in the 1799 *Anti-Jacobin Review*) Godwin's *Political Justice* lies at the foot of the bed.

The Creature leaving Elizabeth, fainted in horror, in Whale's *Frankenstein,* 1931. The pose of her body shows that Whale, too, knew Fuseli's *Nightmare,* but this Elizabeth survives the Creature's assault.

lay the body of Elizabeth, my love, my wife, so lately living, so dear, so worthy. She had been moved from the posture in which I had first beheld her; and now, as she lay, her head upon her arm, and a handkerchief thrown across her face and neck, I might have supposed her asleep. I rushed towards her, and embraced her with ardour;[6] but the deathly languor and coldness of the limbs told me, that what I now held in my arms had ceased to be the Elizabeth whom I had loved and cherished. The murderous mark of the fiend's grasp was on her neck, and the breath had ceased to issue from her lips.

While I still hung over her in the agony of despair, I happened to look up. The windows of the room had before been darkened; and I felt a kind of panic on seeing the pale yellow light of the moon illuminate the chamber.[7] The shutters had been thrown back; and, with a sensation of horror not to be described, I saw at the open window a figure the most hideous and abhorred. A grin was on the

6 Other than Victor's nightmare embrace of Elizabeth in Vol. 1, Ch. IV (prophetic in retrospect), this is the sole heterosexual embrace in the novel. Knoepflmacher sees the Creature acting out Victor's repressed resentment of Elizabeth for her agency in his mother's death. A very different reading is provided by Wolf (290), who reads a scene of sexual competition.

7 Mary Shelley deftly replays the Creature's first gaze on his creator in Vol. I, Ch. IV, where yellow moonlight and the Creature's yellow eyes are in eerie sympathy. Furthermore, the Creature, with finely calculated revenge, has restaged the scene of Frankenstein's destruction of his own intended bride (Vol. III, Ch. III).

face of the monster; he seemed to jeer, as with his fiendish finger he pointed towards the corpse of my wife. I rushed towards the window and, drawing a pistol from my bosom, shot; but he eluded me, leaped from his station, and, running with the swiftness of lightning, plunged into the lake.

The report of the pistol brought a crowd into the room. I pointed to the spot where he had disappeared, and we followed the track with boats; nets were cast, but in vain. After passing several hours, we returned hopeless, most of my companions believing it to have been a form conjured by my fancy. After having landed, they proceeded to search the country, parties going in different directions among the woods and vines.

I did not accompany them; I was exhausted: a film covered my eyes, and my skin was parched with the heat of fever. In this state I lay on a bed, hardly conscious of what had happened; my eyes wandered round the room, as if to seek something that I had lost.

At length I remembered that my father would anxiously expect the return of Elizabeth and myself, and that I must return alone. This reflection brought tears into my eyes, and I wept for a long time; but my thoughts rambled to various subjects, reflecting on my misfortunes, and their cause. I was bewildered in a cloud of wonder and horror. The death of William, the execution of Justine, the murder of Clerval, and lastly of my wife; even at that moment I knew not that my only remaining friends were safe from the malignity of the fiend; my father even now might be writhing under his grasp, and Ernest might be dead at his feet. This idea made me shudder, and recalled me to action. I started up, and resolved to return to Geneva with all possible speed.

There were no horses to be procured, and I must return by the lake; but the wind was unfavourable, and the rain fell in torrents.

However, it was hardly morning, and I might reasonably hope to arrive by night. I hired men to row, and took an oar myself, for I had always experienced relief from mental torment in bodily exercise. But the overflowing misery I now felt, and the excess of agitation that I endured, rendered me incapable of any exertion. I threw down the oar; and, leaning my head upon my hands, gave way to every gloomy idea that arose. If I looked up, I saw the scenes which were familiar to me in my happier time, and which I had contemplated but the day before in the company of her who was now but a shadow and a recollection. Tears streamed from my eyes. The rain had ceased for a moment, and I saw the fish play in the waters as they had done a few hours before; they had then been observed by Elizabeth. Nothing is so painful to the human mind as a great and sudden change. The sun might shine, or the clouds might lour; but nothing could appear to me as it had done the day before. A fiend had snatched from me every hope of future happiness: no creature had ever been so miserable as I was; so frightful an event is single in the history of man.

But why should I dwell upon the incidents that followed this last overwhelming event? Mine has been a tale of horrors; I have reached their *acme,* and what I must now relate can but be tedious to you. Know that, one by one, my friends were snatched away; I was left desolate.[8] My own strength is exhausted; and I must tell, in a few words, what remains of my hideous narration.

I arrived at Geneva. My father and Ernest[9] yet lived; but the former sunk under the tidings that I bore. I see him now, excellent and venerable old man! his eyes wandered in vacancy, for they had lost their charm and their delight—his niece, his more than daughter, whom he doated on with all that affection which a man feels, who, in the decline of life, having few affections, clings more earnestly to those that remain. Cursed, cursed be the fiend that

8   The Creature has succeeded in recreating Frankenstein in his own image.

9   This is his last mention of his brother.

brought misery on his grey hairs, and doomed him to waste in wretchedness! He could not live under the horrors that were accumulated around him; an apoplectic fit was brought on, and in a few days he died in my arms.

What then became of me? I know not; I lost sensation, and chains and darkness were the only objects that pressed upon me. Sometimes, indeed, I dreamt that I wandered in flowery meadows and pleasant vales with the friends of my youth; but awoke, and found myself in a dungeon. Melancholy followed, but by degrees I gained a clear conception of my miseries and situation, and was then released from my prison. For they had called me mad; and during many months, as I understood, a solitary cell had been my habitation.

But liberty had been a useless gift to me had I not, as I awakened to reason, at the same time awakened to revenge. As the memory of past misfortunes pressed upon me, I began to reflect on their cause—the monster whom I had created, the miserable dæmon whom I had sent abroad into the world for my destruction. I was possessed by a maddening rage when I thought of him, and desired and ardently prayed that I might have him within my grasp to wreak a great and signal revenge on his cursed head.

Nor did my hate long confine itself to useless wishes; I began to reflect on the best means of securing him; and for this purpose, about a month after my release, I repaired to a criminal judge in the town, and told him that I had an accusation to make; and that I knew the destroyer of my family; and that I required him to exert his whole authority for the apprehension of the murderer.

The magistrate listened to me with attention and kindness. "Be assured, sir," said he, "no pains or exertions on my part shall be spared to discover the villain."

"I thank you," replied I; "listen, therefore, to the deposition that I have to make. It is indeed a tale so strange that I should fear you would not credit it, were there not something in truth which, however wonderful, forces conviction. The story is too connected to be mistaken for a dream, and I have no motive for falsehood." My manner, as I thus addressed him, was impressive, but calm; I had formed in my heart a resolution to pursue my destroyer to death; and this purpose quieted my agony, and provisionally reconciled me to life. I now related my history briefly, but with firmness and precision, marking the dates with accuracy, and never deviating into or exclamation.

The magistrate appeared at first perfectly incredulous, but as I continued he became more attentive and interested; I saw him sometimes shudder with horror, at others a lively surprise, unmingled with disbelief, was painted on his countenance.

When I had concluded my narration, I said: "This is the being whom I accuse, and for whose detection and punishment I call upon you to exert your whole power. It is your duty as a magistrate, and I believe and hope that your feelings as a man will not revolt from the execution of those functions on this occasion."

This address caused a considerable change in the physiognomy of my auditor. He had heard my story with that half kind of belief that is given to a tale of spirits and supernatural events;[10] but when he was called upon to act officially in consequence, the whole tide of his incredulity returned. He, however, answered mildly, "I would willingly afford you every aid in your pursuit; but the creature of whom you speak appears to have powers which would put all my exertions to defiance. Who can follow an animal which can traverse the sea of ice, and inhabit caves and dens where no man would venture to intrude? Besides, some months have

10 As the first audience of Frankenstein's story, the magistrate doubles Walton as well as the novel's readers. The language of "supernatural events" and the suspension of "disbelief" reflects Coleridge's principles of imagination in two works impinging on *Frankenstein: The Rime of the Ancient Mariner* (republished in 1817) and *Christabel* (1816), a vampire tale that Byron read aloud during the ghost-story week. In *Biographia Literaria* (1817; which the Shelleys read) Coleridge explains his use of "incidents and agents . . . in part at least, supernatural" in *The Rime* and *Christabel*: not shallow sensationalism but an experiment in "the dramatic truth of such emotions, as would naturally accompany such situations, supposing them real . . . so as to transfer from our inward nature a human interest and semblance of truth sufficient to procure for these shadows of imagination that willing suspension of disbelief for the moment, which constitutes poetic faith" (Chap. XIV). This is the mode of *Frankenstein* overall.

11 Revenge is the motive, often on a principle of individual, family, or tribal honor, in much classical epic and drama. In Christian ethics, revenge is more than "vice"; it is a mortal "sin" because it assumes God's prerogative: "Vengeance [is] mine; I will repay, saith the Lord"; the crucial text is St. Paul (Romans 12: 14–21). No matter: revenge remained a powerful motor in literary imagination, from Renaissance drama, to *Paradise Lost,* to eighteenth-century novels (especially the gothic).

12 In the course of describing his agitated behavior, Frankenstein returns to the vanity and sense of self-importance we have heard throughout, attributing his rage to a heroic elevation of mind that is not appreciated by the dull, bourgeois Genevese.

elapsed since the commission of his crimes, and no one can conjecture to what place he has wandered, or what region he may now inhabit."

"I do not doubt that he hovers near the spot which I inhabit; and if he has indeed taken refuge in the Alps, he may be hunted like the chamois, and destroyed as a beast of prey. But I perceive your thoughts: you do not credit my narrative, and do not intend to pursue my enemy with the punishment which is his desert."

As I spoke, rage sparkled in my eyes; the magistrate was intimidated; "You are mistaken," said he, "I will exert myself; and if it is in my power to seize the monster, be assured that he shall suffer punishment proportionate to his crimes. But I fear, from what you have yourself described to be his properties, that this will prove impracticable, and that, while every proper measure is pursued, you should endeavour to make up your mind to disappointment."

"That cannot be; but all that I can say will be of little avail. My revenge is of no moment to you; yet, while I allow it to be a vice, I confess that it is the devouring and only passion of my soul.[11] My rage is unspeakable, when I reflect that the murderer, whom I have turned loose upon society, still exists. You refuse my just demand: I have but one resource; and I devote myself, either in my life or death, to his destruction."

I trembled with excess of agitation as I said this; there was a phrenzy in my manner, and something, I doubt not, of that haughty fierceness, which the martyrs of old are said to have possessed. But to a Genevan magistrate, whose mind was occupied by far other ideas than those of devotion and heroism, this elevation of mind had much the appearance of madness.[12] He endeavoured to soothe me as a nurse does a child, and reverted to my tale as the effects of delirium.

"Man," I cried, "how ignorant art thou in thy pride of wisdom! Cease; you know not what it is you say."

I broke from the house angry and disturbed, and retired to meditate on some other mode of action.

CHAPTER VII

MY PRESENT SITUATION was one in which all voluntary thought was swallowed up and lost. I was hurried away by fury; revenge alone endowed me with strength and composure; it modelled my feelings, and allowed me to be calculating and calm, at periods when otherwise delirium or death would have been my portion.

My first resolution was to quit Geneva for ever; my country, which, when I was happy and beloved, was dear to me, now, in my adversity, became hateful. I provided myself with a sum of money, together with a few jewels which had belonged to my mother, and departed.

And now my wanderings began, which are to cease but with life. I have traversed a vast portion of the earth, and have endured all the hardships which travellers, in deserts and barbarous countries, are wont to meet. How I have lived I hardly know; many times have I stretched my failing limbs upon the sandy plain, and prayed for death. But revenge kept me alive; I dared not die, and leave my adversary in being.

When I quitted Geneva, my first labour was to gain some clue by which I might trace the steps of my fiendish enemy. But my plan was unsettled; and I wandered many hours round the confines of the town, uncertain what path I should pursue. As night approached, I found myself at the entrance of the cemetery where William, Elizabeth, and my father reposed. I entered it, and ap-

1   That is, one without a personal connection to particular grave-sites.

2   The Creature has felt nothing but this agony and despair. The logic of revenge is potentially endless, as each party seeks to return equal misery on its opponent.

3   By using this plural for his passion, Frankenstein evokes the furies of classical mythology, charged with avenging unpunished crimes, and imagines himself trapped inside a Greek tragedy.

proached the tomb which marked their graves. Every thing was silent, except the leaves of the trees, which were gently agitated by the wind; the night was nearly dark; and the scene would have been solemn and affecting even to an uninterested observer.[1] The spirits of the departed seemed to flit around, and to cast a shadow, which was felt but seen not, around the head of the mourner.

The deep grief which this scene had at first excited quickly gave way to rage and despair. They were dead, and I lived; their murderer also lived, and to destroy him I must drag out my weary existence. I knelt on the grass, and kissed the earth, and with quivering lips exclaimed, "By the sacred earth on which I kneel, by the shades that wander near me, by the deep and eternal grief that I feel, I swear; and by thee, O Night, and by the spirits that preside over thee, I swear to pursue the dæmon, who caused this misery, until he or I shall perish in mortal conflict. For this purpose I will preserve my life: to execute this dear revenge, will I again behold the sun, and tread the green herbage of earth, which otherwise should vanish from my eyes for ever. And I call on you, spirits of the dead; and on you, wandering ministers of vengeance, to aid and conduct me in my work. Let the cursed and hellish monster drink deep of agony; let him feel the despair that now torments me."[2]

I had begun my adjuration with solemnity, and an awe which almost assured me that the shades of my murdered friends heard and approved my devotion; but the furies[3] possessed me as I concluded, and rage choked my utterance.

I was answered through the stillness of night by a loud and fiendish laugh. It rung on my ears long and heavily; the mountains re-echoed it, and I felt as if all hell surrounded me with mockery and laughter. Surely in that moment I should have been possessed by phrenzy, and have destroyed my miserable existence, but that

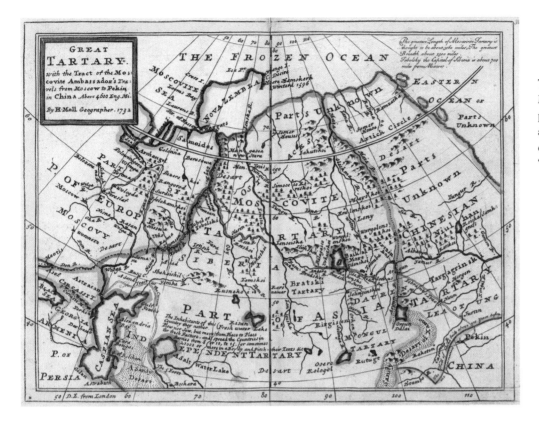

Tartary, engraved map by Herman Moll, geographer, 1732. Victor's pursuit of the Creature leads him across the frontiers beyond the edge of European civilization into "Parts Unknown."

my vow was heard, and that I was reserved for vengeance. The laughter died away; when a well-known and abhorred voice, apparently close to my ear, addressed me in an audible whisper—"I am satisfied: miserable wretch! you have determined to live, and I am satisfied."

I darted towards the spot from which the sound proceeded; but the devil[4] eluded my grasp. Suddenly the broad disk of the moon arose, and shone full upon his ghastly and distorted shape, as he fled with more than mortal speed.[5]

I pursued him; and for many months this has been my task. Guided by a slight clue, I followed the windings of the Rhone, but

4 Mary first wrote *wretch,* then *villain,* then, on Percy's suggestion, *devil,* allowing Frankenstein to cast his Creature as a supernatural and inhuman antagonist.

5 Percy supplied the last clause of this sentence, to highlight the Creature's nightmarish power (*Notebooks* 586–587).

6 Frankenstein joins his Creature in echoing Milton's Satan: "Which way I fly is hell; my self am hell" (*Paradise Lost* IV.75); "the hot hell that always in him burns" (IX.467).

7 In a more precise sense of the day: "complained of difficulties."

8 This whole adventure has a surreal quality; it does not occur to Frankenstein that his Creature is leading him on, keeping him alive.

vainly. The blue Mediterranean appeared; and, by a strange chance, I saw the fiend enter by night, and hide himself in a vessel bound for the Black Sea. I took my passage in the same ship; but he escaped, I know not how.

Amidst the wilds of Tartary and Russia, although he still evaded me, I have ever followed in his track. Sometimes the peasants, scared by this horrid apparition, informed me of his path; sometimes he himself, who feared that if I lost all trace I should despair and die, often left some mark to guide me. The snows descended on my head, and I saw the print of his huge step on the white plain. To you first entering on life, to whom care is new, and agony unknown, how can you understand what I have felt, and still feel? Cold, want, and fatigue, were the least pains which I was destined to endure; I was cursed by some devil, and carried about with me my eternal hell;[6] yet still a spirit of good followed and directed my steps, and, when I most murmured,[7] would suddenly extricate me from seemingly insurmountable difficulties. Sometimes, when nature, overcome by hunger, sunk under the exhaustion, a repast was prepared for me in the desert, that restored and inspirited me. The fare was, indeed, coarse, such as the peasants of the country ate; but I may not doubt that it was set there by the spirits that I had invoked to aid me.[8] Often, when all was dry, the heavens cloudless, and I was parched by thirst, a slight cloud would bedim the sky, shed the few drops that revived me, and vanish.

I followed, when I could, the courses of the rivers; but the dæmon generally avoided these, as it was here that the population of the country chiefly collected. In other places human beings were seldom seen; and I generally subsisted on the wild animals that crossed my path. I had money with me, and gained the friendship of the villagers by distributing it, or bringing with me some food that I had killed, which, after taking a small part, I always presented to those who had provided me with fire and utensils for cooking.

My life, as it passed thus, was indeed hateful to me, and it was during sleep alone that I could taste joy. O blessed sleep! often, when most miserable, I sank to repose, and my dreams lulled me even to rapture. The spirits that guarded me had provided these moments, or rather hours, of happiness, that I might retain strength to fulfil my pilgrimage. Deprived of this respite, I should have sunk under my hardships. During the day I was sustained and inspirited by the hope of night: for in sleep I saw my friends, my wife, and my beloved country; again I saw the benevolent countenance of my father, heard the silver tones of my Elizabeth's voice, and beheld Clerval enjoying health and youth. Often, when wearied by a toil-some march, I persuaded myself that I was dreaming until night should come, and that I should then enjoy reality in the arms of my dearest friends. What agonizing fondness did I feel for them! how did I cling to their dear forms, as sometimes they haunted even my waking hours, and persuade myself that they still lived! At such moments vengeance, that burned within me, died in my heart, and I pursued my path towards the destruction of the dæ-mon more as a task enjoined by heaven, as the mechanical impulse of some power of which I was unconscious, than as the ardent de-sire of my soul.

What his feelings were whom I pursued, I cannot know. Some-times, indeed, he left marks in writing on the barks of the trees, or cut in stone, that guided me, and instigated my fury.[9] "My reign is not yet over," (these words were legible in one of these inscriptions); "you live, and my power is complete. Follow me; I seek the ever-lasting ices of the north, where you will feel the misery of cold and frost, to which I am impassive. You will find near this place, if you follow not too tardily, a dead hare; eat, and be refreshed. Come on,

9 Mary was reading Ariosto's *Orlando Furioso* in 1815. In this romance (already mentioned by Elizabeth and Victor), Orlando is driven to fury upon seeing his beloved's name carved upon trees with the name of another lover.

10   On the retreat of Xenophon's army from Persia through Armenia in the 5th century B.C., the men were ecstatic at the sight of the sea, and of their nearness to home.

my enemy; we have yet to wrestle for our lives; but many hard and miserable hours must you endure, until that period shall arrive."

Scoffing devil! Again do I vow vengeance; again do I devote thee, miserable fiend, to torture and death. Never will I omit my search, until he or I perish; and then with what ecstasy shall I join my Elizabeth, and those who even now prepare for me the reward of my tedious toil and horrible pilgrimage.

As I still pursued my journey to the northward, the snows thickened, and the cold increased in a degree almost too severe to support. The peasants were shut up in their hovels, and only a few of the most hardy ventured forth to seize the animals whom starvation had forced from their hiding-places to seek for prey. The rivers were covered with ice, and no fish could be procured; and thus I was cut off from my chief article of maintenance.

The triumph of my enemy increased with the difficulty of my labours. One inscription that he left was in these words: "Prepare! your toils only begin: wrap yourself in furs, and provide food, for we shall soon enter upon a journey where your sufferings will satisfy my everlasting hatred."

My courage and perseverance were invigorated by these scoffing words; I resolved not to fail in my purpose; and, calling on heaven to support me, I continued with unabated fervour to traverse immense deserts, until the ocean appeared at a distance, and formed the utmost boundary of the horizon. Oh! how unlike it was to the blue seas of the south! Covered with ice, it was only to be distinguished from land by its superior wildness and ruggedness. The Greeks wept for joy when they beheld the Mediterranean from the hills of Asia, and hailed with rapture the boundary of their toils.[10] I did not weep; but I knelt down, and, with a full heart, thanked my guiding spirit for conducting me in safety to the place where I hoped, notwithstanding my adversary's gibe, to meet and grapple with him.

Some weeks before this period I had procured a sledge and dogs, and thus traversed the snows with inconceivable speed. I know not whether the fiend possessed the same advantages; but I found that, as before I had daily lost ground in the pursuit, I now gained on him; so much so that, when I first saw the ocean, he was but one day's journey in advance, and I hoped to intercept him before he should reach the beach. With new courage, therefore, I pressed on, and in two days arrived at a wretched hamlet on the sea-shore. I inquired of the inhabitants concerning the fiend, and gained accurate information.[11] A gigantic monster, they said, had arrived the night before, armed with a gun and many pistols; putting to flight the inhabitants of a solitary cottage, through fear of his terrific appearance. He had carried off their store of winter food,[12] and, placing it in a sledge, to draw which he had seized on a numerous drove of trained dogs, he had harnessed them, and the same night, to the joy of the horror-struck villagers, had pursued his journey across the sea in a direction that led to no land; and they conjectured that he must speedily be destroyed by the breaking of the ice, or frozen by the eternal frosts.

On hearing this information, I suffered a temporary access of despair. He had escaped me; and I must commence a destructive and almost endless journey across the mountainous ices of the ocean,—amidst cold that few of the inhabitants could long endure, and which I, the native of a genial and sunny climate, could not hope to survive. Yet at the idea that the fiend should live and be triumphant, my rage and vengeance returned, and, like a mighty tide, overwhelmed every other feeling. After a slight repose, during which the spirits of the dead hovered round, and instigated me to toil and revenge, I prepared for my journey.

I exchanged my land-sledge for one fashioned for the inequalities of the frozen ocean; and,, purchasing a plentiful stock of provisions, I departed from land.

11   It is unclear if Mary Shelley expected us to imagine Frankenstein speaking Russian.

12   Not only a stark inversion of his care for the De Laceys, this action may condemn these peasants to starvation. Napoleon's armies were notorious for this tactic.

13 This image seeks to top in sublime terror what the Ancient Mariner reports in his already alarming, potentially prophetic, view from his ship of "Ice mast-high" (51).

I cannot guess how many days have passed since then; but I have endured misery, which nothing but the eternal sentiment of a just retribution burning within my heart could have enabled me to support. Immense and rugged mountains of ice often barred up my passage,[13] and I often heard the thunder of the ground sea, which threatened my destruction. But again the frost came, and made the paths of the sea secure.

By the quantity of provision which I had consumed I should guess that I had passed three weeks in this journey; and the continual protraction of hope, returning back upon the heart, often wrung bitter drops of despondency and grief from my eyes. Despair had indeed almost secured her prey, and I should soon have sunk beneath this misery; when once, after the poor animals that carried me had with incredible toil gained the summit of a sloping ice mountain, and one sinking under his fatigue died, I viewed the expanse before me with anguish, when suddenly my eye caught a dark speck upon the dusky plain. I strained my sight to discover what it could be, and uttered a wild cry of ecstasy when I distinguished a sledge, and the distorted proportions of a well-known form within. Oh! with what a burning gush did hope revisit my heart! warm tears filled my eyes, which I hastily wiped away, that they might not intercept the view I had of the dæmon; but still my sight was dimmed by the burning drops, until, giving way to the emotions that oppressed me, I wept aloud.

But this was not the time for delay; I disencumbered the dogs of their dead companion, gave them a plentiful portion of food; and, after an hour's rest, which was absolutely necessary, and yet which was bitterly irksome to me, I continued my route. The sledge was still visible; nor did I again lose sight of it, except at the moments when for a short time some ice rock concealed it with its intervening crags. I indeed perceptibly gained on it; and when, after nearly two days' journey, I beheld my enemy at no more than a mile distant, my heart bounded within me.

But now, when I appeared almost within grasp of my enemy, my hopes were suddenly extinguished, and I lost all trace of him more utterly than I had ever done before. A ground sea was heard; the thunder of its progress, as the waters rolled and swelled beneath me, became every moment more ominous and terrific. I pressed on, but in vain. The wind arose; the sea roared; and, as with the mighty shock of an earthquake, it split, and cracked with a tremendous and overwhelming sound. The work was soon finished: in a few minutes a tumultuous sea rolled between me and my enemy, and I was left drifting on a scattered piece of ice, that was continually lessening, and thus preparing for me a hideous death.

In this manner many appalling hours passed; several of my dogs died; and I myself was about to sink under the accumulation of distress, when I saw your vessel riding at anchor, and holding forth to me hopes of succour and life. I had no conception that vessels ever came so far north, and was astounded at the sight. I quickly destroyed part of my sledge to construct oars; and by these means was enabled, with infinite fatigue, to move my ice-raft in the direction of your ship. I had determined, if you were going southward, still to trust myself to the mercy of the seas, rather than abandon my purpose. I hoped to induce you to grant me a boat with which I could pursue my enemy. But your direction was northward. You took me on board when my vigour was exhausted, and I should soon have sunk under my multiplied hardships into a death, which I still dread,—for my task is unfulfilled.

Oh! when will my guiding spirit, in conducting me to the dæmon, allow me the rest I so much desire; or must I die, and he yet

14   For all his pathos, Frankenstein forgets he was the first maker of a wretch. Creature and creator have become each other's maker.

15   The spirits of these dead.

16   Frankenstein, who at first saw in Walton a version of his own reckless ambition, now attempts to infect him with his own obsession.

17   This inscription appears as that of some later reader or editor.

18   Walton's frame-story returns with a resurgence of explicit horror-genre language. He has shifted from audience to purveyor, and he becomes an actor in the narrative finale. The *like*-clause is Percy's addition (*Notebooks* 604–605), underscoring the vampiric effect of narrative transmission.

live? If I do, swear to me, Walton, that he shall not escape; that you will seek him and satisfy my vengeance in his death. Yet, do I dare ask you to undertake my pilgrimage, to endure the hardships that I have undergone? No; I am not so selfish. Yet, when I am dead, if he should appear; if the ministers of vengeance should conduct him to you, swear that he shall not live—swear that he shall not triumph over my accumulated woes, and live to make another such a wretch as I am.[14] He is eloquent and persuasive; and once his words had even power over my heart: but trust him not. His soul is as hellish as his form, full of treachery and fiend-like malice. Hear him not; call on the manes[15] of William, Justine, Clerval, Elizabeth, my father, and of the wretched Victor, and thrust your sword into his heart. I will hover near, and direct the steel aright.[16]

WALTON, *in continuation.*[17]

August 26th, 17—.

You have read this strange and terrific story, Margaret; and do you not feel your blood congeal with horror, like that which even now curdles mine?[18] Sometimes, seized with sudden agony, he could not continue his tale; at others, his voice broken, yet piercing, uttered with difficulty the words so replete with agony. His fine and lovely eyes were now lighted up with indignation, now subdued to downcast sorrow, and quenched in infinite wretchedness. Sometimes he commanded his countenance and tones, and related the most horrible incidents with a tranquil voice, suppressing every mark of agitation; then, like a volcano bursting forth, his face would suddenly change to an expression of the wildest rage, as he shrieked out imprecations on his persecutor.

His tale is connected, and told with an appearance of the simplest truth; yet I own to you that the letters of Felix and Safie, which he shewed me, and the apparition of the monster, seen from our ship, brought to me a greater conviction of the truth of his narrative than his asseverations, however earnest and connected.[19] Such a monster has then really existence; I cannot doubt it; yet I am lost in surprise and admiration. Sometimes I endeavoured to gain from Frankenstein the particulars of his creature's formation; but on this point he was impenetrable.

"Are you mad, my friend?" said he; "or whither does your senseless curiosity lead you? Would you also create for yourself and the world a demoniacal enemy? Or to what do your questions tend? Peace, peace! learn my miseries, and do not seek to increase your own."

Frankenstein discovered that I made notes concerning his history: he asked to see them, and then himself corrected and augmented them in many places;[20] but principally in giving the life and spirit to the conversations he held with his enemy. "Since you have preserved my narration," said he, "I would not that a mutilated one should go down to posterity."[21]

Thus has a week passed away, while I have listened to the strangest tale that ever imagination formed. My thoughts, and every feeling of my soul, have been drunk up by the interest for my guest, which this tale, and his own elevated and gentle manners have created. I wish to soothe him; yet can I counsel one so infinitely miserable, so destitute of every hope of consolation, to live? Oh, no! the only joy that he can now know will be when he composes his shattered feelings to peace and death. Yet he enjoys one comfort, the offspring of solitude and delirium: he believes, that, when in dreams he holds converse with his friends, and derives from that communion consolation for his miseries, or excitements to his vengeance, they are not the creations of his fancy, but the real beings who visit him from the regions of a remote world. This faith gives a solemnity to his reveries that render them to me almost as imposing and interesting as truth.

19   Textual transmissions—letters (hallmark of the epistolary novel); notebooks and narrative notes; and even the literary works that influence the characters—remain a crucial resource for infusing various reports and tales with credibility. At the same time, the assembly of these disparate components into one document, a manuscript to be transmitted, makes the novel itself a secondary "Frankenstein" creation. More than one reviewer described it as a monstrous production.

20   Mary Shelley reflects her relationship with Percy Shelley's textual service: his correcting and augmenting her draft in many places.

21   In editorial terminology, "mutilated" refers to a text corrupted by a transcriber or printer. Frankenstein's devotion to this unmutilated creation ironically evokes his mutilated Creature, whom he would now control in narration. His phrase for the career of "his history," *down to posterity,* echoes the opening sentence of his narrative, boasting of his ancestry and of a father's plan of "bestowing on the state sons who might carry his virtues and his name down to posterity"—the novel's only two instances of the word *posterity.* Frankenstein exposes his hideous, gothic perversion of bestowal (uttered with more pride in Mary Shelley's description of her novel, in the Introduction of 1831, as her "hideous progeny").

"The Crews of H.M.S. Hecla & Griper Cutting Into Winter Harbour, Sept. 26th, 1819" is an illustration in *Journal of a Voyage for the Discovery of a North-West Passage from the Atlantic to the Pacific: Performed in the Years, 1819-20, in His Majesty's Ships Hecla and Griper, Under the Orders of William Edward Parry; With an Appendix Containing the Scientific and Other Observations* (The Library at The Mariners' Museum, 1821). This expedition, commanded by Sir William Edward Parry (1790–1855), was Friedrich's inspiration for *Mer de Glace.* Having reached a record latitude, more than half the distance from Greenland to the Bering Strait, Parry was compelled to retreat. He returned to England in November 1820, comforted by the success of proving the possibility of a northwest passage. Parry undertook further polar expeditions in 1821–1823, and again in 1824—all unsuccessful, but admired for their purpose and daring.

In mid-September, Walton's crew is alarmed by the increasing perils, even as their novice captain remains devoted to a northward push. The crews depicted in this engraving are digging a water-path through the ice to establish a winter harbor, knowing that by September they must await the longer days and warmer temperatures of spring for the ice to break.

In 1827 the Arctic explorer Sir William Edward Parry (1790–1855) again attempted to reach the North Pole, traveling farther north than any previous expedition. His record stood for almost fifty years.

Our conversations are not always confined to his own history and misfortunes. On every point of general literature he displays unbounded knowledge, and a quick and piercing apprehension. His eloquence is forcible and touching; nor can I hear him, when he relates a pathetic incident, or endeavours to move the passions of pity or love, without tears. What a glorious creature must he have been in the days of his prosperity when he is thus noble and godlike in ruin.[22] He seems to feel his own worth, and the greatness of his fall.[23]

"When younger," said he, "I felt as if I were destined for some great enterprise. My feelings are profound; but I possessed a coolness of judgment that fitted me for illustrious achievements. This

22 Milton's fallen Satan appears in Hell as "Arch-angel ruin'd, and th' excess / Of glory obscur'd" (*Paradise Lost* I.593–594)—an image of Victor Frankenstein that Walton approached in Letter IV (see p. 82, above).

23 Echoing Frankenstein's view of himself as a victim of destiny and overwhelming forces, Walton represents his story in the terminology of Greek tragedy—in contrast to the other impressive story of man's fall marked on the novel's title page, *Paradise Lost*. Mary presents a complex character. She imprints Victor Frankenstein with many elements of Percy's idealism and felt sense of persecution by an unappreciative world. Yet she also scripts Frankenstein's last actions and self-accounting (as Shakespeare does with Othello) in terms that may strain our sympathy.

24 Those with a project (scientists or entrepreneurs).

25 After allowing himself (in the comparison of the previous sentence) one more expression of pride, Frankenstein then debases himself lower than the dust that is the fate of the mortal herd. His shifting between extremes continues until the bitter end.

26 For his presumption, Satan (formerly the archangel Lucifer) is plunged to "bottomless perdition, there to dwell / In adamantine chains and penal fire" (*Paradise Lost* I.47–48). Frankenstein enrolls himself in the fraternity of Romantic Satans: noble, daring, tragic, tormented transgressors of conventional morality.

27 Losing his soul mate, Walton relapses to his original loneliness. In the first sentence of this paragraph, Mary first wrote "creature," then decided on "admirable being" (*Notebooks* 610–611).

28 Naming Clerval before Elizabeth may respect the chronology of their deaths, but it also reflects the intense male affections in this tale.

sentiment of the worth of my nature supported me, when others would have been oppressed; for I deemed it criminal to throw away in useless grief those talents that might be useful to my fellow-creatures. When I reflected on the work I had completed, no less a one than the creation of a sensitive and rational animal, I could not rank myself with the herd of common projectors.[24] But this feeling, which supported me in the commencement of my career, now serves only to plunge me lower in the dust.[25] All my speculations and hopes are as nothing; and, like the archangel who aspired to omnipotence, I am chained in an eternal hell.[26] My imagination was vivid, yet my powers of analysis and application were intense; by the union of these qualities I conceived the idea, and executed the creation of a man. Even now I cannot recollect, without passion, my reveries while the work was incomplete. I trod heaven in my thoughts, now exulting in my powers, now burning with the idea of their effects. From my infancy I was imbued with high hopes and a lofty ambition; but how am I sunk! Oh! my friend, if you had known me as I once was, you would not recognize me in this state of degradation. Despondency rarely visited my heart; a high destiny seemed to bear me on, until I fell, never, never again to rise."

Must I then lose this admirable being? I have longed for a friend; I have sought one who would sympathize with and love me.[27] Behold, on these desert seas I have found such a one; but, I fear, I have gained him only to know his value, and lose him. I would reconcile him to life, but he repulses the idea.

"I thank you, Walton," he said, "for your kind intentions towards so miserable a wretch; but when you speak of new ties, and fresh affections, think you that any can replace those who are gone? Can any man be to me as Clerval was; or any woman another Elizabeth?[28] Even where the affections are not strongly moved by any superior excellence, the companions of our child-

hood always possess a certain power over our minds, which hardly any later friend can obtain. They know our infantine dispositions, which, however they may be afterwards modified, are never eradicated; and they can judge of our actions with more certain conclusions as to the integrity of our motives. A sister or a brother can never, unless indeed such symptoms have been shewn early, suspect the other of fraud or false dealing, when another friend, however strongly he may be attached, may, in spite of himself, be invaded with suspicion. But I enjoyed friends, dear not only through habit and association, but from their own merits; and, wherever I am, the soothing voice of my Elizabeth, and the conversation of Clerval, will be ever whispered in my ear. They are dead; and but one feeling in such a solitude can persuade me to preserve my life. If I were engaged in any high undertaking or design, fraught with extensive utility to my fellow-creatures, then could I live to fulfil it. But such is not my destiny; I must pursue and destroy the being to whom I gave existence; then my lot on earth will be fulfilled, and I may die."

A whaling expedition meets a catastrophe in the harsh ice-world of winter. The image is from *An account of several late voyages and discoveries: 4 vols., IV: F. Marten's voyage to Spitzbergen and Greenland,* by Sir John Narbrough, 2nd edition (1724), facing p. 4.

29 The overt sense is *destined*.

30 This first-century Roman Stoic was condemned to suicide by his former pupil Nero after an unsuccessful conspiracy to overthrow his tyranny. He calmly carried out the order, true to his philosophy of emotional detachment.

31 This is richly ironic: even as Frankenstein's compassionate encouragements mask his agenda to keep a course north in order to pursue the Creature, he has warned Walton about the Creature's "eloquent and persuasive" rhetorical "power."

September 2d.

MY BELOVED SISTER,

I write to you, encompassed by peril, and ignorant whether I am ever doomed[29] to see again dear England, and the dearer friends that inhabit it. I am surrounded by mountains of ice, which admit of no escape, and threaten every moment to crush my vessel. The brave fellows, whom I have persuaded to be my companions, look towards me for aid; but I have none to bestow. There is something terribly appalling in our situation, yet my courage and hopes do not desert me. We may survive; and if we do not, I will repeat the lessons of my Seneca, and die with a good heart.[30]

Yet what, Margaret, will be the state of your mind? You will not hear of my destruction, and you will anxiously await my return. Years will pass, and you will have visitings of despair, and yet be tortured by hope. Oh! my beloved sister, the sickening failings of your heart-felt expectations are, in prospect, more terrible to me than my own death. But you have a husband, and lovely children; you may be happy: heaven bless you, and make you so!

My unfortunate guest regards me with the tenderest compassion. He endeavours to fill me with hope; and talks as if life were a possession which he valued. He reminds me how often the same accidents have happened to other navigators, who have attempted this sea, and, in spite of myself, he fills me with cheerful auguries. Even the sailors feel the power of his eloquence: when he speaks, they no longer despair; he rouses their energies, and, while they hear his voice, they believe these vast mountains of ice are mole-hills, which will vanish before the resolutions of man.[31] These feelings are transitory; each day's expectation delayed fills them with fear, and I almost dread a mutiny caused by this despair.

September 5th.

A scene has just passed of such uncommon interest, that although it is highly probable that these papers may never reach you, yet I cannot forbear recording it.

We are still surrounded by mountains of ice, still in imminent danger of being crushed in their conflict. The cold is excessive, and many of my unfortunate comrades have already found a grave amidst this scene of desolation.[32] Frankenstein has daily declined in health: a feverish fire still glimmers in his eyes; but he is exhausted, and, when suddenly roused to any exertion, he speedily sinks again into apparent lifelessness.

I mentioned in my last letter the fears I entertained of a mutiny. This morning, as I sat watching the wan countenance of my friend—his eyes half closed, and his limbs hanging listlessly,—I was roused by half a dozen of the sailors, who desired admission into the cabin. They entered; and their leader addressed me. He told me that he and his companions had been chosen by the other sailors to come in deputation to me, to make me a demand, which, in justice, I could not refuse.[33] We were immured in ice, and should probably never escape; but they feared that if, as was possible, the ice should dissipate, and a free passage be opened, I should be rash enough to continue my voyage, and lead them into fresh dangers, after they might happily have surmounted this. They desired, therefore, that I should engage with a solemn promise, that if the vessel should be freed, I would instantly direct my course southward.

This speech troubled me. I had not despaired; nor had I yet conceived the idea of returning, if set free. Yet could I, in justice, or even in possibility, refuse this demand? I hesitated before I answered; when Frankenstein, who had at first been silent, and, indeed, appeared hardly to have force enough to attend, now roused himself; his eyes sparkled, and his cheeks flushed with momentary vigour.[34] Turning towards the men, he said—

32 The dying of Walton's crew repeats in human beings the dwindling of Frankenstein's sled-dogs, exposing the life-wasting obsession that grips both men.

33 This deputation to Walton, a potential prelude to mutiny, would recall to nineteenth-century readers the sensational mutiny on the *HMS Bounty* in 1789 and, more generally, widespread discussion in the age about political justice and revolution.

34 This is the final scene of re-animation in the novel: Frankenstein stirs himself back to life for one last heroic volley.

View of the Racehorse and Carcass August 7th 1773, when inclosed in the ice in Lat. 80° 37.N. Engraved for Payne's *Universal Geography,* V:
481, after John Cleveley. Horatio Nelson was a midshipman on the *Carcass.* Setting off in June, this expedition managed to reach within ten degrees of the North Pole before getting icebound. When the ice broke with a shift in the wind, they were able to make it back to Britain by September. This close call is reprised in *Frankenstein* when a shift in the wind on September 11 (see p. 316, below) saves Walton's icebound crew.

"What do you mean? What do you demand of your captain? Are you then so easily turned from your design? Did you not call this a glorious expedition? and wherefore was it glorious? Not because the way was smooth and placid as a southern sea, but because it was full of dangers and terror; because, at every new incident, your fortitude was to be called forth, and your courage exhibited; because danger and death surrounded, and these dangers you were to brave and overcome. For this was it a glorious, for this was it an honourable undertaking. You were hereafter to be hailed as the benefactors of your species;[35] your name adored, as belonging to brave men who encountered death for honour and the benefit of mankind. And now, behold, with the first imagination of danger, or, if you will, the first mighty and terrific trial of your courage, you shrink away, and are content to be handed down as men who had not strength enough to endure cold and peril; and so, poor souls, they were chilly, and returned to their warm fire-sides. Why, that requires not this preparation; ye need not have come thus far, and dragged your captain to the shame of a defeat, merely to prove yourselves cowards. Oh! be men, or be more than men. Be steady to your purposes, and firm as a rock. This ice is not made of such stuff as your hearts might be; it is mutable, cannot withstand you, if you say that it shall not. Do not return to your families with the stigma of disgrace marked on your brows. Return as heroes who have fought and conquered, and who know not what it is to turn their backs on the foe."[36]

He spoke this with a voice so modulated to the different feelings expressed in his speech, with an eye so full of lofty design and heroism, that can you wonder that these men were moved. They looked at one another, and were unable to reply. I spoke; I told them to retire, and consider of what had been said: that I would not lead them further north, if they strenuously desired the contrary; but that I hoped that, with reflection, their courage would return.

35 No small irony attends this phrase. The language of idealism, honor, and glory in Walton's initial spirit of adventure and Frankenstein's scientific enthusiasm is here exposed as manipulative rhetoric. The Shelleys despised this rhetoric of honor and glory in military recruitment, often to serve the personal vengeances and ambitions of national leaders.

36 A reader may hear echoed many famous battle speeches, including Shakespeare's Henry V inspiring his outnumbered troops at Agincourt. The closest and far more sinister model is Dante's Ulysses exhorting his men to leave home and family for one more voyage to the western islands—a quest in defiance of the boundaries set by Hercules, in which they all perish. Dante and Virgil hear this speech in *Inferno* (Canto XXVI). Like Milton's infernal Satan, Ulysses is a complex compound of rhetorical eloquence and immoral self-interest.

37   Thus spoke Julius Caesar in 49 B.C. on crossing the Rubicon River heading south toward Rome—in effect, a declaration of civil war. The phrase became the slogan of an irrevocable step ("die" is singular of "dice"). Wolf (321) notes the ironic pun in the wake of "I had rather die, than return shamefully" (near the end of Walton's previous entry). Walton translates Caesar's defiant declaration into a sigh of bitter defeat.

38   *1818:* "19th"; the past tense "began" and "11th" (7 lines down) indicate a printer's error; Mary's draft has 9th (*Notebooks* 622–623). *1823* corrects to "9th" (Ch. II, 260). The missing date, September 10th, 1797, is that of Mary Wollstonecraft's death.

They retired, and I turned towards my friend; but he was sunk in languor, and almost deprived of life.

How all this will terminate, I know not; but I had rather die, than return shamefully,—my purpose unfulfilled. Yet I fear such will be my fate; the men, unsupported by ideas of glory and honour, can never willingly continue to endure their present hardships.

September 7th.

The die is cast;[37] I have consented to return, if we are not destroyed. Thus are my hopes blasted by cowardice and indecision; I come back ignorant and disappointed. It requires more philosophy than I possess, to bear this injustice with patience.

September 12th.

It is past; I am returning to England. I have lost my hopes of utility and glory;—I have lost my friend. But I will endeavour to detail these bitter circumstances to you, my dear sister; and, while I am wafted towards England, and towards you, I will not despond.

September 9th,[38] the ice began to move, and roarings like thunder were heard at a distance, as the islands split and cracked in every direction. We were in the most imminent peril; but, as we could only remain passive, my chief attention was occupied by my unfortunate guest, whose illness increased in such a degree, that he was entirely confined to his bed. The ice cracked behind us, and was driven with force towards the north; a breeze sprung from the west, and on the 11th the passage towards the south became perfectly free. When the sailors saw this, and that their return to their native country was apparently assured, a shout of tumultuous joy broke from them, loud and long-continued. Frankenstein, who was dozing, awoke, and asked the cause of the tumult. "They shout," I said, "because they will soon return to England."

"Do you then really return?"

"Alas! yes; I cannot withstand their demands. I cannot lead them unwillingly to danger, and I must return."

"Do so, if you will; but I will not. You may give up your purpose; but mine is assigned to me by heaven, and I dare not. I am weak; but surely the spirits who assist my vengeance will endow me with sufficient strength." Saying this, he endeavoured to spring from the bed, but the exertion was too great for him; he fell back, and fainted.

It was long before he was restored; and I often thought that life was entirely extinct. At length he opened his eyes, but he breathed with difficulty, and was unable to speak. The surgeon gave him a composing draught, and ordered us to leave him undisturbed. In the mean time he told me, that my friend had certainly not many hours to live.

His sentence was pronounced; and I could only grieve, and be patient. I sat by his bed watching him; his eyes were closed, and I thought he slept; but presently he called to me in a feeble voice, and, bidding me come near, said—"Alas! the strength I relied on is gone; I feel that I shall soon die, and he, my enemy and persecutor, may still be in being. Think not, Walton, that in the last moments of my existence I feel that burning hatred, and ardent desire of revenge, I once expressed, but I feel myself justified in desiring the death of my adversary. During these last days I have been occupied in examining my past conduct; nor do I find it blameable. In a fit of enthusiastic madness I created a rational creature, and was bound towards him, to assure, as far as was in my power, his happiness and well-being. This was my duty; but there was another still paramount to that. My duties towards my fellow-creatures[39] had greater claims to my attention, because they included a greater proportion of happiness or misery. Urged by thisview, I refused, and I did right in refusing, to create a compan-

39   One might think, against Frankenstein, that the Creature has a claim to this class; in *1831* Mary Shelley revised the phrasing to terms that emphatically exile the Creature: "towards the beings of my own species" (196).

40 Frankenstein, one last time, rehearses and refuses the lesson modeled on Raphael's instruction to Adam in *Paradise Lost:*

> heav'n is for thee too high
> To know what passes there; be lowlie wise:
> Think only what concerns thee and thy being;
> Dream not of other worlds, what creatures there
> Live, in what state, condition or degree . . . (VIII.172–176)

Having warned against ambition, Frankenstein's final words leave open the alluring possibility of another's success—once again aligning himself with Ulysses, Faustus, and predicting the Hollywood film-makers who seized on the open-endedness of such desires to create sequels to his story.

ion for the first creature. He shewed unparalleled malignity and selfishness, in evil: he destroyed my friends; he devoted to destruction beings who possessed exquisite sensations, happiness, and wisdom; nor do I know where this thirst for vengeance may end. Miserable himself, that he may render no other wretched, he ought to die. The task of his destruction was mine, but I have failed. When actuated by selfish and vicious motives, I asked you to undertake my unfinished work; and I renew this request now, when I am only induced by reason and virtue.

"Yet I cannot ask you to renounce your country and friends, to fulfill this task; and now, that you are returning to England, you will have little chance of meeting with him. But the consideration of these points, and the well-balancing of what you may esteem your duties, I leave to you; my judgment and ideas are already disturbed by the near approach of death. I dare not ask you to do what I think right, for I may still be misled by passion.

"That he should live to be an instrument of mischief disturbs me; in other respects this hour, when I momentarily expect my release, is the only happy one which I have enjoyed for several years. The forms of the beloved dead flit before me, and I hasten to their arms. Farewell, Walton! Seek happiness in tranquility, and avoid ambition, even if it be only the apparently innocent one of distinguishing yourself in science and discoveries. Yet why do I say this? I have myself been blasted in these hopes, yet another may succeed."[40]

His voice became fainter as he spoke; and at length, exhausted by his effort, he sunk into silence. About half an hour afterwards he attempted again to speak, but was unable; he pressed my hand feebly, and his eyes closed forever, while the irradiation of a gentle smile passed away from his lips.

Margaret, what comment can I make on the untimely extinction of this glorious spirit? What can I say, that will enable you to understand the depth of my sorrow? All that I should express would be inadequate and feeble. My tears flow; my mind is overshadowed by a cloud of disappointment. But I journey towards England, and I may there find consolation.

I am interrupted. What do these sounds portend? It is midnight; the breeze blows fairly, and the watch on deck scarcely stir. Again; there is a sound as of a human voice, but hoarser; it comes from the cabin where the remains of Frankenstein still lie. I must arise, and examine. Good night, my sister.

Great God! what a scene has just taken place! I am yet dizzy with the remembrance of it. I hardly know whether I shall have the power to detail it; yet the tale which I have recorded would be incomplete without this final and wonderful catastrophe.

I entered the cabin, where lay the remains of my ill-fated and admirable friend. Over him hung a form which I cannot find words to describe; gigantic in stature, yet uncouth and distorted in its proportions. As he hung over the coffin, his face was concealed by long locks of ragged hair; but one vast hand was extended, in colour and apparent texture like that of a mummy. When he heard the sound of my approach, he ceased to utter exclamations of grief and horror, and sprung towards the window. Never did I behold a vision so horrible as his face, of such loathsome, yet appalling hideousness. I shut my eyes involuntarily, and endeavoured to recollect what were my duties with regard to this destroyer. I called on him to stay.

He paused, looking on me with wonder;[41] and, again turning towards the lifeless form of his creator, he seemed to forget my presence, and every feature and gesture seemed instigated by the wildest rage of some uncontrollable passion.

41 This is only the second time the Creature has not been immediately repelled and abused. Though appalled, Walton cannot bring himself to enact Frankenstein's vengeance and, stunned into silence, listens to the Creature's self-accounting. This is the final courtroom scene (metaphorically) in the novel.

42 The Creature intends a synonym for *generous: self-devoted* means *devoting of self.* Our modern sense of *devoted-to-self* is anachronistic but not irrelevant. Percy depended on the older sense to ameliorate his own stigma of monstrosity. In the wake of his first wife's suicide, he wrote to Leigh Hunt on December 8, 1816, describing himself as an "outcast from human society," "an object" whom "all . . . abhor and avoid," except for those "few" who "believe in self-devotion and generosity because they are themselves generous and self devoted" (*Letters PBS* 2: 530).

43 Mary Shelley's manuscript underlines *"I"*; the printer failed to italicize.

"That is also my victim!" he exclaimed; "in his murder my crimes are consummated; the miserable series of my being is wound to its close! Oh, Frankenstein! generous and self-devoted[42] being! what does it avail that I now ask thee to pardon me? I, who irretrievably destroyed thee by destroying all thou lovedst. Alas! he is cold; he may not answer me."

His voice seemed suffocated; and my first impulses, which had suggested to me the duty of obeying the dying request of my friend, in destroying his enemy, were now suspended by a mixture of curiosity and compassion. I approached this tremendous being; I dared not again raise my looks upon his face, there was something so scaring and unearthly in his ugliness. I attempted to speak, but the words died away on my lips. The monster continued to utter wild and incoherent self-reproaches. At length I gathered resolution to address him, in a pause of the tempest of his passion: "Your repentance," I said, "is now superfluous. If you had listened to the voice of conscience, and heeded the stings of remorse, before you had urged your diabolical vengeance to this extremity, Frankenstein would yet have lived."

"And do you dream?" said the dæmon; "do you think that I[43] was then dead to agony and remorse?—He," he continued, pointing to the corpse, "he suffered not more in the consummation of the deed;—oh! not the ten-thousandth portion of the anguish that was mine during the lingering detail of its execution. A frightful selfishness hurried me on, while my heart was poisoned with remorse. Think ye that the groans of Clerval were music to my ears? My heart was fashioned to be susceptible of love and sympathy; and, when wrenched by misery to vice and hatred, it did not endure the violence of the change without torture, such as you cannot even imagine.

"After the murder of Clerval, I returned to Switzerland, heart-broken and overcome. I pitied Frankenstein; my pity amounted to horror: I abhorred myself. But when I discovered that he, the author at once of my existence and of its unspeakable torments, dared to hope for happiness; that while he accumulated wretchedness and despair upon me, he sought his own enjoyment in feelings and passions from the indulgence of which I was forever barred, then impotent envy and bitter indignation filled me with an insatiable thirst for vengeance. I recollected my threat, and resolved that it should be accomplished. I knew that I was preparing for myself a deadly torture; but I was the slave, not the master of an impulse, which I detested, yet could not disobey. Yet when she died!—nay, then I was not miserable. I had cast off all feeling, subdued all anguish to riot in the excess of my despair. Evil thenceforth became my good.[44] Urged thus far, I had no choice but to adapt my nature to an element which I had willingly chosen. The completion of my demoniacal design became an insatiable passion. And now it is ended; there is my last victim!"

I was at first touched by the expressions of his misery; yet when I called to mind what Frankenstein had said of his powers of eloquence and persuasion,[45] and when I again cast my eyes on the lifeless form of my friend, indignation was re-kindled within me. "Wretch!" I said, "it is well that you come here to whine over the desolation that you have made. You throw a torch into a pile of buildings, and when they are consumed you sit among the ruins, and lament the fall. Hypocritical fiend! if he whom you mourn still lived, still would he be the object, again would he become the prey of your accursed vengeance. It is not pity that you feel; you lament only because the victim of your malignity is withdrawn from your power."

"Oh, it not thus—not thus," interrupted the being;[46] "yet such must be the impression conveyed to you by what appears to be the purport of my actions. Yet I seek not a fellow-feeling in my misery. No sympathy may I ever find. When I first sought it, it was the

44 The Creature consciously echoes Satan, arrived in Eden to do his worst: "Farwell remorse: all good to me is lost; / Evil, be thou my good" (*Paradise Lost* IV.109–110).

45 Walton's affection for Frankenstein blinds him to Frankenstein's similar powers.

46 This singularly neutral marker reflects Walton's unexpected suspension of prejudice and judgment—perhaps because the Creature condemns himself.

47 In Heaven, Satan was archangel Lucifer (light-bearer): "Lucifer from heav'n . . . / Fell with his flaming legions through the deep" (*Paradise Lost* VII.131–134).

48 The Creature again identifies with the tragic grandeur of Shakespeare's Lear, "a man / More sinned against than sinning" (*King Lear* 3.2.59–60). P. B. Shelley's review takes this cue, commenting that "the crimes and malevolence of the single Being, though indeed withering and tremendous," are no "offspring of any unaccountable propensity to evil . . . Treat a person ill, and he will become wicked. Requite affection with scorn;—let one being be selected, for whatever cause, as the refuse of his kind—divide him, a social being, from society and you impose upon him the irresistible obligations—malevolence and selfishness" (*Athenaeum,* November 10, 1832, 730).

love of virtue, the feelings of happiness and affection with which my whole being overflowed, that I wished to be participated. But now, that virtue has become to me a shadow, and that happiness and affection are turned into bitter and loathing despair, in what should I seek for sympathy? I am content to suffer alone, while my sufferings shall endure: when I die, I am well satisfied that abhorrence and opprobrium should load my memory. Once my fancy was soothed with dreams of virtue, of fame, and of enjoyment. Once I falsely hoped to meet with beings, who, pardoning my outward form, would love me for the excellent qualities which I was capable of bringing forth. I was nourished with high thoughts of honour and devotion. But now vice has degraded me beneath the meanest animal. No crime, no mischief, no malignity, no misery, can be found comparable to mine. When I call over the frightful catalogue of my deeds, I cannot believe that I am he whose thoughts were once filled with sublime and transcendant visions of the beauty and the majesty of goodness. But it is even so; the fallen angel becomes a malignant devil.[47] Yet even that enemy of God and man had friends and associates in his desolation; I am quite alone.

"You, who call Frankenstein your friend, seem to have a knowledge of my crimes and his misfortunes. But, in the detail which he gave you of them, he could not sum up the hours and months of misery which I endured, wasting in impotent passions. For whilst I destroyed his hopes, I did not satisfy my own desires. They were for ever ardent and craving; still I desired love and fellowship, and I was still spurned. Was there no injustice in this? Am I to be thought the only criminal, when all human kind sinned against me?[48] Why do you not hate Felix, who drove his friend from his door with contumely? Why do you not execrate the rustic who sought to destroy the saviour of his child? Nay, these are virtuous and immaculate beings! I, the miserable and abandoned, am an abortion,[49] to be spurned at, and kicked, and trampled on. Even now my blood boils at the recollection of this injustice.

"But it is true that I am a wretch. I have murdered the lovely and the helpless; I have strangled the innocent as they slept, and grasped to death his throat who never injured me or any other living thing. I have devoted my creator, the select specimen of all that is worthy of love and admiration among men, to misery; I have pursued him even to that irremediable ruin. There he lies, white and cold in death. You hate me; but your abhorrence cannot equal that with which I regard myself. I look on the hands which executed the deed; I think on the heart in which the imagination of it was conceived, and long for the moment when they will meet my eyes, when it will haunt my thoughts no more.

"Fear not that I shall be the instrument of future mischief. My work is nearly complete. Neither your's nor any man's death is needed to consummate the series of my being, and accomplish that which must be done; but it requires my own. Do not think that I shall be slow to perform this sacrifice. I shall quit your vessel on the ice-raft which brought me hither, and shall seek the most northern extremity of the globe; I shall collect my funeral pile, and consume to ashes this miserable frame, that its remains may afford no light to any curious and unhallowed wretch, who would create such another as I have been. I shall die. I shall no longer feel the agonies which now consume me, or be the prey of feelings unsatisfied, yet unquenched. He is dead who called me into being; and when I shall be no more, the very remembrance of us both will speedily vanish. I shall no longer see the sun or stars, or feel the winds play on my cheeks. Light, feeling, and sense, will

49 This word has several meanings, indicating any kind of failed or deformed conception. This is the sole instance of this word in the novel (here, with a phonic echo of *abhor*) in place of Frankenstein's usual terminology, "the devil" (*Notebooks* 638–639). P. B. Shelley suggested this word and used it himself in his planned anonymous review, embedding it in a sympathetic understanding of how monsters become abortions of the human community: "The Being in 'Frankenstein' . . . was an abortion and an anomaly; and though his mind was such as its first impressions framed it, affectionate and full of moral sensibility, yet the circumstances of his existence are so monstrous and uncommon, that, when the consequences of them became developed in action, his original goodness was gradually turned into inextinguishable misanthropy and revenge" (*Athenaeum,* November 10, 1832, 730).

50 The pile, we may realize, is to be assembled from the Creature's sledge, perhaps also from Frankenstein's, and the shipwrecks of unlucky expeditions. Shipwrecks were frequent elements in paintings, and later photographs, of the arctic sublime. The projected conflagration is a complex involute of classical heroic self-immolation, the female versions (such as Dido's) that mime a marriage bed, and the then legal custom in India of a widow's enforced suttee. The promised pyre, notes critic Andrew Griffin, fulfills Walton's fantasy of a warm spot in the polar climes. That this denouement is only promised leaves open the imagination of some other conclusion, or perpetuation, of the Creature's history.

51 Percy Shelley's review closed in admiration for "the more than mortal enthusiasm and grandeur" of the Creature's speech: "an exhibition of intellectual and imaginative power, which we think the reader will acknowledge has seldom been surpassed."

52 Mary Shelley ends her novel short of the spectacle of the promised suicide. Her manuscript reads: "he was carried away by the waves and I soon lost sight of him in the darkness & distance" (*Notebooks* 642–643). Her revision to "borne away" nicely sounds a final pun on what the Creature never was, *born,* leaving implicit the subjective "I" witness, for whom this whole history has the quality of an overwhelming nightmare—a darkness and distance that is as psychic in its terrain as it is global and geographical.

pass away; and in this condition must I find my happiness. Some years ago, when the images which this world affords first opened upon me, when I felt the cheering warmth of summer, and heard the rustling of the leaves and the chirping of the birds, and these were all to me, I should have wept to die; now it is my only consolation. Polluted by crimes, and torn by the bitterest remorse, where can I find rest but in death?

"Farewell! I leave you, and in you the last of human kind whom these eyes will ever behold. Farewell, Frankenstein! If thou wert yet alive, and yet cherished a desire of revenge against me, it would be better satiated in my life than in my destruction. But it was not so; thou didst seek my extinction, that I might not cause greater wretchedness; and if yet, in some mode unknown to me, thou hast not yet ceased to think and feel, thou desirest not my life for my own misery. Blasted as thou wert, my agony was still superior to thine; for the bitter sting of remorse may not cease to rankle in my wounds until death shall close them for ever.

"But soon," he cried, with sad and solemn enthusiasm, "I shall die, and what I now feel be no longer felt. Soon these burning miseries will be extinct. I shall ascend my funeral pile triumphantly, and exult in the agony of the torturing flames.[50] The light of that conflagration will fade away; my ashes will be swept into the sea by the winds. My spirit will sleep in peace; or if it thinks, it will not surely think thus. Farewell."[51]

He sprung from the cabin-window, as he said this, upon the ice-raft which lay close to the vessel. He was soon borne away by the waves, and lost in darkness and distance.[52]

THE END.

EDITORS' INTRODUCTION

The "new" *Frankenstein: or, The Modern Prometheus* published in 1831 reflects the expanding popularity of the novel by an anonymous "Author" that debuted in 1818. In 1823, on the stimulus of its stage success, *Frankenstein* was republished in two volumes, with minor corrections and now with "Mary Wollstonecraft Shelley" on the title page. Soon after, Shelley started to sketch out some revisions, and she kept at it over the decade. It seems clear that she intended a second version. One notable alteration is in the character of Victor Frankenstein, whose Percy Shelley elements were now a matter of idealizing elegy for a husband who drowned in 1822. The most striking feature of the 1831 version, however, is the new Introduction, recounting the genesis of the novel at Villa Diodati in 1816. This became an intriguing narrative in its own right, one that mirrors many of the conflicted elements of the now famous tale it prefaces.

If Mary Shelley was somewhat uneasy about fame, by 1831 she had become a professional writer. She approached Charles Ollier, in February 1831, to test his interest in a new version of *Frankenstein* for Colburn and Bentley's Standard Novels series. Back in 1817, as a publisher, Ollier had turned down *Frankenstein;* but now as Colburn and Bentley's chief literary advisor, he recognized success and supported Shelley's proposal, which was accepted in June 1831. She sold the firm her copyright for £30, the last sum she or her heirs would gain from this signature success. Even so, Shelley was eager to tell her story: "remember that I have a short passage to add to the Introduction" (that is, the original Preface); "Do not fail me with regard to this—it will be only a few lines —& those not disagreeable to C.&B.—but the contrary."[1]

Shelley's "short passage" quickly became an autobiographical short story. Cast as an anecdote, it also capitalized on the fame of *Frankenstein,* recounting its inception fifteen years earlier, and before then, in the nurture of her girlhood imagination. Her story of origins links her creative project to Victor Frankenstein's, both of them "authors" of terrifying constructions. This was not the usual self-accounting for a proper female novelist, and Colburn and Bentley could not have been more delighted. Early in September 1831, the firm put an advertisement on the front page of *The Morning Chronicle:* "Mrs. Shelley's popular Romance, Frankenstein, Revised by the Author, with a New Introduction explanatory of the origin of the Story." Further advertisements followed across the subsequent weeks. In the October 19 *Chronicle,* excitement swelled when an article on Thomas Moore's *Life of Byron* quoted Byron on the entertainments of June 1816: "The most memorable result, indeed, of their story-telling compact was Mrs. Shelley's powerful romance of 'Frankenstein'—one of those original conceptions that take hold of the public mind at once, and for ever" (4). Meanwhile, Colburn's *Court Journal* ran advertisements throughout September, then previewed the "new Introduction" in the October 22 issue (724). Everything was primed for the Halloween return of *Frankenstein.*

Frankenstein appeared in Bentley's Standard Novels, No. IX, a gathering of three tales in two volumes: *Frankenstein,* the main attraction, was "complete" at the front of volume 1, followed by the first part of an English translation of Friedrich Schiller's mysterious novel *The Ghost-Seer,* which Mary read in an earlier translation in 1816 (readers had to buy volume 2 for the continuation of this tale and the enjoyment of Charles Brockden Brown's American gothic novel, *Edgar Huntley; or, The Sleep Walker*). The packaging reflects a commercial regard of Shelley's novel as less a philosophical romance than a gothic thriller. Within days *The Chronicle* reported that "demand" had been "so great as to absorb on the first day the whole supply"—with assurances to "those who were disappointed in their applications for the volume" that "another impression has been produced, and copies may be had either at the publishers, or at the retail booksellers."

For the new *Frankenstein* the publishers commissioned two illustrations. A frontispiece presented a picture by Theodor von Holst, engraved by W. Chevalier—the first time a pictorial image of the Creature appeared in the novel itself. The facing title page had an image by the same artists of Frankenstein's parting from Elizabeth (either going off to college, or on his "tour" of England). The mirroring elements of the pair (two

Frontispiece and title page to the 1831 edition of *Frankenstein*. The two new illustrations, on facing pages at the front of the novel, establish Victor as one who is always departing, whether in fear or sorrow. Shared compositional features (narrow arches and Victor departing on the right) imply a pattern.

arches, two departures) at once counterpoint and correlate the sentimental and gothic tableaux. At the top of the Victor-Elizabeth recto we read "Frankenstein, by Mary W. Shelley." The internal title page gives the subtitle and a fuller authorial reputation.

Gone is the epigraph from *Paradise Lost* and the dedication to William Godwin. This is not to be taken as a novel of political philosophy. The new Introduction was placed before the 1818 Preface.

Colburn and Bentley set an initial print run of 4,500, which sold out, and another run was quickly called for; 500 more copies were issued in 1832, and the demand produced reprintings, by the thousands, across this decade alone. The 1831 *Frankenstein,* though not always in the 1831 format, was the only one widely known until the 1970s, when scholars, drawn to the historical importance and distinctive literary qualities of the Romantic-era original, developed new editions of the 1818 novel. Even so, these editions always include the 1831 Introduction, which has become integral. It is memorably acted out in the opening of James Whale's sequel, *The Bride of Frankenstein* (1935), where Elsa Lanchester (who will reappear as the "Bride") is a self-possessed Mary Shelley, embroidering by the fireplace, while a self-dramatizing "Byron" expresses his admiration for this "astonishing creature": the "bland and lovely" girl who produced such a horrific tale, and whose spellbinding narration draws us into the sequel.

NOTE

1. *MWS Letters* 2: 129. Bentley wanted both new material and different text (with corrections, or better, revisions) in order to be able to claim a new copyright that, if not legally impregnable, would be respected within the industry. For authors who couldn't be bothered, Bentley would assign a professional reviser. For this history, see William St. Clair, *The Godwins and the Shelleys: The Biography of a Family* (New York: Norton, 1989), 360–362.

MARY SHELLEY'S INTRODUCTION

The Publishers of the Standard Novels, in selecting "Frankenstein" for one of their se-ries, expressed a wish that I should furnish them with some account of the origin of the story. I am the more willing to comply, because I shall thus give a general answer to the question, so very frequently asked me—"How I, then a young girl, came to think of, and to dilate upon, so very hideous an idea?"[1] It is true that I am very averse to bringing myself forward in print; but as my account will only appear as an appendage to a for-mer production, and as it will be confined to such topics as have connection with my authorship alone, I can scarcely accuse myself of a personal intrusion.[2]

It is not singular that, as the daughter of two persons of distinguished literary celeb-rity, I should very early in life have thought of writing.[3] As a child I scribbled; and my favourite pastime, during the hours given me for recreation, was to "write stories." Still I had a dearer pleasure than this, which was the formation of castles in the air—the indulging in waking dreams—the following up trains of thought, which had for their subject the formation of a succession of imaginary incidents. My dreams were at once more fantastic and agreeable than my writings. In the latter I was a close imitator—rather doing as others had done, than putting down the suggestions of my own mind. What I wrote was intended at least for one other eye—my childhood's companion and friend; but my dreams were all my own; I accounted for them to nobody; they were my refuge when annoyed—my dearest pleasure when free.[4]

I lived principally in the country as a girl, and passed a considerable time in Scotland. I made occasional visits to the more picturesque parts; but my habitual residence was on the blank and dreary northern shores of the Tay, near Dundee. Blank and dreary on retrospection I call them; they were not so to me then. They were the eyry of freedom, and the pleasant region where unheeded I could commune with the creatures of my fancy.[5] I wrote then—but in a most common-place style. It was beneath the trees of the grounds belonging to our house, or on the bleak sides of the woodless mountains near, that my true compositions, the airy flights of my imagination, were born and fostered. I did not make myself the heroine of my tales. Life appeared to me too common-place an affair as regarded myself. I could not figure to myself that romantic woes or wonderful events would ever be my lot; but I was not confined to my own identity, and I could people the hours with creations far more interesting to me at that age, than my own sensations.[6]

After this my life became busier, and reality stood in place of fiction. My husband, however, was, from the first, very anxious that I should prove myself worthy of my parentage, and enrol myself on the page of fame.[7] He was for ever inciting me to obtain literary reputation, which even on my own part I cared for then, though since I have become infinitely indifferent to it. At this time he desired that I should write, not so much with the idea that I could produce any thing worthy of notice, but that he might himself judge how far I possessed the promise of better things hereafter. Still I did nothing. Travelling, and the cares of a family, occupied my time; and study, in the way of reading, or improving my ideas in communication with his far more cultivated mind, was all of literary employment that engaged my attention.

In the summer of 1816, we visited Switzerland, and became the neighbours of Lord Byron. At first we spent our pleasant hours on the lake, or wandering on its shores; and Lord Byron, who was writing the third canto of Childe Harold, was the only one among us who put his thoughts upon paper. These, as he brought them successively to us, clothed in all the light and harmony of poetry, seemed to stamp as divine the glories of heaven and earth, whose influences we partook with him.

But it proved a wet, ungenial summer, and incessant rain often confined us for days to the house. Some volumes of ghost stories, translated from the German into French, fell into our hands.[8] There was the History of the Inconstant Lover, who, when he thought to clasp the bride to whom he had pledged his vows, found himself in the arms of the pale ghost of her whom he had deserted.[9] There was the tale of the sinful founder

Portrait of William Godwin, by James Northcote, circa 1802. A dramatically lit image of Mary's father and famous man of letters.

John Opie's 1797 portrait of a wistful Mary Wollstonecraft, pregnant with Mary, and dressed in plain attire quietly signifying her refusal of "feminine" ornamentation in favor of intellectual seriousness. James Heath's engraving of this portrait appeared as the frontispiece of Godwin's *Memoirs* of Wollstonecraft (1798).

of his race, whose miserable doom it was to bestow the kiss of death on all the younger sons of his fated house, just when they reached the age of promise. His gigantic, shadowy form, clothed like the ghost in Hamlet, in complete armour, but with the beaver up, was seen at midnight, by the moon's fitful beams, to advance slowly along the gloomy avenue.[10] The shape was lost beneath the shadow of the castle walls; but soon a gate swung back, a step was heard, the door of the chamber opened, and he advanced to the couch of the blooming youths, cradled in healthy sleep.[11] Eternal sorrow sat upon his face as he bent down and kissed the forehead of the boys, who from that hour with-

Thomas Phillips, *Portrait of a Nobleman (Lord Byron),* 1814, commissioned by Byron's publisher John Murray, with plans for reproductions to be sold separately to admirers of Byron's poetical works. Along with Westall's *Byron,* this was the most widely circulated image of the poet in his lifetime.

ered like flowers snapt upon the stalk. I have not seen these stories since then; but their incidents are as fresh in my mind as if I had read them yesterday.

"We will each write a ghost story," said Lord Byron; and his proposition was acceded to. There were four of us. The noble author began a tale, a fragment of which he printed at the end of his poem of Mazeppa. Shelley, more apt to embody ideas and sentiments in the radiance of brilliant imagery, and in the music of the most melodious verse that adorns our language, than to invent the machinery of a story, commenced one founded on the experiences of his early life. Poor Polidori had some terrible idea about a skull-headed lady, who was so punished for peeping through a key-hole—what to see I forget—something very shocking and wrong of course; but when she was reduced to a worse condition than the renowned Tom of Coventry, he did not know what to do with her, and was obliged to despatch her to the tomb of the Capulets, the only place for which she was fitted.[12] The illustrious poets also, annoyed by the platitude of prose, speedily relinquished their uncongenial task.

I busied myself *to think of a story,*—a story to rival those which had excited us to this task.[13] One which would speak to the mysterious fears of our nature, and awaken thrilling horror—one to make the reader dread to look round, to curdle the blood, and quicken the beatings of the heart. If I did not accomplish these things, my ghost story would be unworthy of its name. I thought and pondered—vainly. I felt that blank incapability of invention which is the greatest misery of authorship, when dull Nothing replies to our anxious invocations. *Have you thought of a story?* I was asked each morning, and each morning I was forced to reply with a mortifying negative.[14]

Every thing must have a beginning, to speak in Sanchean phrase; and that beginning must be linked to something that went before.[15] The Hindoos give the world an elephant to support it, but they make the elephant stand upon a tortoise. Invention, it must be humbly admitted, does not consist in creating out of void, but out of chaos; the materials must, in the first place, be afforded: it can give form to dark, shapeless substances, but cannot bring into being the substance itself. In all matters of discovery and

This image is from William Beattie, M.D., *Switzerland, In a Series of Views Taken Expressly for this Work by W. H. Bartlett, Esq.* (London: Virtue, 1838). Villa Diodati is the chateau center left; Geneva is directly across. The attraction of this famous site was enhanced by its reputation as the residence of the Byron-Shelley circle in 1816.

John William Polidori, by F. G. Gainsford, 1817. Polidori (1795–1821) was part of the Villa Diodati household in June 1816. His effort in the ghost-story contest was *The Vampyre*. His suicide was the result of gambling debts and a falling out with Byron, whom he adored and resented.

335

Engraving from Luigi Galvani, *De Viribus Electricitatis in Motu Musculari* (1791). On the table at left is an electrostatic machine, on the right, a Leyden Jar, which holds an electric charge. Galvani (1737–1798) discovered animal electricity by accident in 1771, when he found that an electrical charge could make a dead frog's leg kick.

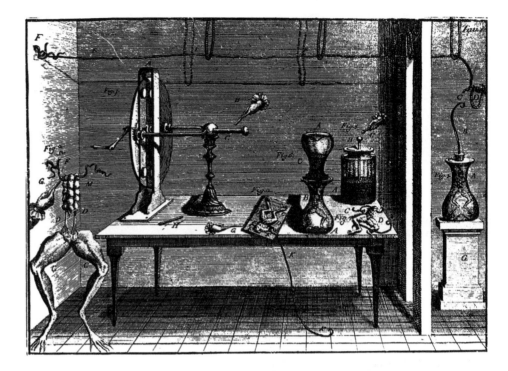

invention, even of those that appertain to the imagination, we are continually reminded of the story of Columbus and his egg.[16] Invention consists in the capacity of seizing on the capabilities of a subject, and in the power of moulding and fashioning ideas suggested to it.

Many and long were the conversations between Lord Byron and Shelley, to which I was a devout but nearly silent listener.[17] During one of these, various philosophical doctrines were discussed, and among others the nature of the principle of life, and whether there was any probability of its ever being discovered and communicated. They talked of the experiments of Dr. Darwin, (I speak not of what the Doctor really did, or said that he did, but, as more to my purpose, of what was then spoken of as having been done by him,) who preserved a piece of vermicelli in a glass case, till by some extraordinary means it began to move with voluntary motion. Not thus, after all, would life be given. Perhaps a corpse would be re-animated; galvanism had given token of such things: perhaps the component parts of a creature might be manufactured, brought together, and endued with vital warmth.[18]

Night waned upon this talk; and even the witching hour had gone by, before we retired to rest. When I placed my head on my pillow, I did not sleep, nor could I be said

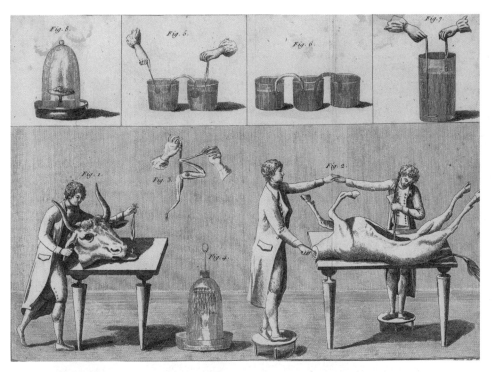

Giovanni Aldini, Plate IV (lower panel) in Giovannni Aldini, *Essai théorique et expérimental sur le galvanisme* (Paris: Fournier Fils, 1804). The engraving is based on a drawing by Pecheux. This nephew of Luigi Galvani conducted electrical experiments on corpses of decapitated convicts in Italy, 1802. At a public experiment at Newgate Prison in London in 1803, he applied an electrical stimulus to the body of the executed murderer George Forster. One of the corpse's eyes opened, his fist clenched, and his legs moved. Aldini conducted performances of electrical "reanimation" across Europe, using a variety of animal and human body parts.

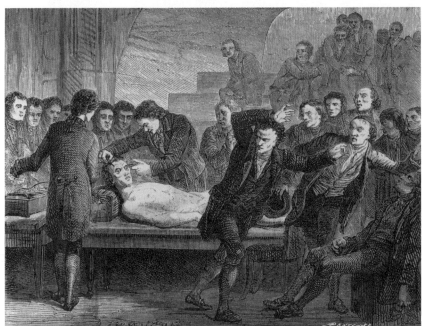

Le docteur Ure galvanisant le corps de l'assassin Clydsdale, from Louis Figuier, *Les merveilles de la Science* (Paris, 1867), p. 653. Shortly after *Frankenstein* was published, Dr. Andrew Ure, inspired by Galvani's experiments on frogs, tested his theory of "Animal Electricity" on the corpse of an executed criminal. Before a curious public, in the Anatomy Theater of Glasgow University, he produced some bizarre effects, including apparent breathing, violent leg extension, and extreme facial expressions: "every muscle in his countenance was simultaneously thrown into fearful action; rage, horror, despair, anguish, and ghastly smiles, united their hideous expressions in the murderer's face, surpassing far the wildest representations of Fuseli or a Kean. At this period several of the spectators were forced to leave the apartment from terror or sickness, and one gentleman fainted" ("An Account of some Experiments made on the body of a Criminal immediately after Execution, with Physiological and Practical Observations," *Quarterly Journal of Science and the Arts*, vol. 6, 1819, p. 290).

Samuel John Stump, portrait of a woman, 1831, long thought to be Mary Shelley, around the time that she wrote this Introduction to a new edition of *Frankenstein*. She now appears as a successful woman of letters, with the tools of her trade.

to think. My imagination, unbidden, possessed and guided me, gifting the successive images that arose in my mind with a vividness far beyond the usual bounds of reverie. I saw—with shut eyes, but acute mental vision,—I saw the pale student of unhallowed arts kneeling beside the thing he had put together. I saw the hideous phantasm of a man stretched out, and then, on the working of some powerful engine, show signs of life, and stir with an uneasy, half vital motion. Frightful must it be; for supremely frightful would be the effect of any human endeavour to mock the stupendous mechanism of the Creator of the world.[19] His success would terrify the artist; he would rush away from his odious handywork, horror-stricken. He would hope that, left to itself, the slight spark of life which he had communicated would fade; that this thing, which had received such imperfect animation, would subside into dead matter; and he might sleep in the belief that the silence of the grave would quench for ever the transient existence of the hideous corpse which he had looked upon as the cradle of life. He sleeps; but he is awakened; he opens his eyes; behold the horrid thing stands at his bedside, opening his curtains, and looking on him with yellow, watery, but speculative eyes.[20]

I opened mine in terror. The idea so possessed my mind, that a thrill of fear ran through me, and I wished to exchange the ghastly image of my fancy for the realities around. I see them still; the very room, the dark *parquet,* the closed shutters, with the moonlight struggling through, and the sense I had that the glassy lake and white high Alps were beyond.[21] I could not so easily get rid of my hideous phantom; still it haunted me. I must try to think of something else. I recurred to my ghost story,—my tiresome unlucky ghost story! O! if I could only contrive one which would frighten my reader as I myself had been frightened that night![22]

Swift as light and as cheering was the idea that broke in upon me.[23] "I have found it! What terrified me will terrify others; and I need only describe the spectre which had haunted my midnight pillow." On the morrow I announced that I had *thought of a story.* I began that day with the words, *It was on a dreary night of November,* making only a transcript of the grim terrors of my waking dream.

At first I thought but of a few pages—of a short tale; but Shelley urged me to develope the idea at greater length. I certainly did not owe the suggestion of one incident, nor scarcely of one train of feeling, to my husband, and yet but for his incitement, it would never have taken the form in which it was presented to the world.[24] From this declaration I must except the preface. As far as I can recollect, it was entirely written by him.

And now, once again, I bid my hideous progeny go forth and prosper.[25] I have an affection for it, for it was the offspring of happy days, when death and grief were but words, which found no true echo in my heart.[26] Its several pages speak of many a walk, many a drive, and many a conversation, when I was not alone; and my companion was one whom, in this world, I shall never see more. But this is for myself; my readers have nothing to do with these associations.[27]

I will add but one word as to the alterations I have made. They are principally those of style. I have changed no portion of the story, nor introduced any new ideas or circumstances. I have mended the language where it was so bald as to interfere with the interest of the narrative; and these changes occur almost exclusively in the beginning of the first volume. Throughout they are entirely confined to such parts as are mere adjuncts to the story, leaving the core and substance of it untouched.

M. W. S.

London, October 15. 1831.

NOTES

1. With the rhetorical and obstetrical term *dilate* Shelley figures the production of the novel as creative and procreative, a birth in both senses.

2. Shelley's disclaimers reflect the general strictures against female authorship and self-declaration.

3. Wollstonecraft and Godwin remain unnamed. Godwin may have lived down his controversial reputation from the 1790s, but Wollstonecraft's would not be rehabilitated for decades. Even so, Shelley knows that her notorious parents are of interest.

4. The childhood companion is Isabel Baxter, the daughter of William Baxter, one of Godwin's admirers. Mary lived with the family in two intervals across June 1812–March 1814.

5. An *eyry* is an eagle's nest, or high remote perch. By a pun two sentences on, Shelley links her happy sojourn with the Baxters to her first "airy flights" of imagination.

6. In a sentence in *1818* that Percy provided, Elizabeth experiences the world as "a vacancy, which she sought to people with imaginations of her own" (Vol. I, Ch. I; *Notebooks* 10–11). Did he remember something that Mary said about her own childhood, or is Mary here remembering his characterization of Elizabeth? Whatever the origin, it is striking that Mary's account of her girlhood imagination also echoes Frankenstein's fantasy of populating the world with "a new species" (Vol. I, Ch. III).

7. They did not marry until December 1816, after Harriet Shelley's suicide.

8. *Fantasmagoria* (French trans. 1812); for more, see the 1818 Preface.

9. This lurid tale infuses Frankenstein's nightmare after animating the Creature: he embraces Elizabeth, who becomes the corpse of his mother (Vol. I, Ch. IV). All these fables seem to imprint *Frankenstein,* with Mary remembering some of her inspirations.

10. A beaver is a helmet-visor; the allusion is to the ghost of Hamlet's murdered, revenge-seeking father (*Hamlet* 1.2.226–230).

11. The somewhat misrecalled tales are *La Morte Fiancée (The Dead Fiancée)* and *Les Portraits de Famille (The Family Portraits).*

12. The "vampyre" heroes in the tales of Polidori and Byron mirror one term in Victor's lexicon for his Creature. Polidori's tale *The Vampyre, A Tale* generated a theatrical success that preceded the stage-play of *Frankenstein.* Tom of Coventry is the legendary "Peeping Tom" of the thirteenth century who was struck blind for disobeying an edict not to peek at Lady Godiva as she rode naked through Coventry. In *Romeo and Juliet,* the tragic suicides of the young lovers occur in the Capulet family tomb.

13. The italics in this paragraph mirror the only italic sentence in *1818: "I will be with you on your wedding-night,"* Victor recalls, shifting the Creature's *shall* to a determined *will* (257, 280, above). In *1831,* both iterations, with *will,* are italic (149, 168).

14. Meaning humiliating or embarrassing, *mortifying* by its etymology (death-making) collates stymied creation with the death from which life is to be retrieved.

15. Mary Shelley was reading *Don Quixote* in 1816. Even though he lacks experience, the Don's squire Sancho Panza is confident that he can govern his own island: "in this matter of government everything depends upon the beginning" (2.33).

16. In classical rhetoric, *Inventio* (from the Latin *invenire: to find, to come upon*) is the method for discovering an argument. The ancient Hindu myth is cited in Shaftesbury's *Characteristicks* (2nd ed., 1715) and Wollstonecraft's *Rights of Woman* (Ch. V, section iv). Archangel Raphael visits Adam in Eden and relates the creation of the world from materials in Chaos (*Paradise Lost* VII.220–242). In a famous legend, recounted by Washington Irving in *The Life and Voyages of Christopher Columbus* (1828; Book 5, chap. 8), Columbus, challenged on his boast that he could stand an egg on end, tapped off one end and stood it up, citing the trick to demonstrate how a seemingly impossible task, such as sailing to the Americas, once demonstrated, was easily repeated.

17. Mary's devoted attention is analogous to the Creature's rapt curiosity as he silently absorbs Safie's education by Felix De Lacey.

18. In *The Temple of Nature, or, The Origin of Society: A Poem* (1803), Erasmus Darwin has a few lines of poetry ("Hence without parent by spontaneous birth / Rise the first specks of animated earth" [I.247–248]) and a long prose footnote on the theory of spontaneous vitality. The improbable sounding pasta experiment of animating vermicelli probably derives (as Wolf notes, 4) from a confusion of Darwin's references to microscopic animals in a paste of flour and

water (which contains animalcules) and his reference to vorticella (microscopic animals) "coming to life after being dried" (Wolf cites a personal communication from Darwin's biographer, Desmond King-Hele). The conflation was probably encouraged by the etymology of *vermicelli: little worms.* (Byron enjoyed punning on "celli" and "Shelley.") Galvinism used electrical current to induce spasms in dead frog legs. The process received a sensational, widely reported demonstration when Giovanni Aldini (Luigi Galvani's nephew) "animated" the corpse of an executed convict, stirring into motion its hand and legs and opening one eye. One observer "died of fright" soon after (*Newgate Calendar,* 1803).

19. The verb "mock" means "imitate presumptuously."

20. Shelley retells the most startling, most controversial episode (the opening of Vol. I, Ch. IV) as her generative reverie, one in which her point of view complements that of her protagonist Victor Frankenstein. At the same time, her framing of her inspiration as an unbidden half-dream, of which she was the passive recipient, aligns her with Victor's helpless fascination with his horrid creation.

21. Recent research by a team headed by Donald Olson, professor of astronomy at Texas State University San Marcos, has confirmed an unusually brilliant full moon in mid-June 1816; "Scientist: Sky confirms 'shining moon' behind Frankenstein," by Jim Forsyth, Monday, September 26, 2011 (http://www.reuters.com/article/2011/09/26/us-frankenstein-astronomer-texas).

22. This is a gothic version of Horace's dictum, in *Ars Poetica:* "si vis me flere, dolendum est primum ipse tibi" (if you wish me to weep, you yourself must first feel sorrow).

23. Again, in imaginative consonance with her protagonist, Shelley echoes her representation of Frankenstein's report of his discovery of the "change from life to death, and death to life": "from the midst of this darkness a sudden light broke in upon me—a light so brilliant and wondrous, yet so simple, that . . . I became dizzy with the immensity of the prospect which it illustrated" (Vol. I, Ch. III).

24. Mary Shelley protects her claim to authorship while crediting Percy Shelley for making possible her new identity as "The Author of *Frankenstein.*"

25. Shelley plays on a convention reaching back to classical times, of authors bidding fond farewell to their textual progeny, a gesture made notable in English poetry by Chaucer's "Go, litel bok" (*Troilus and Criseyde*) and Spenser's "Goe little booke" *(The Shepheardes Calender),* echoed parodically by Byron at the end of Canto I of *Don Juan* (1819). Shelley's gothic turn on this parental pride complements Victor Frankenstein's hideous bequest to posterity.

26. Not only Percy but all their progeny, save Percy Florence, were dead by 1822. So was Polidori; Byron died in 1824.

27. In this sentence, M. W. S. may feel, retrospectively, an affinity with the Creature. In 1831 the novel *Frankenstein* is the survivor of this history of family deaths.

SAMPLE OF REVISED PASSAGES

Victor's Childhood, the Adoption of Elizabeth

In this extended revision, a remarkable episode is the adoption of Elizabeth. Beholding a double for herself rescued by Alphonse Frankenstein, Victor's mother rescues this "orphan and a beggar." Her ethical benevolence coincides with ethnic and class aesthetics. A "different stock" from the peasant foster family, fair-skinned, blue-eyed, golden-haired Elizabeth is discovered to be half-German and the daughter of a "nobleman," and so quite assimilable to the Frankensteins. Such qualifications possess the Frankensteins throughout the novel, most strikingly in Victor's recoil from a Creature whose failure to be beautiful casts him out as a different "species." Shelley's revision also complicates Victor's relationship with Elizabeth. Pleasing his mother's longing for a daughter, this new family member could have generated a bitter sibling rivalry, but Victor accepts his mother's proposal to regard Elizabeth as a gift to him, an asset to his own self-esteem. This new text follows "When my father became a husband and a parent . . ." (Vol. I, Ch. I; 88, above, bottom paragraph).

> There was a considerable difference between the ages of my parents, but this circumstance seemed to unite them only closer in bonds of devoted affection. There was a sense of justice in my father's upright mind, which rendered it necessary

that he should approve highly to love strongly. Perhaps during former years he had suffered from the late-discovered unworthiness of one beloved, and so was disposed to set a greater value on tried worth. There was a show of gratitude and worship in his attachment to my mother, differing wholly from the doating fondness of age, for it was inspired by reverence for her virtues, and a desire to be the means of, in some degree, recompensing her for the sorrows she had endured, but which gave inexpressible grace to his behaviour to her. Every thing was made to yield to her wishes and her convenience. He strove to shelter her, as a fair exotic is sheltered by the gardener, from every rougher wind, and to surround her with all that could tend to excite pleasurable emotion in her soft and benevolent mind. Her health, and even the tranquillity of her hitherto constant spirit, had been shaken by what she had gone through. During the two years that had elapsed previous to their marriage my father had gradually relinquished all his public functions; and immediately after their union they sought the pleasant climate of Italy, and the change of scene and interest attendant on a tour through that land of wonders, as a restorative for her weakened frame.

From Italy they visited Germany and France. I, their eldest child, was born at Naples, and as an infant accompanied them in their rambles.[1] I remained for several years their only child. Much as they were attached to each other, they seemed to draw inexhaustible stores of affection from a very mine of love to bestow them upon me. My mother's tender caresses, and my father's smile of benevolent pleasure while regarding me, are my first recollections. I was their plaything and their idol, and something better—their child, the innocent and helpless creature bestowed on them by Heaven, whom to bring up to good, and whose future lot it was in their hands to direct to happiness or misery, according as they fulfilled their duties towards me. With this deep consciousness of what they owed towards the being to which they had given life, added to the active spirit of tenderness that animated both, it may be imagined that while during every hour of my infant life I received a lesson of patience, of charity, and of self-control, I was so guided by a silken cord, that all seemed but one train of enjoyment to me.

For a long time I was their only care. My mother had much desired to have a daughter, but I continued their single offspring.[2] When I was about five years old, while making an excursion beyond the frontiers of Italy, they passed a week on the shores of the Lake of Como. Their benevolent disposition often made them enter the cottages of the poor. This, to my mother, was more than a duty; it was a necessity, a passion,—remembering what she had suffered, and how she had been relieved,—for her to act in her turn the guardian angel to the afflicted. During one of their walks a poor cot in the foldings of a vale attracted their notice, as being singularly disconsolate, while the number of half-clothed children gathered about it, spoke of penury in its worst shape. One day, when my father had gone by himself to Milan, my mother, accompanied by me, visited this abode. She found a peasant and his wife, hard working, bent down by care and labour, distributing a scanty meal to five hungry babes. Among these there was one which attracted my mother far above all the rest. She appeared of a different stock. The four others were dark-eyed, hardy little vagrants; this child was thin, and very fair. Her hair was the brightest living gold, and, despite the poverty of her clothing, seemed to set a crown of distinction on her head. Her brow was clear and ample, her blue eyes cloudless, and her lips and the moulding of her face so expressive of sensibility[3] and sweetness, that none could behold her without looking on her as of a distinct species, a being heaven-sent, and bearing a celestial stamp in all her features.[4]

The peasant woman, perceiving that my mother fixed eyes of wonder and admiration on this lovely girl, eagerly communicated her history. She was not her child, but the daughter of a Milanese nobleman. Her mother was a German, and had died on giving her birth.[5] The infant had been placed with these good people to nurse: they were better off then.[6] They had not been long married, and their eldest child was but just born. The father of their charge was one of those Italians nursed in the memory of the antique glory of Italy,—one among the *schiavi ognor frementi*, who exerted himself to obtain the liberty of his country.[7] He became the victim of its weakness. Whether he had died, or still lingered in the dungeons of Austria, was not known. His property was confiscated, his child became an orphan and a beggar. She continued with her foster parents, and bloomed in their rude abode, fairer than a garden rose among dark-leaved brambles.

When my father returned from Milan, he found playing with me in the hall of our villa, a child fairer than pictured cherub—a creature who seemed to shed radiance from her looks, and whose form and motions were lighter than the chamois[8] of the hills. The apparition was soon explained. With his permission my mother prevailed on her rustic guardians to yield their charge to her. They were fond of the sweet orphan. Her presence had seemed a blessing to them; but it would be unfair to her to keep her in poverty and want, when Providence afforded her such powerful protection. They consulted their village priest, and the result was, that Elizabeth Lavenza became the inmate of my parents' house—my more than sister—the beautiful and adored companion of all my occupations and my pleasures.[9]

Every one loved Elizabeth. The passionate and almost reverential attachment with which all regarded her became, while I shared it, my pride and my delight. On the evening previous to her being brought to my home, my mother had said playfully,—"I have a pretty present for my Victor—to-morrow he shall have it." And when, on the morrow, she presented Elizabeth to me as her promised gift, I, with childish seriousness, interpreted her words literally, and looked upon Elizabeth as mine—mine to protect, love, and cherish. All praises bestowed on her, I received as made to a possession of my own. We called each other familiarly by the name of cousin. No word, no expression could body forth the kind of relation in which she stood to me—my more than sister, since till death she was to be mine only.[10]

Chapter II

We were brought up together; there was not quite a year difference in our ages. I need not say that we were strangers to any species of disunion or dispute. Harmony was the soul of our companionship, and the diversity and contrast that subsisted in our characters drew us nearer together. Elizabeth was of a calmer and more concentrated disposition; but, with all my ardour, I was capable of a more intense application, and was more deeply smitten with the thirst for knowledge. She busied herself with following the aerial creations of the poets; and in the majestic and wondrous scenes which surrounded our Swiss home—the sublime shapes of the mountains; the changes of the seasons, tempest and calm; the silence of winter, and the life and turbulence of our Alpine summers,—she found ample scope for admiration and delight. While my companion contemplated with a serious and satisfied spirit the magnificent appearances of things, I delighted in investigating their causes. The world was to me a secret which I desired to divine. Curiosity, earnest research to learn the hidden laws of nature, gladness akin to rapture, as they were unfolded to me, are among the earliest sensations I can remember.

On the birth of a second son, my junior by seven years, my parents gave up entirely their wandering life, and fixed themselves in their native country. We possessed a house in Geneva, and a *campagne*[11] on Belrive, the eastern shore of the lake, at the distance of rather more than a league from the city. We resided principally in the latter, and the lives of my parents were passed in considerable seclusion. It was my temper to avoid a crowd and to attach myself fervently to a few. I was indifferent, therefore, to my schoolfellows in general; but I united myself in the bonds of the closest friendship to one among them. Henry Clerval was the son of a merchant of Geneva. He was a boy of singular talent and fancy. He loved enterprise, hardship, and even danger, for its own sake. He was deeply read in books of chivalry and romance.[12] He composed heroic songs, and began to write many a tale of enchantment and knightly adventure. He tried to make us act plays, and to enter into masquerades, in which the characters were drawn from the heroes of Roncesvalles,[13] of the Round Table of King Arthur, and the chivalrous train who shed their blood to redeem the holy sepulchre from the hands of the infidels.[14]

No human being could have passed a happier childhood than myself. My parents were possessed by the very spirit of kindness and indulgence. We felt that they were not the tyrants to rule our lot according to their caprice, but the agents and creators of all the many delights which we enjoyed. When I mingled with other families, I distinctly discerned how peculiarly fortunate my lot was, and gratitude assisted the development of filial love.

My temper was sometimes violent, and my passions vehement; but by some law in my temperature they were turned, not towards childish pursuits, but to an eager desire to learn, and not to learn all things indiscriminately.[15] I confess that neither the structure of languages, nor the code of governments, nor the politics of various states, possessed attractions for me. It was the secrets of heaven and earth that I desired to learn; and whether it was the outward substance of things or the inner spirit of nature and the mysterious soul of man that occupied me, still my enquiries were directed to the metaphysical, or, in its highest sense, the physical secrets of the world.

Meanwhile Clerval occupied himself, so to speak, with the moral relations of things. The busy stage of life, the virtues of heroes, and the actions of men, were his theme; and his hope and his dream was to become one among those whose names are recorded in story, as the gallant and adventurous benefactors of our species.[16] The saintly soul of Elizabeth shone like a shrine-dedicated lamp in our peaceful home. Her sympathy was ours; her smile, her soft voice, the sweet glance of her celestial eyes, were ever there to bless and animate us. She was the living spirit of love to soften and attract: I might have become sullen in my study, rough through the ardour of my nature, but that she was there to subdue me to a semblance of her own gentleness. And Clerval—could aught ill entrench on the noble spirit of Clerval?—yet he might not have been so perfectly humane, so thoughtful in his generosity—so full of kindness and tenderness amidst his passion for adventurous exploit, had she not unfolded to him the real loveliness of beneficence, and made the doing good the end and aim of his soaring ambition.

[1818 *resumes:* "I feel pleasure in dwelling on the recollections of childhood . . ." (91, above)]

Frankenstein's Anguish over Justine (*1831,* Chapter VIII)

Shelley elaborates Victor's anguished paralysis at Justine's doom, his apprehensions for his family, and his anxieties about creating a She-Creature. This new text replaces the end of Vol. I, Ch. VII, the paragraph that opens: "As we returned . . ." (153, above).

And on the morrow Justine died. Elizabeth's heart-rending eloquence failed to move the judges from their settled conviction in the criminality of the saintly sufferer. My passionate and indignant appeals were lost upon them. And when I received their cold answers, and heard the harsh unfeeling reasoning of these men, my purposed avowal died away on my lips. Thus I might proclaim myself a madman, but not revoke the sentence passed upon my wretched victim. She perished on the scaffold as a murderess!

From the tortures of my own heart, I turned to contemplate the deep and voiceless grief of my Elizabeth. This also was my doing! And my father's woe, and the desolation of that late so smiling home—all was the work of my thrice-accursed hands! Ye weep, unhappy ones; but these are not your last tears! Again shall you raise the funeral wail, and the sound of your lamentations shall again and again be heard! Frankenstein, your son, your kinsman, your early, much-loved friend; he who would spend each vital drop of blood for your sakes—who has no thought nor sense of joy, except as it is mirrored also in your dear countenances—who would fill the air with blessings, and spend his life in serving you—he bids you weep—to shed countless tears; happy beyond his hopes, if thus inexorable fate be satisfied, and if the destruction pause before the peace of the grave have succeeded to your sad torments!

Thus spoke my prophetic soul, as, torn by remorse, horror, and despair, I beheld those I loved spend vain sorrow upon the graves of William and Justine, the first hapless victims to my unhallowed arts.

Frankenstein's Agony and Desire for Oblivion (*1831*, Chapter IX)

New agonies for Frankenstein after Elizabeth's question, "what can disturb our tranquillity?" (Vol. II, Ch. I, 161, top, above.)

And could not such words from her whom I fondly prized before every other gift of fortune, suffice to chase away the fiend that lurked in my heart? Even as she spoke I drew near to her, as if in terror; lest at that very moment the destroyer had been near to rob me of her.

Thus not the tenderness of friendship, nor the beauty of earth, nor of heaven, could redeem my soul from woe: the very accents of love were ineffectual. I was encompassed by a cloud which no beneficial influence could penetrate. The wounded deer dragging its fainting limbs to some untrodden brake, there to gaze upon the arrow which had pierced it, and to die—was but a type of me.[17]

Sometimes I could cope with the sullen despair that overwhelmed me: but sometimes the whirlwind passions of my soul drove me to seek, by bodily exercise and by change of place, some relief from my intolerable sensations. It was during an access of this kind that I suddenly left my home, and bending my steps towards the near Alpine valleys, sought in the magnificence, the eternity of such scenes, to forget myself and my ephemeral, because human, sorrows.

The She-Creature (*1831,* Chapter XVIII)

New text after "I was delighted with the idea of spending a year or two in change of scene and variety of occupation" (Vol. III, Ch. I, 237, bottom, above).

I had an insurmountable aversion to the idea of engaging myself in my loathsome task in my father's house, while in habits of familiar intercourse with those I loved. I knew that a thousand fearful accidents might occur, the slightest of which would disclose a tale to thrill all connected with me with horror. I was aware also that I should often lose all self-command, all capacity of hiding the harrowing sensations that would possess me during the progress of my unearthly occupation. I must absent myself from all I loved while thus employed. Once commenced, it would quickly be achieved, and I might be restored to my family in peace and happiness. My promise fulfilled, the monster would depart for ever. Or (so my fond fancy imaged) some accident might meanwhile occur to destroy him

[Then follows: "and put an end to my slavery for ever." (238, top)]

Victor's Apprehensions for His Family (*1831,* Chapter XXI)

Replacing the two short paragraphs, "I remember . . . so much misery" (Vol. III, Ch. I, 275, top, above), Shelley amplifies Victor's longing for oblivion in the image of himself as one of the walking dead.

Yet one duty remained to me, the recollection of which finally triumphed over my selfish despair. It was necessary that I should return without delay to Geneva, there to watch over the lives of those I so fondly loved; and to lie in wait for the murderer, that if any chance led me to the place of his concealment, or if he dared again to blast me by his presence, I might, with unfailing aim, put an end to the existence of the monstrous Image which I had endued with the mockery of a soul still more monstrous. My father still desired to delay our departure, fearful that I could not sustain the fatigues of a journey: for I was a shattered wreck,—the shadow of a human being. My strength was gone. I was a mere skeleton; and fever night and day preyed upon my wasted frame.

New sentences for Vol. III, Ch. V, ¶2 (276, above) elaborate Victor's anguish at his father's concern for him.

My father's care and attentions were indefatigable; but he did not know the origin of my sufferings, and sought erroneous methods to remedy the incurable ill. He wished me to seek amusement in society. I abhorred the face of man. Oh, not abhorred! they were my brethren, my fellow beings, and I felt attracted even to the most repulsive among them, as to creatures of an angelic nature and celestial mechanism. But I felt that I had no right to share their intercourse. I had unchained an enemy among them, whose joy it was to shed their blood, and to revel in their groans. How they would, each and all, abhor me, and hunt me from the world, did they know my unhallowed acts, and the crimes which had their source in me!

NOTES

1. This revises Frankenstein's boast in *1818* of being "Genevese" (Swiss) "by birth"; a birth in Italy makes him more compatible with his new "sister" Elizabeth Lavenza.

2. Reciprocating her own parents' expectation of a son, Shelley has Victor remember his mother's wish for a daughter.

3. "Sensibility" had a range of meanings; here, emotional sensitivity and spiritual character.

4. Sharpening the contrasts with the Creature's doomed hopes, Shelley elaborates the racialized aesthetic values.

5. Shelley again remembers her own mother.

6. A "wet-nurse," in lactation from nursing her own child, nurses a child not her own.

7. An echo of Alfieri's *Misogallo,* sonnet 18: "Servi siam sì, ma servi ognor frementi" (We are slaves, yes, but *slaves still quivering* [with rage and defiance]). The Italian poet and dramatist Vittorio Alfieri (1749–1803) championed the American Revolution and Italian independence from Austria.

8. Small mountain antelope.

9. The primary sense in 1831 was "inhabitant." (The modern sense of inmate as "prisoner" was just emerging.)

10. In *1818* Elizabeth uses *sister* as a term of affection for adoptee Justine Moritz. Every Frankenstein is "more than": Elizabeth is also an intended spouse; Victor is also a virtual father, a

brother, and for a while doted-on only son; Alphonse is a father, and fatherly husband; Caroline is a wife who is like a daughter.

11. A *campagne* is a country house (in distinction from the town house).

12. "Romance" is the literary genres of knightly exploits and exotic adventures.

13. Roncesvalles Pass in the Pyrenees is famed in Spain's legendary past and in the recent Napoleonic wars. It was here in 778 that Roland, the most renowned of Charlemagne's Christian knights, in an ambush of his retreating army of 20,000, was killed by a band of Basque mountaineers—represented in *Chanson de Roland* (11th c.) as an attack force of 400,000 Muslims.

14. King Arthur and his Knights of the Round Table are part of England's legendary Christian past. The Crusades of 1095–1243 were a pan-European war to reclaim the "Holy Lands" from the "Infidels," the Muslim populations of the eastern Mediterranean world. Though traditionally celebrated in the literature of Christian Romance, by the end of the eighteenth century this phase of Western history was coming to be regarded by thinkers such as the Godwins and the Shelleys as brutal imperialism.

15. "Temperature" is used here in the older sense of character being tempered by a mixture of impulses or humors.

16. Compare Robert Walton's self-representation in Letter I.

17. This icon for a tortured soul, as old as Virgil's *Aeneid,* was memorably versed in William Cowper's poem *The Task* (1785): "I was a stricken deer that left the herd / Long since; with many an arrow deep infixt / My panting side was charged when I withdrew / To seek a tranquil death in distant shades" (3.108–111).

The notations of dates and time-spans throughout *Frankenstein* have tempted many a reader to plot a chronology of internal events and to coordinate this calendar with external history. A timeline exposes intriguing coordinates not explicit in the narrative— for instance, the birth of Victor Frankenstein, Henry Clerval, and Justine Moritz all in the same year; Robert Walton's birth in the year Alphonse Frankenstein meets Caroline Beaufort (Victor's mother); the inception of Victor's studies at Ingolstadt the same year Walton begins to train for his polar voyage, 1789, the year of the French Revolution. Yet for all the allure, the execution meets with several complications. We attempt to address these before we sketch a fictional timeline in relation to key events in the history of Mary Shelley and her family, and in literary, political, and cultural history.

In its internal calendrics, *Frankenstein* inscribes two specific day-dates, both locatable on an actual calendar. One is in Walton's Letter IV: "Monday (July 31st)," when his crew beholds a strange being driving a sledge across the distant ice. All his letters bear a blank decade "17—." For several reasons, the 1790s comprise the most appealing decade in which to imagine the events of the novel reaching conclusion. It's not just that the Creature overhears readings from Volney's *Ruins of Empires* (II.V; he would have heard the French, *Les Ruines, ou méditations sur les révolutions des empires*), published in 1791. The 1790s in general are the years in which the ideals that launched the French Revolution in 1789 descended into civil war ("The Terror"), then Napoleon's wars against European monarchies (extinguishing the republics of Venice and Switzerland, too)—not to end until his defeat by allied British and Prussian forces at Waterloo in June 1815. The 1790s also have intense significance for Mary Wollstonecraft (Godwin) Shelley: in this decade her parents made their reputations with controversial political tracts and novels, met, re-met, and married. Her mother became pregnant in December 1796; Mary was born on August 30, 1797 (the month most probable for Frankenstein's encounter with Robert Walton); her mother died from septic complications on September 10, 1797. Collating this calendar with the event of July 31 on Monday in 1797, Anne Mellor ingeniously proposes December 11, 1796–September 12, 1797, as the timeline of Walton's letters and journal, the "womb" that brings "Mary Shelley's literary pregnancy to full term" (54–55).

The Frankenstein family calendar up to Walton's voyage proves more of a challenge. The second specific date in *Frankenstein* is "Thursday (May 7th)": the date of little William's murder (Vol. I, Ch. VI). Mary Shelley took care here: the manuscript shows "May 26," then "May 28th," and then in *1818* "May 7."[1] In the 1790s the year with Thursday, May 7, is 1795 (May 28 is also a Thursday in 1795). Yet for all Shelley's care, we see why Mellor would re-set this event to a fictive "Thursday May 7, 1794" (238). A one-year-earlier date can be reconciled to Frankenstein's later chronology—given "with firmness and precision, marking the dates with accuracy" (Vol. III, Ch. VI)—of his nervous breakdown and pursuit of the Creature into the arctic across "many months" (Vol. III, Ch. VII).[2] In a compromise with Mellor, we accept Nora Crook's suggestion that Thursday, May 8, 1794, was meant: this is an actual date on the calendar.[3] Yet to vex our brains this way is to overwork Frankenstein's late-term delivery, in which calendric accuracy, even when most asserted by characters within the novel, seems maddeningly elusive.[4]

Further challenges are at hand in the several anachronistic references to literary works. Walton alludes, with a casual familiarity, to Coleridge's *Rime of the Ancyent Marinere* (1798), assuming that his sister needs no gloss on his reference or quotation. Frankenstein quotes from *The Rime* by memory, as well as from Wordsworth's *Tintern Abbey*—both first published in October 1798 in *Lyrical Ballads*. He also alludes, casually, to Charles Lamb's lyric "The Old Familiar Faces" (1798) and quotes from Percy Shelley's "Mutability" (1816)—all references impossible in 1797. Anachronism is a venerable practice in English literature since Shakespeare, and its warp on the fictive chronology of *Frankenstein* may have a purpose that trumps the calendar: the array of references constitutes, in effect, an anthology that marks Mary Shelley's tacit solidarity with her Romantic-era contemporaries.[5]

Mary Shelley is not writing documentary history but rendering an illusion of historical events, in which a calendar in the 1790s is overlaid with her literary and intellectual interests, the years of her first three pregnancies, and European history in the aftermath of Waterloo. She is acutely mindful of her own origins in the 1790s, mindful of the literary culture from which her novel emerges, and mindful of her life with Percy Shelley from 1814 to 1817, which included their elopement to the Continent, the birth and death of their first child, an unnamed daughter, the birth of their first son, and the birth of a second daughter. When Mary was writing *Frankenstein*, William was a toddler, and she was pregnant with Clara in December 1816 (twenty years after her mother became pregnant with her). Clara was born on September 2, 1817, just three days after her own twentieth birthday and her completion of the draft of *Frankenstein*. In this decade, too, Walton's adventure, though located in the 1790s, has counterparts: after the long war with France was over, British naval captains and admirals competed for prize money to find a polar passage to the northern Pacific.

Our fictional timelines now anchored, we can work our way backward from May 8, 1794. Ernest Frankenstein, six years Victor's junior, is "not yet sixteen" on March 18, 1793; if he turns sixteen later in 1793, that makes him born in 1777, and so Victor was born in 1771. As for Walton: on December 11, 17[96], he writes that "six years have passed" since he resolved on his "present undertaking." This resolution would likely have occurred just after his twenty-first birthday, when his inheritance from his cousin would come into his control. This would make him twenty-seven by December 11, 1796; on March 28, 1797, he says he's "twenty-eight"—and so born in the early months of 1769. In our calendar, fictional events in *Frankenstein* appear in *italic* to distinguish these from "external" history. Parenthetical references to *Frankenstein* give volume and chapter (sometimes, just to give the basis in the novel for our speculative dating).

1752   On a dark and stormy afternoon, Ben Franklin attaches his kite to a silk string, with an iron key tied at the other end, to capture electricity from a lightning discharge.

1755   Immanuel Kant dubs Franklin "The Prometheus of Modern Times."

1756   Birth of Mary Shelley's father, William Godwin.

1759 Birth of Mary Shelley's mother, Mary Wollstonecraft.

1769 *Before March 28, Robert Walton is born. Alphonse Frankenstein rescues destitute Caroline Beaufort from Lucerne, taking her to Geneva (I.I).*

August 15: Napoleon Bonaparte is born.

1770 *Alphonse Frankenstein and Caroline Beaufort marry (I.I).*

1771 *Victor Frankenstein is born (I.I). Justine Moritz is born (I.V). Henry Clerval is born (III.IV).*

1773 Fifteen-year-old Horatio Nelson (later naval hero in the war against Napoleon) travels on a polar expedition to discover a Northwest passage. From north Greenland, the team embarks on June 4, and by the end of July reaches a latitude of just over 80° North, becomes icebound, and returns in September.

Poet Laureate Robert Southey's popular *Life of Nelson* (1813) reports that Nelson chased a polar bear across the ice in pursuit of a trophy-skin to present to his father.

1774 Louis XVI becomes king of France. Goethe's *Sorrows of Young Werther* is published, creating a sensation of readerly self-identifications, and more than a few suicides. *(From this novel the Creature will learn the language of emotion.)*

1775 *When Victor is "four years of age" (I.I), Alphonse Frankenstein's sister, married to an Italian surnamed Lavenza, dies; her widower, remarrying rather quickly, asks Alphonse to adopt his infant daughter, Elizabeth Lavenza.*

1776 May 1: The Order of the Illuminati is founded at the University of Ingolstadt, involving freethinkers, philosophers, and freemasons. This secret society is believed to be conspiring to overthrow European monarchies, and to be laying the groundwork for the French Revolution in 1789. *(Victor will begin his scientific studies at Ingolstadt in 1789.)*

1778   Victor's brother Ernest ("nearly sixteen" on March 18, 1793) is born (I.I).

1778   July 2:   Death of Jean-Jacques Rousseau, author of education tracts, of political theory that inspired the French Revolution, and father of several children abandoned to a foundling hospital.

1782   Henri Fuseli's painting *The Nightmare* is exhibited at the Royal Academy in London.

1783   Justine Moritz, age twelve, comes to live with the Frankensteins. At age fourteen Walton, having read only stories of sea voyages, discovers the celebrated English poets and dreams of becoming a poet himself (Letter II).

1784   After "one year" of this dream (Letter I), at age fifteen Walton gives up the idea of becoming a poet. With an inheritance from a cousin, he returns to his dream of seafaring adventure (Letter I). Victor ("I was thirteen") reads occult science: Cornelius Agrippa, Albertus Magnus, Paracelsus (I.I).

1786   Victor, "about fifteen," sees a lightning bolt shatter an old oak and becomes fascinated by electrical power; he studies mathematics in Geneva (I.II).

First recorded ascent of Mont Blanc.

1787   Victor's brother William is born (he is an "infant" when Victor is "the age of seventeen") (I.I).

First ascent of Mont Blanc by an Englishman.

1788   By "the age of seventeen" (I.II), Victor is adept at mathematics, proficient in Latin, Greek, and fluent in German and English (his native language is French). His parents decide to send him to the University of Ingolstadt, Germany, where he hopes to study science. This plan is delayed for three months by scarlet fever in the family; Elizabeth recovers but his mother succumbs (I.II). Late fall, Victor travels to Ingolstadt (I.II; I.VI). Justine, age seventeen, resident with the Frankensteins for five years (I.VII), is called back home by her mother (I.V).

1789 *Frankenstein begins his studies. Walton, age twenty-one, dedicates himself to polar adventure (Letter I) and trains in the skills and rigors by accompanying whalers on North Sea expeditions. In the early fall, Mme. Moritz dies, and Justine rejoins the Frankensteins (I.V).*

The storming of the Bastille prison on July 14 launches the French Revolution. Luigi Galvani experiments with electrically induced muscular contractions. Mutiny on the *HMS Bounty* against a tyrannical captain, during a voyage from Tahiti to collect "breadfruit" as a potential cheap food for slaves being transported from Africa to new-world markets. In Germany J. W. von Goethe's poem "Prometheus" receives its first authorized publication.

1789–1790: *Frankenstein becomes a notable student of chemical science (I.III).*

1790 October: Starving Parisians march seventeen miles to Versailles, to force the royal family to abandon the palace for a residence in Paris. November: Edmund Burke's *Reflections on the Revolution in France* denounces the Revolution. Wollstonecraft's rapid response, *Vindication of the Rights of Men,* denounces the *ancien régime.*

1791: *After two transformative years at Ingolstadt, Frankenstein is about to visit home when he suddenly discovers the secret of life (I.III). He throws himself into research for the rest of the year (and into the next).*

William Godwin and Mary Wollstonecraft (Mary's parents) meet. Volney's *Les Ruines . . . des empires* is published in Paris. Another answer to Burke, Tom Paine's *The Rights of Man,* is published in London and becomes an international best seller. Pope Pius VI condemns the French Constitution. June: Louis XVI tries to flee France and is arrested, returned to Paris, and forced to accept the Constitution. Erasmus Darwin's two-part poem, *The Botanic Garden,* is published. William Wilberforce's bill for the abolition of the slave trade fails in Parliament.

1792 January: Wollstonecraft's treatise *A Vindication of the Rights of Woman* is published. August 4: Percy Bysshe Shelley is born.

From spring to fall, Frankenstein devotes himself to creating a "human being."⁶ November: He animates a Creature, who vanishes; Henry Clerval arrives for study at Ingolstadt; finding Frankenstein in a state of collapse, he postpones his plans to care for his friend. Across the winter, the Creature fends for himself in the woods. The De Lacey family is exiled from Paris.

Counter-revolutionary uprisings rock France, spurred by high food prices. Paine's *Rights of Man*, Part 2, is published. By March, the revolutionary regime in France urges the overthrow of the monarchy and the clergy, and the export of revolution across Europe. June: Mobs invade the Paris residence of the royal family; August: overthrow of the monarchy. After another attempt to escape, the royal family is imprisoned. September: The "Terror" emerges with the massacre of 12,000 prisoners in Paris alone (ordinary criminals, priests, aristocrats, counter-revolutionaries, and servants of these people); eyewitnesses Wollstonecraft and William Wordsworth are horrified. December: Louis XVI is tried and condemned for treason.

1793   Winter: The Creature discovers the De Lacey's cottage and becomes the family's secret benefactor, living in an adjoining "kennel." By April (two weeks after receiving Elizabeth's letter of March 18) Victor has recovered his health and spends the year with Clerval studying languages (I.V). Spring: Safie joins the De Laceys; she and the Creature learn French. The Creature finds a satchel of books (August). Late fall/early winter: His hopes for acceptance by the De Laceys meet catastrophic failure.

January: Louis XVI is guillotined. France declares war on Britain, Holland, and Spain, and Britain declares war on France, where the radicals rise to power. Wollstonecraft begins an affair with American adventurer Gilbert Imlay and is pregnant by August. October: Marie Antoinette is guillotined. Godwin publishes *Enquiry Concerning Political Justice*. Blake's epic satire *The Marriage of Heaven and Hell* is published.

1794   Winter weather thwarts a return to Geneva; Frankenstein and Clerval remain in Ingolstadt until the spring. In May they take a two-week "pedestrian tour in the environs" (I.V). The Creature, having learned some of his origin, travels to Geneva. On "Thursday May [8]" he kills William Frankenstein (age seven). Friday, May 9: The body is discovered. Monday, May 12: Alphonse writes to Victor with this news.

William Godwin's journal, August 30, 1797, recording the birth of his and Mary Wollstonecraft's daughter: "Birth of Mary 20 minutes after 11 at night." Godwin kept meticulous records, filling 32 octavo notebooks, starting April 6, 1788, and continuing to March 26, 1836, less than two weeks before his death.

May: Birth of Wollstonecraft and Imlay's child, Françoise (in honor of her birthplace), later anglicized to Fanny.

July: In internal conflicts with the radical faction in France, Danton, Robespierre, and St. Just are all executed; the Terror ends.

August: Early in this month, on returning to Switzerland, Victor catches sight of the Creature. By the end of August, Justine is tried and executed for the murder of William. The Frankensteins seek solace in Chamounix, where the Creature finds Victor, tells his story, and demands a mate. Postponing marriage to Elizabeth, Victor departs for England. September: He meets Clerval in Strasbourgh; they journey down the Rhine to Rotterdam. October: They sail to England (III.I / III.II) and spend the winter in London—all the time shadowed by the Creature.

Published: Wollstonecraft's *Historical and Moral View of the French Revolution;* Godwin's political novel *Adventures of Caleb Williams;* Erasmus Darwin's *Zoonomia; or, The Laws of Organic Life;* Ann Radcliffe's gothic novel *The Mysteries of Udolpho,* a sensational success that Mary Godwin (later Mary Shelley) will read in 1815. Rousseau is interred as a national hero in the Panthéon in Paris.

1795   *Leaving London on March 27, Clerval and Frankenstein head up to Scotland.*

April: Wollstonecraft returns to London. May: In despair over Imlay's new lover, she attempts suicide. June: She travels, with infant Fanny and a maid, to Scandinavia on business for Imlay.

July: Parting from Clerval at Perth, Frankenstein sets up a workshop in the northern Orkney Islands, where by August ("nearly a year" since leaving Geneva [III.III]), he has constructed a female creature. He destroys his work, disposing of the parts at sea; blown by winds to Ireland, he finds himself arrested for the murder of a man who turns out to be Clerval.

August 1: Birth of Harriet Westbrook (to be Percy Shelley's first wife and mother of his two eldest children). September: Returning to London, Wollstonecraft discovers Imlay with yet another lover.

By October ("two months" later [III.IV]), Alphonse comes to Ireland. Victor is acquitted in late November and leaves with his father in December (III.V).

October: Wollstonecraft again attempts suicide. Napoleon suppresses a royalist revolt. Volney's *Ruins of Empires* is published in English.

1796   January: Wollstonecraft's *Letters, Written during a Short Residence in Sweden, Norway, and Denmark* is published. March: Her final meeting with Imlay; Napoleon invades Italy, inaugurating his war of European expansion. April: Wollstonecraft re-meets Godwin, who has read *Letters* and fallen in love with the author; she begins *The Wrongs of Woman; or Maria,* a political-gothic novel that includes the inset story of a bastard girl who is treated as a "monster."

May 8: Victor and his father are in Le Havre (III.V). During "a few weeks" in Paris, Victor receives a letter from Elizabeth in Geneva, dated "May 18th, 17—."

June: "after two years of exile" for Victor (III.I), they return to Geneva (III.V). Victor marries Elizabeth, who is murdered on their wedding night; his father dies a few days later. Summer: Victor is confined in a madhouse (III.VI). Fall: A month after his release he tells his story to a judge, to no avail. He begins a lone pursuit of the Creature across Europe. December 11: Robert Walton writes to his sister, from St. Petersburg, Russia, at the start of his polar adventure.

Mid-December: Wollstonecraft is pregnant (with Mary).

1797   Winter: *Frankenstein travels to the Black Sea and into Russia. March 28: Walton (Letter II) is at Archangel, a port on the North Sea.*

March 29: Wollstonecraft and Godwin marry. May: Napoleon invades Venice and extinguishes the Republic.

"Monday July 31, 17—." (Letter IV), Walton's crew sees a gigantic being on the far ice, driving a dogsled. August 1: Frankenstein is taken aboard Walton's vessel. By August 5, he is recovering; from the 13th to the 26th he tells his story to Walton.

August 30: Mary Wollstonecraft Godwin is born.

September 2: Walton fears a mutiny from the crew of his ice-bound ship.

20 minutes before 8. ———

Montagu, M, miss G & Fanny dine.
Carlisle calls: Montagu at tea.

Johnson & H n call: Montagu &
miss G at tea.

H n, Ogive n & Dyson n call: mus t
removes: Fenwicks sup from Fordyce:
write to Inchbald, Tuthil & Pass.

Write to mrs Cotton. Barbauld on Devotion, p. 22. Fenwicks & PV sup.

Funeral: M's lodgings. Write to Carlisle.
Pursley, p. 50. Fawcet dines; adv. Fenwicks.

Pursley, p. 186: Mary, p. 187, fin. Call
on Mkerveley, w. Fenwick: Fawcet dines: Fanny at home: Ht calls.

William Godwin's journal, the morning of Mary Wollstonecraft's death, September 10, 1797. All Godwin could do was record the time, "20 minutes before 8," and draw two blank lines.

Title page of William Godwin's *Memoirs of the Author of Vindication of the Rights of Woman,* 1798. While Godwin presented what he imagined to be an admirable and candid account of his late wife, his disclosure of scandalous personal details managed to ruin Wollstonecraft's reputation for almost a century.

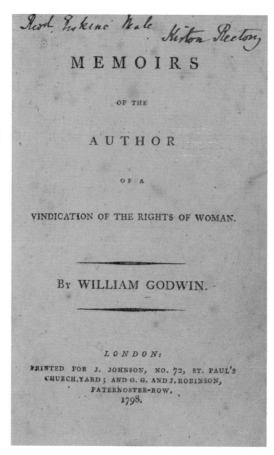

September 4: Napoleon's coup d'état consolidates his leadership in France.

September 5: Frankenstein urges the crew to persist north. September 7: Walton consents to turn south should the ice break. September 9: The ice begins to break.

September 10: Wollstonecraft dies from septic poisoning.

September 11: A passage opens to the south. September 12: Bitterly disappointed, Walton reports that he is returning to England. Frankenstein dies. The Creature appears on ship.

Radcliffe's gothic novel *The Italian,* set in the eighteenth century, is published; Mary Godwin reads the book in 1815.

1798   In Ireland 100,000 peasants revolt, with approximately 25,000 deaths; the Irish Parliament is abolished. Napoleon invades Rome, then the Republic of Switzerland (the Frankensteins' home); he sails for Egypt, but loses the Battle of the Nile to Britain; Britain, Austria, and Russia form an alliance against France.

Published: Godwin's *Memoirs* of Wollstonecraft; *Lyrical Ballads,* an unsigned volume opening with Coleridge's *Rime of the Ancyent Marinere* and closing with Wordsworth's *Tintern Abbey.*

1799   Napoleon returns to France; in a coup d'état (November 9–10) he becomes First Consul. Godwin publishes *St. Leon,* whose hero discovers the alchemy of transmuting base metals into gold, and the elixir of life, granting immortality.

1800   Napoleon crosses the Alps into Austria with an army of 4,000. Humphry Davy publishes studies in chemistry. Alessandro Volta produces electricity from a cell and creates the first electric battery. The University of Ingolstadt closes.

1801   December 21:   William Godwin marries Mary Jane Clairmont, already pregnant by him, and already mother of Charles (age seven) and Mary Jane/Claire (four), their father(s) unknown.

1802   April: William Godwin, Jr., is born and dies soon after. The Peace of Amiens between England and France allows Britons to travel to the Continent for the first time in many years; France reoccupies Switzerland. Davy's *Discourse, Introductory* to his lectures on chemistry published.

1803   England again declares war on France. A second William Godwin, Jr., is born, on March 28. John Aldini publishes his treatise *Galvanism,* with an *Appendix, Containing the author's Experiments on the body of a Malefactor Executed at Newgate.*

1804   Napoleon crowns himself Emperor of the French; Pope Pius VII is in attendance.

William Powell Frith, *The Lover's Seat* (1877). A sentimental Victorian imagining of the now famous clandestine courtship of Percy Bysshe Shelley and teenage Mary Godwin at St. Pancras Churchyard. Frith's better-known paintings include *The Crossing-Sweeper* (1858; a poor boy, hopeful of a tip, sweeping the street for rich indifferent swell) and *A Private View at the Royal Academy* (1881), featuring Oscar Wilde holding forth to the assembly at this art gallery.

1805 Horatio Nelson dies during his victory over the French fleet at Trafalgar; Napoleon defeats allied Austrian and Russian forces.

1806 J. M. W. Turner paints *Mer de Glace* (where Frankenstein and the Creature converge). Napoleon wages war against Prussia and Russia and closes the Continent to British trade. Mary hears Coleridge recite *The Rime of the Ancient Mariner* on a visit to Godwin; she publishes a fanciful poem with M. J. Godwin & Co., the firm founded by her father and stepmother. Charles Lamb publishes his *Specimens of English Dramatic Poets who Lived About the Time of Shakespeare*, including generous excerpts from Christopher Marlowe's *Dr Faustus* (which Mary and Percy read in 1817).

1807 Napoleon invades Spain and Portugal. The British support uprisings. Parliament abolishes the slave trade in the British Empire (colonial slavery remains legal until 1833).

1808 Goethe's *Faust*, Part I, is published.

1809 Byron takes his seat in the House of Lords. Napoleon's army is defeated in Austria. Lamarck's *Philosophie Zoologique* proposes a theory of evolution, against the theory of fixed, unchanging species.

1811 January: Percy Shelley meets Harriet Westbrook. March: He is expelled from Oxford University for his pamphlet *The Necessity of Atheism* (the refusal of institutional religion). August: He elopes with Harriet to Scotland.

George III is deemed incompetent. The Prince of Wales becomes Prince Regent. Luddite riots against weaving frames. Jane Austen publishes her first novel, *Sense and Sensibility,* anonymously.

1812 January: Shelley introduces himself to his idol, Godwin. February: Shelley is in Ireland distributing pamphlets against religion, protesting the injustice of poverty and bans on free assembly. June–November: Godwin sends Mary to live with the

Baxter family in Dundee, Scotland. Shelley meets and frequently visits Godwin; Mary meets him and his wife in November.

Lord Byron's *Childe Harold's Pilgrimage* is an overnight sensation. Napoleon invades Russia in June and retreats from Moscow in December, abandoning his troops in the winter to fend for themselves, with horrific losses (500,000 of 600,000 men).

1813   Mary returns to Scotland for ten months. Percy and Harriet Shelley's daughter Ianthe is born. Published: Austen's *Pride and Prejudice* (anonymous); Southey's *Life of Horatio Nelson;* Shelley's *Queen Mab,* protesting Kingcraft, Statecraft, and Priestcraft.

Austria joins the alliance against France; Napoleon is defeated at Leipzig and re-treats from Spain, Holland, Italy, and Switzerland. Wars of liberation erupt throughout Europe.

1814   February: Harriet Shelley is pregnant. March: She and Shelley remarry to guarantee legitimacy for Ianthe. Mary Godwin returns from Scotland on March 30, and Shelley is smitten with her; by June she, too, is pregnant. Harriet declines Shelley's offer that she live with him and Mary as his "sister." July 8: Godwin tries to break up Percy and Mary. July 28: Mary elopes with Percy to the Continent, taking along her stepsister, Claire Clairmont. They tour France, Germany, Switzerland, and Holland, and return in September to an enraged Godwin, who refuses to receive the lovers. He does not see Mary for three years. November 30: Percy and Harriet Shelley's son Charles is born.

The Allies invade France. April: Napoleon abdicates and is exiled to Elba; the reaction-ary Bourbon dynasty is restored, and British tourism is again possible. Henry Cary's translation of *The Divine Comedy* is published; Byron publishes *The Corsair* and *Lara,* to record-breaking sales, consolidating his celebrity with these "Eastern tales." Austen publishes *Mansfield Park* anonymously.

1815   January 5:   From his grandfather's will, Percy Shelley receives an annuity of £1,000 and funds to settle his debts. February 22: Mary and Percy's daughter is born prematurely and dies on March 6. June 6: Percy gives Mary *Paradise Lost,* possibly to commemorate their first meeting in early June 1814. August 3: They live at Bishopsgate, Great Windsor Park. Late August/early September: They tour Windsor and Oxford.

January: Byron weds a wealthy heiress; their daughter Ada is born in December. Austen's *Emma* is published by John Murray (anonymously, though she is now famous).

Napoleon escapes from Elba, enters France in March, is defeated at Waterloo, and is exiled to St. Helena, an island in the Atlantic Ocean; the restoration of several reactionary European monarchies.

1816   January 24:   Mary and Percy's son William is born. May 2: With Claire Clairmont, they travel to Switzerland, arriving on May 13. May 27: Byron and Percy Shelley meet for the first time. By June 10, Byron is resident at Villa Diodati, on Lake Geneva, the site of a ghost-story contest (June 16) during which *Frankenstein* is conceived. Byron recites some of Coleridge's *Christabel,* which gives Percy a nightmare. Percy is reading Volney's *Ruins of Empire* and will soon work on a translation of Aeschylus's *Prometheus Bound.* July: Claire, Mary, and Percy visit Chamounix (Mont Blanc and Mer de Glace). September: They return to England. Mary works on *Frankenstein* throughout the autumn, reading Davy's studies of chemistry and sea-voyaging literature; perhaps she drafts the Walton frame. October 9: Mary's half-sister, Fanny, commits suicide. October 26: Percy (writing in Mary's journal) describes *Frankenstein* as a "book." October 28: Mary reads Davy's book on chemistry. Late November/early December: Harriet Shelley (living as "Harriet Smith"), pregnant by someone else and still wearing Percy's wedding ring, drowns herself in the Serpentine canal, London. Her body is discovered on December 10; Mary and Percy hear the news on December 15 and marry December 30. Mary is reconciled with her father. She is again pregnant.

January: Lady Byron leaves Byron, a little more than a year into the marriage, taking with her their newborn. April: With a decree of separation, Byron leaves England forever, never again to see his wife or their daughter. Claire Clairmont seeks him out and they begin an affair; she becomes pregnant. Byron works on *Manfred* (its hero, a scientist of occult arts, is doomed to misery for some unnamable sin) and a short lyric *Prometheus.* December: Byron's *Childe Harold's Pilgrimage, Canto III* is published to electric success; on Byron's urging, John Murray publishes a volume of Coleridge's poetry, *Christabel, Kubla Khan,* and *The Pains of Sleep.*

June 1816–April 1817: Mary reads intensively and works steadily on *Frankenstein*. December: She is pregnant again.

1817   January 12: Residing in Bath with the Shelleys, Claire gives birth to Allegra, her daughter by Byron. March: The Shelleys, Claire, and Allegra move to Marlow. March 17: Chancery Court denies Percy custody of his children by Harriet. Across April and May, Mary corrects (with Percy's advice) and transcribes *Frankenstein*, completing it by May 13; Percy seeks a publisher. Byron's *Manfred* is published in June. August 22: Lackington & c accepts *Frankenstein* (Percy submitted it on behalf of the "author," an unnamed "friend"). The Shelleys' daughter Clara is born (September 2); a few weeks later Mary gives Percy "carte blanche" to correct proofs for *Frankenstein* and make whatever "alterations you please." From September to November, he and William Godwin read proofs. November 6: *History of a Six Weeks' Tour* "by Percy Bysshe Shelley" is published in London. (Assembled after Mary Shelley completed her first draft of *Frankenstein*, this history recounts the travels of summer 1814, and includes "descriptive" letters from summer 1816 by them both, as well as Percy's poem *Mont Blanc*.)

November 6: death of Princess Charlotte from complications in the delivery of a stillborn child; national mourning.

December: *Frankenstein* advertised in the London press (*Literary Panorama*, London *Observer*, London *Times*).

1818   January 1:   *Frankenstein* published by Lackington & c. The Shelleys send a copy to Walter Scott, who reviews it favorably in *Blackwood's Edinburgh Magazine* (March), assuming the author to be Percy Shelley; other reviews appear, during the year, in *"Scots" Edinburgh Magazine*, *La Belle Assemblée*, the *British Critic*, *Gentleman's Magazine*, the *Monthly Review*, and the *Quarterly Review*. March 11: The Shelleys, Claire, and children leave for Italy. Moving from Milan to Pisa to Livorno, they settle in Bagni di Lucca in June. Percy brings Claire and Allegra to Byron in Venice; Mary and children follow in August; baby Clara dies in Venice from heat exhaustion on September 24. The family moves to Este (where Percy Shelley begins *Prometheus Unbound*), then to Rome in November, and Naples in December. Godwin, in increasing financial straits, hounds the Shelleys for money.

Two parodies of the gothic novel are published: Austen's *Northanger Abbey* and T. L. Peacock's *Nightmare Abbey*. Canto IV of Byron's *Childe Harold's Pilgrimage* is published.

1819   March: The Shelleys go to Rome. June 7: Their son William dies of malaria. They move to Livorno (Leghorn), then Montenero; Percy writes *The Cenci*, a play about incest-rape and murder, and a lyric drama *Prometheus Unbound,* both published in 1820. October: The family moves to Florence. November 12: Percy Florence is born, the only child to survive into adulthood.

Byron's vampire "Fragment," a work from that ghost-story night, is published as a page-filler in *Mazeppa*. April 1: J. W. Polidori's *The Vampyre* appears in *New Monthly Magazine,* attributed to Byron. May 15: Byron tells publisher Murray that Mary Shelley, not Percy Shelley, is the author of *Frankenstein.*

December: William Parry embarks on his Arctic expedition.

1820   The Shelleys move to Pisa (January), Livorno (June–August), Bagni di San Guiliano (August–October), and back to Pisa; Byron sends Allegra away from her mother, to live in the country. Mary Shelley begins her next novel, *Valperga*.

1821   Enamored of Teresa (Emilia) Viviani, Percy Shelley writes a visionary romance of union with her, *Epipsychidion,* with harsh allusions to Mary's coldness (published anonymously in May). The Shelleys meet Jane and Edward Williams; Percy falls in love with Jane. The Shelleys move to Bagni di San Guiliano (April), then to Pisa (October) to be near Byron. Byron publishes *Cain* in December and sends Allegra to a convent. Polidori commits suicide.

1822   April: Byron and Claire's daughter, Allegra, dies of typhus. May: The Shelleys and the Williamses move to Casa Magni on the Bay of Lerici. June 16: Mary suffers a nearly fatal miscarriage, her life saved by Percy's care. July: Leigh Hunt, with his large family, arrives in Pisa to join Byron and Percy Shelley in publishing *The Liberal*. Percy Shelley and Edward Williams sail over to greet them and drown in a storm on the return trip (July 8). Mary and Percy Florence move, with Byron and the Hunts, to Genoa (September).

Mary Shelley's grave, at St. Peter's Church, Bournemouth, England. According to family legend, she was buried with Percy Shelley's heart, which Edward Trelawny had snatched from Shelley's funeral pyre in Italy.

1823 February: *Valperga* is published by Colburn and Bentley (who will publish the 1831 *Frankenstein*). Quarreling with Byron, Mary returns with Percy Florence to London in the summer. July 29: R. B. Peake's musical-comedy melodrama *Presumption; or, The Fate of Frankenstein* opens at the English Opera House. Mary attends on August 29. Motivated by its success, Godwin manages a two-volume reprint of *Frankenstein*, which appears on August 11, with "Mary Wollstonecraft Shelley" on the title page—"for my benefit," she marvels (*Letters* 1: 379). August 18: H. M. Milner's *Frankenstein; or The Demon of Switzerland* opens at the Royal Coburg Theatre. Then some lesser successes—September 1: *Presumption and the Blue Demon* opens at Davis's Royal Amphitheatre, and *Humgumption; or, Dr. Frankenstein and the Hobgoblin of Hoxton* at the New Surrey. October 20: Peake's *Another Piece of Presumption* opens at the Adelphi Theatre.

1824 March 16: Foreign Secretary Canning invokes *Frankenstein* in Parliament, to warn of the dangers of liberating slaves. Mary Shelley begins her next novel, *The Last Man,* and publishes Percy Shelley's *Posthumous Poems,* which his father suppresses. December: *Frank-in-Steam; or, The Modern Promise to Pay* opens at the Olympic Theatre.

1825 Godwin declares bankruptcy; Mary Shelley declines a proposal of marriage from American playwright John Howard Payne.

1826 *The Last Man,* "By the Author of *Frankenstein,*" is published. When Charles Shelley (Percy's son by his first wife) dies, Percy Florence becomes the Shelley heir. June: *Le Monstre et le Magicien* by J.-T. Merle and A. N. Beraud, an adaptation of *Frankenstein,* opens in Paris at Theatre de la Porte Saint-Martin; after ninety-four performances, it moves to another theater. July, in London: Milner's melodrama *The Man and the Monster* opens at the Royal Coburg, and the English translation of the French play, *The Monster and the Magician,* opens at the New Royal West Theatre.

1827 Sir William Edward Parry's expedition gets closer to the North Pole (82°45′N) than any attempt in the previous fifty years.

1828 Mary Shelley contracts smallpox in Paris.

1831   September–October: Bentley and Colburn advertise *Frankenstein* as forthcoming. October 22: Mary Shelley's new "Introduction" is pre-published in Colburn's *Court Journal.* October 31 (Halloween): *Frankenstein* is published in a print run of 4,020, priced at 6 shillings.

1832   Five hundred more copies of *Frankenstein* are printed. Percy Shelley's review of *Frankenstein* appears in *The Athenæum* in a series of posthumous papers, organized by his cousin Thomas Medwin. Medwin's translation of Aeschylus's *Prometheus Bound,* on which Percy Shelley collaborated, is published. Mary Shelley's half-brother, William Godwin, Jr., dies in a pan-national cholera epidemic.

1833   Slavery is abolished in British colonies.

1836   William Godwin dies.

1838   William Hazlitt, Jr., seeks to publish *Frankenstein* in his series, *The Best Works of the Best Authors,* but the copyright-holders (Colburn and Bentley) refuse, wanting to retain the franchise.

1839   Colburn and Bentley reprint *Frankenstein.*

1844   Sir Timothy Shelley dies; Percy Florence Shelley inherits the title and estate, and he and Mary Shelley are now financially secure.

1849   Mary Shelley joins the household of Percy Florence and his wife. Colburn and Bentley reprint *Frankenstein.* A political burlesque, *Frankenstein; or, The Model Man,* by W. and R. Brough, opens at the Adelphi. Herman Melville reads *Frankenstein.*

1851   February 1:   Mary Shelley, age fifty-three, dies from a brain tumor.

1880   Now out of copyright, *Frankenstein* goes into vigorous reprinting, selling more copies than all previous editions together (William St. Clair, *The Godwins and the Shelleys: The Biography of a Family* [New York: Norton, 1989], 365).

1887 *Frankenstein; or The Vampyre's Victim,* a musical comedy by R. Butler and H. C. Newton, opens on Christmas Eve.

1910 Valentine's Day: Thomas Edison's *Frankenstein,* a fifteen-minute silent film, is released.

1927 Peggy Webling's *Frankenstein: An Adventure in the Macabre,* a melodrama with all sorts of distortions, including a rampant wild "monster," opens in Lancashire.

1930 Webling's *Frankenstein* plays seventy-two performances in London.

1931 Universal Studios buys the rights to a revision of Webling's play by John Balderston, who thought hers "illiterate" and "inconceivably crude." James Whale's *Frankenstein* (with Boris Karloff) is released, one hundred years after the third (revised) edition of the novel.

1935 Whale's film *The Bride of Frankenstein* is released; "Mary Shelley" in the prologue is doubled as the "Bride" in the story (both played by Elsa Lanchester).

NOTES

1. For the manuscript, see Robinson, *Frankenstein Notebooks* 1: 154–155.

2. Nora Crook remarks that the historical "Thursday (May 7th)," 1795, would set Walton's letters in 1798, and so negate "Monday July 31st" as a day in 1797. The dates in the novel, she suggests, were either intended to give an illusion of history or reflect Shelley's error in her calendar work (51, note).

3. Even though we accept this advice, we find it curious that as Shelley made other corrections, she let stand "May 7th" both in *1823* (I: 135) and in *1831* (Vol. I, Ch. VII, 57).

4. Facing the "impasse" of incoherent years, Wolf resorts to a bare time-sequencing calibrated from age differences and internal year spans ("A Chronology of Events in *Frankenstein,*" 340–342). Another internal calendar problem (not even crossing his radar) is the history of Justine that Elizabeth gives in her first letter (I.V) and court testimony (I.VII). She says Justine joined the household at "twelve," was recalled to her mother "five" years on (just after Victor goes to Ingolstadt), and returns some months later, "nearly two years" before the death of Wil-

liam. Her chronology would have William murdered in May 1792 (not even the historically possible 1794); it was accepted at the trial (even though her testimony was in general disregarded).

5. Crook proposes that the literary anachronisms be read as the additions of a later fictive editor, the hand that may also have blanked-out the dates on Walton's letters (9)—perhaps Margaret [Walton] Saville, proxy for author "M. W. S." (Mellor, 54).

6. Frankenstein's narrative in Chapter III gives the impression that his research and "labour" in "the creation of a human being" spanned a year: "Winter, spring, and summer," a nine-month gestation in gothic perversion of human sexual conception. Yet in Chapter IV he says this was "nearly two years" (making the animation happen in November 1792). So, too, in retrospect from William's death, he says, "Two years had now nearly elapsed since the night on which he first received life" (Vol. I, Ch. VI). In late summer 1795, he says it was "three years before" (Vol. III, Ch. III).

FURTHER READING AND VIEWING

Mary Wollstonecraft Godwin Shelley: Biography, Letters, and Journals

Garrett, Martin. *The British Library Writers' Lives: Mary Shelley.* Oxford: Oxford University Press, 2002.

Mellor, Anne K. *Mary Shelley: Her Life, Her Fiction, Her Monsters.* New York: Methuen, 1988.

Nitchie, Elizabeth. *Mary Shelley, Author of "Frankenstein."* New Brunswick, NJ: Rutgers University Press, 1953.

St. Clair, William. *The Godwins and the Shelleys: The Biography of a Family.* New York: Norton, 1989.

Shelley, Mary Wollstonecraft. *The Journals of Mary Shelley, 1814–1844.* Edited by Paula R. Feldman and Diana Scott-Kilvert. Oxford: Oxford University Press, 1987; Baltimore: Johns Hopkins University Press, 1995.

———. *The Letters of Mary Wollstonecraft Shelley.* Edited by Betty T. Bennett, 3 vols. Baltimore: Johns Hopkins University Press, 1980–1988.

———. "Rousseau." In *Lives of the Most Eminent Literary and Scientific Men of France.* In Dionysius Lardner's *Cabinet Cyclopaedia,* 2: 111–174. London: Longman & c; John Taylor, 1839. Rousseau's genius and carelessness of his domestic responsibilities and social duty.

Sunstein, Emily. *Mary Wollstonecraft Shelley: Romance and Reality.* Boston: Little, Brown, 1989.

Walling, William. *Mary Shelley.* New York: Twayne, 1972.

Other Texts of *Frankenstein*

Anobile, Richard J., ed. *Frankenstein.* New York: Universe ("a Darien House book"), 1971. James Whale's 1931 film text, with over 1,000 sequentially arranged frame photos.

Crook, Nora, ed. *Frankenstein; or The Modern Prometheus.* London: Chatto and Pickering, 1996. Scholarly, with detailed footnotes, all textual variants, and the page numbering of the 1818 edition.

Rieger, James, ed. *Frankenstein, the 1818 text.* Chicago: University of Chicago Press, 1974, 1982. Includes revisions begun in 1823, the 1831 variants, Byron's and Polidori's ghost stories.

Robinson, Charles. *The Frankenstein Notebooks. A Facsimile Edition of Mary Shelley's Manuscript Novel, 1816–17 (with Alterations in the Hand of Percy Bysshe Shelley) as it Survives in Draft and Fair Copy Deposited by Lord Abinger in the Bodleian Library, Oxford* (Dep. c. 477/1 and Dep. c. 534/1-2), 2 vols. Garland Publishing, 1996. The premier reference for all questions of authorship, textual genetics, and revision.

———, ed. *Frankenstein or The Modern Prometheus: The Original Two-Volume Novel of 1816-1817 from the Bodleian Library Manuscripts.* By Mary Wollstonecraft Shelley (with Percy Bysshe Shelley). Oxford: Bodleian Library, 2008. In this more accessible version, Robinson presents a basic transcription distinguishing the two hands, and redacts Mary's pre-Percy draft—enabling us to see how the 1818 publication emerged.

Shelley, Mary Wollstonecraft. *Frankenstein: or, The Modern Prometheus.* "A New Edition." 2 vols. London: G. and W. B. Whittaker, 1823. Photofacsimile reprint: New York: Woodstock Books, 1993. Also on Google Books.

———. *Frankenstein: or, The Modern Prometheus*. London: Henry Colburn and Richard Bentley, 1832. Also on Google Books.

———. *Frankenstein*. Edited by Johanna Smith, 2nd ed. Boston: Bedford/St. Martin's, 2000. The 1831 version, with biographical and historical materials, critical history, and some critical essays.

Wolf, Leonard, ed. *The Annotated Frankenstein*. New York: Clarkson Potter, 1977. Maps, illustrations, commentary. The facsimile reproduction of the *1818* text (though not the 1818 page divisions) is valuable for this record and for its supplements, but the facsimile is flawed in several places, chopping off Shelley's footnotes and rearranging the pages.

Wolfson, Susan J., ed. *Mary Wollstonecraft Shelley's Frankenstein*. A Longman Cultural Edition. New York: Longman, 2003. A wealth of contextual materials, including the ghost stories by Byron and Polidori, Peake's play of 1823, *Presumption,* passages from Coleridge, Byron, Shelley, and Milton relevant to the novel, and excerpts from Dr. Benjamin Spock's *Baby and Child Care*.

Websites

Curran, Stuart, ed. *Frankenstein,* by Mary Shelley. A Romantic Circles Electronic Edition. Expertly edited, with massive supplementary resources. Complete texts of 1818 and 1831. http://www.rc.umd.edu/editions/frankenstein/.

Mary Shelley, Chronology and Resource site, by Shanon Lawson. http://www.rc.umd.edu/reference/chronologies/mschronology/mws.html.

Reviews of *Presumption; or, The Fate of Frankenstein* (1823). http://www.rc.umd.edu/reference/chronologies/mschronology/reviews/mprev.html.

The 1818 *Frankenstein:* http://www.boutell.com/frankenstein/. Not entirely accurate, but very useful for word searches.

Visual media: http://www.imdb.com/find?s=all&q=Frankenstein.

Critical Issues

Baldick, Chris. *In Frankenstein's Shadow: Myth, Monstrosity, and Nineteenth-Century Writing*. Oxford: Clarendon Press, 1987.

Behrendt, Stephen C. "Language and Style in *Frankenstein*." In Behrendt, *Approaches to Teaching,* 78–84.

———. "Mary Shelley, *Frankenstein,* and the Woman Writer's Fate." In *Romantic Women Writers: Voices and Counter-Voices,* ed. Paula R. Feldman and Theresa M. Kelley, 69–87. Hanover, NH: University Press of New England, 1995.

———, ed. *Approaches to Teaching Shelley's* Frankenstein. Modern Language Association, 1990. Enjoyable as "approaches to reading," nineteen essays on a range of topics; bibliography; filmography.

Bennett, Betty T. "*Frankenstein* and the Uses of Biography." In Behrendt, *Approaches to Teaching,* 78–84.

Bloom, Harold. "*Frankenstein,* Or, The New Prometheus." In M. Shelley, *Frankenstein.* New York: New American Library. Signet *Frankenstein,* 1965. On Prometheus, and the doubling of creator and creature.

Botting, Fred. *Making Monstrous: Frankenstein, Criticism, Theory.* Manchester: Manchester University Press, 1991.

Brooks, Peter. "'Godlike Science / Unhallowed Arts': Language, Nature, and Monstrosity." In Levine and Knoepflmacher, 205–220.

Brown, Marshall. "*Frankenstein:* A Child's Tale." *Novel* 36, no. 2 (2003): 145–175. Reprinted in *The Gothic Text,* 183–208. Stanford, CA: Stanford University Press, 2005. In its elements of fairy-tale, folk-lore and fantasy, the novel embodies a child's unformed, inchoate experience of the world.

Butler, Marilyn. "The First *Frankenstein* and Radical Science." *Times Literary Supplement* 9 (April 1993): 12–14. On Enlightenment ideals, experiments, and anxieties.

Cantor, Paul. "The Nightmare of Romantic Idealism." In *Creature and Creator: Myth-Making and English Romanticism,* 103–132. Cambridge: Cambridge University Press, 1984.

Duyfhuizen, Bernard. "Periphrastic naming in Mary Shelley's *Frankenstein.*" *Studies in the Novel* (1995): 477–492. What names mean, and who has them.

Ellis, Kate. "Monsters in the Garden: Mary Shelley and the Bourgeois Family." In Levine and Knoepflmacher, 123–142. Sharp reading of social ideologies.

Favret, Mary A. "The Letters of *Frankenstein.*" *Genre* 20 (1987): 3–24.

Ferguson, Frances. "The Gothicism of the Gothic Novel." In *Solitude and the Sublime,* 97–113. New York: Routledge, 1992.

———."Generationalizing: Romantic Social Forms and the Case of Mary Shelley's *Frankenstein,*" *Partial Answers: Journal of Literature and the History of Ideas* 8, no. 1 (2010): 97–118.

Gigante, Denise. "Facing the Ugly: The Case of *Frankenstein,*" *ELH: English Literary History* 67 (2000): 565–587. Canny reading of this anti-aesthetic aesthetic.

Gilbert, Sandra, and Susan Gubar. "Horror's Twin: Mary Shelley's Monstrous Eve." In *The Madwoman in the Attic: The Woman Writer and the Nineteenth-Century Literary Imagination,* 213–247. New Haven: Yale University Press, 1979. Groundbreaking feminist analysis.

Griffin, Andrew. "Fire and Ice in *Frankenstein.*" In Levine and Knoepflmacher, 49–73. The symbolic landscape, human tempers and temperatures.

Hitchcock, Susan Tyler. *Frankenstein: A Cultural History.* New York: W. W. Norton, 2007.

Homans, Margaret. "Bearing Demons: *Frankenstein*'s Circumvention of the Maternal." In *Bearing the Word: Language and Female Experience in Nineteenth-Century Women's Writing,* 100–119. Chicago: University of Chicago Press, 1986.

Itard, E. M. [Jean-Marc Gaspard]. *An Historical Account of the Discovery and Education of a Savage Man, or The First Developments, Physical and Moral, of the Young Savage Caught in the Woods Near Aveyron in the Year 1798.* London: Richard Phillips, 1802.

Jacobus, Mary. "Is There a Woman in This Text?" *New Literary History* 14 (1982): 117–141. Reprinted in *Reading Woman: Essays in Feminist Criticism,* 83–109. New York: Columbia University Press, 1986.

Johnson, Barbara. "My Monster/My Self." *Diacritics* 12, no. 2 (1982): 2–10. Reprinted in *A World of Difference,* 144–154. Baltimore: Johns Hopkins University Press, 1987.

Kincaid, James R. "'Words Cannot Express': *Frankenstein*'s Tripping on the Tongue." *Novel* 24 (1990): 26–47. Reprinted in *Annoying the Victorians,* 181–206. New York: Routledge, 1995.

Knoepflmacher, U. C. "Thoughts on the Aggression of Daughters." In Levine and Knoepflmacher, 88–119.

Levine, George. "The Ambiguous Heritage of *Frankenstein.*" In Levine and Knoepflmacher, 3–30.

———. "*Frankenstein* and the Tradition of Realism." *Novel* 7 (1973): 14–30. Revised in Chapter 2 of *The Realistic Imagination: English Fiction from* Frankenstein *to* Lady Chatterly's Lover. Chicago: University of Chicago Press, 1981.

———, and U. C. Knoepflmacher, eds. *The Endurance of Frankenstein: Essays on Mary Shelley's Novel.* Berkeley: University of California Press, 1979. A wealth of essays, with various approaches: thematic, psychoanalytic, linguistic, philosophical, socio-historical, film, popular culture.

London, Bette. "Mary Shelley, *Frankenstein,* and the Spectacle of Masculinity." *PMLA* 108 (1993): 253–267.

Marshall, David. *The Surprising Effects of Sympathy.* Chicago: University of Chicago Press, 1988.

Mellor, Anne K. "Frankenstein, Racial Science and the Yellow Peril." *Nineteenth-Century Contexts* 23 (2001): 1–28.

Moers, Ellen. "Female Gothic." Chapter 5, *Literary Women.* Doubleday, 1976. Excerpted in Levine and Knoepflmacher, *Endurance of Frankenstein,* 77–87.

Morton, Timothy, ed. *A Routledge Literary Sourcebook on Mary Shelley's Frankenstein.* London: Routledge, 2002.

Newman, Beth. "Narratives of Seduction and the Seductions of Narrative: The Frame Structure of *Frankenstein.*" *ELH: English Literary History* 53, no. 1 (1986): 141–163.

Oates, Joyce Carol. "*Frankenstein*'s Fallen Angel." *Critical Inquiry* 10, no. 3 (March 1984): 543–554.

O'Rourke, James. "'Nothing more unnatural': Mary Shelley's Revision of Rousseau." *ELH: English Literary History* 56, no. 3 (Fall 1989): 543–569.

———. "The 1831 Introduction and Revisions to *Frankenstein:* Mary Shelley Dictates Her Legacy." *Studies in Romanticism* 38 (1999): 365–385.

Poovey, Mary. "My Hideous Progeny: Mary Shelley and the Feminization of Romanticism." *PMLA* 95 (1980): 332–347. Reprinted in *The Proper Lady and the Woman Writer: Ideology as Style,* 114–142. Chicago: University of Chicago Press, 1984.

Rauch, Alan. "The Monstrous Body of Knowledge in Mary Shelley's *Frankenstein.*" *Studies in Romanticism* 34 (1995): 227–254.

Richardson, Alan. "From *Emile* to *Frankenstein:* The Education of Monsters." *European Romantic Review* 1, no. 2 (1991): 147–162.

Rubenstein, Marc. "'My Accursed Origin': The Search for the Mother in *Frankenstein.*" *Studies in Romanticism* 15 (1976): 165–194.

St. Clair, William. "Frankenstein." In *The Reading Nation in the Romantic Period,* 357–373. Cambridge: Cambridge University Press, 2004.

Scott, Peter Dale. "Vital Artifice: Mary, Percy, and the Psychopolitical Integrity of *Frankenstein.*" In Levine and Knoepflmacher, 172–202.

Sherwin, Paul. "Creation as Catastrophe." *PMLA* 96 (1981): 883–903.

Skal, David J. *The Monster Show: A Cultural History of Horror.* New York: Norton, 1993.

Small, Christopher. *Mary Shelley's Frankenstein: Tracing the Myth.* Pittsburgh: University of Pittsburgh Press, 1973.

Spivak, Gayatri Chakravorty. "Three Women's Texts and a Critique of Imperialism." *Critical Inquiry* 12 (1985–86): 243–261.

Sterrenberg, Lee. "Mary Shelley's Monster: Politics and Psyche in *Frankenstein.*" In Levine and Knoepflmacher, 143–171.

Stevick, Philip. "*Frankenstein* as Comedy." In Levine and Knoepflmacher, 221–239.

Stewart, Garrett. "In the Absence of Audience: Of Reading and Dread in Mary Shelley." In *Dear Reader: The Conscripted Audience in Nineteenth-Century British Fiction,* 113–132. Baltimore: Johns Hopkins University Press, 1996.

Tropp, Martin. *Mary Shelley's Monster: The Story of Frankenstein.* Boston: Houghton Mifflin, 1976.

Veeder, William. *Mary Shelley and Frankenstein: The Fate of Androgyny.* Chicago: University of Chicago Press, 1986.

Wolfson, Susan. "Feminist Inquiry and *Frankenstein.*" In Behrendt, *Approaches to Teaching,* 50–59.

———. "Reconstructing *Frankenstein.*" *Review* 20 (1998): 1–15.

Gene Wilder as a descendant of Victor Frankenstein and Peter Boyle as a new Creature in Mel Brooks's *Young Frankenstein* (1974). Shelley's tale, almost from its inception, has been adapted and revised in many directions, including the comic. Here, the Creature's education culminates in his debut as a sophisticated man about town, with a performance of "Puttin' on the Ritz" (Irving Berlin's song, 1930). The outfitting in top hat and tails is a nod to Fred Astaire's performance in *Blue Skies* (1946).

On the Stage and Film Versions

Branagh, Kenneth. *Mary Shelley's Frankenstein: The Classic Tale of Terror Reborn on Film.* New York: Newmarket Press, 1994.

Dixon, Wheeler. "The Films of *Frankenstein.*" In Behrendt, *Approaches to Teaching,* 166–179.

Forry, Steven E. *Hideous Progenies: Dramatizations of Frankenstein, from Mary Shelley to the Present.* Philadelphia: University of Pennsylvania Press, 1990.

Heffernan, James A. W. "Looking for the Monster: *Frankenstein* and Film." *Critical Inquiry* 24 (August 1997): 133–158.

La Valley, Albert J. "The Stage and Film Children of *Frankenstein:* A Survey." In Levine and Knoepflmacher, *Endurance* 243–259.

Some Film Versions and Sequels

1910 *Frankenstein.* "A Liberal Adaptation from Mrs. Shelley's Famous Story for Edison Productions." Circa fifteen minutes. Silent. Mad scientist, lab-science, the animation, Frankenstein's wedding, mirror scenes, final confrontation.

1931 *Frankenstein.* Fixing the image of the Creature with flattened head and electrodes—inarticulate, but still poignant. Directed by James Whale. Boris Karloff (Creature), Colin Clive (Frankenstein). Based on the stage play by Peggy Webling.

1935 *The Bride of Frankenstein.* Directed by James Whale. Boris Karloff (Creature), Colin Clive (Frankenstein), Elsa Lanchester (Mary Shelley and the Bride). Begins with the summer of 1816. *Bride of* refers to genesis, not possession.

1939 *Son of Frankenstein.* Basil Rathbone (son), Boris Karloff (Creature).

1942 *The Ghost of Frankenstein.* Cedrick Hardwicke (another son), Lon Chaney, Jr. (Creature), Ralph Bellamy, Evelyn Ankers, Lionel Atwill, Bela Lugosi.

1943 *Frankenstein Meets the Wolfman.* Bela Lugosi (Creature).

1944 *House of Frankenstein.* Glenn Strange (Creature), Boris Karloff (mad doctor).

1948 *Abbott and Costello Meet Frankenstein.* Also with Lon Chaney, Jr. (Creature), Bela Lugosi (Dracula).

1957 *The Curse of Frankenstein.* Christopher Lee (Creature), Peter Cushing (Frankenstein).
I Was a Teenage Frankenstein. Gary Conway (Creature), Whit Bissell (Frankenstein).

1974 *Young Frankenstein.* Mel Brooks's sublime satire. Gene Wilder (Frankenstein), Peter Boyle (Creature), Madeline Kahn, Cloris Leachman, Marty Feldman (Igor).

Kenneth Branagh's *Mary Shelley's Frankenstein,* 1994, is a hyperbolic and often visually arresting version of the tale, featuring Robert Di Niro as the Creature and Branagh as his Creator/father/alter ego. The Creature's athleticism is given full play as he descends on Frankenstein for a compelled meeting on the Mer de Glace outside Geneva.

1975 *Rocky Horror Picture Show.* Tim Curry as the transvestite from Transylvania, Dr. Frank-N-Furter. Preceded by *The Rocky Horror Show* on the London stage, also spiced with Curry.

1986 *The Bride.* Sting (Frankenstein), Jennifer Beals.
     Gothic. Directed by Ken Russell. Surreal summer of 1816. Natasha Richardson, Gabriel Byrne, Julian Sands.

1987 *Making Mr. Right.* Comedy. Frankie Stone, tired of the singles scene, gets involved in educating an android (John Malkovich); they fall for each other.

1988 *Haunted Summer* (of 1816). Eric Stolz as Percy B. Shelley.

1994 *Mary Shelley's Frankenstein.* Directed by Kenneth Branagh (also Frankenstein), Robert De Niro (Creature). Spectacular on the sublimities; De Niro is poignant.

1998 *Gods and Monsters.* The demons in the mind of a dying James Whale—director of *Frankenstein* and *The Bride of Frankenstein*—closeted homosexual in the homophobic Hollywood of the 1950s, still traumatized by the horrors of trench warfare in WWI. Ian McKellan is brilliant.

ILLUSTRATION CREDITS

The Creature confronts his maker, wood engraving by Lynd Ward. From Mary Wollstonecraft Shelley, *Frankenstein* (New York: Harrison Smith and Robert Haas, 1934), after p. 106. Copyright Estate of Lynd Ward, 2007. Courtesy of Houghton Library, Harvard University. *frontispiece, 173*

Mary Wollstonecraft by John Opie, 1790–91. © Tate, London, 2011. *3*

Title page of Mary Wollstonecraft, *A Vindication of the Rights of Woman* (London, 1792). Courtesy of Rare Books Division, Department of Rare Books and Special Collections, Princeton University Library. *4*

Title page of William Godwin, *An Enquiry Concerning Political Justice,* 2 vols. (London, 1793). Courtesy of Rare Books Division, Department of Rare Books and Special Collections, Princeton University Library. *4*

Portrait of William Godwin by J. W. Chandler, 1798. © Tate, London, 2012. *5*

Title page of William Godwin, *Things as They Are; or, the Adventures of Caleb Williams* (London, 1794). Courtesy of Houghton Library, Harvard University. *5*

Portrait of Percy Shelley by Amelia Curran, 1819. © National Portrait Gallery, London. *7*

Engraving of St. Pancras Churchyard in 1815–1816. From John Britton and Edward Wedlake Brayley, *The beauties of England and Wales, or, Delineations, topographical, historical, and descriptive, of each county: embellished with engravings* (London: printed by T. Maiden for Vernor and Hood, 1801–1816). Courtesy of Princeton University Library. *9*

George Gordon, Lord Byron, by Richard Westall, 1813. © National Portrait Gallery, London. *10*

Villa Diodati, near Geneva, Switzerland, residence of Lord Byron and the Shelley entourage in 1816. Steel engraving, 1833. The Granger Collection, New York. *11*

Portrait of Mary Shelley by Richard Rothwell, c. 1840. © National Portrait Gallery, London. *13*

First film version of the Creature from Edison Studios, *Frankenstein* (1910). *The Edison Kinetogram,* vol. 1, no. 1 (April 15, 1910). U.S. Dept of Interior, National Park Service, Edison National Historic Site. Courtesy of the British Film Institute. *18*

Imploring hands of Boris Karloff as the Creature in James Whale's *Frankenstein* (1931). *19*

Athletic Creature, wood engraving by Lynd Ward. From Mary Wollstonecraft Shelley, *Frankenstein* (New York: Harrison Smith and Robert Haas, 1934), 151. Copyright Estate of Lynd Ward, 2007. Courtesy of Houghton Library, Harvard University. *20*

Colin Clive as Frankenstein and Boris Karloff as his Creature, viewed through the gears of the windmill in James Whale's *Frankenstein* (1931). *21*

Prometheus Creating Man [*L'Homme formé par Prométhée et animé par Minerve*], detail, 1802. Painted by Jean-Simon Berthélemy, 1802; painted again by Jean-Baptiste Mauzaisse, 1826. Ceiling of the Rotunda of Mars. Inv.: INV20043.

Photo: Hervé Lewandowski. Réunion des Musées Nationaux / Art Resource, New York. *23*

Prometheus Bound by Peter Paul Rubens, 1611–1612. Inv.P.115. Photo: Hervé Lewandowski. Réunion des Musées Nationaux / Art Resource, New York. *26*

Thomas Potter Cooke as the unnamed being in the first staging of *Frankenstein*, 1823. The Carl H. Pforzheimer Collection of Shelley and His Circle, The New York Public Library, Astor, Lenox, and Tilden Foundations. *27*

Cover illustration of the publication text of Richard Brinsley Peake's *Frankenstein*, the performance text, in Dicks' Standard Plays, No. 431. *27*

Frontispiece from Henry M. Milner, *Frankenstein, or, The Man and the Monster!* (London: J. Duncombe, 1826). Courtesy of Houghton Library, Harvard University. *28*

Endless Entertainment, Friday, June 17, 1825, 97–119; cover, p. 97. P.P.5814.q. © The British Library Board. *29*

The Modern Prometheus, or Downfall of Tyranny by George Cruikshank, 1814, print published in London. © The Trustees of the British Museum. *30*

Detail of the newly animated Creature, picture by Theodor von Holst, engraved by W. Chevalier. Frontispiece, from Mary Wollstonecraft Shelley, *Frankenstein*, rev., corr., and illustrated, with a new Introduction by the author (London: Henry Colburn and Richard Bentley, 1831). Courtesy of Houghton Library, Harvard University. *31*

Benjamin Franklin Drawing Electricity from the Sky by Benjamin West, ca. 1816. Gift of Mr. and Mrs. Wharton Sinkler, 1958. The Philadelphia Museum of Art / Art Resource, New York. *34*

Village mob and burning windmill in James Whale's *Frankenstein* (1931). *39*

Boris Karloff as the captured Creature in James Whale's *Bride of Frankenstein* (1935). *39*

Milton Dictating to His Daughter by Henry Fuseli, 1793–1794. Preston O. Morton Memorial Purchase Fund for Older Paintings, 1973.303, The Art Institute of Chicago. Photography © The Art Institute of Chicago. *48*

Mary Shelley's copy of John Milton, *Paradise Lost. A Poem in Twelve Books* (Dublin, 1747). Courtesy of Rare Books Division, Department of Rare Books and Special Collections, Princeton University Library. *49*

Title page of John Milton, *Paradise Regained. A Poem in Four Books* (Dublin, 1752). Courtesy of Rare Books Division, Department of Rare Books and Special Collections, Princeton University Library. *52*

Last page of the Introduction, from Mary Wollstonecraft Shelley, *Frankenstein*, rev., corr., and illustrated, with a new Introduction by the author (London: Henry Colburn and Richard Bentley, 1831), xii. Courtesy of Houghton Library, Harvard University. *52*

Title page of Mary Wollstonecraft Shelley, *Frankenstein, or The modern Prometheus: in three volumes*, vol. 1 (London, 1818). Courtesy of Rare Books Division, Department of Rare Books and Special Collections, Princeton University Library. *57*

Dedication page of Mary Wollstonecraft Shelley, *Frankenstein, or The modern Prometheus: in three volumes* (London, 1818). Courtesy of Rare Books Division, Department of Rare Books and Special Collections, Princeton University Library. *59*

P. B. Shelley in the Baths of Caracalla, writing *Prometheus Unbound*, posthumous portrait by Joseph Severn, 1845. Keats-Shelley Memorial House, Rome, Italy / The Bridgeman Art Library. *63*

The Palace Embankment seen from the Peter and Paul Fortress, St. Petersburg by Fyodor Yakovlevich Alekseyev, 1794. State Russian Museum, St. Petersburg, Russia / The Bridgeman Art Library. *67*

A Map of the Countries Thirty Degrees round the North Pole by Samuel John Neele, from Clement Crutwell, *Atlas to Crutwell's Gazetteer* (London, 1799). Newberry Library, Chicago / The Bridgeman Art Library. *68*

The Explorer A. E. Nordenskiöld by Georg von Rosen, 1886. © Nationalmuseum, Stockholm / The Bridgeman Art Library. *72*

Ice ship, steel engraving for *The Rime of the Ancient Mariner* by Gustave Doré, 1870. Courtesy of Special Collections, Fine Arts Library, Harvard University. *74*

Albatross, engraving for *The Rime of the Ancient Mariner*, Gustave Doré, 1870. Courtesy of Special Collections, Fine Arts Library, Harvard University. *75*

Das Eismeer [The Ice Sea] by Caspar David Friedrich, 1823–1824. Hamburger Kunsthalle, Hamburg / The Bridgeman Art Library. *77*

Geneva, the walled city, around the historical time of Frankenstein. The National Library of Israel, Eran Laor Cartographic Collection, Shapell Family

Digitization Project, and The Hebrew University of Jerusalem, Department of Geography, Historic Cities Research Project. *87*

Jean-Jacques Rousseau by Maurice Quentin de la Tour. Musée de la Ville de Paris, Musée Carnavalet, Paris. Giraudon / The Bridgeman Art Library. *91*

The Great Magic Circle of Agrippa for the Evocation of Demons, copy of an illustration from *Les Oevres Magiques de Henri Corneille Agrippa* (Rome, 1744), used in a *History of Magic* (late 19th century). Private collection. The Stapleton Collection / Bridgeman Art Library. *92*

Robert Boyle's Air Pump, from Robert Boyle, *New experiments physico-mechanicall, touching the spring of the air and its effects* (Oxford, 1660), vol. 1, plate 1. Courtesy of Houghton Library, Harvard University. *94*

An Experiment on a Bird in the Air Pump by Joseph Wright of Derby, 1768. National Gallery, London. The Bridgeman Art Library. *95*

Lake of Geneva as Seen from Montreux by J. M. W. Turner, c. 1810. Adele S. Browning Memorial Collection, donated by Mildred Browning and Judge Lucius Peyton Green. Digital Image © 2012 Museum Associates / LACMA. Licensed by Art Resource, New York. *96*

The Philosopher and His Kite, Henry S. Sadd. Courtesy of Library of Congress. *97*

Manuscript (1816–1817) for the opening of Volume I, Chapter IV, the animation of the Creature. Dep. c. 477/1 folio 21 recto. The Bodleian Libraries, The University of Oxford. *115*

Opening of Chapter IV from Mary Wollstonecraft Shelley, *Frankenstein, or The modern Prometheus: in three volumes* (London, 1818). Courtesy of Rare Books Division, Department of Rare Books and Special Collections, Princeton University Library. *115*

Colin Clive as Frankenstein concentrates his gaze on the hand of Boris Karloff as the Creature in James Whale's *Frankenstein* (1931). *117*

Colin Clive as Frankenstein heralds his accomplishment, from James Whale's *Frankenstein* (1931). *118*

First frontal view of Boris Karloff as Creature in James Whale's *Frankenstein* (1931). *121*

The judges at Justine's trial, wood engraving by Lynd Ward. From Mary Wollstonecraft Shelley, *Frankenstein* (New York: Harrison Smith and Robert Haas, 1934), 83. Copyright Estate of Lynd Ward, 2007. Courtesy of Houghton Library, Harvard University. *150*

Title page of Mary Wollstonecraft Shelley, *Frankenstein, or The modern Prometheus: in three volumes,* vol. 2 (London, 1818). Courtesy of Rare Books Division, Department of Rare Books and Special Collections, Princeton University Library. *155*

Mont Blanc, from William Beattie, M.D., *Switzerland, In a Series of Views Taken Expressly for this Work by W. H. Bartlett, Esq.* (London: Virtue, c. 1838). Courtesy of Houghton Library, Harvard University. *162*

The Source of the Averon by Marc Theodore Bourrit, from *Description des glacières de Savoye,* 1773 (English translation, Norwich, 1775–1776). Courtesy of Houghton Library, Harvard University. *163*

Mer de Glace, Aiguille du Géant et Grandes Jorasses, Chamonix, France. Courtesy of the Library of Congress. *167*

Vue de la mer de glace et de l'hopital de Blair vue du sommet de Montavert dans le mois d'aout 1781 by Carl Ludwig Hackert. Bibliothèque de Genève. *168*

Vüe de la Mer de Glace du montanvert from Marc-Théodore Bourrit, *Nouvelle description des glaciers . . .* (Geneva: P. Barde, 1785). *169*

The Creature crosses icy terrain, wood engraving by Lynd Ward. From Mary Wollstonecraft Shelley, *Frankenstein* (New York: Harrison Smith and Robert Haas, 1934), 242. Copyright Estate of Lynd Ward, 2007. Courtesy of Houghton Library, Harvard University. *171*

Reunion of Creature and Creator from James Whale's *Frankenstein* (1931). *174*

Mary Shelley's manuscript of the first page of the Creature's story; originally Volume II, Chapter I. Dep. c. 534/1, folio 1 verso. The Bodleian Libraries, The University of Oxford. *177*

Victor of Aveyron, "the wild child," from E. M. Itard, *An historical account of the discovery and education of a savage man, or: of the first developments, physical and moral, of the young savage caught in the woods near Aveyron in the year 1798* (France, 1801; London: Richard Phillips, 1802). Courtesy of Houghton Library, Harvard University. *178*

The stoning of the Creature, wood engraving by Lynd Ward. From Mary Wollstonecraft Shelley, *Frankenstein* (New York: Harrison Smith and Robert Haas, 1934), after p. 114. Copyright Estate of Lynd Ward, 2007. Courtesy of Houghton Library, Harvard University. *181*

The Creature sees his image reflected, wood engraving by Lynd Ward. From Mary Wollstonecraft Shelley, *Frankenstein* (New York: Harrison Smith and Robert Haas, 1934), after p. 124. Copyright Estate of Lynd Ward, 2007. Courtesy of Houghton Library, Harvard University. *191*

William Shelley, age 3½, by Amelia Curran. The Carl H. Pforzheimer Collection of Shelley and His Circle, The New York Public Library, Astor, Lenox, and Tilden Foundations. *223*

Title page of Mary Wollstonecraft Shelley, *Frankenstein, or The modern Prometheus: in three volumes*, vol. 3 (London, 1818). Courtesy of Rare Books Division, Department of Rare Books and Special Collections, Princeton University Library. *233*

Buttermere Lake, with Part of Cromackwater, Cumberland, a Shower, by J. M. W. Turner, 1798. © Tate, London, 2011. *245*

Abandoned farmhouse on North Ronaldsay, Orkney Islands, Scotland. Paul Glendell / Alamy. *248*

The Irish villagers who greet Victor with suspicion, wood engraving by Lynd Ward. From Mary Wollstonecraft Shelley, *Frankenstein* (New York: Harrison Smith and Robert Haas, 1934), 199. Copyright Estate of Lynd Ward, 2007. Courtesy of Houghton Library, Harvard University. *263*

Movie poster for 1931 *Frankenstein*. © 1931 Universal Pictures Company, Inc. The likeness of Boris Karloff is licensed by Karloff Enterprises / Sara Karloff. *288*

The Nightmare by Johann Heinrich Fuseli, 1781. Detroit Institute of Arts, Founders Society purchase with Mr. and Mrs. Bert L. Smokler and Mr. and Mrs. Lawrence A. Fleischman funds. The Bridgeman Art Library. *290*

Creature leaving Elizabeth, fainted in horror, in James Whale's *Frankenstein* (1931). *291*

Tartary, engraved map by Herman Moll, geographer, 1732. Courtesy of the David Rumsey Map Collection, www.davidrumsey.com. *299*

"The Crews of H.M.S. Hecla & Griper Cutting Into Winter Harbour, Sept. 26th, 1819," *Journal of a Voyage for the Discovery of a North-West Passage from the Atlantic to the Pacific: Performed in the Years, 1819–20, in His Majesty's Ships Hecla and Griper, Under the Orders of William Edward Parry; With an Appendix Containing the Scientific and Other Observations* (The Library at The Mariners' Museum, 1821). Courtesy of Houghton Library, Harvard University. *308*

William Edward Parry. Courtesy of Houghton Library, Harvard University. *309*

An account of several late voyages and discoveries, vol. 4: *F. Marten's voyage to Spitzbergen and Greenland*, by Sir John Narbrough, 2nd ed. (1724), facing p. 4. Courtesy of Houghton Library, Harvard University. *311*

View of the Racehorse and Carcass August 7th 1773, when inclosed in the ice in Lat. 80° 37.N. Engraved for Payne's *Universal Geography*, V: 481, after John Cleveley. Private collection. The Stapleton Collection / The Bridgeman Art Library. *314*

Picture by Theodor von Holst, engraved by W. Chevalier. Frontispiece and title page from 1831 edition of Mary Wollstonecraft Shelley, *Frankenstein, or the Modern Prometheus* (London: Bentley, 1839). Courtesy of Rare Books Division, Department of Rare Books and Special Collections, Princeton University Library. *329*

Portrait of William Godwin by James Northcote, ca. 1802. © National Portrait Gallery, London. *333*

Mary Wollstonecraft by John Opie, 1797. © National Portrait Gallery, London. *333*

Portrait of a Nobleman (Lord Byron), by Thomas Phillips, 1814. Private collection. The Bridgeman Art Library. *334*

Lake Geneva, with Villa Diodati at center left, from William Beattie, M.D., *Switzerland, In a Series of Views Taken Expressly for this Work by W. H. Bartlett, Esq.* (London: Virtue, c. 1838). Courtesy of Houghton Library, Harvard University. *335*

John William Polidori by F. G. Gainsford, 1817. © National Portrait Gallery, London. *335*

Plate engraving from Luigi Galvani, *De Viribus Electricitatis in Motu Musculari* (1791). Photo by Universal History Archive / Getty Images. *336*

Theoretical and Experimental Test on Galvanism by Giovanni Aldini, 1804. Litho from Giovanni Aldini, *Essai théorique et expérimental sur le galvanisme* (Paris: Fournier Fils, 1804), plate 4 (lower panel). The engraving is based on a drawing by Pecheux. Private collection. Courtesy of Swann Auction Galleries / The Bridgeman Art Library. *337*

"Le docteur Ure galvanisant le corps de l'assassin Clydsdale." Engraving from Louis Figuier, *Les merveilles de la Science* (Paris: Furne, Jouvet et Cie., 1867), p. 653, fig. 333. Courtesy of Houghton Library, Harvard University. *337*

Portrait of a woman long thought to be Mary Shelley by Samuel John Stump, 1831. © National Portrait Gallery, London. *338*

Godwin's journal, recording "Birth of Mary 20 minutes after 11 at night," August 30, 1797. *The Diary of William Godwin,* ed. Victoria Myers, David O'Shaughnessy, and Mark Philp (Oxford: Oxford Digital Library, 2010). http://godwindiary.bodleian.ox.ac.uk. *360*

Godwin's journal, the morning of Wollstonecraft's death, September 10, 1797. *The Diary of William Godwin,* ed. Victoria Myers, David O'Shaughnessy, and Mark Philp (Oxford: Oxford Digital Library, 2010). http://godwindiary.bodleian.ox.ac.uk. *363*

Title page of William Godwin, *Memoirs of the Author of A Vindication of the Rights of Woman* (London, 1798). Courtesy of Houghton Library, Harvard University. *364*

The Lover's Seat, Shelley and Mary Godwin in Old St. Pancras Churchyard, by William Powell Frith, 1877. Private collection. The Bridgeman Art Library. *366*

Grave of Mary Shelley, St. Peter's Churchyard, Bournemouth, Dorset. The Bridgeman Art Library. *371*

Gene Wilder as a descendant of Victor Frankenstein and Peter Boyle as a new Creature in Mel Brooks's *Young Frankenstein* (1974). *380*

Robert Di Niro as the Creature and Kenneth Branagh as his Creator in Kenneth Branagh's *Mary Shelley's Frankenstein* (1994). *381*

ACKNOWLEDGMENTS

Unlike Victor Frankenstein, we could not have beheld the accomplishment of our toils on *The Annotated Frankenstein* without considerable assistance and generous support.

We are grateful, first and foremost, to our editor at Harvard University Press, John Gregory Kulka, for proposing this project, and securing such a splendid result, with all manner of courtesies, advice, encouragement, and practical assistance along the way. Among the most materially valuable for us was his happy assignment of Heather M. Hughes as our illustration researcher and manager, as well as, at a crucial moment, our textual proofreader. Another happy resource at Harvard University Press was Christine Thorsteinsson, our copyeditor and cheerful interrogator. The press's advisory readers, Garrett Stewart and Anne Mellor, provided timely, astute encouragement.

We thank Princeton University and several colleagues there for valuable, practical assistance: Kevin Mensch helped with a dossier of visual scans; Paula Brett with screen captures; Charles Green, Ben Primer, and Gabriel Swift granted gratis permission for us to use the wealth of images efficiently and cheerfully secured by AnnaLee Pauls from collections at the university's library.

We are in debt to many others who have answered questions, thought through problems, or provided practical assistance: Richard Levao, Thomas Kauffman, Joseph Terry, Katherine Fletcher and Sarah Howe (curators of the Darkness Visible exhibit at Christ's College Cambridge University), Nora Crook and Charles Robinson (each the editor of important editions of *Frankenstein*), and Esther Schor.

Unlike Victor Frankenstein, too, we are happy to acknowledge our debts to the existing science—in our case, the labors of previous editors and the critical literature and scholarship noted throughout our volume, and especially in our list for further reading and viewing. "And now, once again, I bid my hideous progeny go forth and prosper," said Mary Shelley, the heart and soul of it all, in October 1831. One hundred and eighty-one years later, we are especially happy to recall her prophetic wish.